Quirk's Quest

INTO THE OUTLANDS

Robert Christie   Deborah Lang

:01

First Second

New York

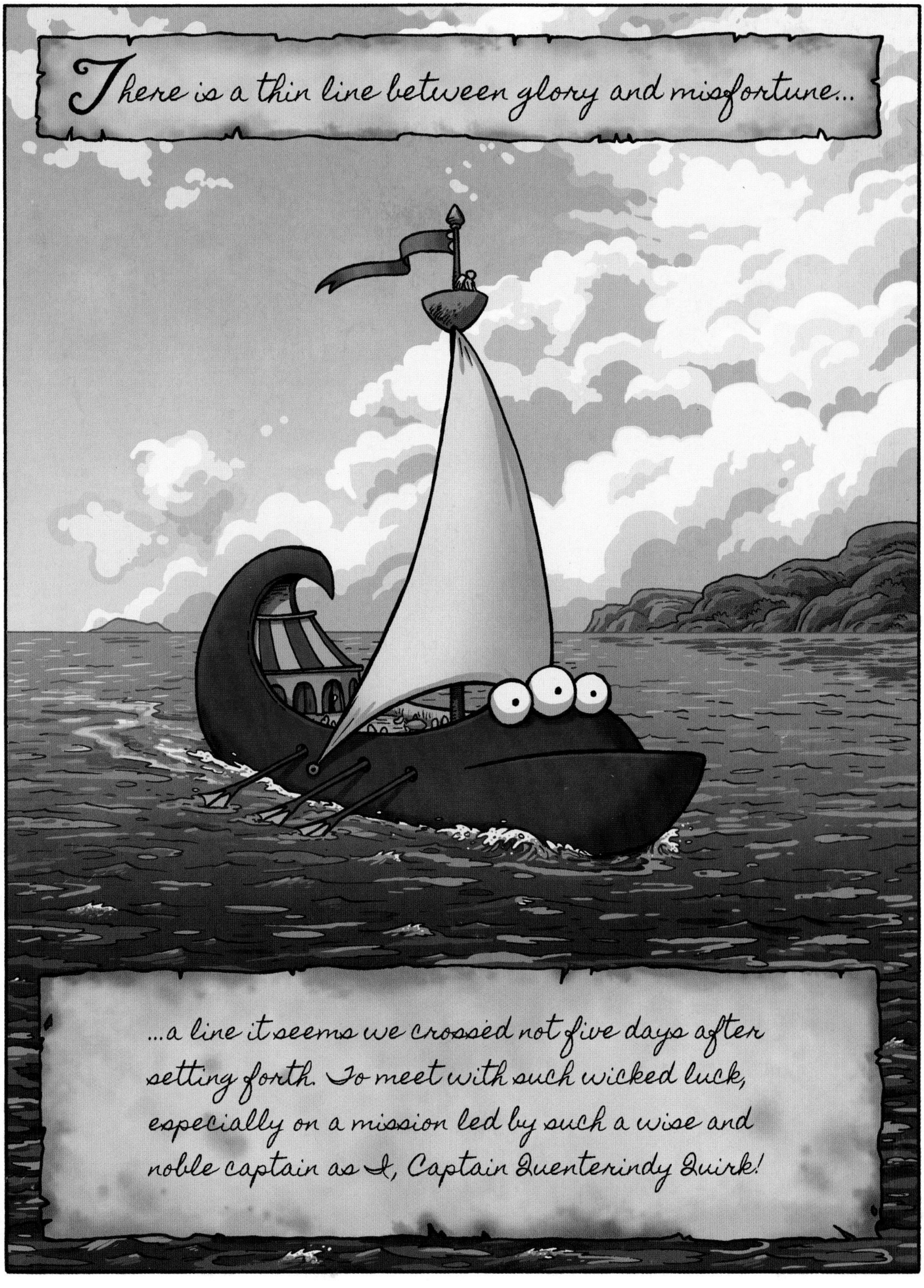
There is a thin line between glory and misfortune...
...a line it seems we crossed not five days after setting forth. To meet with such wicked luck, especially on a mission led by such a wise and noble captain as I, Captain Quenterindy Quirk!

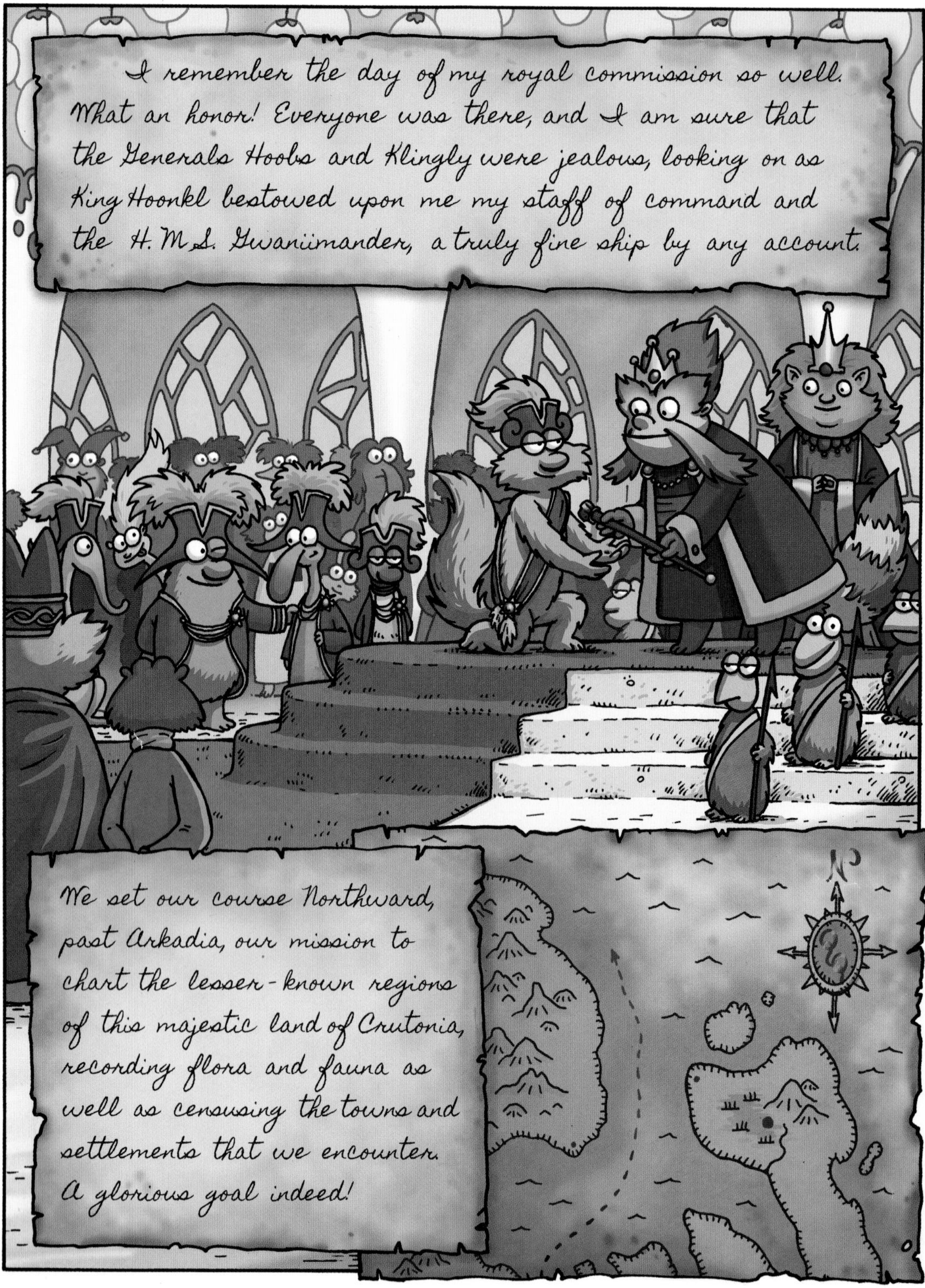
I remember the day of my royal commission so well. What an honor! Everyone was there, and I am sure that the Generals Hoobs and Klingly were jealous, looking on as King Hoonkl bestowed upon me my staff of command and the H.M.S. Gwaniimander, a truly fine ship by any account.
We set our course Northward, past Arkadia, our mission to chart the lesser-known regions of this majestic land of Crutonia, recording flora and fauna as well as censusing the towns and settlements that we encounter. A glorious goal indeed!

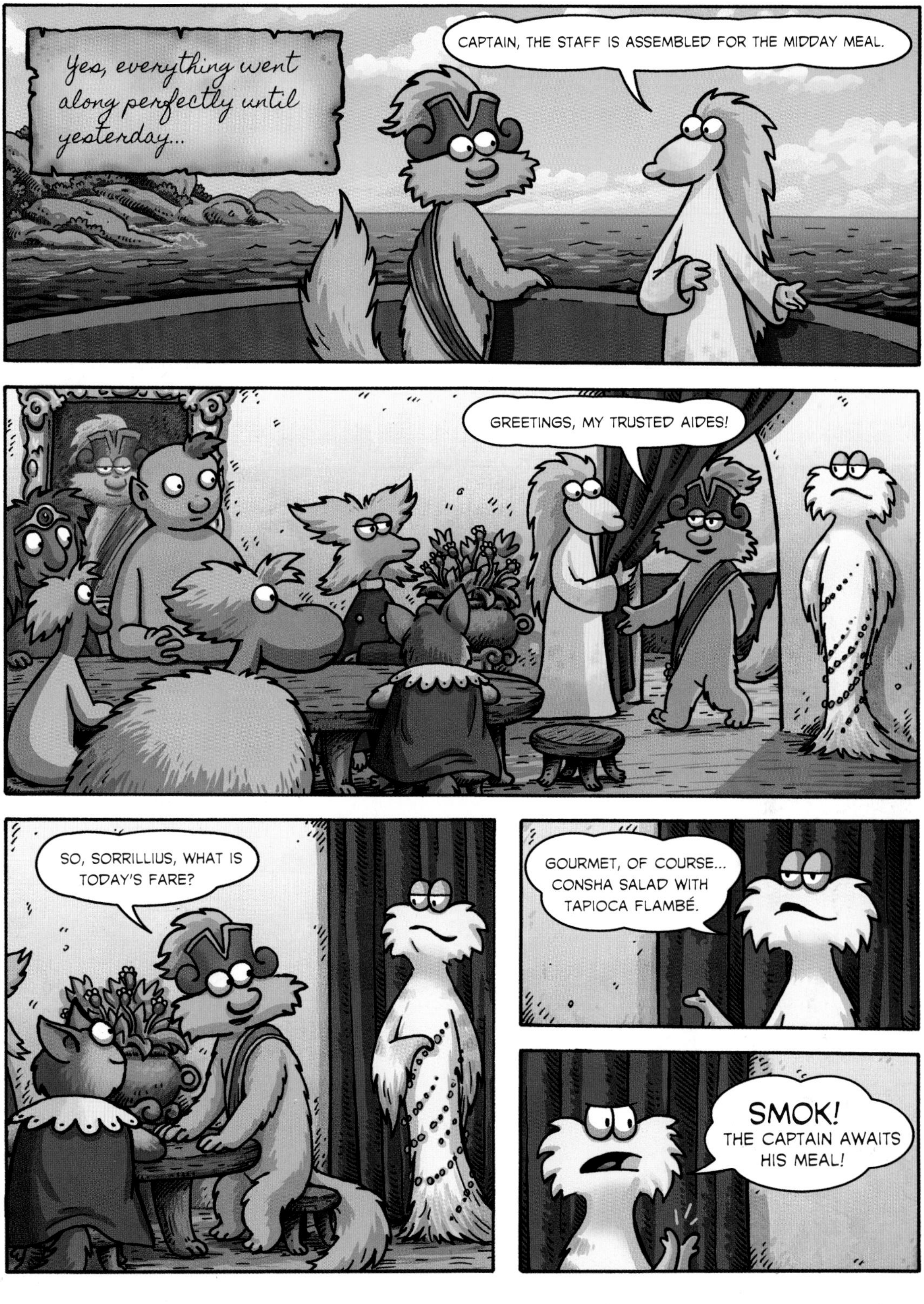
Yes, everything went along perfectly until yesterday...
CAPTAIN, THE STAFF IS ASSEMBLED FOR THE MIDDAY MEAL.
GREETINGS, MY TRUSTED AIDES!
SO, SORRILLIUS, WHAT IS TODAY'S FARE?
GOURMET, OF COURSE... CONSHA SALAD WITH TAPIOCA FLAMBÉ.
SMOK! THE CAPTAIN AWAITS HIS MEAL!

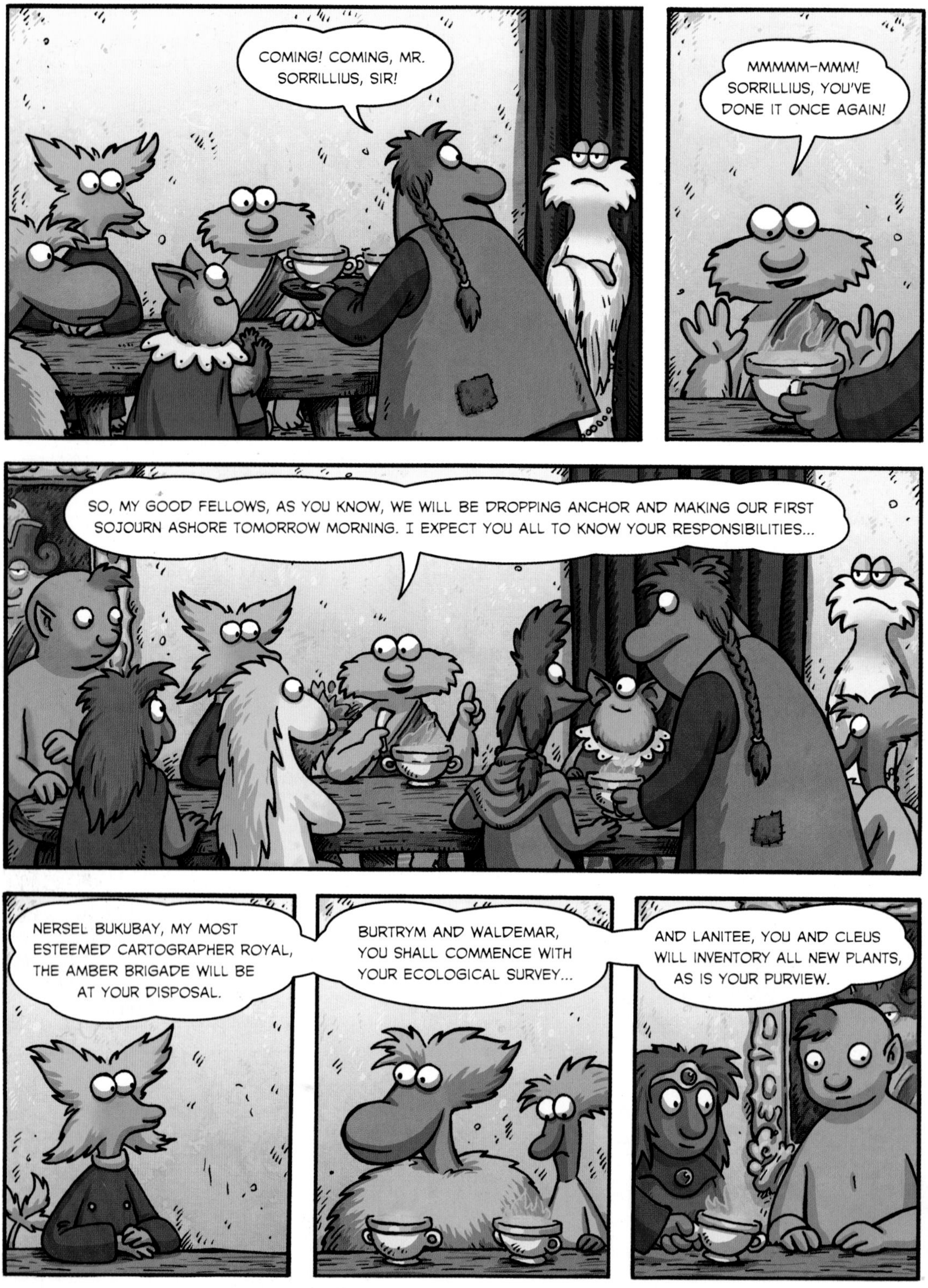
COMING! COMING, MR. SORRILLIUS, SIR!
MMMMM-MMM! SORRILLIUS, YOU'VE DONE IT ONCE AGAIN!
SO, MY GOOD FELLOWS, AS YOU KNOW, WE WILL BE DROPPING ANCHOR AND MAKING OUR FIRST SOJOURN ASHORE TOMORROW MORNING. I EXPECT YOU ALL TO KNOW YOUR RESPONSIBILITIES...
NERSEL BUKUBAY, MY MOST ESTEEMED CARTOGRAPHER ROYAL, THE AMBER BRIGADE WILL BE AT YOUR DISPOSAL.
BURTRYM AND WALDEMAR, YOU SHALL COMMENCE WITH YOUR ECOLOGICAL SURVEY...
AND LANITEE, YOU AND CLEUS WILL INVENTORY ALL NEW PLANTS, AS IS YOUR PURVIEW.

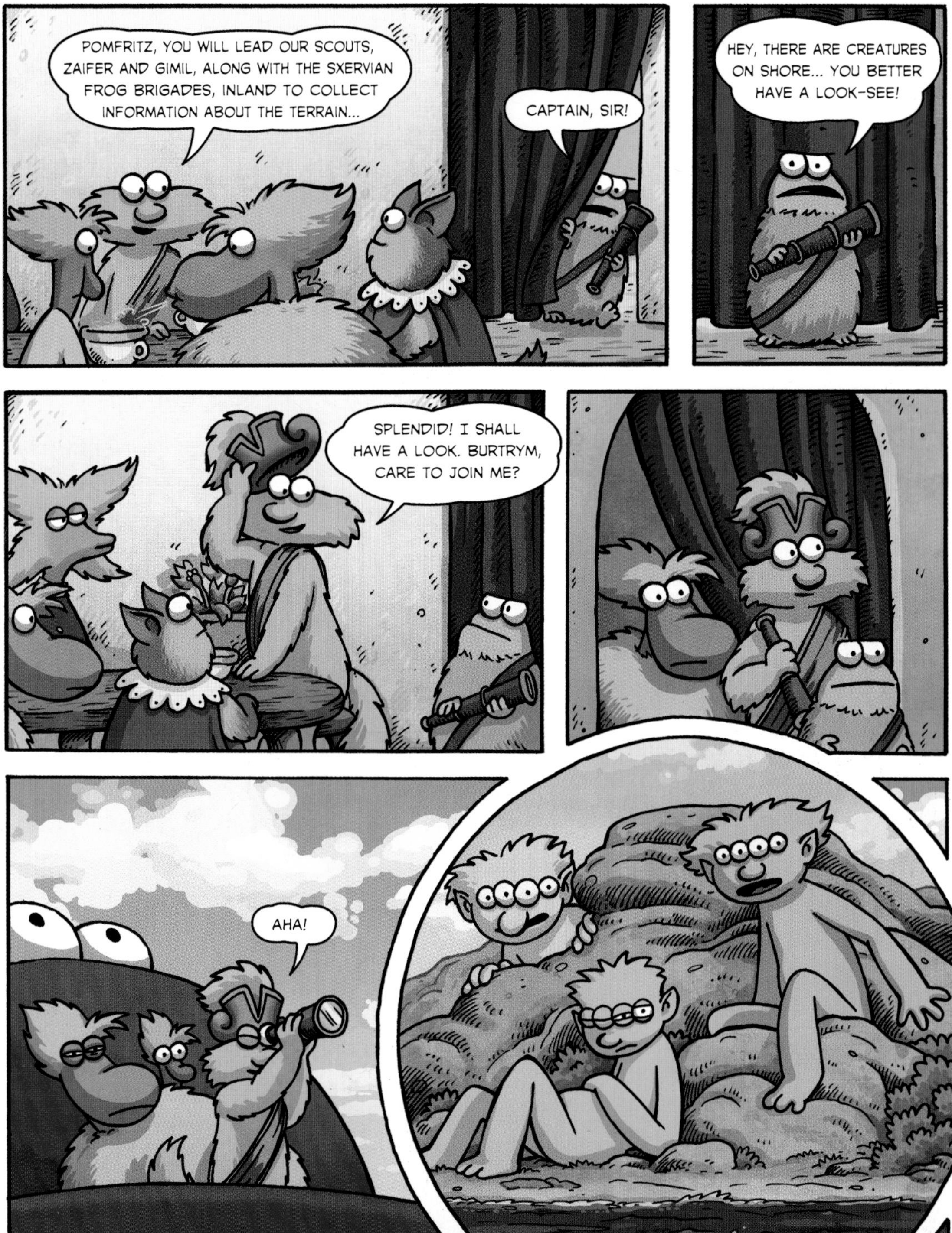
POMFRITZ, YOU WILL LEAD OUR SCOUTS, ZAIFER AND GIMIL, ALONG WITH THE SXERVIAN FROG BRIGADES, INLAND TO COLLECT INFORMATION ABOUT THE TERRAIN...
CAPTAIN, SIR!
HEY, THERE ARE CREATURES ON SHORE... YOU BETTER HAVE A LOOK-SEE!
SPLENDID! I SHALL HAVE A LOOK. BURTRYM, CARE TO JOIN ME?
AHA!

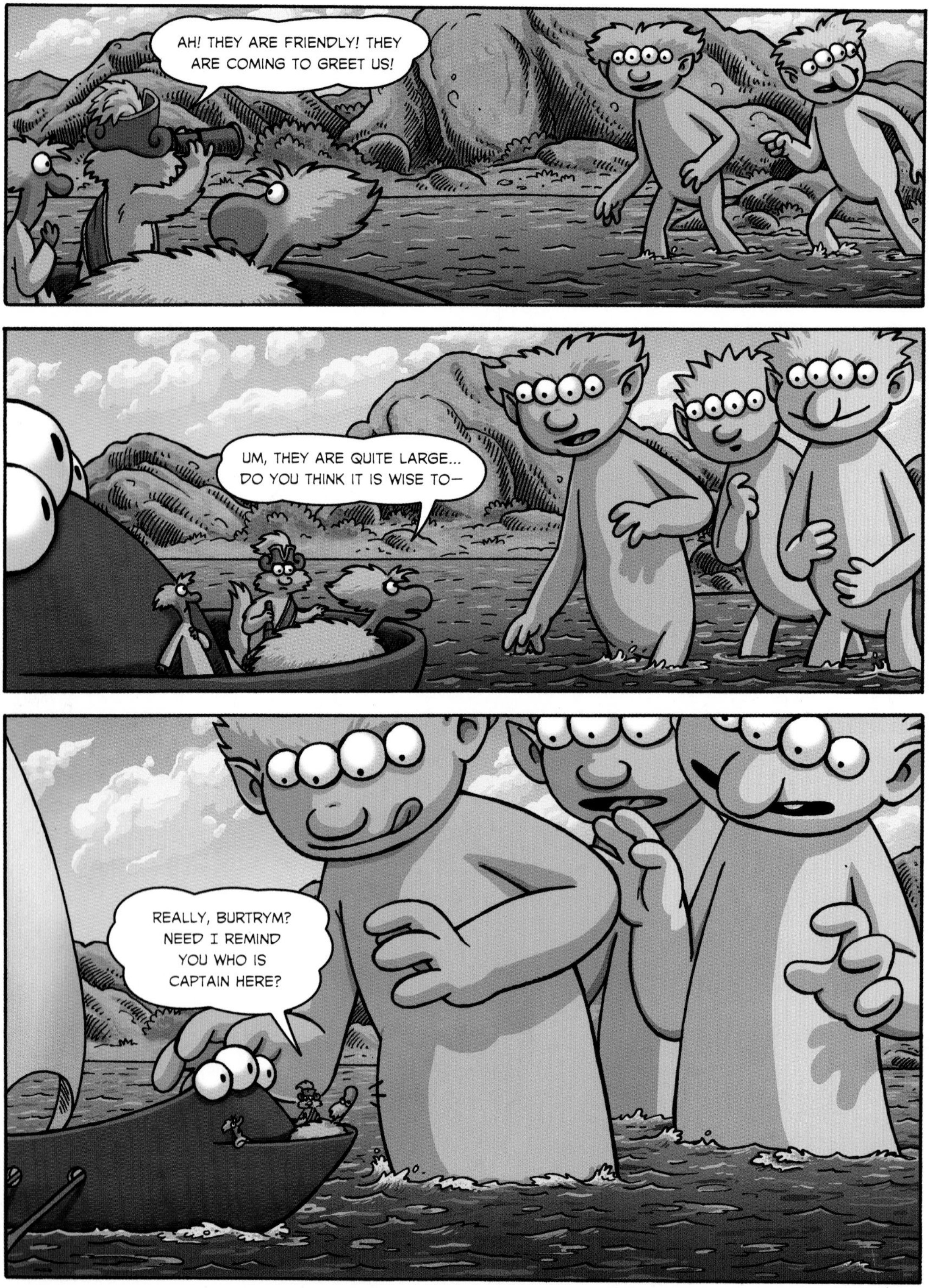
AH! THEY ARE FRIENDLY! THEY ARE COMING TO GREET US!
UM, THEY ARE QUITE LARGE... DO YOU THINK IT IS WISE TO—
REALLY, BURTRYM? NEED I REMIND YOU WHO IS CAPTAIN HERE?

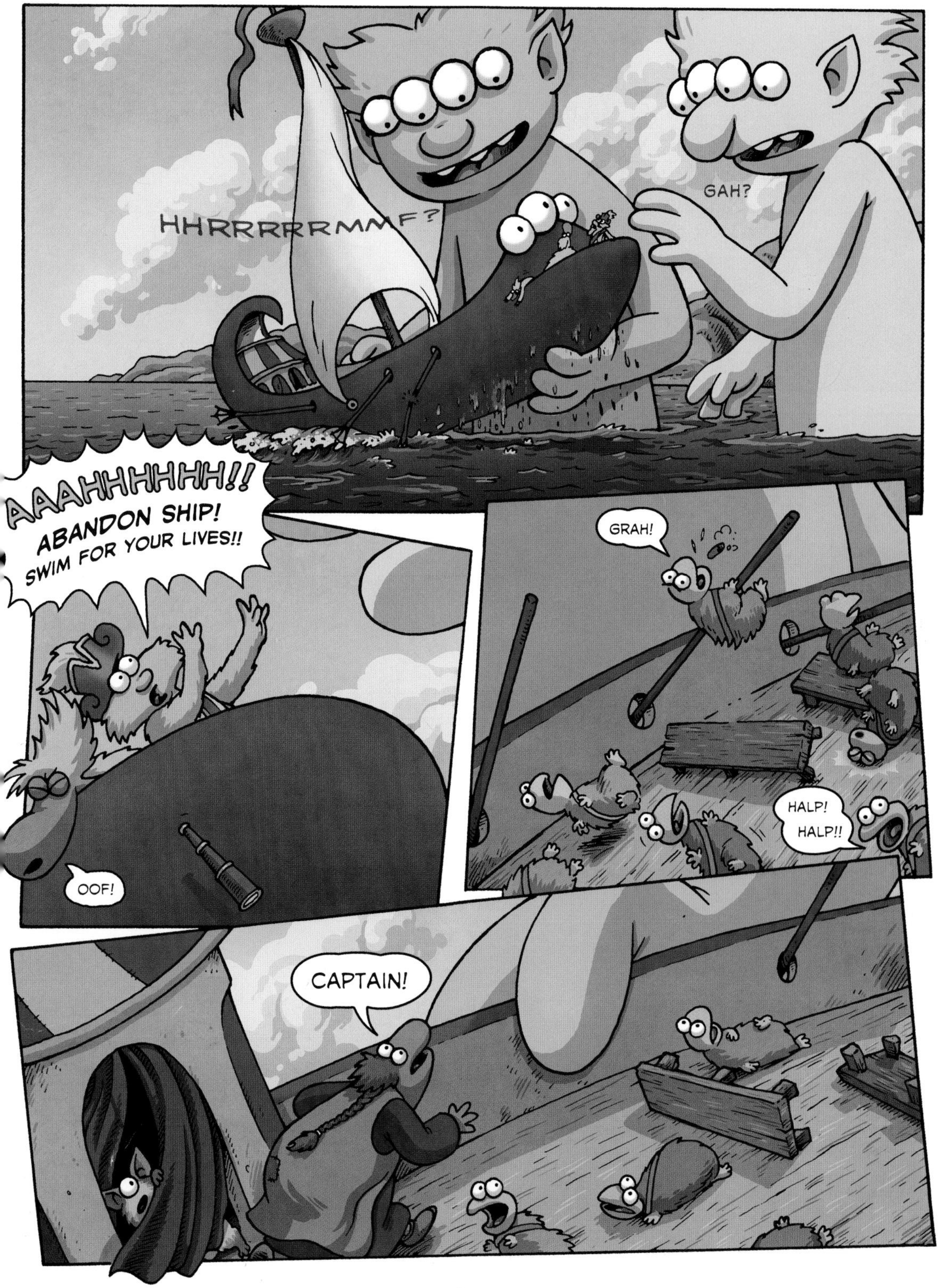
HHRRRRRRMMF?
GAH?
AAAHHHHHH!!
ABANDON SHIP!
SWIM FOR YOUR LIVES!!
OOF!
GRAH!
HALP!
HALP!!
CAPTAIN!

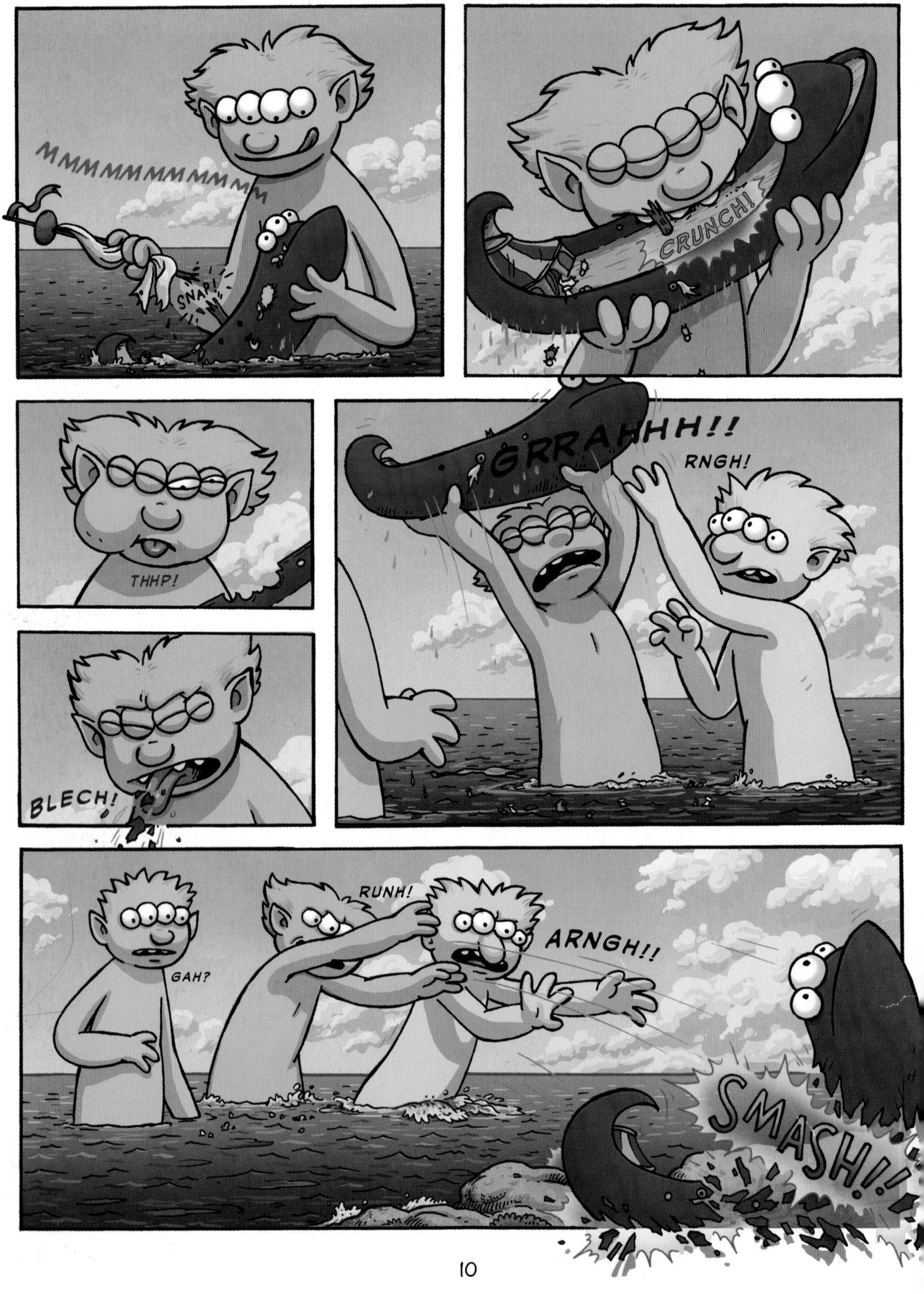
MMMMMMMMMMMMM
SNAP!
CRUNCH!
THHP!
BLECH!
GRRAHHH!!
RNGH!
RUNH!
GAH?
ARNGH!!
SMASH!!

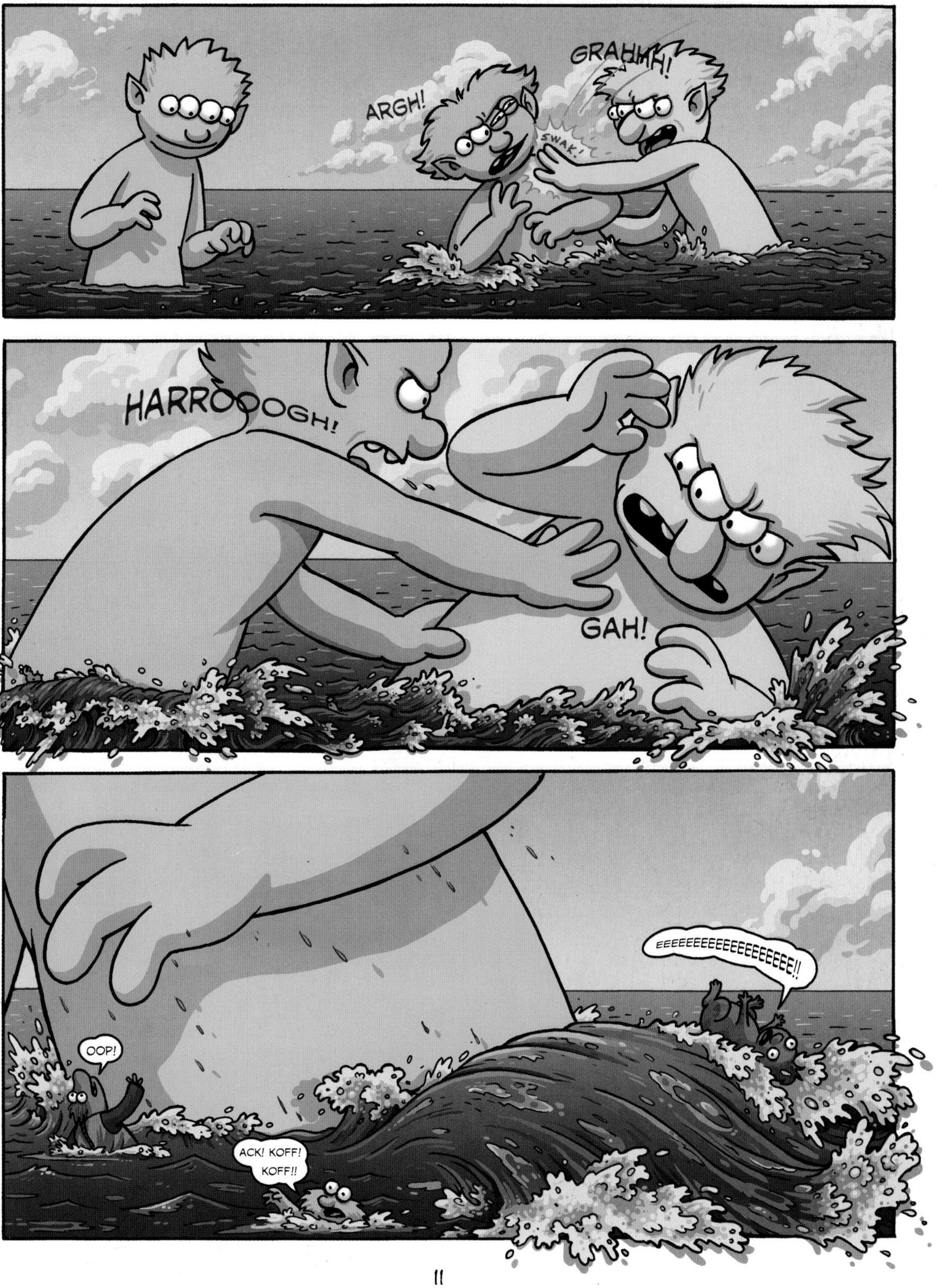
ARGH!
GRAHHHH!
SWAK!
HARROOOGH!
GAH!
EEEEEEEEEEEEEEEEEEE!!
OOP!
ACK! KOFF! KOFF!!

HELP! HELP! I CAN'T SWIM! SOMEONE HELP!!

SOMEONE! ANYONE!! ⸗COUGH COUGH⸗ PLEASE! SOMEBODY BLUBB GLUBB

HACK! COUGH!!

YOU SAVED ⸗COUGH⸗ ME!? THANK YOU ⸗HACK⸗ THANK YOU FROM THE VERY BOTTOM OF MYSELF!

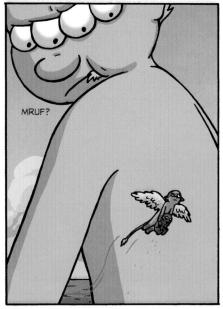

MRUF?

SWAK!

THWAK!

OOF!

ACK!

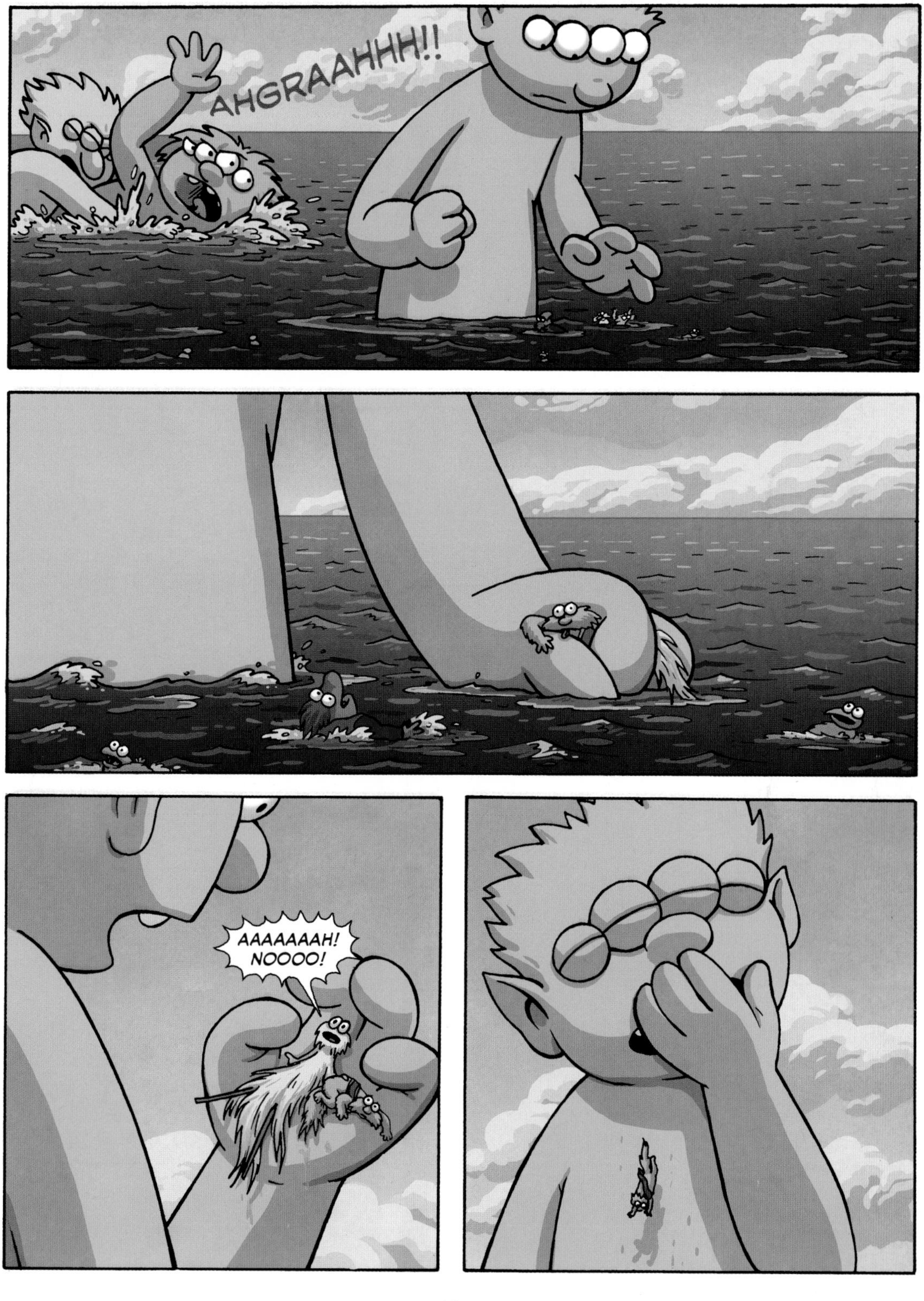
AHGRAAHHH!!
AAAAAAAH! NOOOO!

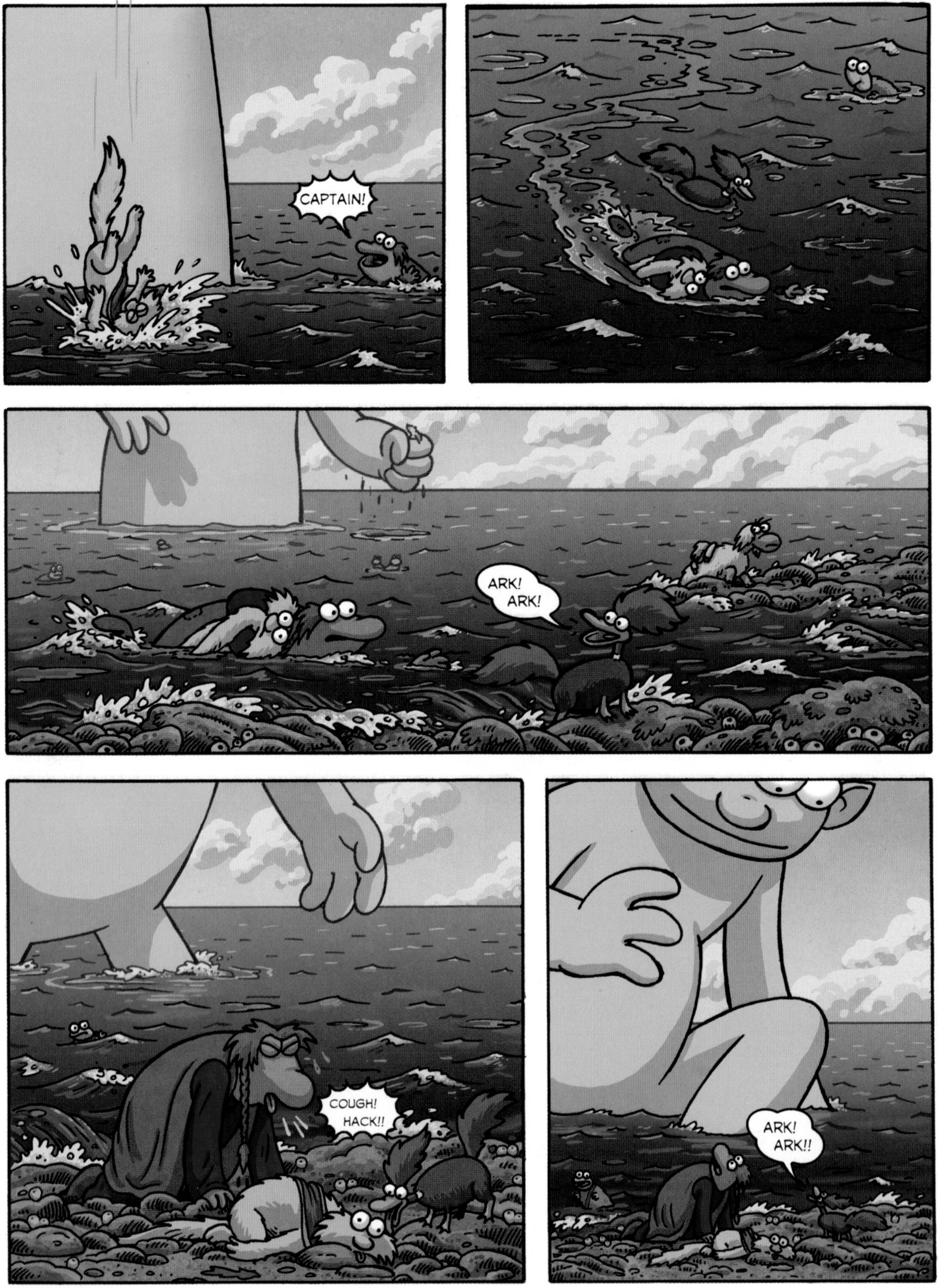
CAPTAIN!
ARK! ARK!
COUGH! HACK!!
ARK! ARK!!

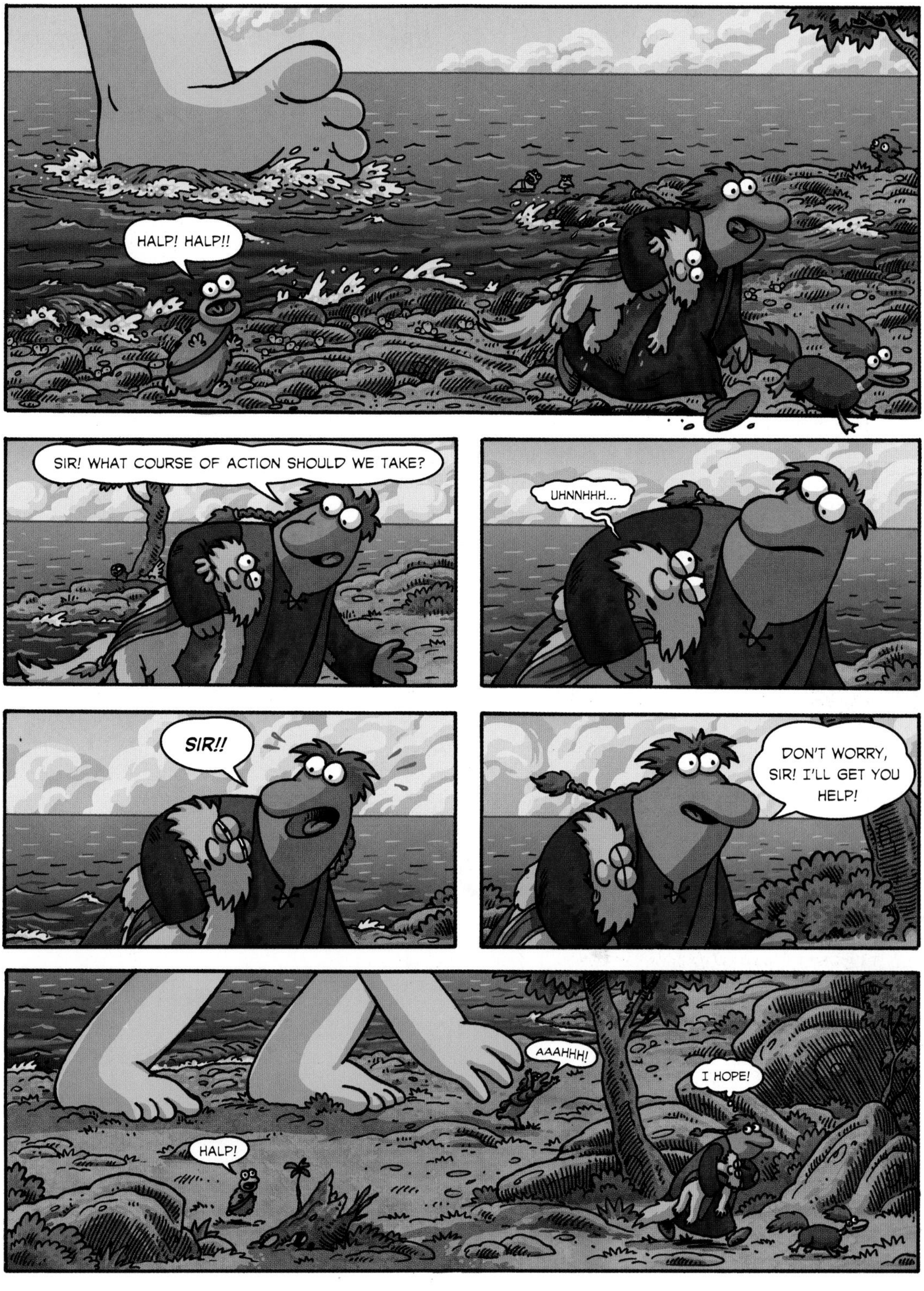
HALP! HALP!!
SIR! WHAT COURSE OF ACTION SHOULD WE TAKE?
UHNNHHH...
SIR!!
DON'T WORRY, SIR! I'LL GET YOU HELP!
AAAHHH!
I HOPE!
HALP!

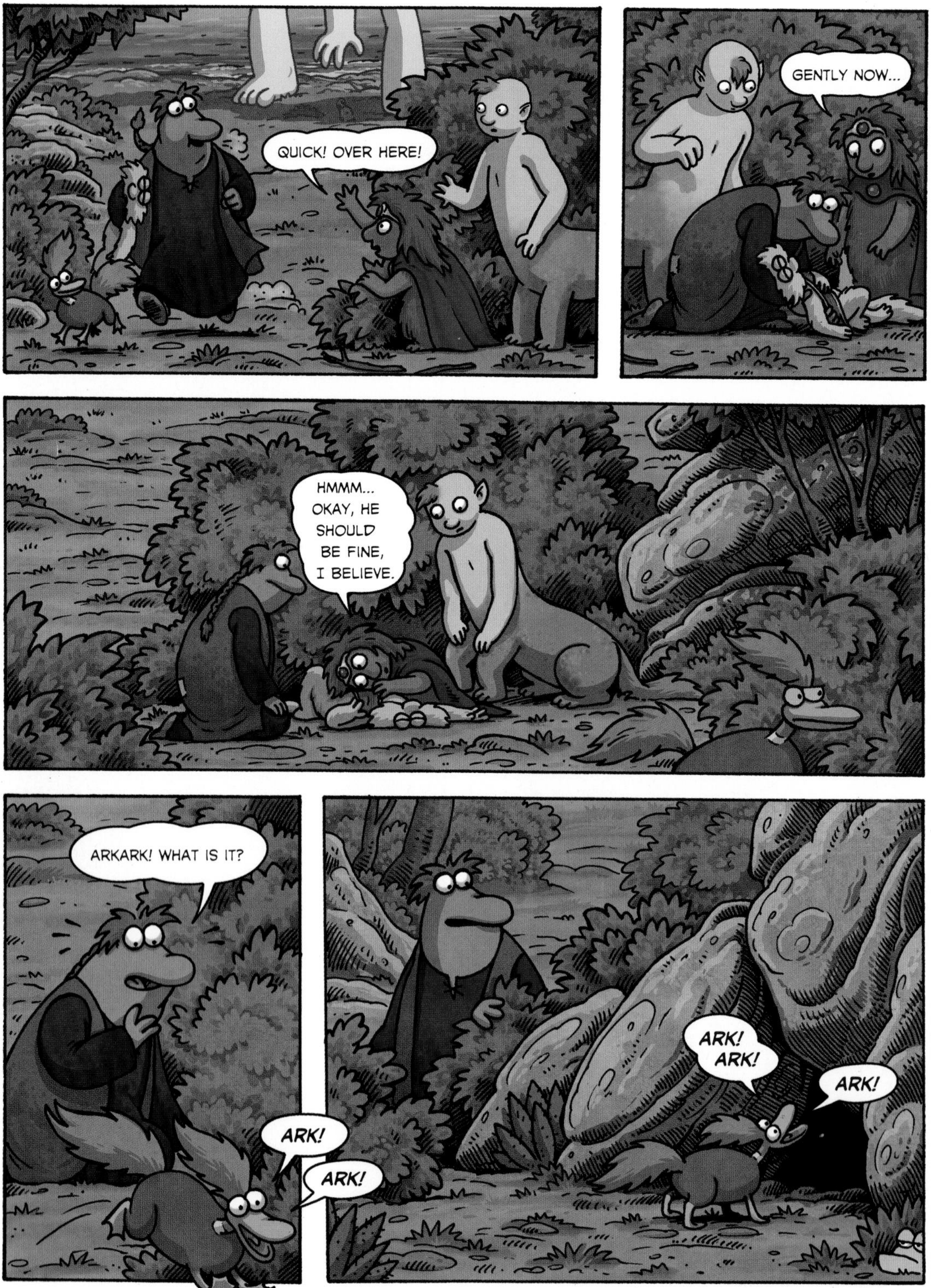
QUICK! OVER HERE!
GENTLY NOW...
HMMM... OKAY, HE SHOULD BE FINE, I BELIEVE.
ARKARK! WHAT IS IT?
ARK!
ARK!
ARK! ARK!
ARK!

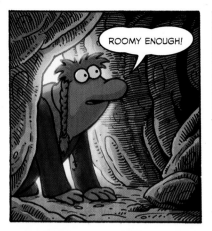

ROOMY ENOUGH!

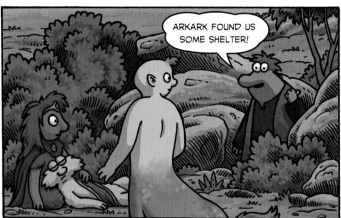

ARKARK FOUND US SOME SHELTER!

YES... THIS CAVE WILL DO NICELY. JUST WHAT WE NEED TO SHELTER US FROM THOSE MONSTERS!

CLEUS, YOU SHOULD GO WITH... UM, WHAT'S YOUR NAME AGAIN?

SMOK.

OF COURSE. GO WITH SMOK TO SEE IF YOU CAN FIND ANY MORE CREW MEMBERS AND BRING THEM HERE. BE CAREFUL!

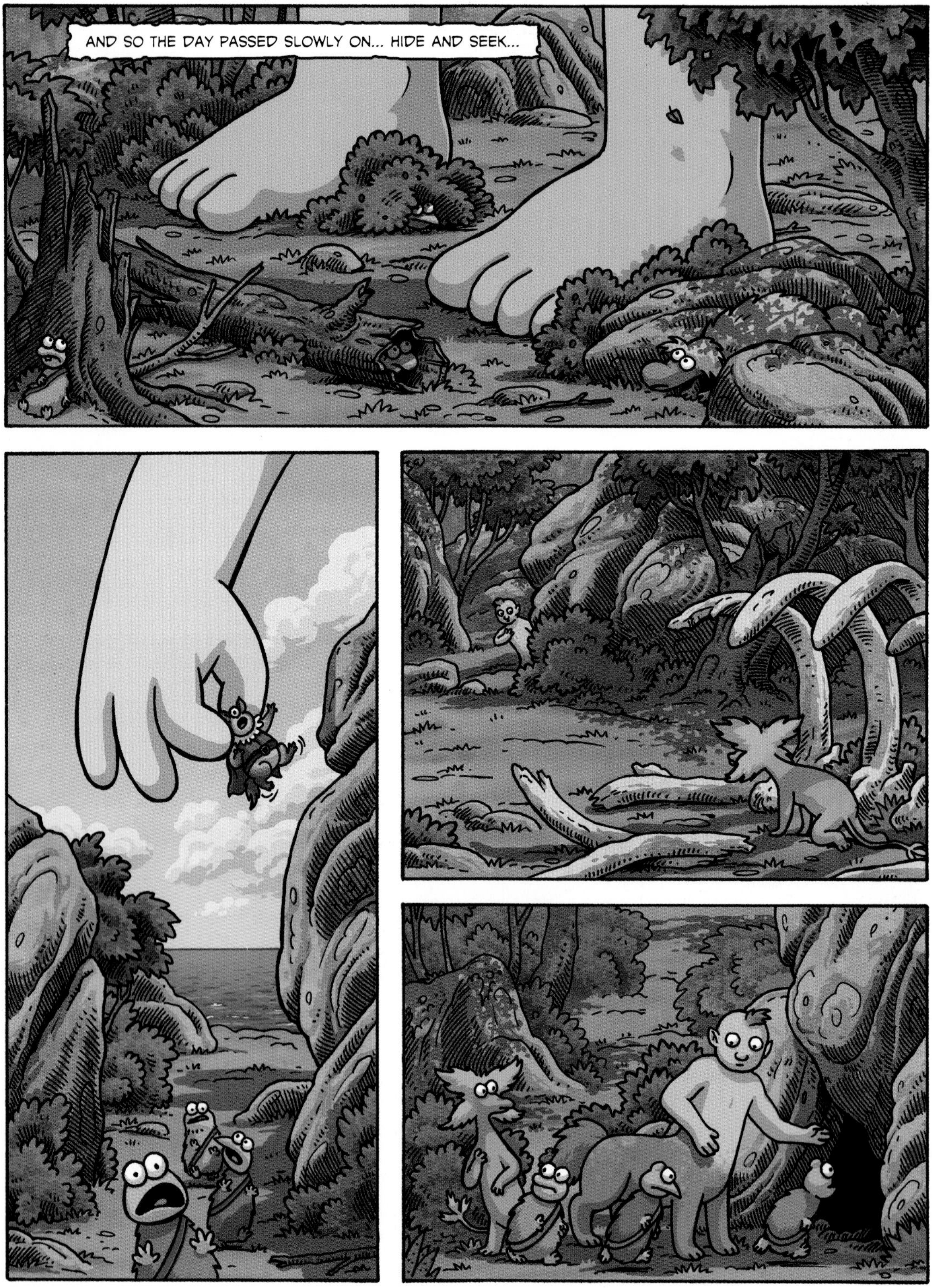
AND SO THE DAY PASSED SLOWLY ON... HIDE AND SEEK...

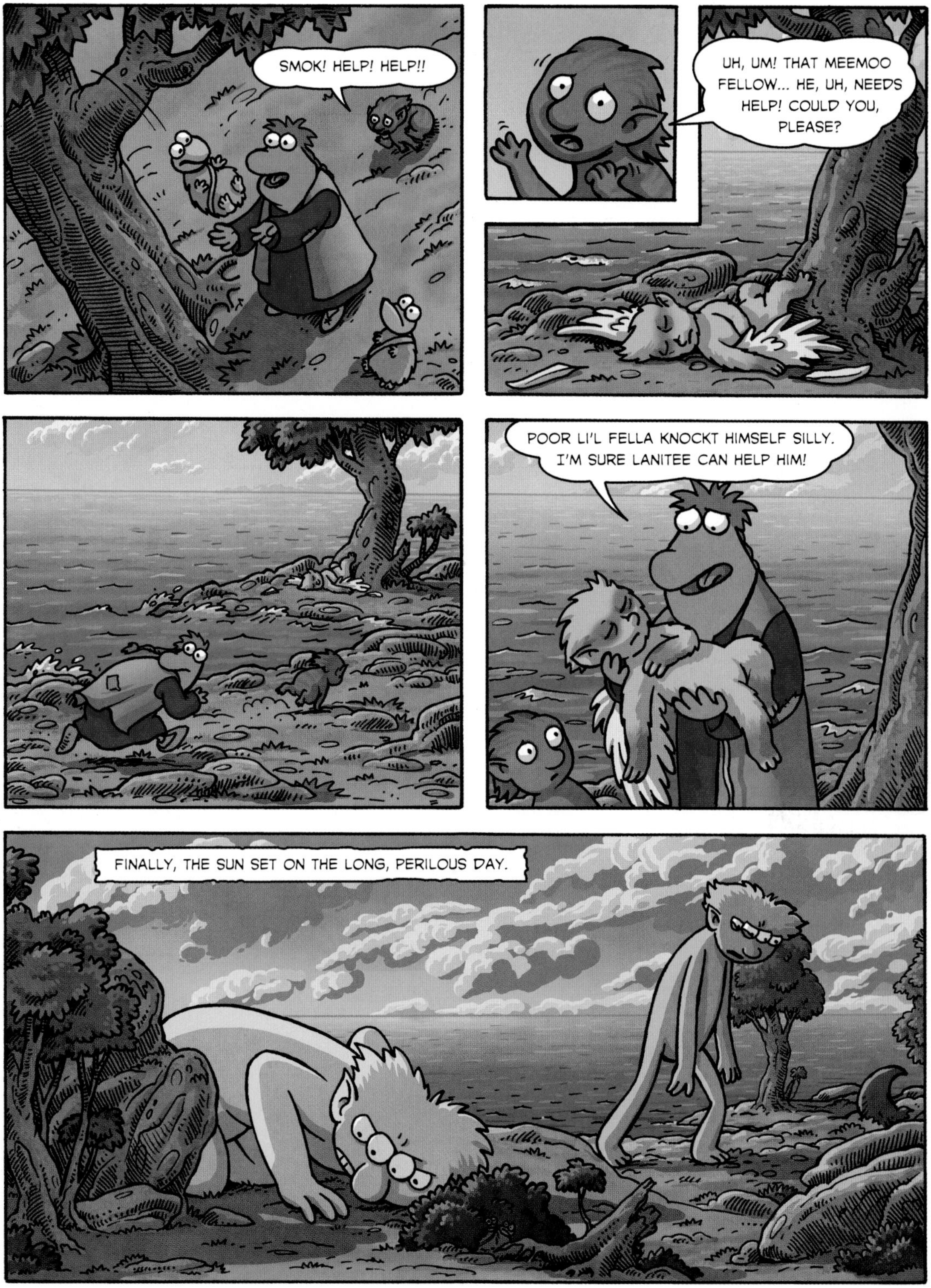
SMOK! HELP! HELP!!
UH, UM! THAT MEEMOO FELLOW... HE, UH, NEEDS HELP! COULD YOU, PLEASE?
POOR LI'L FELLA KNOCKT HIMSELF SILLY. I'M SURE LANITEE CAN HELP HIM!
FINALLY, THE SUN SET ON THE LONG, PERILOUS DAY.

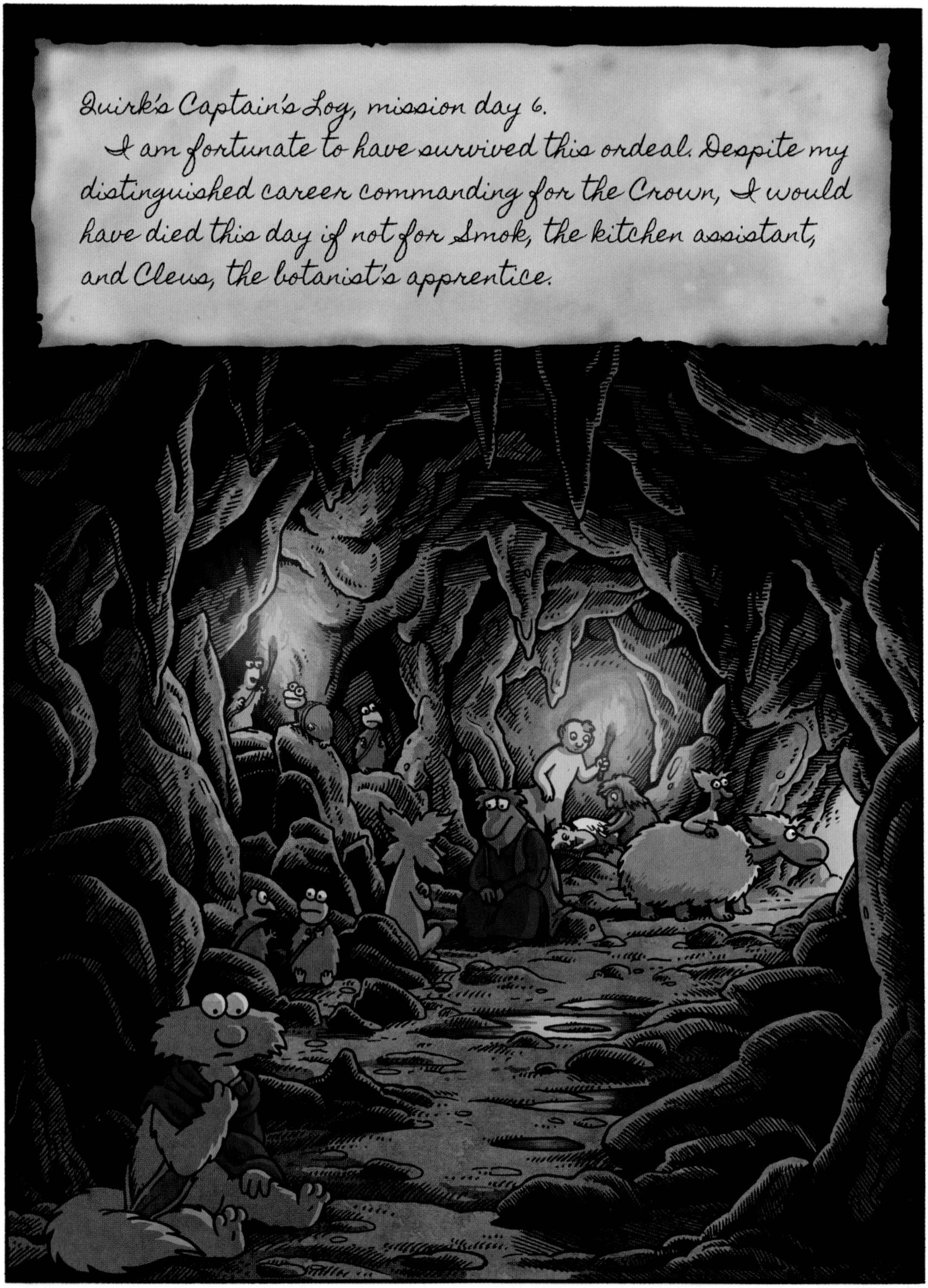
Quirk's Captain's Log, mission day 6.
I am fortunate to have survived this ordeal. Despite my distinguished career commanding for the Crown, I would have died this day if not for Smok, the kitchen assistant, and Cleus, the botanist's apprentice.

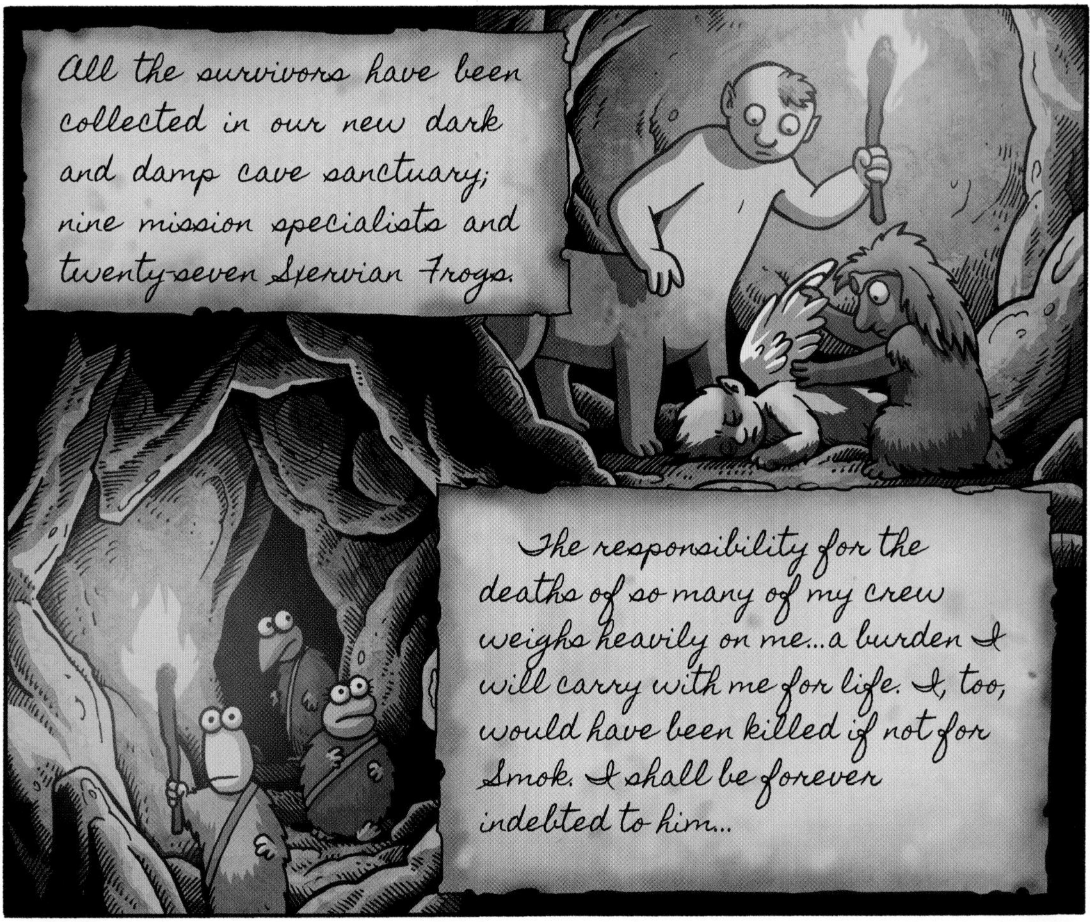
All the survivors have been collected in our new dark and damp cave sanctuary; nine mission specialists and twenty-seven Sjervian Frogs.
The responsibility for the deaths of so many of my crew weighs heavily on me...a burden I will carry with me for life. I, too, would have been killed if not for Smok. I shall be forever indebted to him...

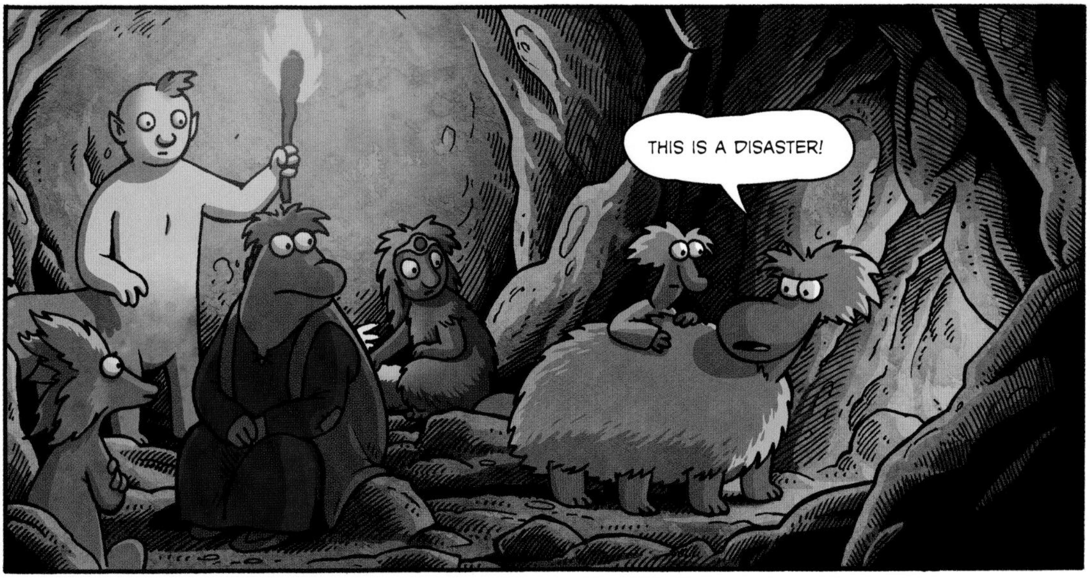
THIS IS A DISASTER!

I'M COLD AND HUNGRY. THESE CONDITIONS ARE INTOLERABLE!

I CONCUR... HOW AM I TO WORK WITHOUT EVEN THE MOST BASIC OF TOOLS?

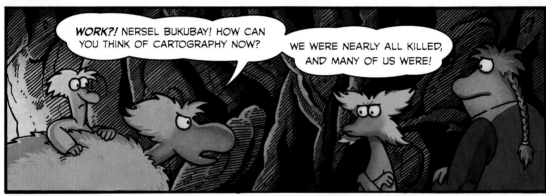

WORK?! NERSEL BUKUBAY! HOW CAN YOU THINK OF CARTOGRAPHY NOW?

WE WERE NEARLY ALL KILLED, AND MANY OF US WERE!

THAT MEEMOO IS GOING TO DIE, TOO, AND WE WILL PROBABLY HAVE TO EAT HIM TO SURVIVE!

HORRIBLE!

GHASTLY!!

HEY! HEY! NO NEED TO SNACK ON EACH OTHER!

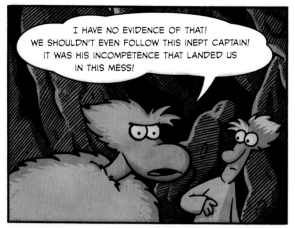

I HAVE NO EVIDENCE OF THAT! WE SHOULDN'T EVEN FOLLOW THIS INEPT CAPTAIN! IT WAS HIS INCOMPETENCE THAT LANDED US IN THIS MESS!

NO, BURTRYM! YOU CAN'T MEAN THAT! OUR CAPTAIN IS A GREAT LEADER AND MUST HAVE A PLAN!

RIGHT, CAPTAIN?

UM, FOR EXAMPLE, I'M SURE HE WANTS TA SEND OUT THE SCOUTS—UH, I MEAN THE SCOUT—TA SEE IF THEM MONSTERS ARE STILL ABOUT... AN' ALSO TA SEE IF ANY OF OUR STUFF WASHED UP.

SIR?

UM... PRECISELY.

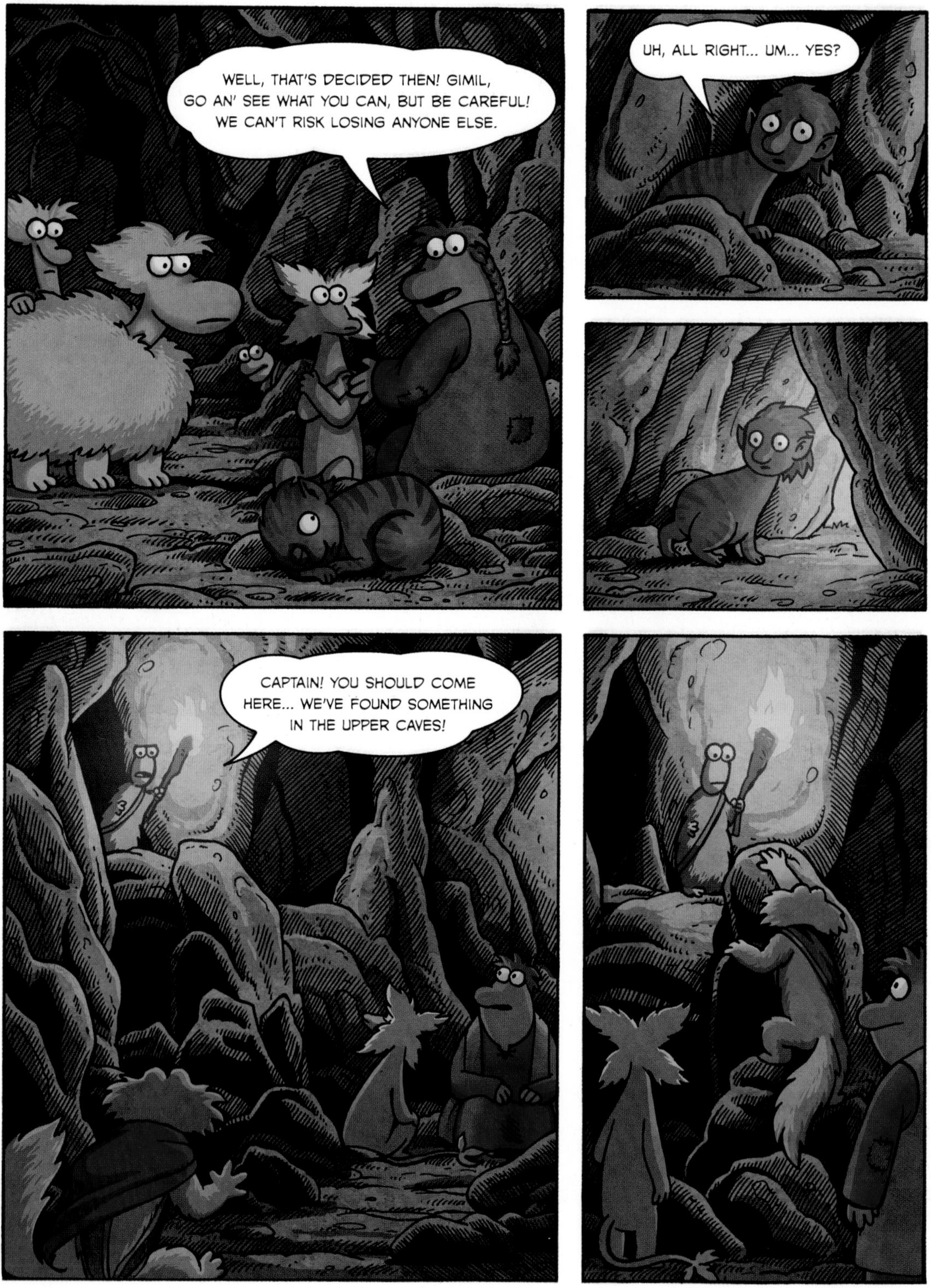
WELL, THAT'S DECIDED THEN! GIMIL, GO AN' SEE WHAT YOU CAN, BUT BE CAREFUL! WE CAN'T RISK LOSING ANYONE ELSE.
UH, ALL RIGHT... UM... YES?
CAPTAIN! YOU SHOULD COME HERE... WE'VE FOUND SOMETHING IN THE UPPER CAVES!

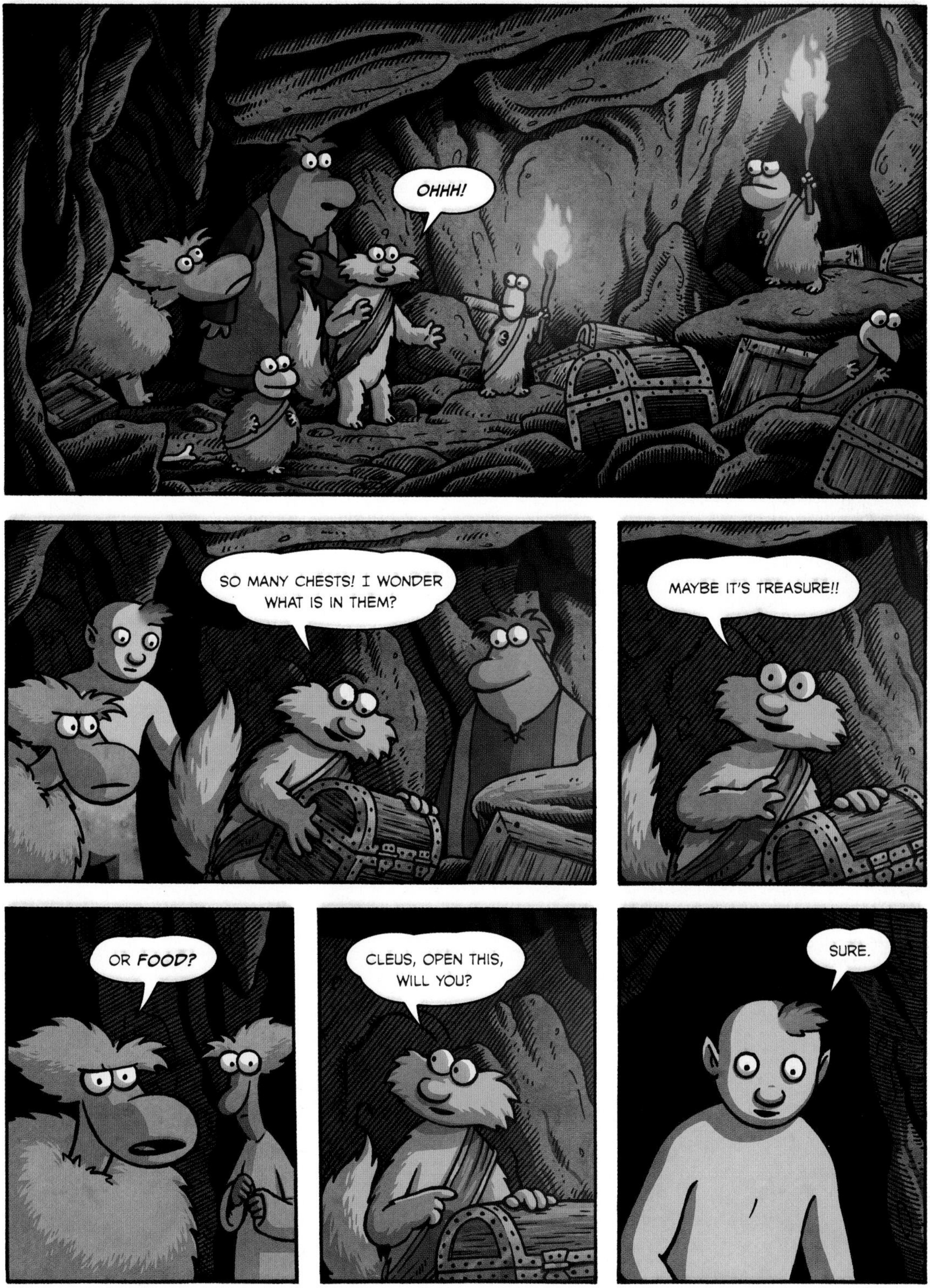
OHHH!
SO MANY CHESTS! I WONDER WHAT IS IN THEM?
MAYBE IT'S TREASURE!!
OR FOOD?
CLEUS, OPEN THIS, WILL YOU?
SURE.

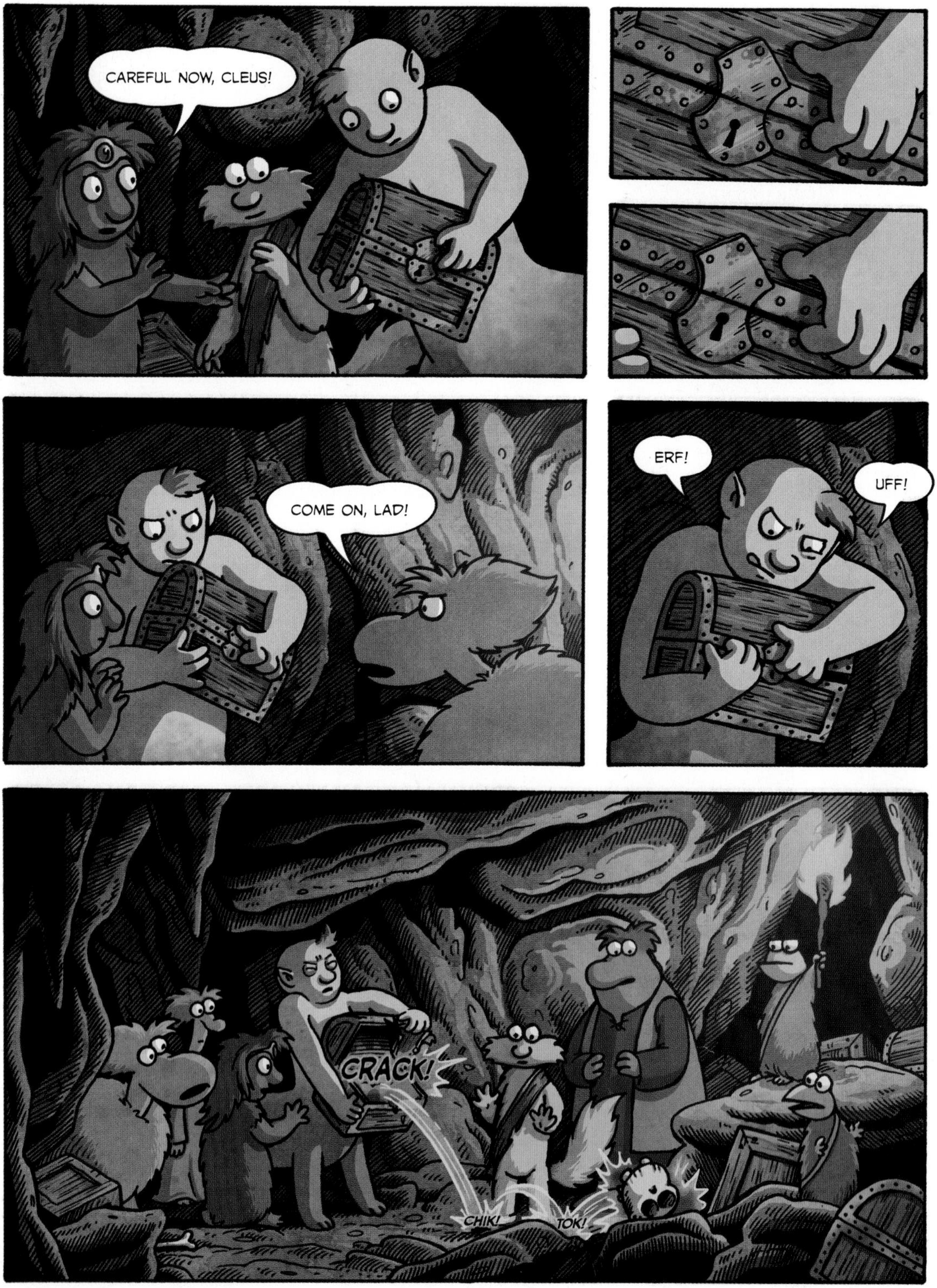
CAREFUL NOW, CLEUS!
COME ON, LAD!
ERF!
UFF!
CRACK!
CHIK!
TOK!

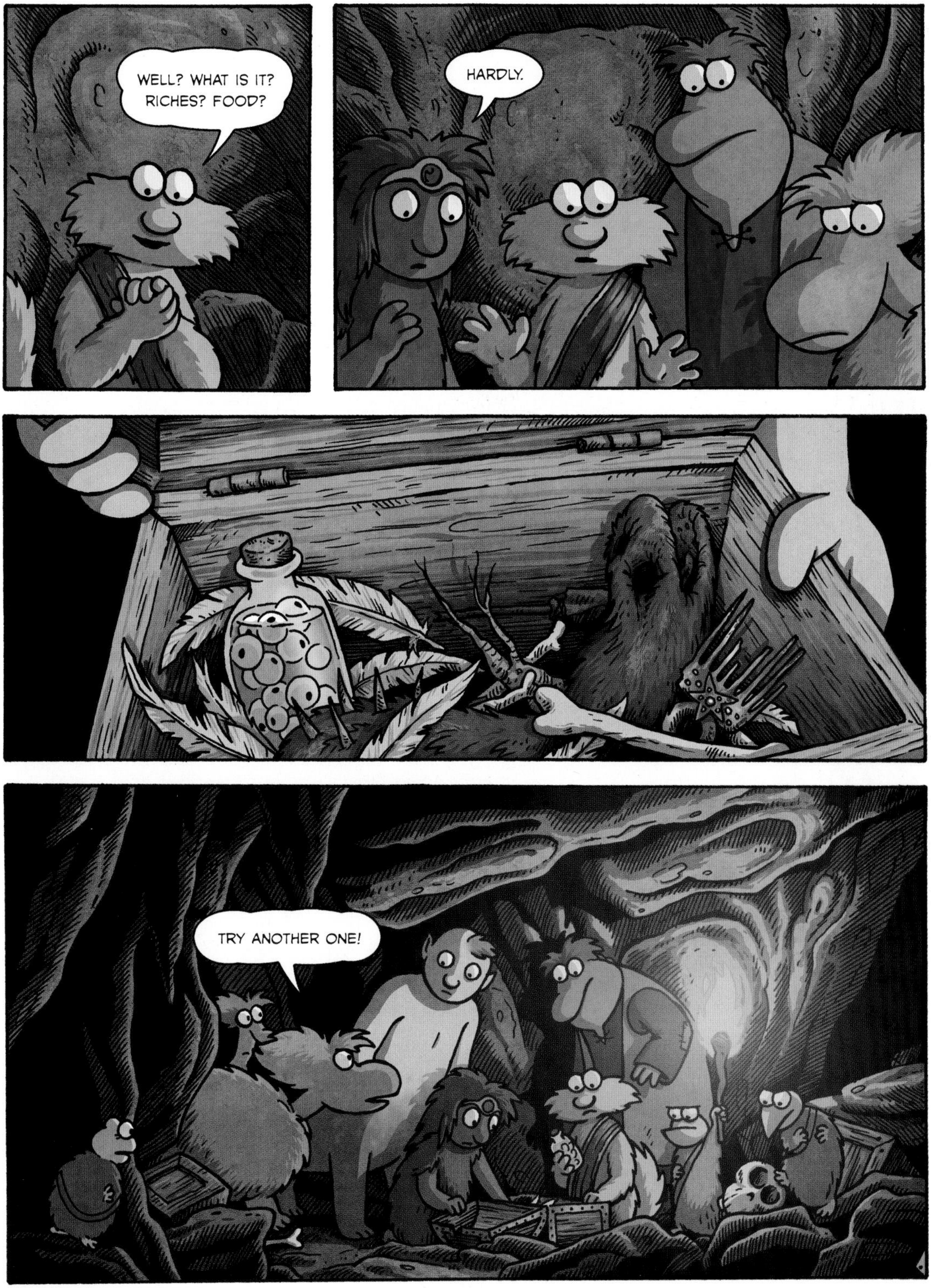
WELL? WHAT IS IT? RICHES? FOOD?
HARDLY.
TRY ANOTHER ONE!

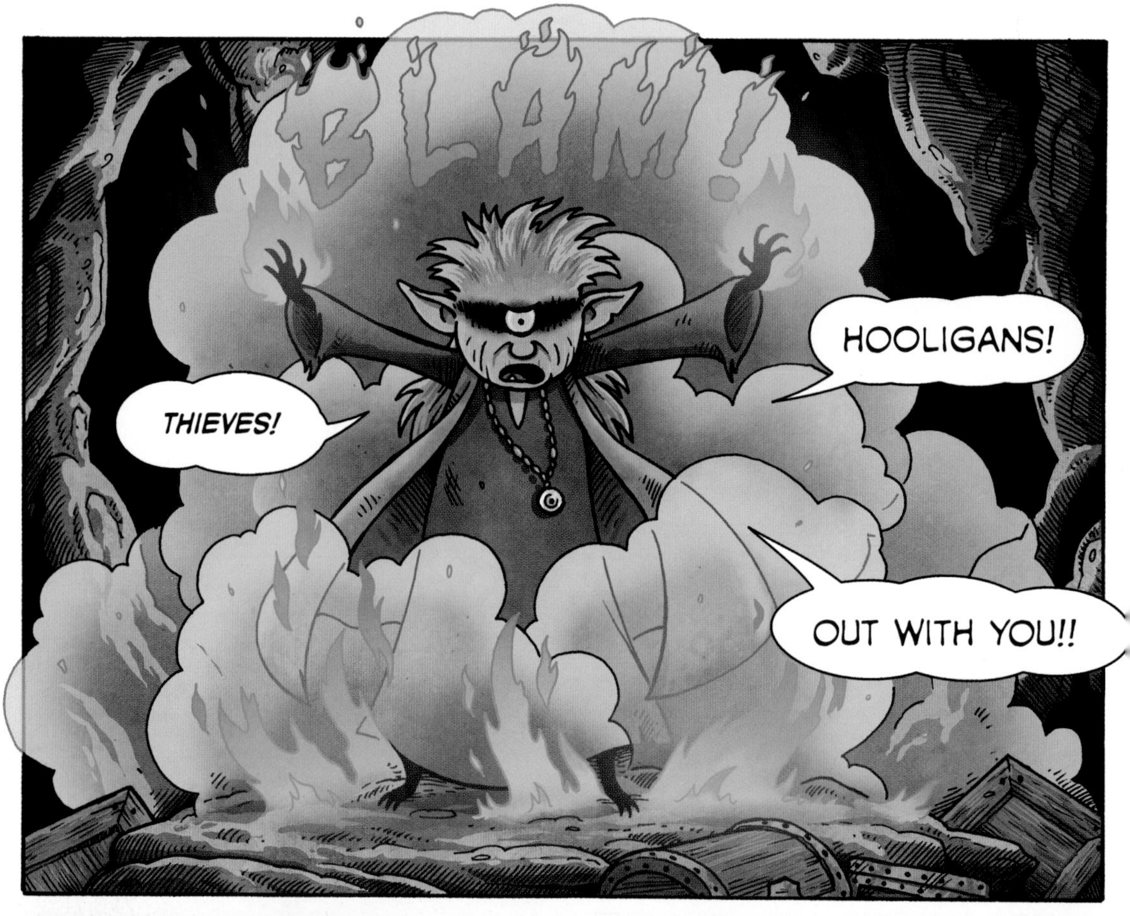
BLAM!
THIEVES!
HOOLIGANS!
OUT WITH YOU!!

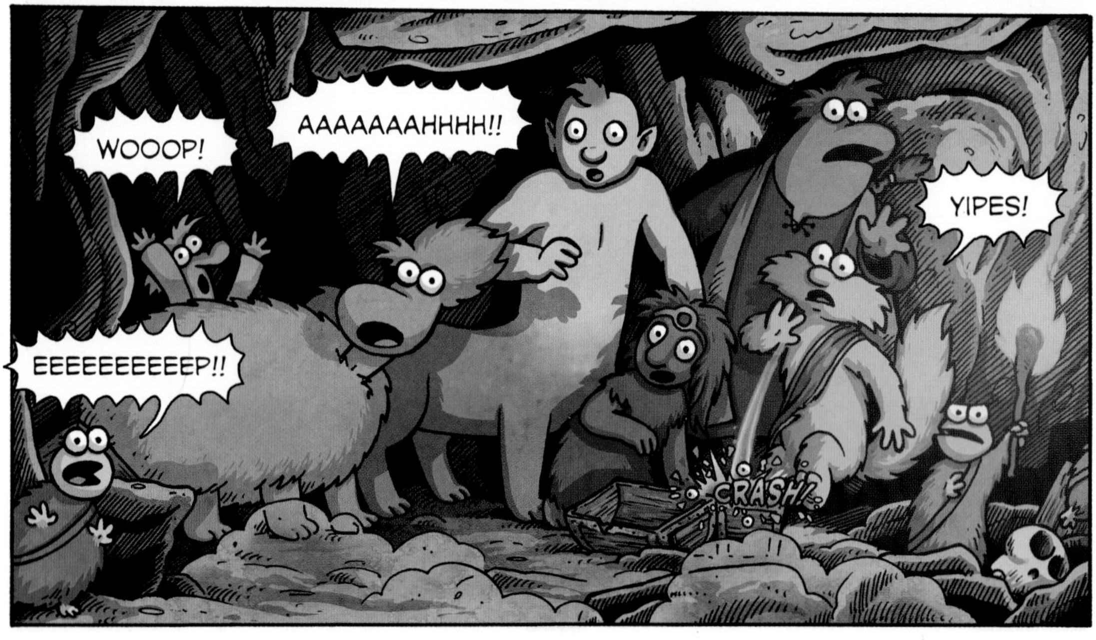
WOOOP!
AAAAAAAHHHH!!
YIPES!
EEEEEEEEEEEP!!
CRASH!

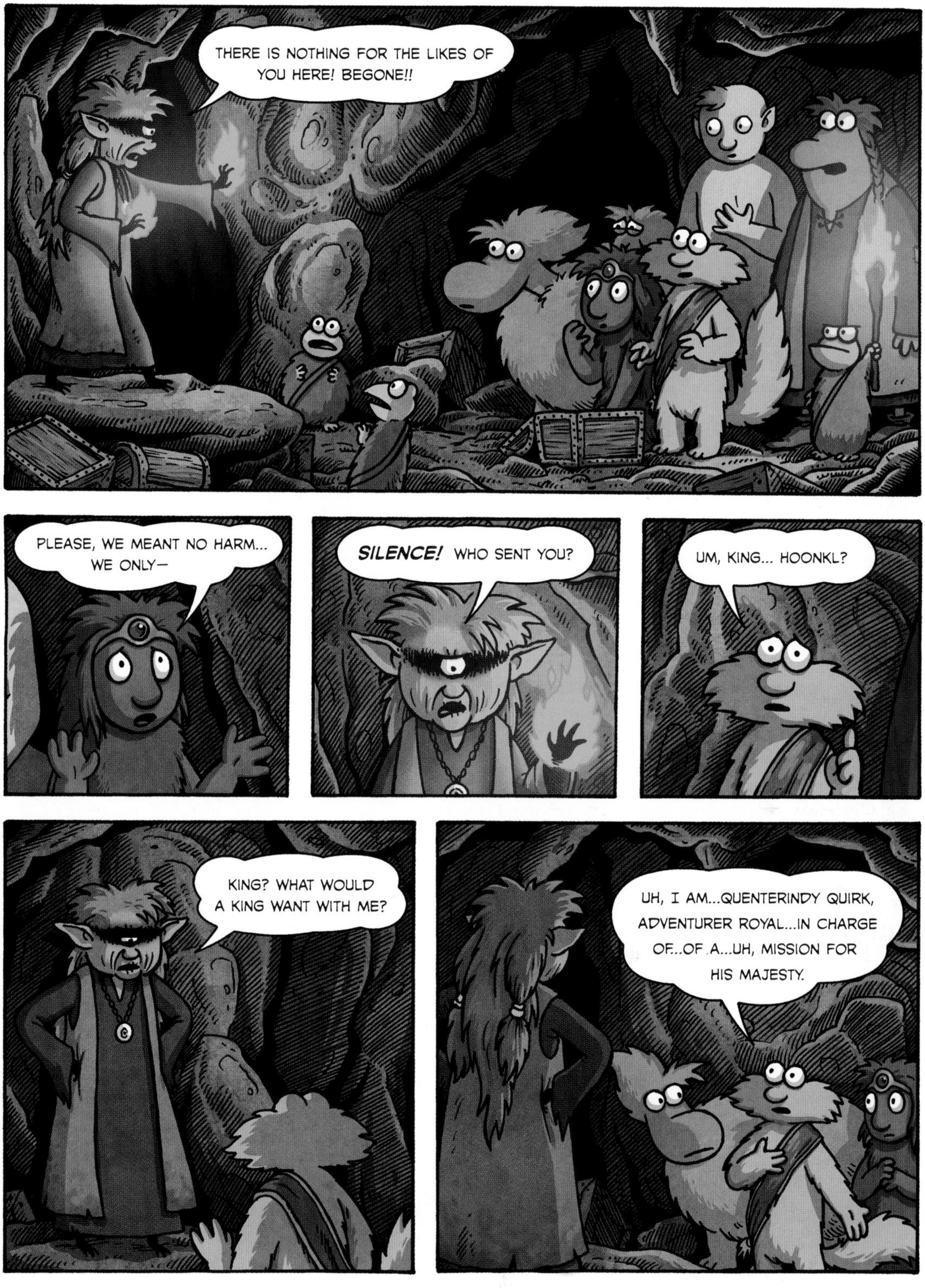
THERE IS NOTHING FOR THE LIKES OF YOU HERE! BEGONE!!
PLEASE, WE MEANT NO HARM... WE ONLY—
SILENCE! WHO SENT YOU?
UM, KING... HOONKL?
KING? WHAT WOULD A KING WANT WITH ME?
UH, I AM...QUENTERINDY QUIRK, ADVENTURER ROYAL...IN CHARGE OF...OF A...UH, MISSION FOR HIS MAJESTY.

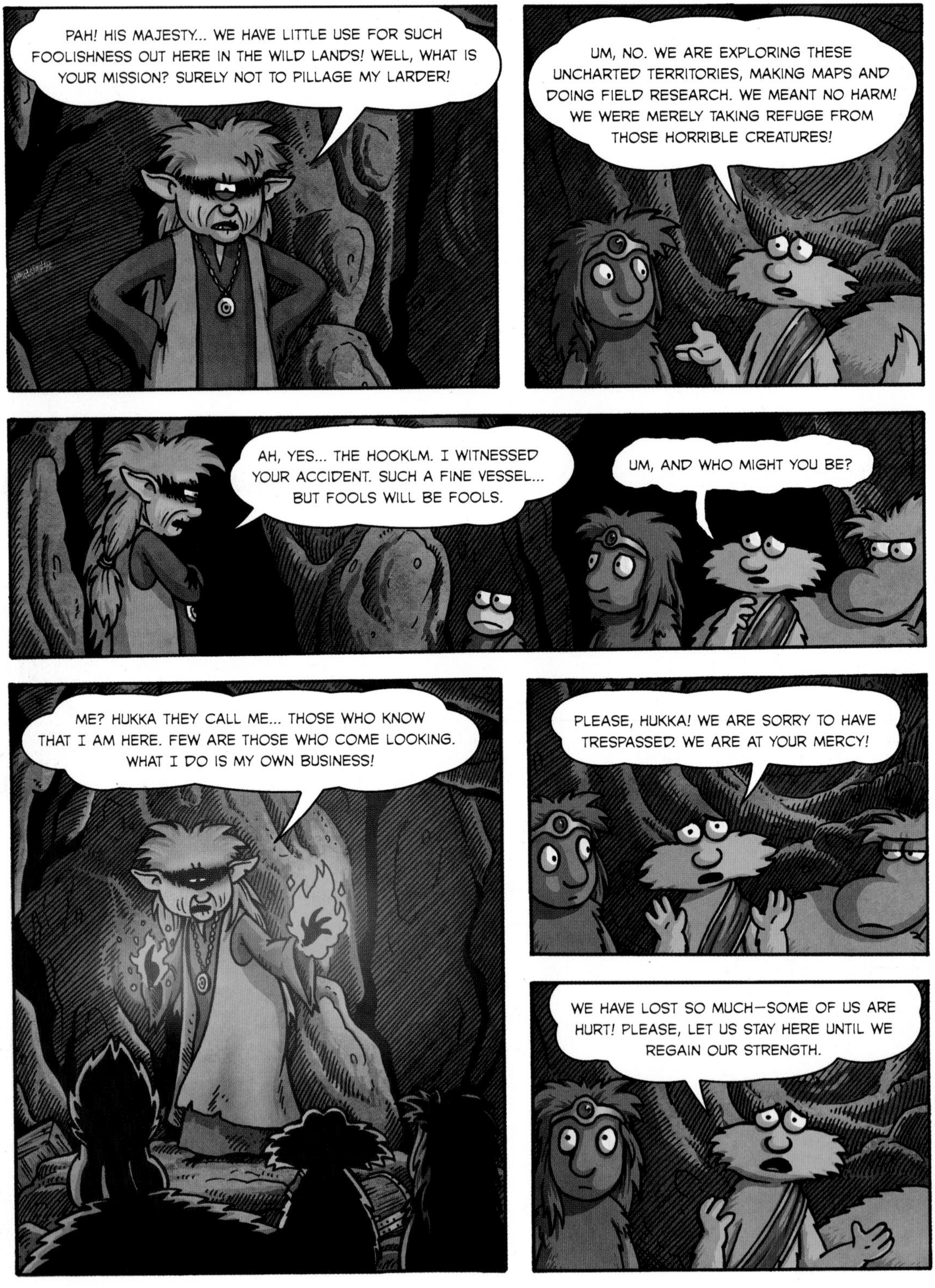

PAH! HIS MAJESTY... WE HAVE LITTLE USE FOR SUCH FOOLISHNESS OUT HERE IN THE WILD LANDS! WELL, WHAT IS YOUR MISSION? SURELY NOT TO PILLAGE MY LARDER!
UM, NO. WE ARE EXPLORING THESE UNCHARTED TERRITORIES, MAKING MAPS AND DOING FIELD RESEARCH. WE MEANT NO HARM! WE WERE MERELY TAKING REFUGE FROM THOSE HORRIBLE CREATURES!
AH, YES... THE HOOKLM. I WITNESSED YOUR ACCIDENT. SUCH A FINE VESSEL... BUT FOOLS WILL BE FOOLS.
UM, AND WHO MIGHT YOU BE?
ME? HUKKA THEY CALL ME... THOSE WHO KNOW THAT I AM HERE. FEW ARE THOSE WHO COME LOOKING. WHAT I DO IS MY OWN BUSINESS!
PLEASE, HUKKA! WE ARE SORRY TO HAVE TRESPASSED. WE ARE AT YOUR MERCY!
WE HAVE LOST SO MUCH—SOME OF US ARE HURT! PLEASE, LET US STAY HERE UNTIL WE REGAIN OUR STRENGTH.

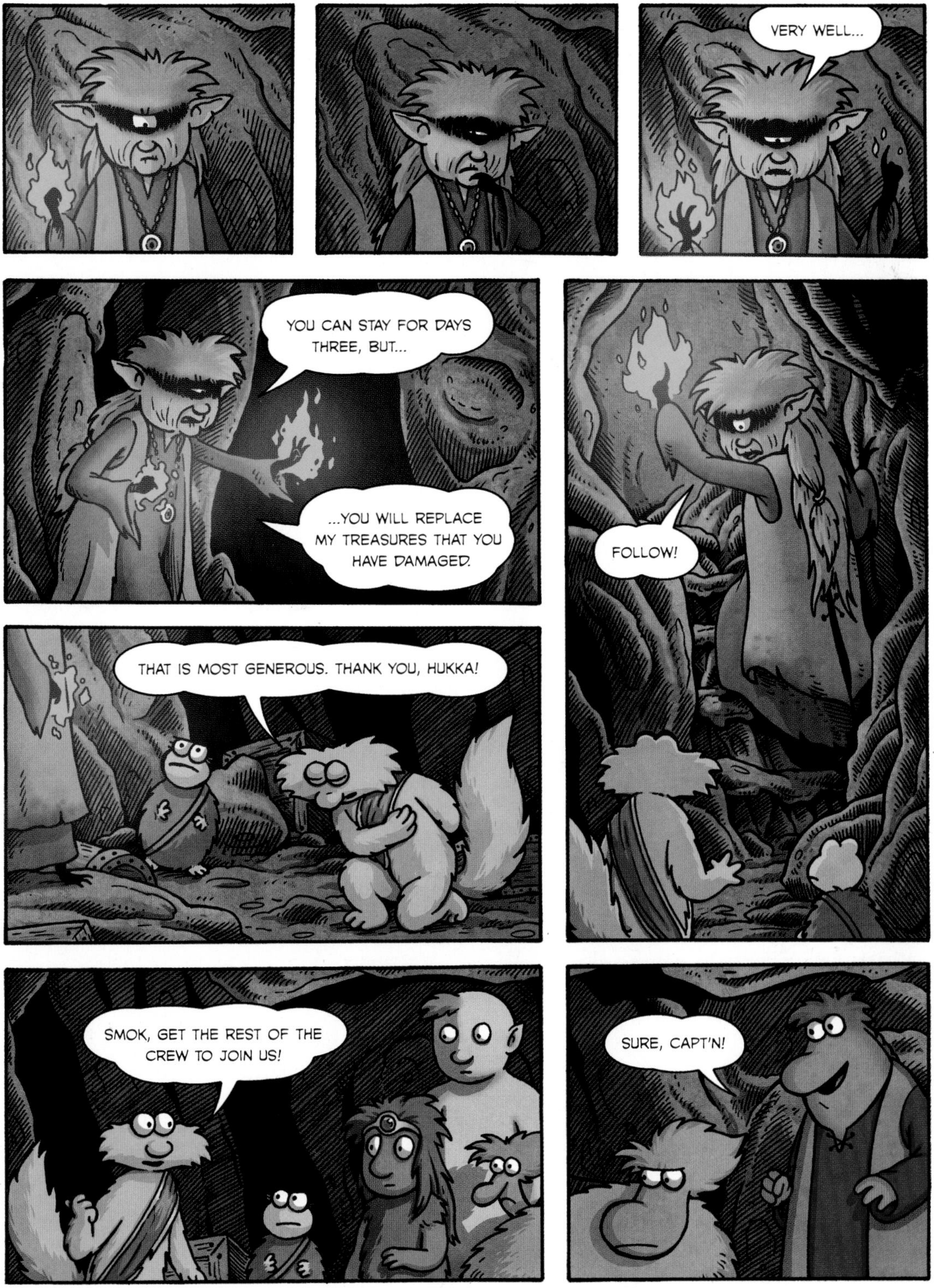
VERY WELL...
YOU CAN STAY FOR DAYS THREE, BUT...
...YOU WILL REPLACE MY TREASURES THAT YOU HAVE DAMAGED.
FOLLOW!
THAT IS MOST GENEROUS. THANK YOU, HUKKA!
SMOK, GET THE REST OF THE CREW TO JOIN US!
SURE, CAPT'N!

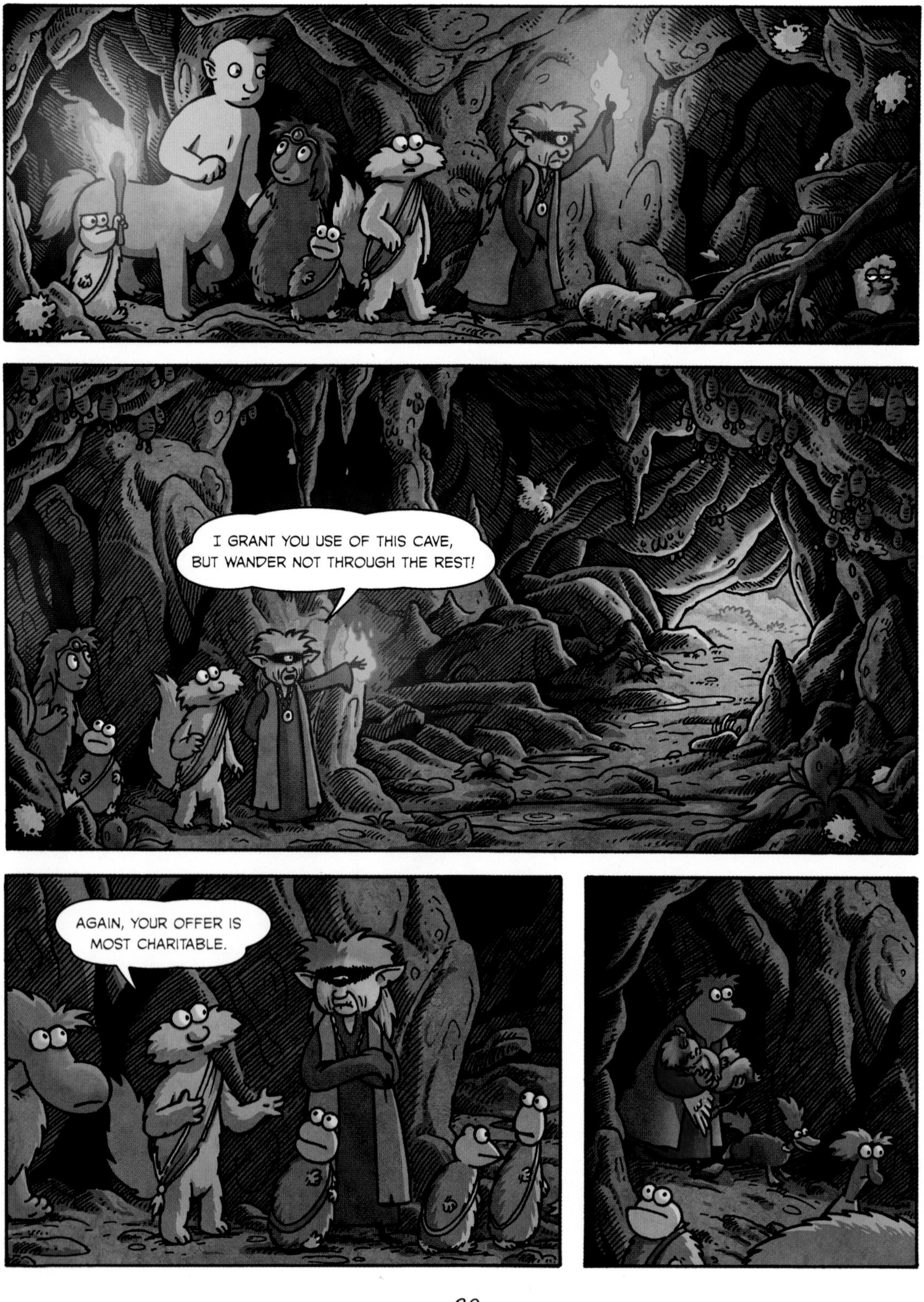
I GRANT YOU USE OF THIS CAVE,
BUT WANDER NOT THROUGH THE REST!
AGAIN, YOUR OFFER IS
MOST CHARITABLE.

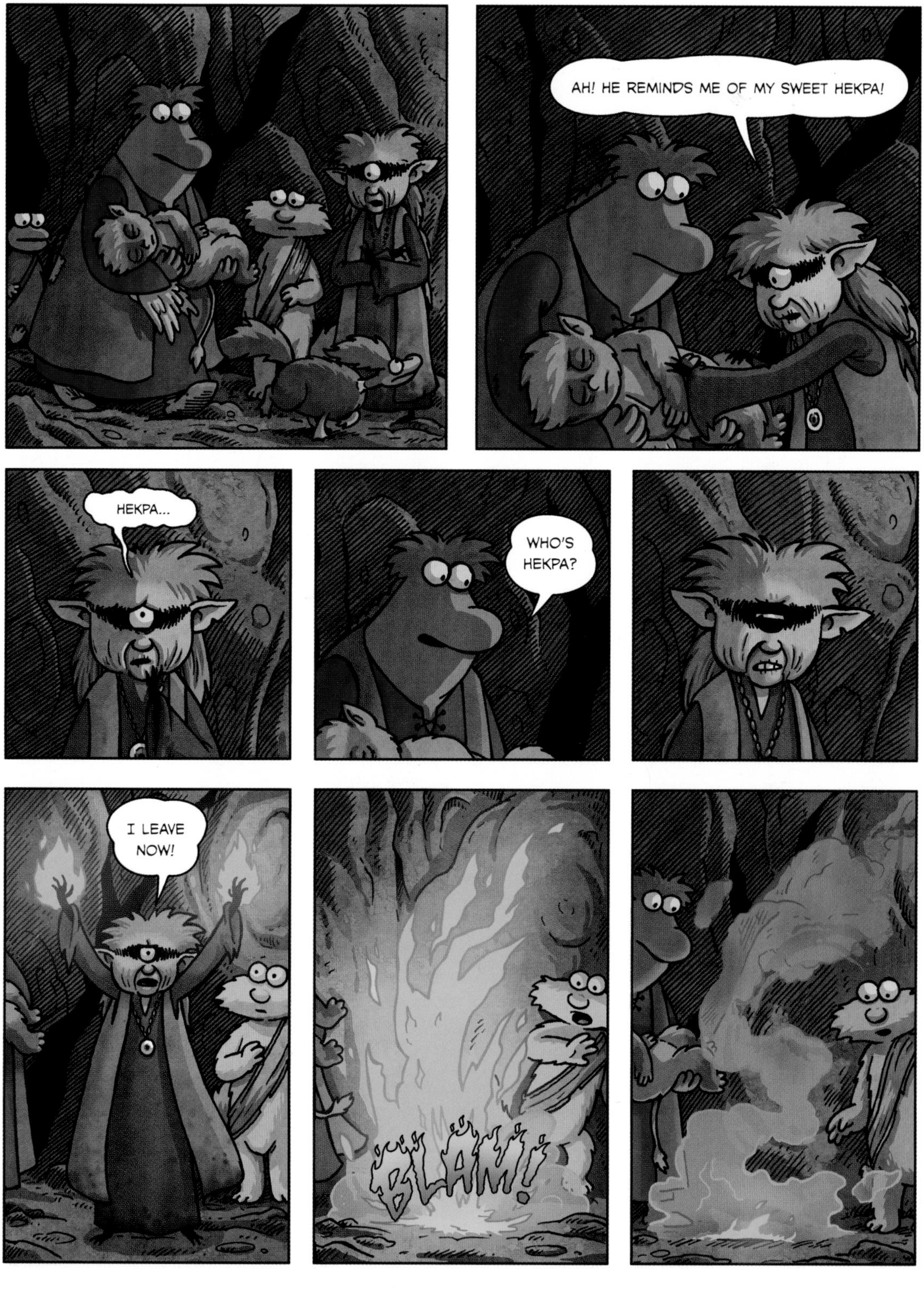
AH! HE REMINDS ME OF MY SWEET HEKPA!
HEKPA...
WHO'S HEKPA?
I LEAVE NOW!
BLAM!

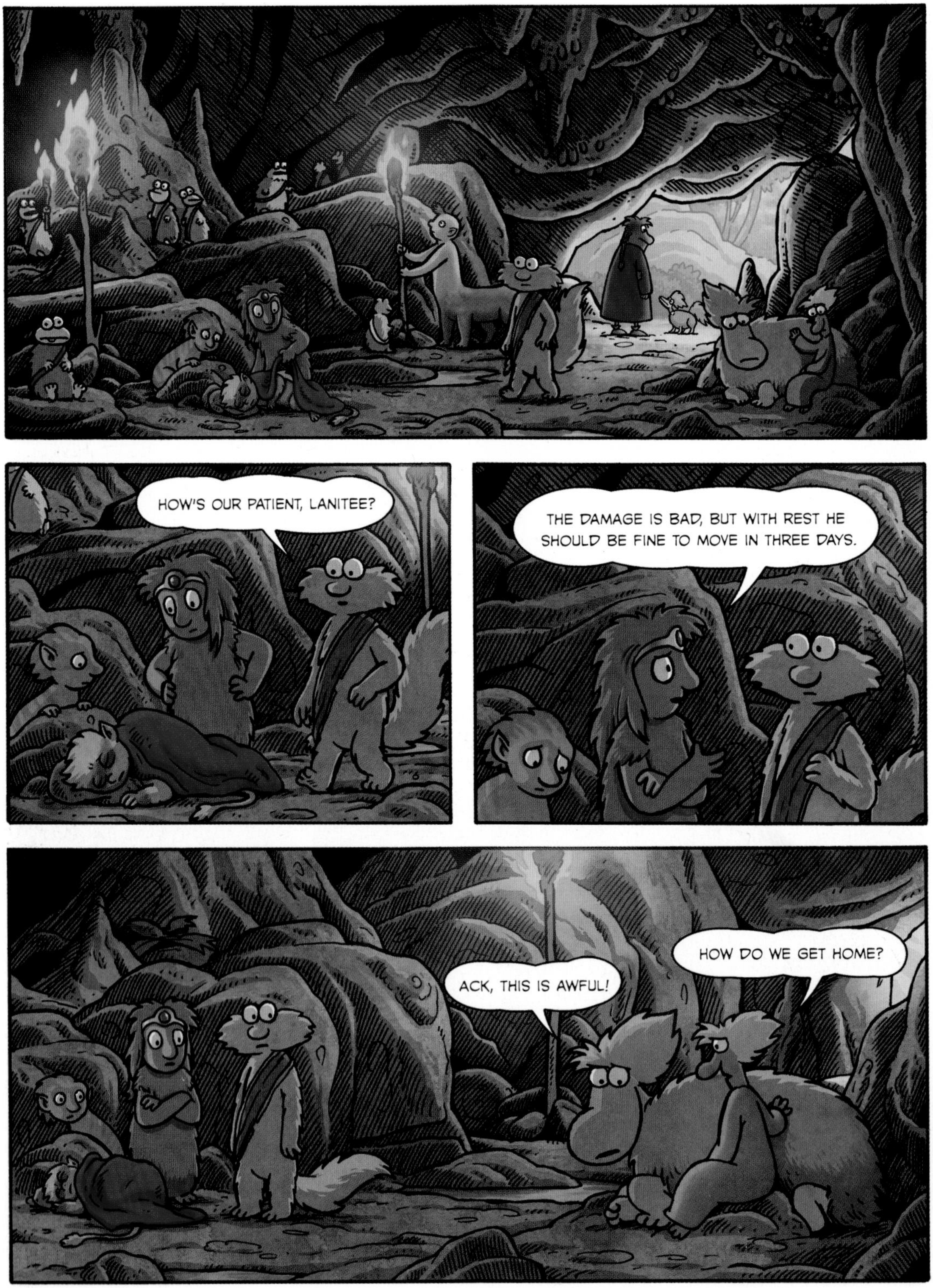
HOW'S OUR PATIENT, LANITEE?
THE DAMAGE IS BAD, BUT WITH REST HE SHOULD BE FINE TO MOVE IN THREE DAYS.
ACK, THIS IS AWFUL!
HOW DO WE GET HOME?

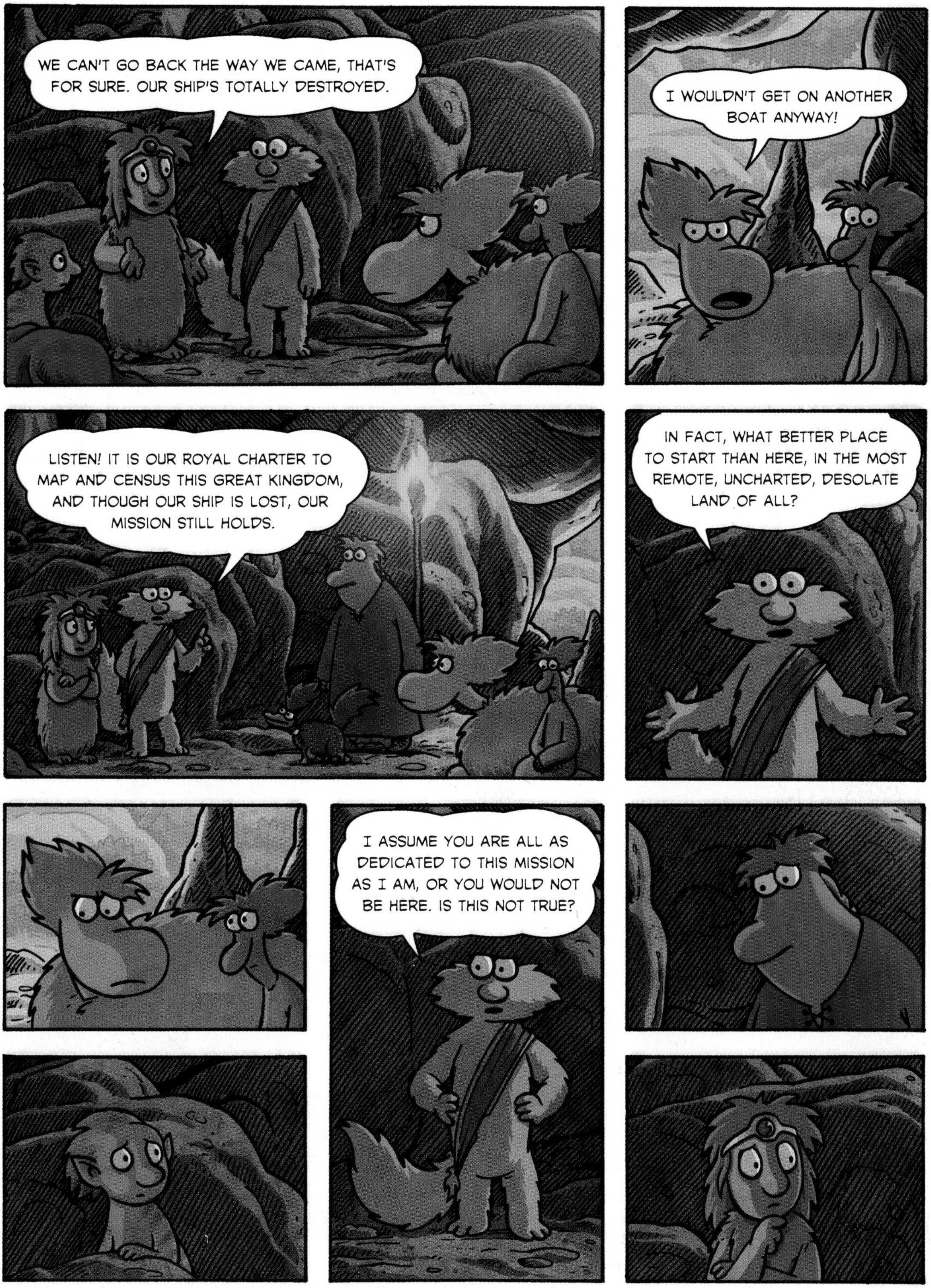
WE CAN'T GO BACK THE WAY WE CAME, THAT'S FOR SURE. OUR SHIP'S TOTALLY DESTROYED.
I WOULDN'T GET ON ANOTHER BOAT ANYWAY!
LISTEN! IT IS OUR ROYAL CHARTER TO MAP AND CENSUS THIS GREAT KINGDOM, AND THOUGH OUR SHIP IS LOST, OUR MISSION STILL HOLDS.
IN FACT, WHAT BETTER PLACE TO START THAN HERE, IN THE MOST REMOTE, UNCHARTED, DESOLATE LAND OF ALL?
I ASSUME YOU ARE ALL AS DEDICATED TO THIS MISSION AS I AM, OR YOU WOULD NOT BE HERE. IS THIS NOT TRUE?

BUT WHAT IS YOUR ACTUAL PLAN? WHERE WILL WE GO WHEN OUR THREE DAYS ARE UP AND HUKKA KICKS US OUT?

WELL, GIMIL HAS INFORMED ME THAT QUITE A LOT OF OUR CARGO HAS WASHED ASHORE... UNFORTUNATELY, THOSE GIANT CREATURES ARE STILL LINGERING ABOUT, IMPEDING ANY HOPE OF RECOVERY FOR NOW.

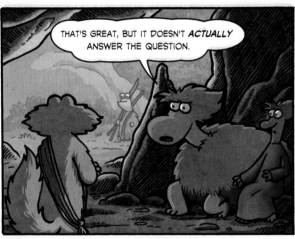

THAT'S GREAT, BUT IT DOESN'T *ACTUALLY* ANSWER THE QUESTION.

HMMM... WELL, PERHAPS *YOU* SHOULD ASSESS THE SITUATION FOR US.

GO AND HAVE A LOOK. GIMIL WILL TAKE YOU.

BUT THAT'S NOT MY JOB!

YOUR JOB IS TO FOLLOW MY ORDERS. NOW STOP COMPLAINING AND *GET TO IT!*

HMPH! YES, SIR.

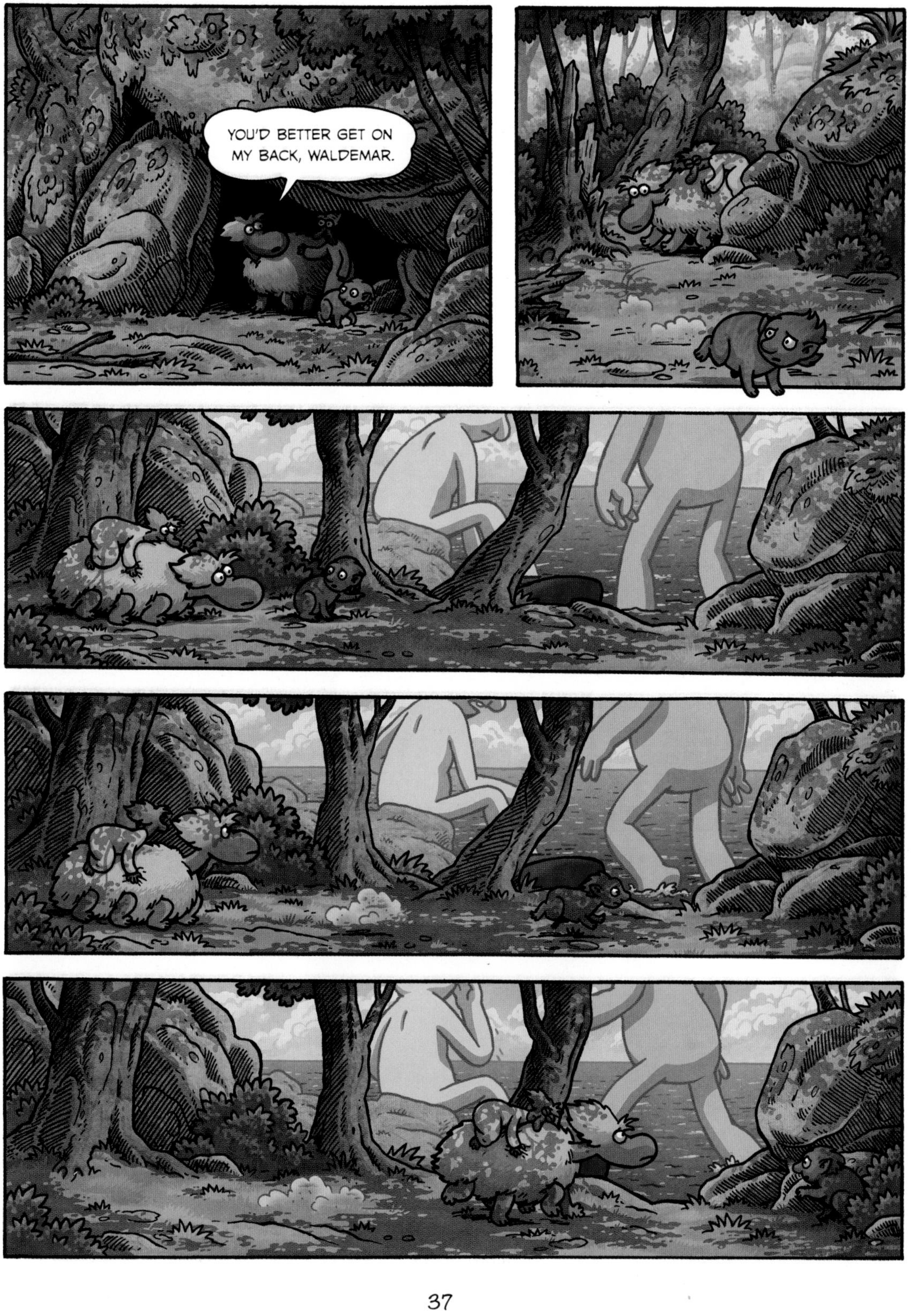
YOU'D BETTER GET ON MY BACK, WALDEMAR.

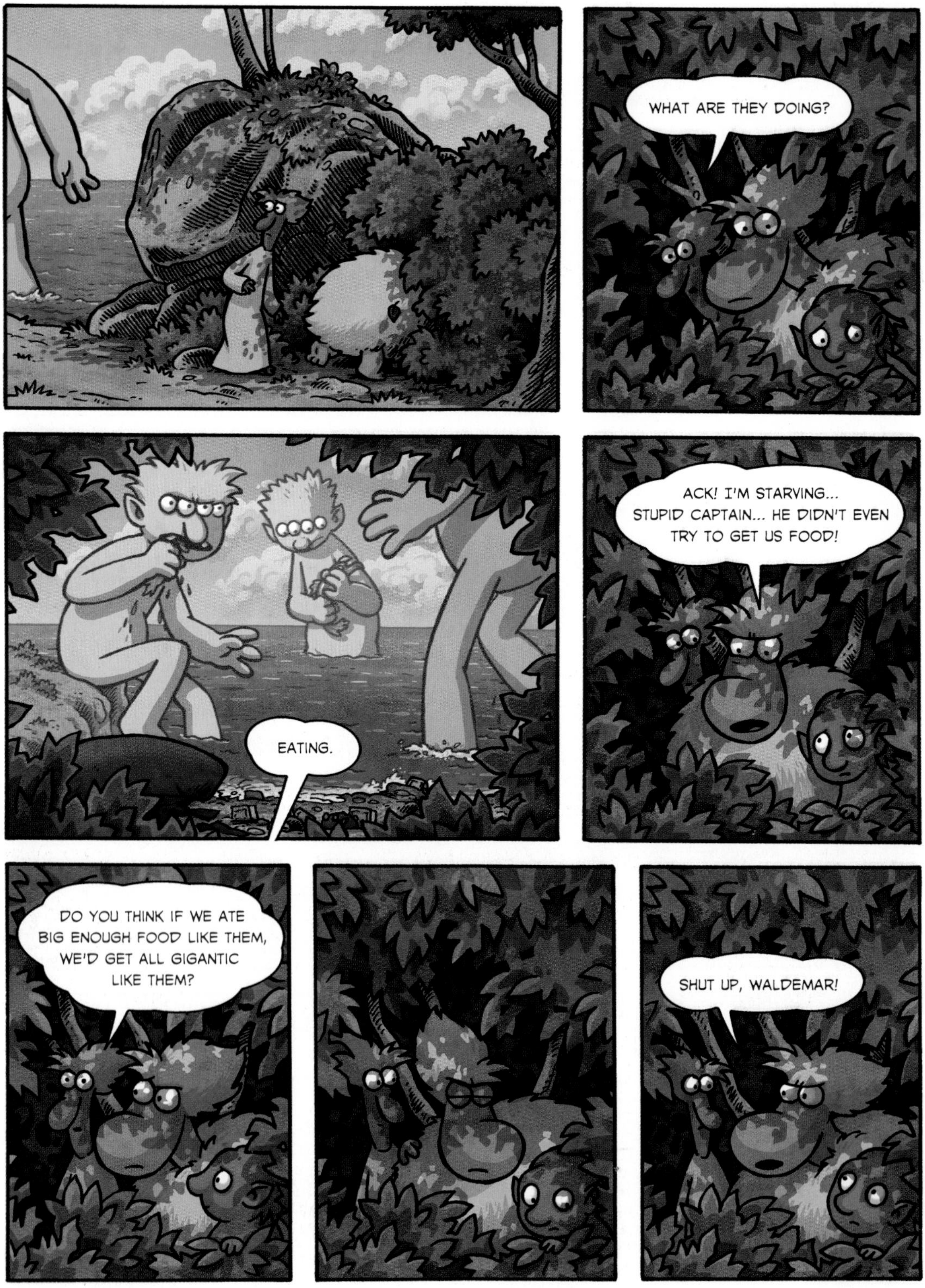
WHAT ARE THEY DOING?
EATING.
ACK! I'M STARVING... STUPID CAPTAIN... HE DIDN'T EVEN TRY TO GET US FOOD!
DO YOU THINK IF WE ATE BIG ENOUGH FOOD LIKE THEM, WE'D GET ALL GIGANTIC LIKE THEM?
SHUT UP, WALDEMAR!

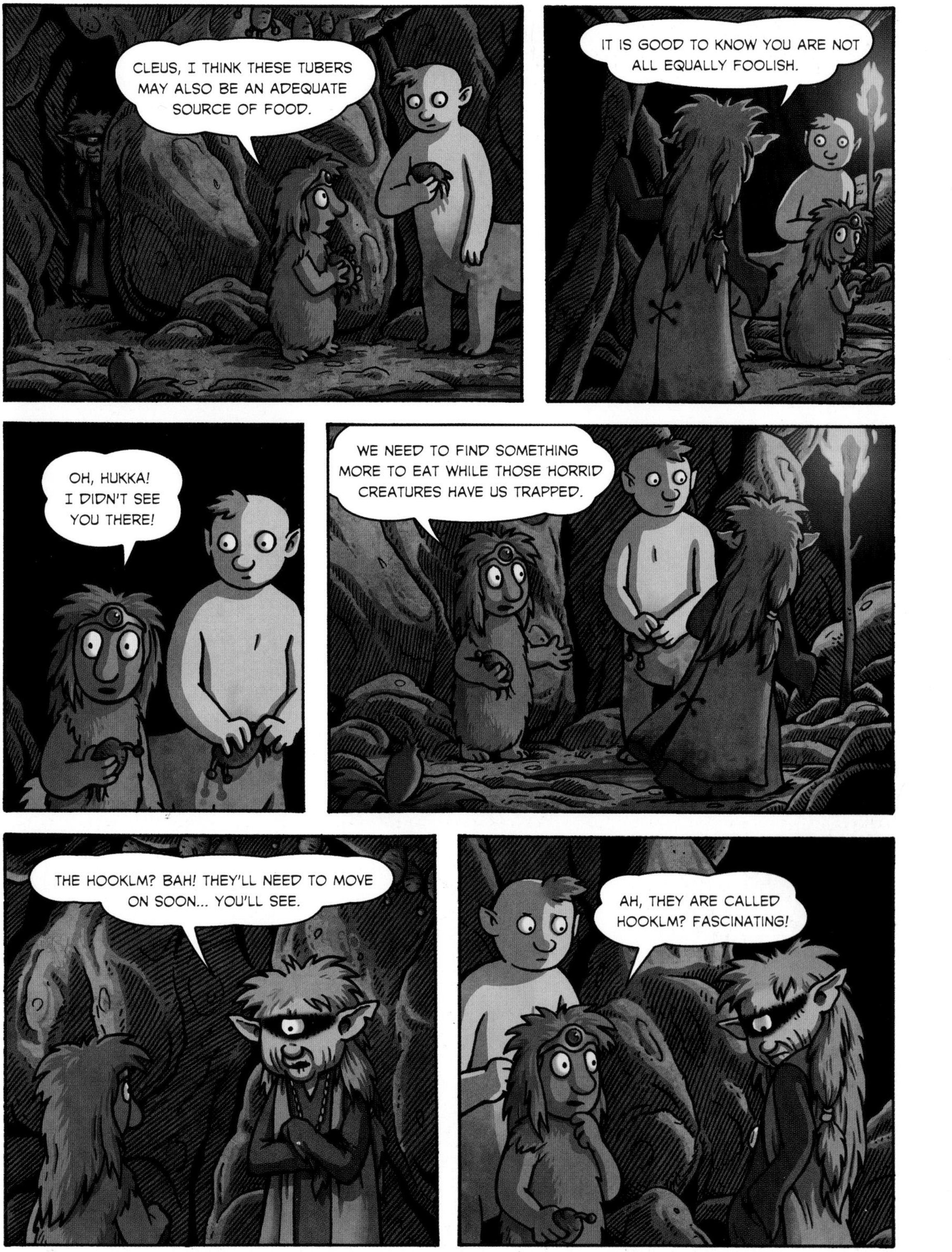
CLEUS, I THINK THESE TUBERS MAY ALSO BE AN ADEQUATE SOURCE OF FOOD.
IT IS GOOD TO KNOW YOU ARE NOT ALL EQUALLY FOOLISH.
OH, HUKKA! I DIDN'T SEE YOU THERE!
WE NEED TO FIND SOMETHING MORE TO EAT WHILE THOSE HORRID CREATURES HAVE US TRAPPED.
THE HOOKLM? BAH! THEY'LL NEED TO MOVE ON SOON... YOU'LL SEE.
AH, THEY ARE CALLED HOOKLM? FASCINATING!

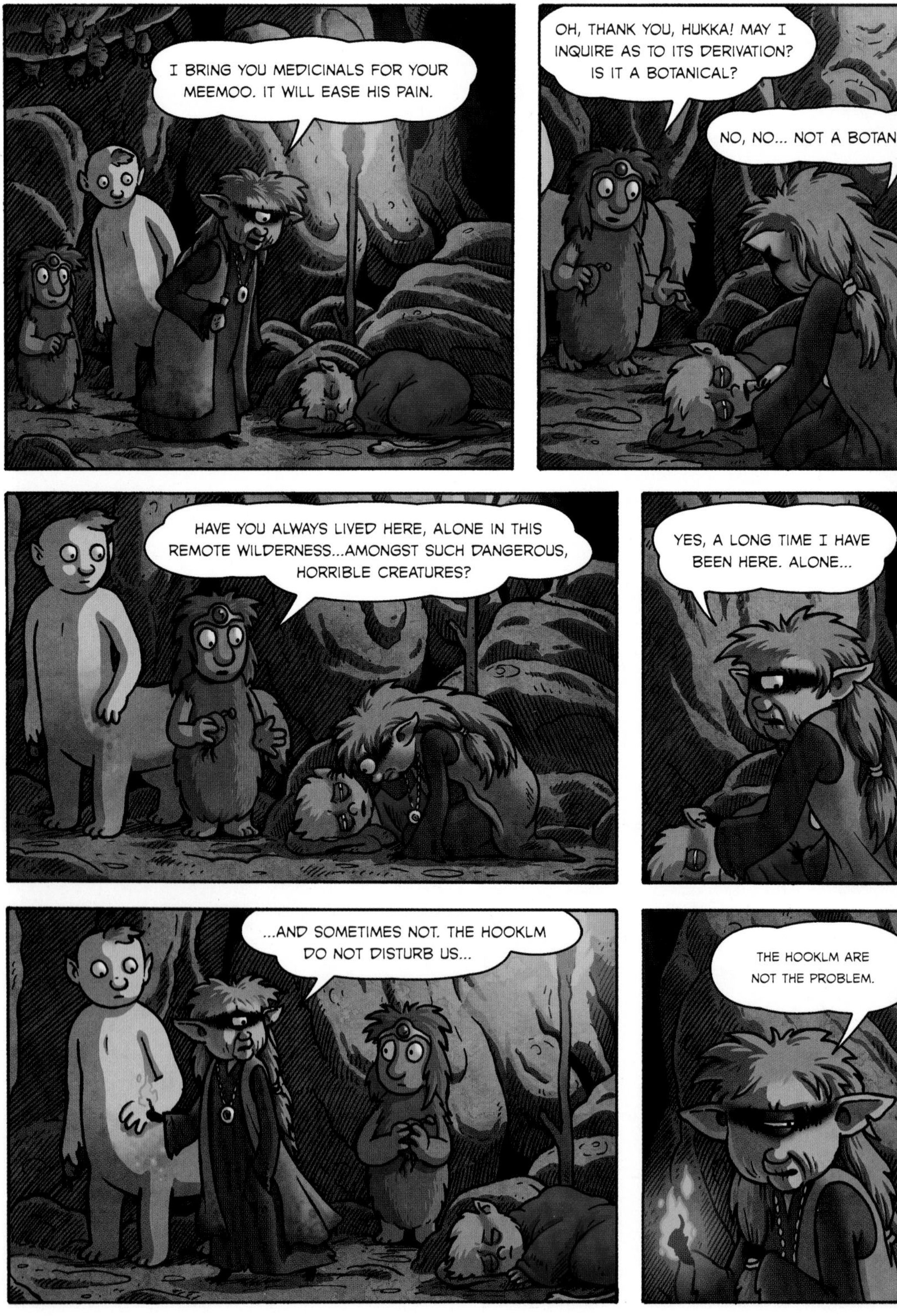
I BRING YOU MEDICINALS FOR YOUR MEEMOO. IT WILL EASE HIS PAIN.
OH, THANK YOU, HUKKA! MAY I INQUIRE AS TO ITS DERIVATION? IS IT A BOTANICAL?
NO, NO... NOT A BOTANICAL...
HAVE YOU ALWAYS LIVED HERE, ALONE IN THIS REMOTE WILDERNESS...AMONGST SUCH DANGEROUS, HORRIBLE CREATURES?
YES, A LONG TIME I HAVE BEEN HERE. ALONE...
...AND SOMETIMES NOT. THE HOOKLM DO NOT DISTURB US...
THE HOOKLM ARE NOT THE PROBLEM.

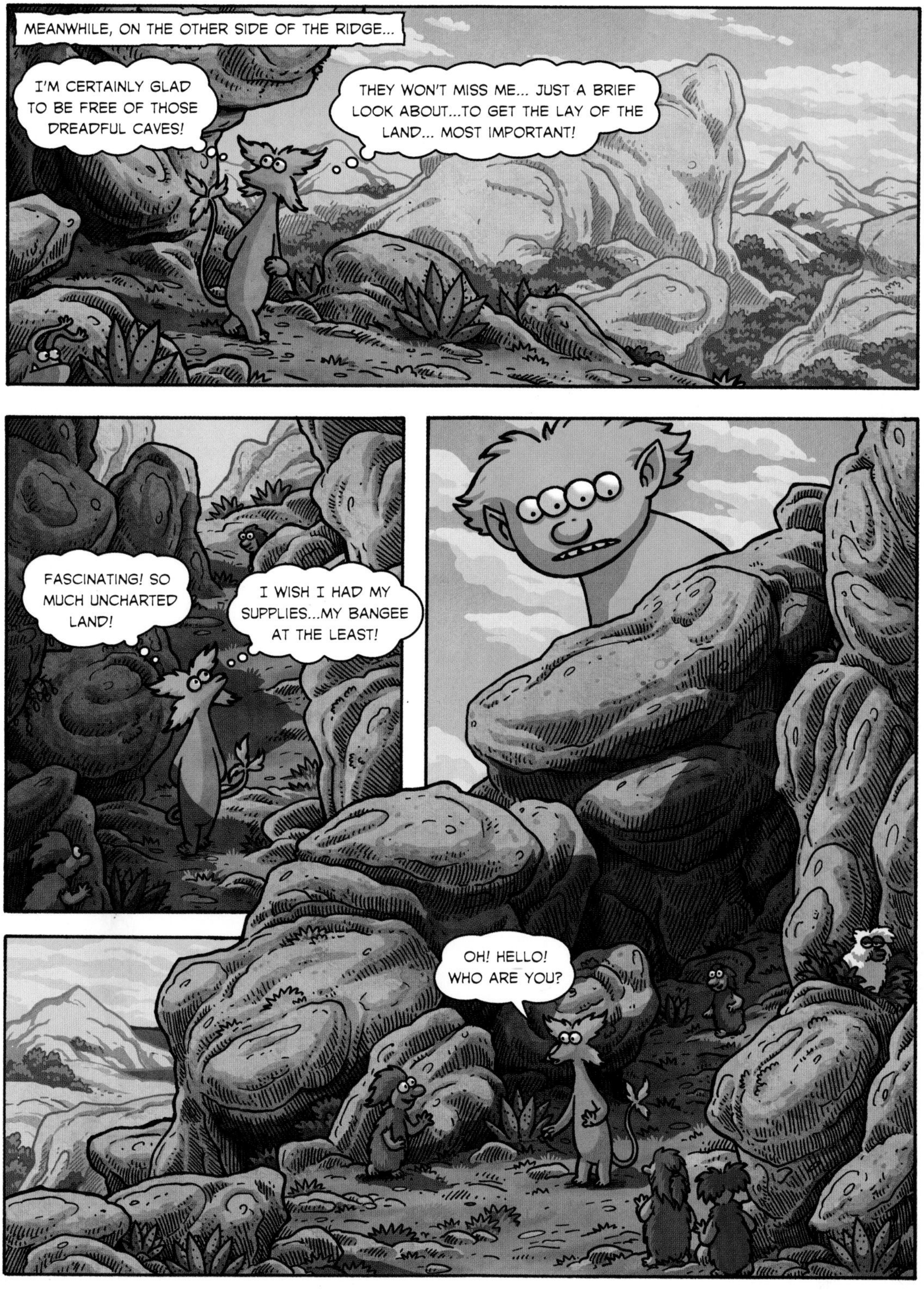
MEANWHILE, ON THE OTHER SIDE OF THE RIDGE...
I'M CERTAINLY GLAD TO BE FREE OF THOSE DREADFUL CAVES!
THEY WON'T MISS ME... JUST A BRIEF LOOK ABOUT...TO GET THE LAY OF THE LAND... MOST IMPORTANT!
FASCINATING! SO MUCH UNCHARTED LAND!
I WISH I HAD MY SUPPLIES...MY BANGEE AT THE LEAST!
OH! HELLO! WHO ARE YOU?

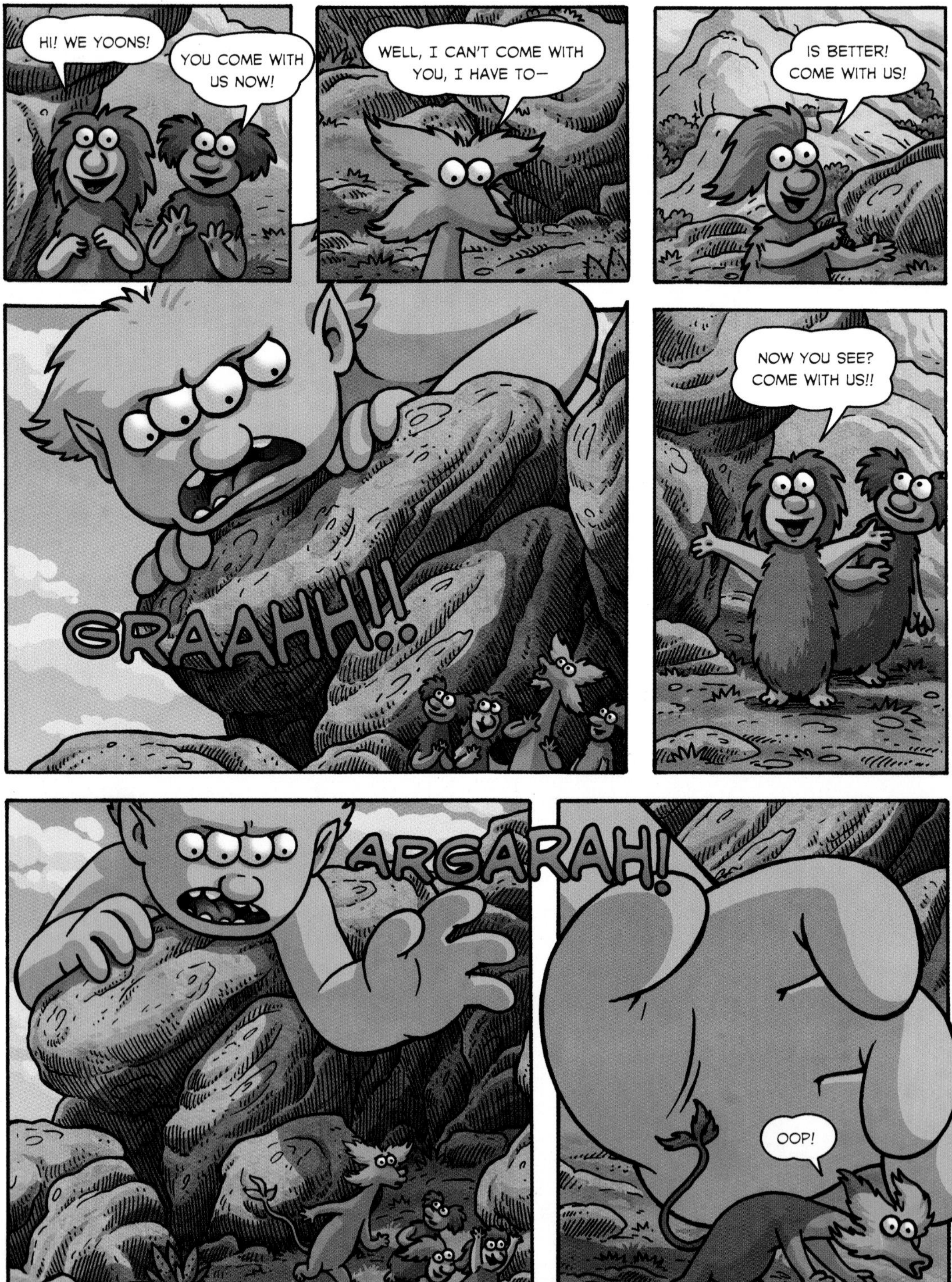
HI! WE YOONS!
YOU COME WITH US NOW!
WELL, I CAN'T COME WITH YOU, I HAVE TO—
IS BETTER! COME WITH US!
GRAAHH!!
NOW YOU SEE? COME WITH US!!
ARGARAH!
OOP!

UP, UP! HURRY!

GET ME OUT OF HERE!!

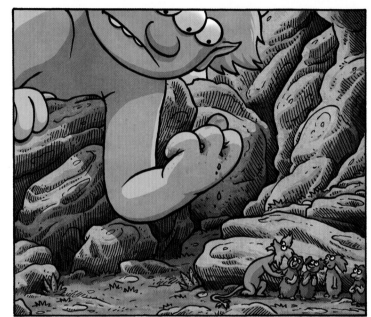

HOORAY!!

GRAHH!!!

43

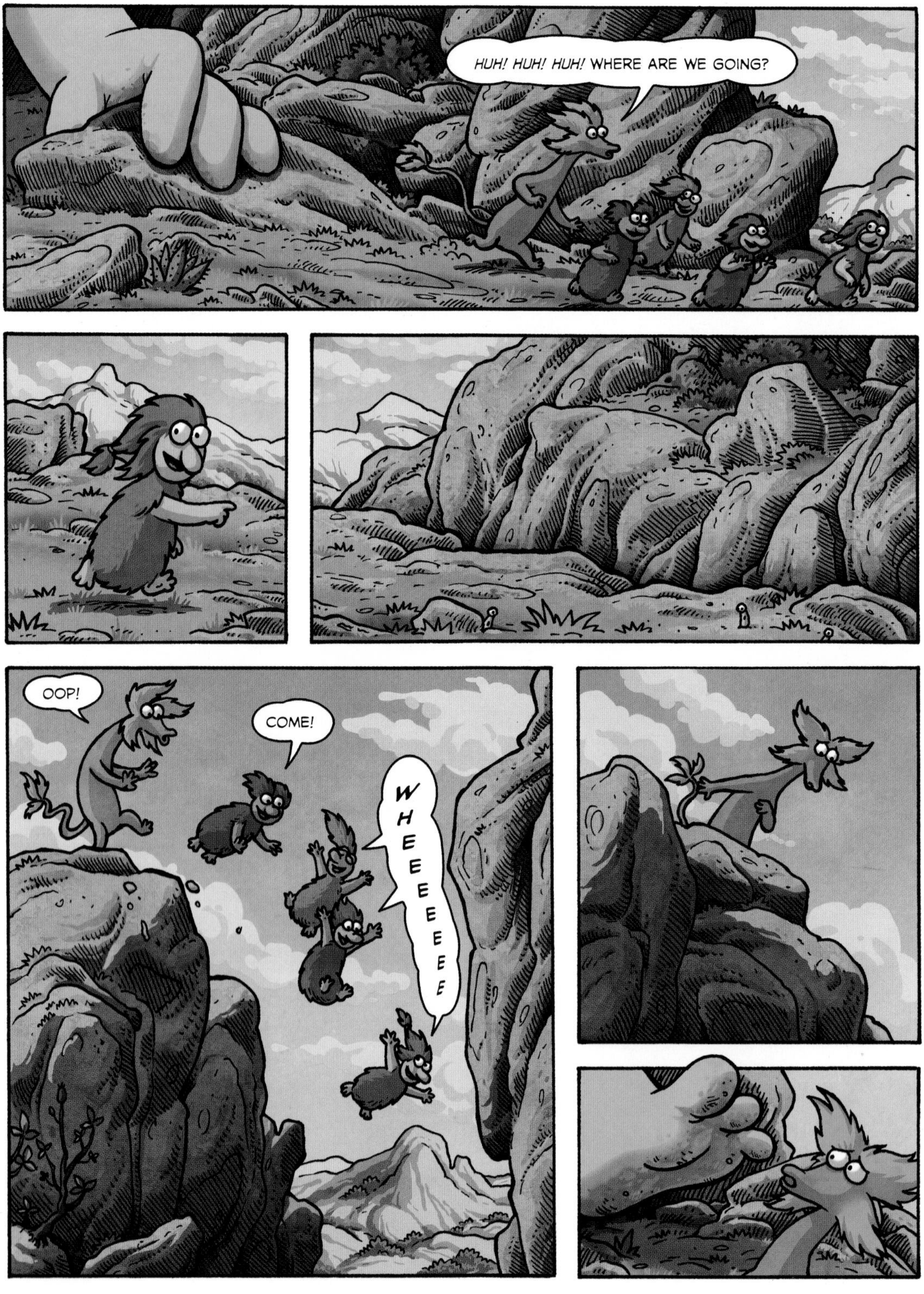
HUH! HUH! HUH! WHERE ARE WE GOING?
OOP!
COME!
WHEEEEEEEE

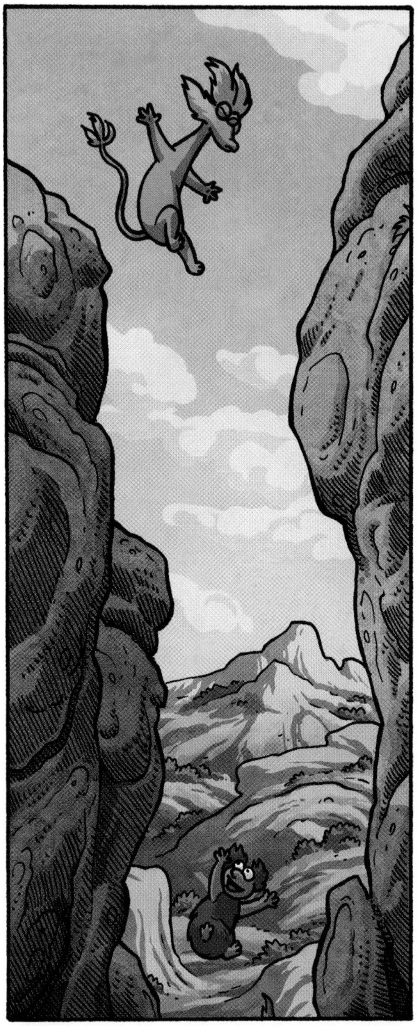

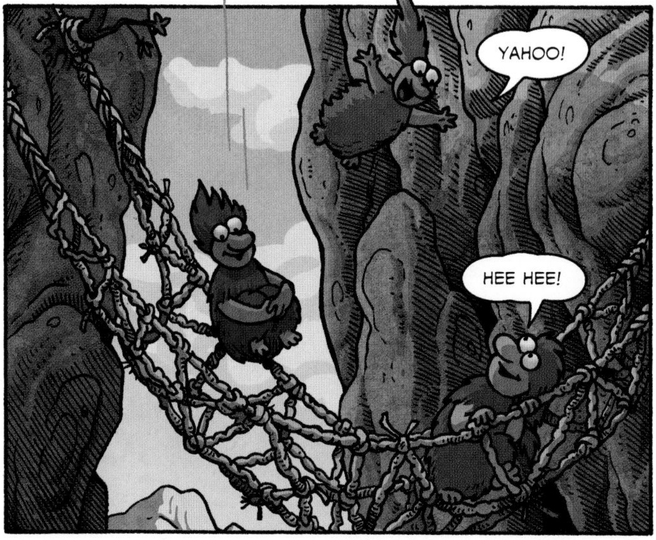
YAHOO!
HEE HEE!

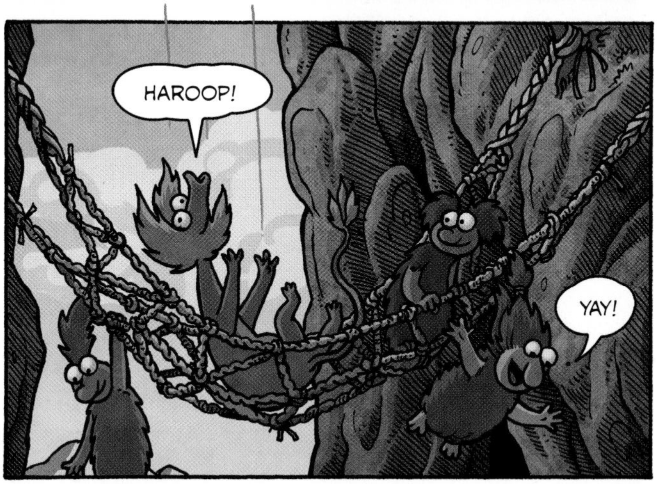
HAROOP!
YAY!

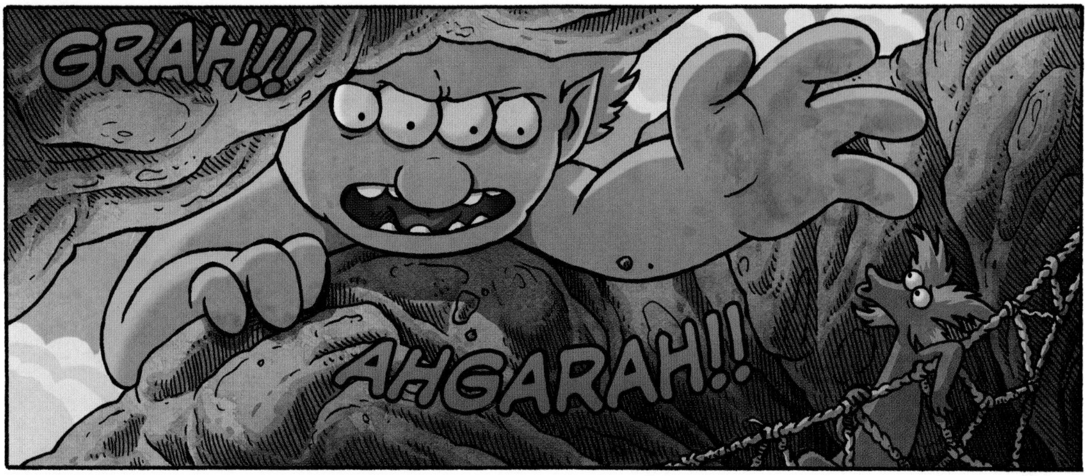
GRAH!!
AHGARAH!!

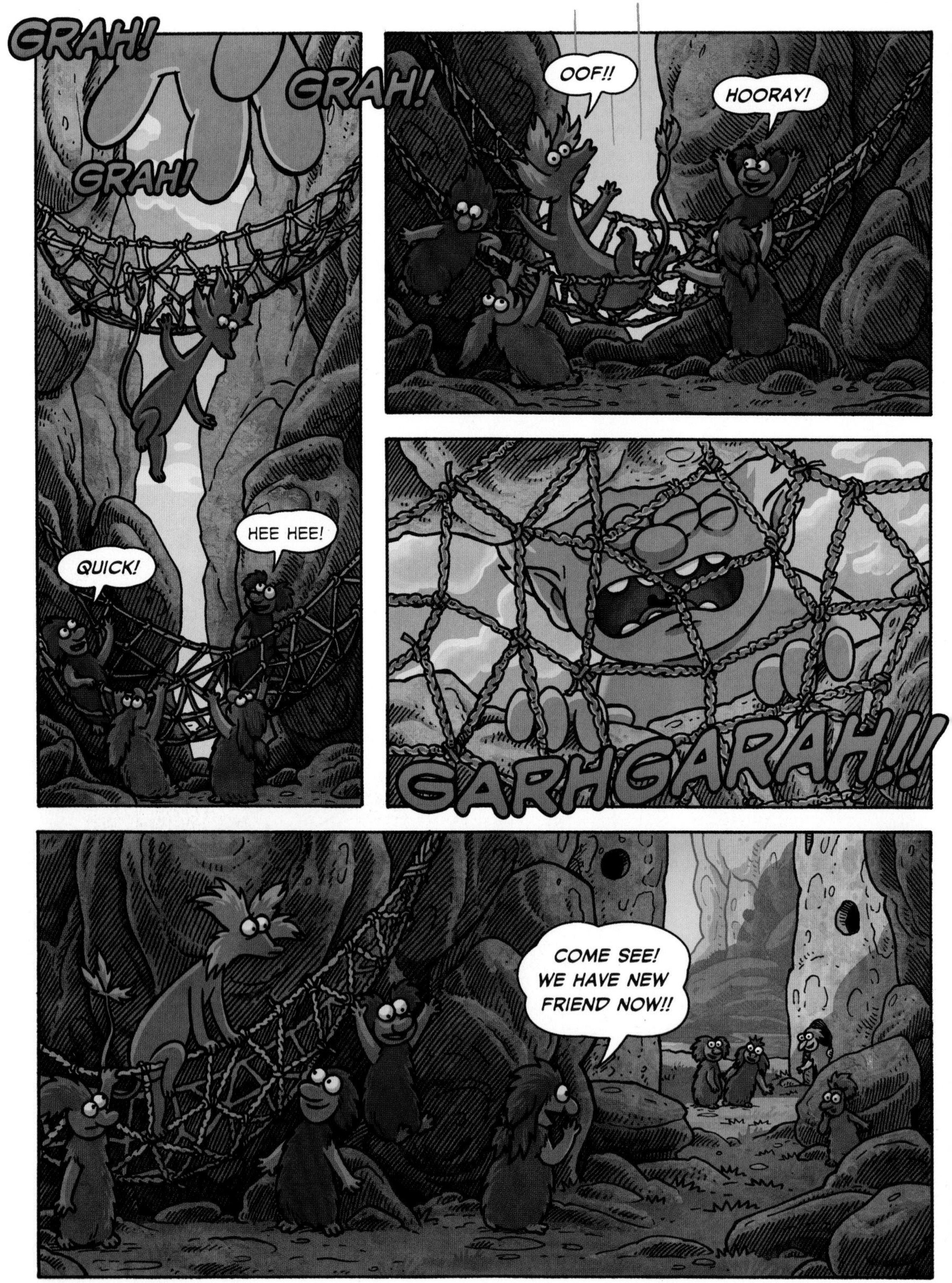
GRAH!
GRAH!
GRAH!
QUICK!
HEE HEE!
OOF!!
HOORAY!
GARHGARAH!!!
COME SEE! WE HAVE NEW FRIEND NOW!!

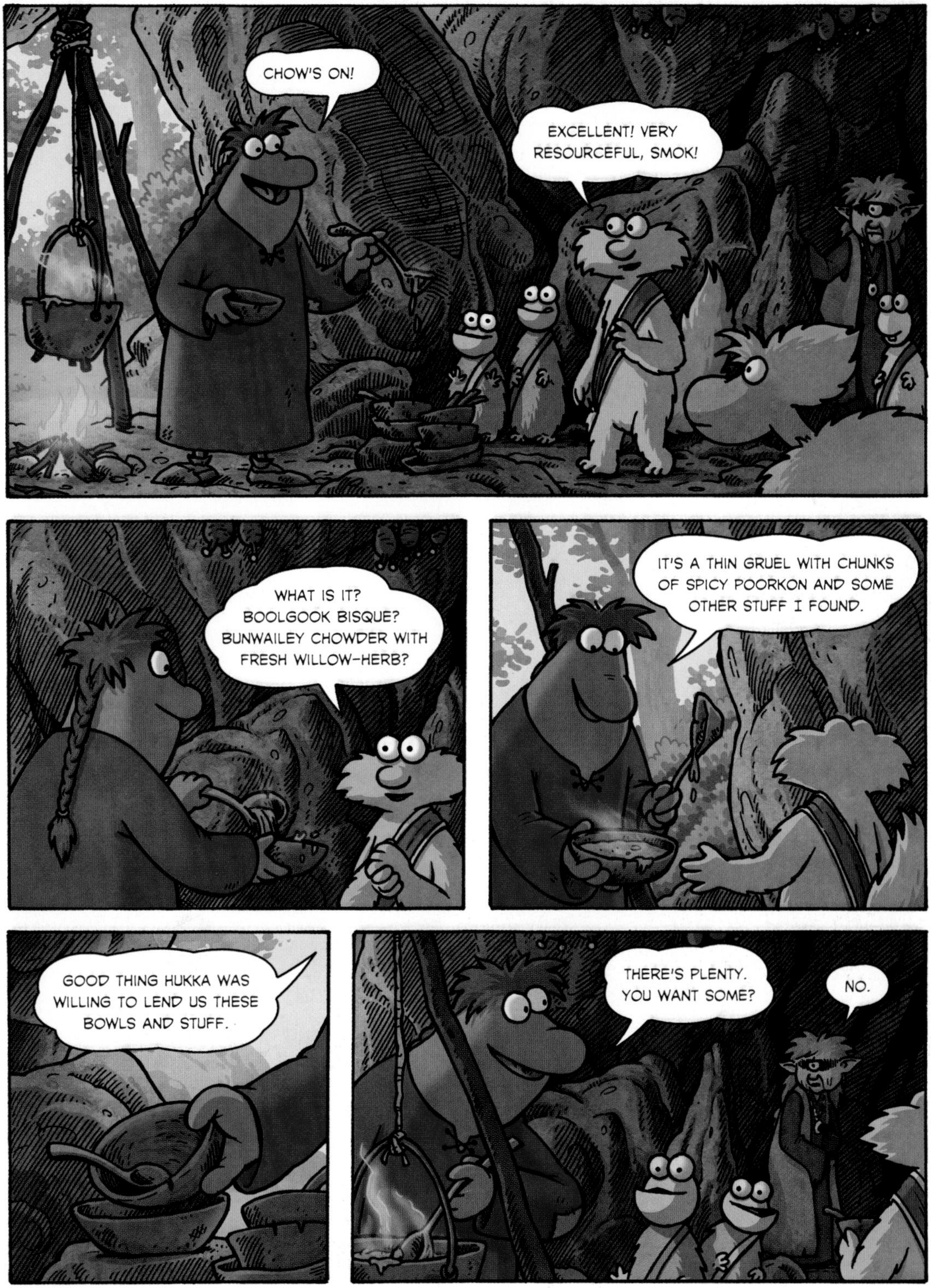
CHOW'S ON!
EXCELLENT! VERY RESOURCEFUL, SMOK!
WHAT IS IT? BOOLGOOK BISQUE? BUNWAILEY CHOWDER WITH FRESH WILLOW-HERB?
IT'S A THIN GRUEL WITH CHUNKS OF SPICY POORKON AND SOME OTHER STUFF I FOUND.
GOOD THING HUKKA WAS WILLING TO LEND US THESE BOWLS AND STUFF.
THERE'S PLENTY. YOU WANT SOME?
NO.

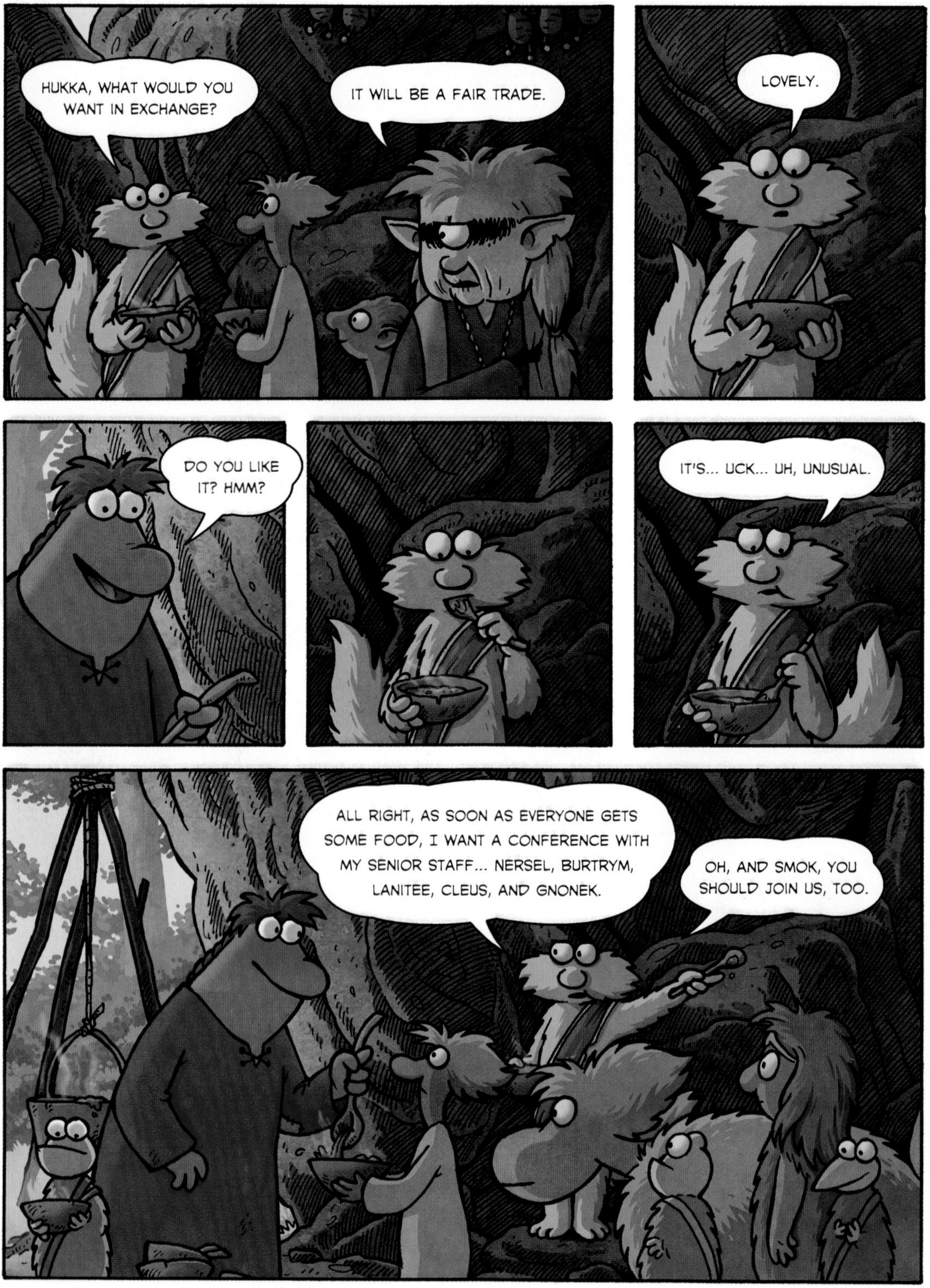
HUKKA, WHAT WOULD YOU WANT IN EXCHANGE?
IT WILL BE A FAIR TRADE.
LOVELY.
DO YOU LIKE IT? HMM?
IT'S... UCK... UH, UNUSUAL.
ALL RIGHT, AS SOON AS EVERYONE GETS SOME FOOD, I WANT A CONFERENCE WITH MY SENIOR STAFF... NERSEL, BURTRYM, LANITEE, CLEUS, AND GNONEK.
OH, AND SMOK, YOU SHOULD JOIN US, TOO.

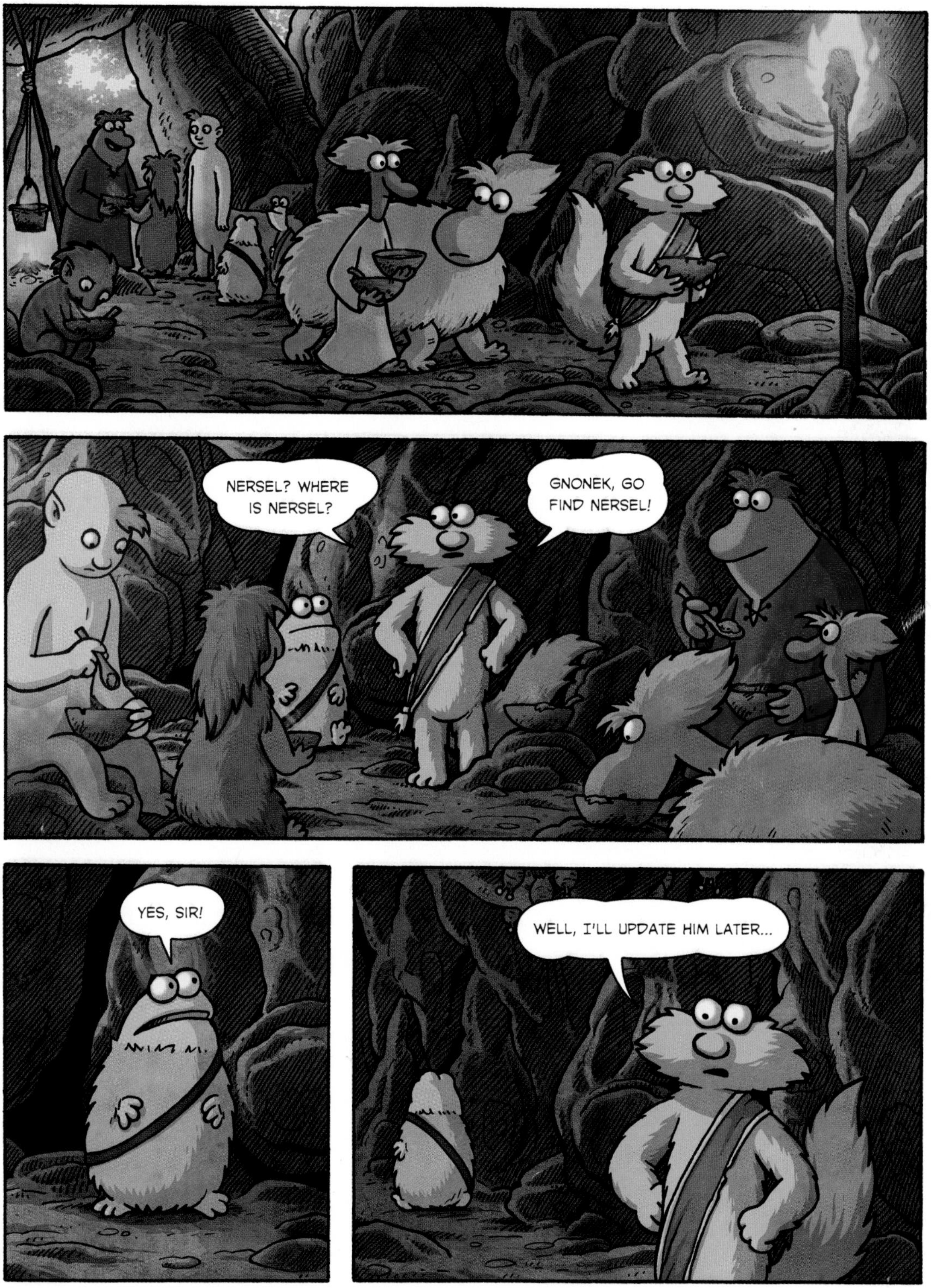
NERSEL? WHERE IS NERSEL?
GNONEK, GO FIND NERSEL!
YES, SIR!
WELL, I'LL UPDATE HIM LATER...

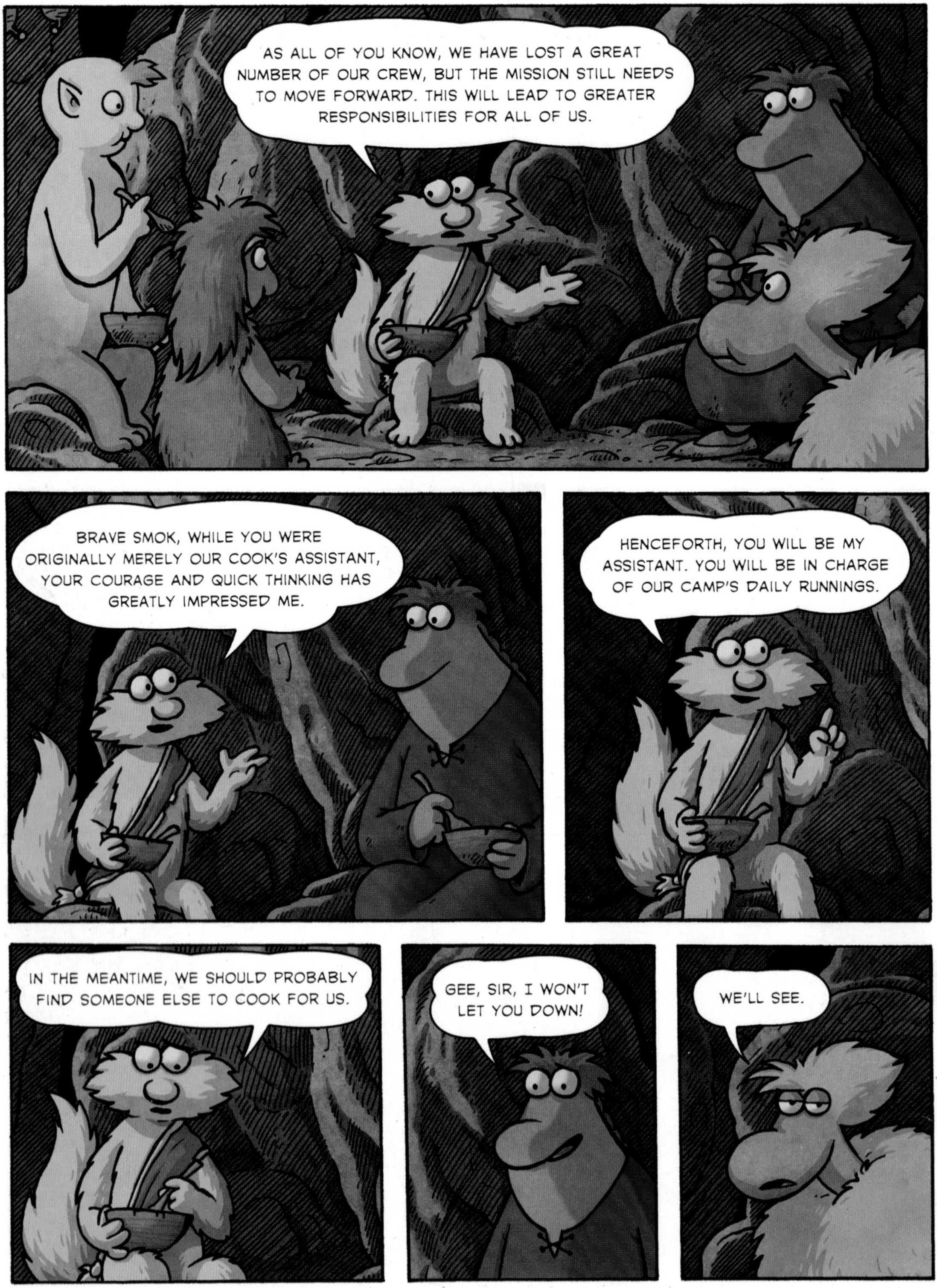
AS ALL OF YOU KNOW, WE HAVE LOST A GREAT NUMBER OF OUR CREW, BUT THE MISSION STILL NEEDS TO MOVE FORWARD. THIS WILL LEAD TO GREATER RESPONSIBILITIES FOR ALL OF US.
BRAVE SMOK, WHILE YOU WERE ORIGINALLY MERELY OUR COOK'S ASSISTANT, YOUR COURAGE AND QUICK THINKING HAS GREATLY IMPRESSED ME.
HENCEFORTH, YOU WILL BE MY ASSISTANT. YOU WILL BE IN CHARGE OF OUR CAMP'S DAILY RUNNINGS.
IN THE MEANTIME, WE SHOULD PROBABLY FIND SOMEONE ELSE TO COOK FOR US.
GEE, SIR, I WON'T LET YOU DOWN!
WE'LL SEE.

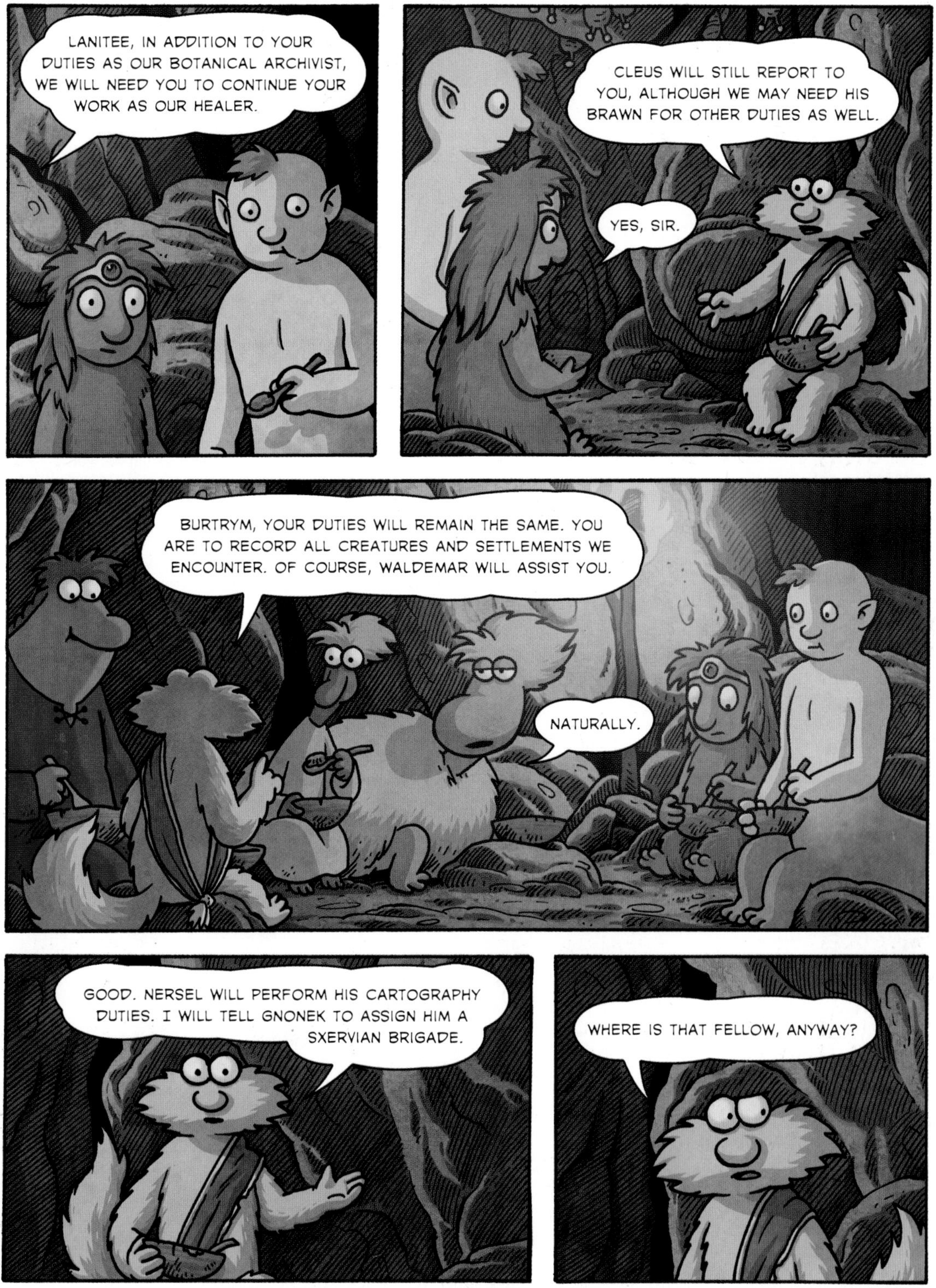
LANITEE, IN ADDITION TO YOUR DUTIES AS OUR BOTANICAL ARCHIVIST, WE WILL NEED YOU TO CONTINUE YOUR WORK AS OUR HEALER.
CLEUS WILL STILL REPORT TO YOU, ALTHOUGH WE MAY NEED HIS BRAWN FOR OTHER DUTIES AS WELL.
YES, SIR.
BURTRYM, YOUR DUTIES WILL REMAIN THE SAME. YOU ARE TO RECORD ALL CREATURES AND SETTLEMENTS WE ENCOUNTER. OF COURSE, WALDEMAR WILL ASSIST YOU.
NATURALLY.
GOOD. NERSEL WILL PERFORM HIS CARTOGRAPHY DUTIES. I WILL TELL GNONEK TO ASSIGN HIM A SXERVIAN BRIGADE.
WHERE IS THAT FELLOW, ANYWAY?

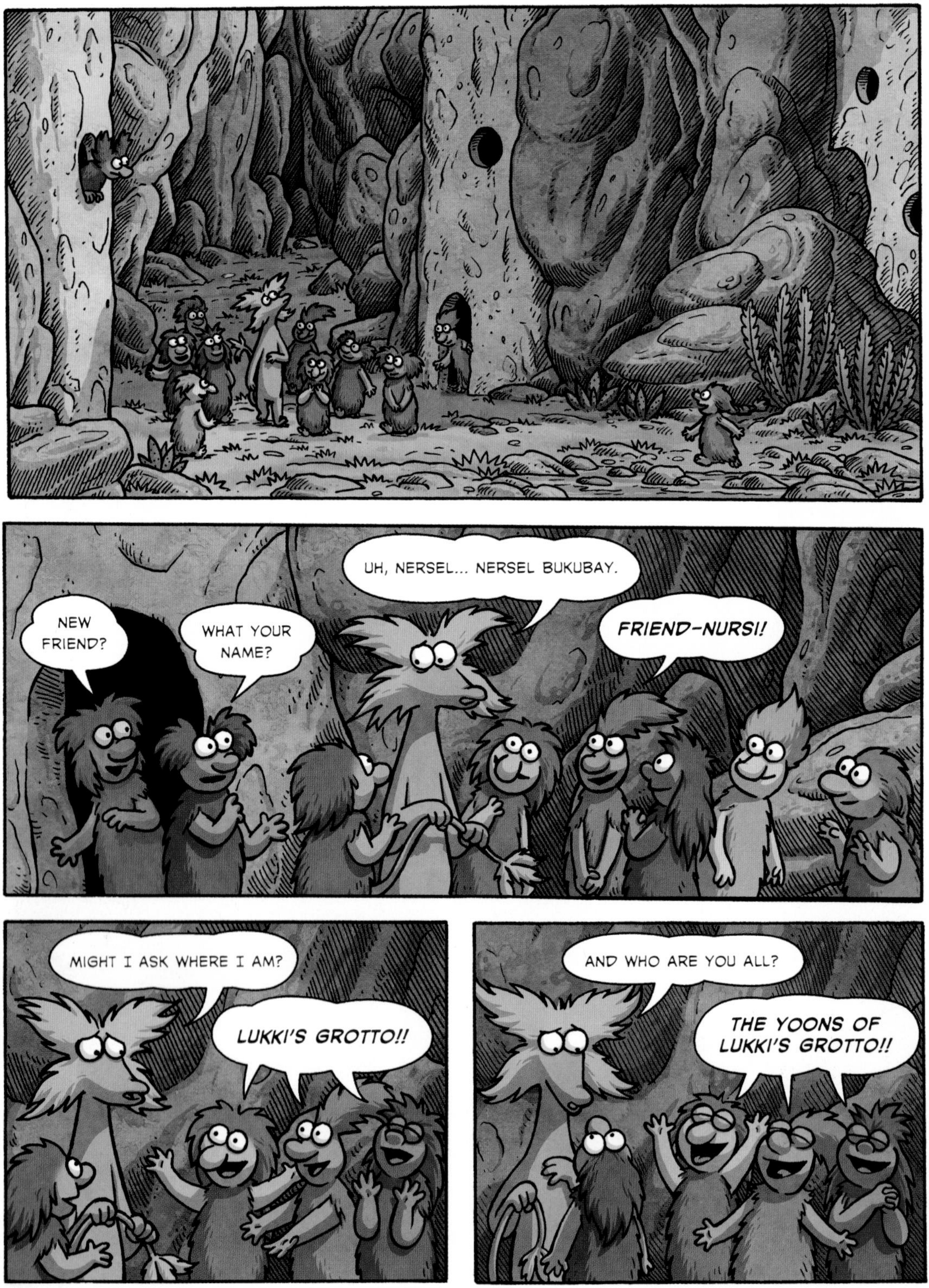
NEW FRIEND?
WHAT YOUR NAME?
UH, NERSEL... NERSEL BUKUBAY.
FRIEND-NURSI!
MIGHT I ASK WHERE I AM?
LUKKI'S GROTTO!!
AND WHO ARE YOU ALL?
THE YOONS OF LUKKI'S GROTTO!!

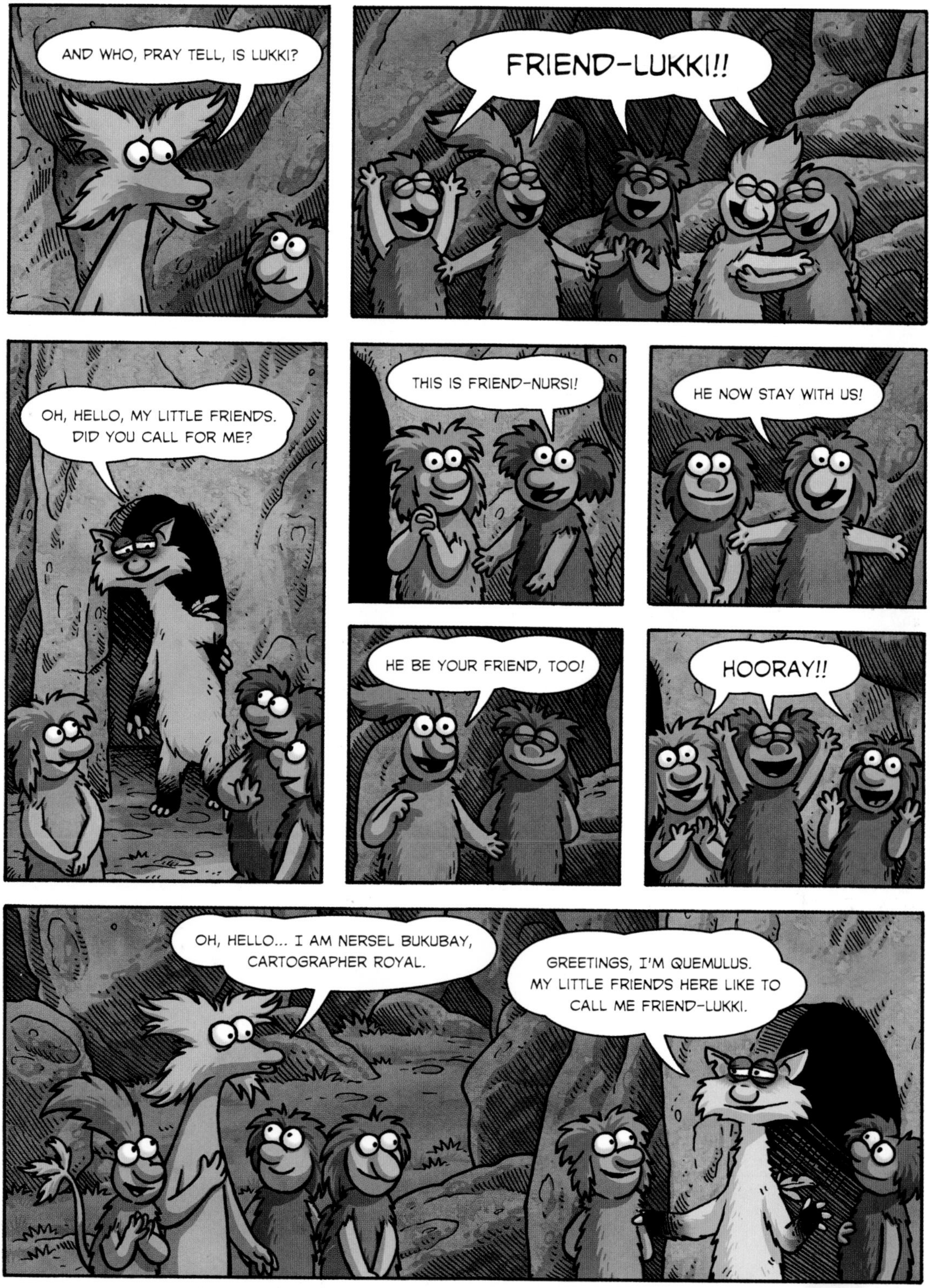
AND WHO, PRAY TELL, IS LUKKI?
FRIEND-LUKKI!!
OH, HELLO, MY LITTLE FRIENDS. DID YOU CALL FOR ME?
THIS IS FRIEND-NURSI!
HE NOW STAY WITH US!
HE BE YOUR FRIEND, TOO!
HOORAY!!
OH, HELLO... I AM NERSEL BUKUBAY, CARTOGRAPHER ROYAL.
GREETINGS, I'M QUEMULUS. MY LITTLE FRIENDS HERE LIKE TO CALL ME FRIEND-LUKKI.

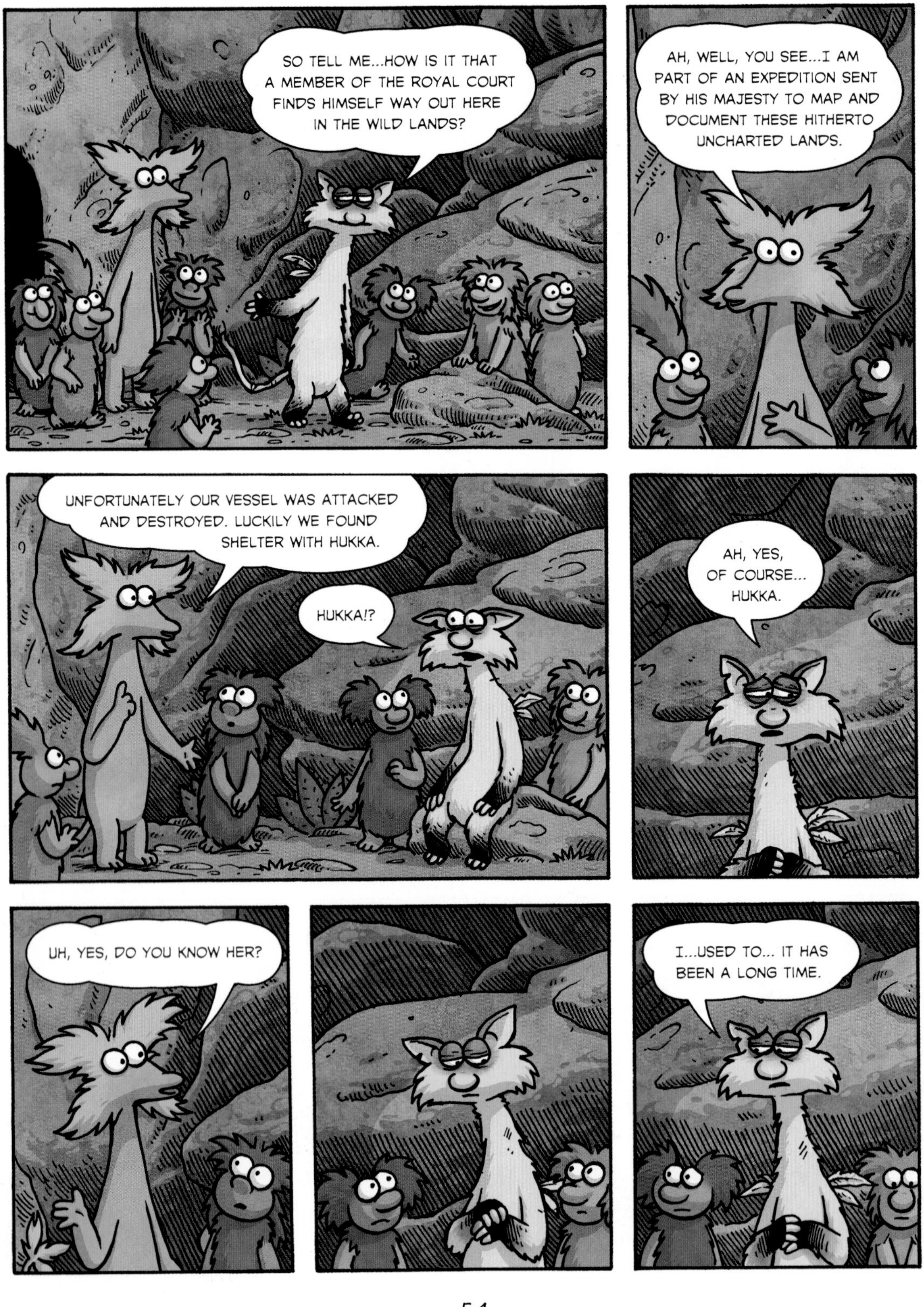
SO TELL ME...HOW IS IT THAT A MEMBER OF THE ROYAL COURT FINDS HIMSELF WAY OUT HERE IN THE WILD LANDS?
AH, WELL, YOU SEE...I AM PART OF AN EXPEDITION SENT BY HIS MAJESTY TO MAP AND DOCUMENT THESE HITHERTO UNCHARTED LANDS.
UNFORTUNATELY OUR VESSEL WAS ATTACKED AND DESTROYED. LUCKILY WE FOUND SHELTER WITH HUKKA.
HUKKA!?
AH, YES, OF COURSE... HUKKA.
UH, YES, DO YOU KNOW HER?
I...USED TO... IT HAS BEEN A LONG TIME.

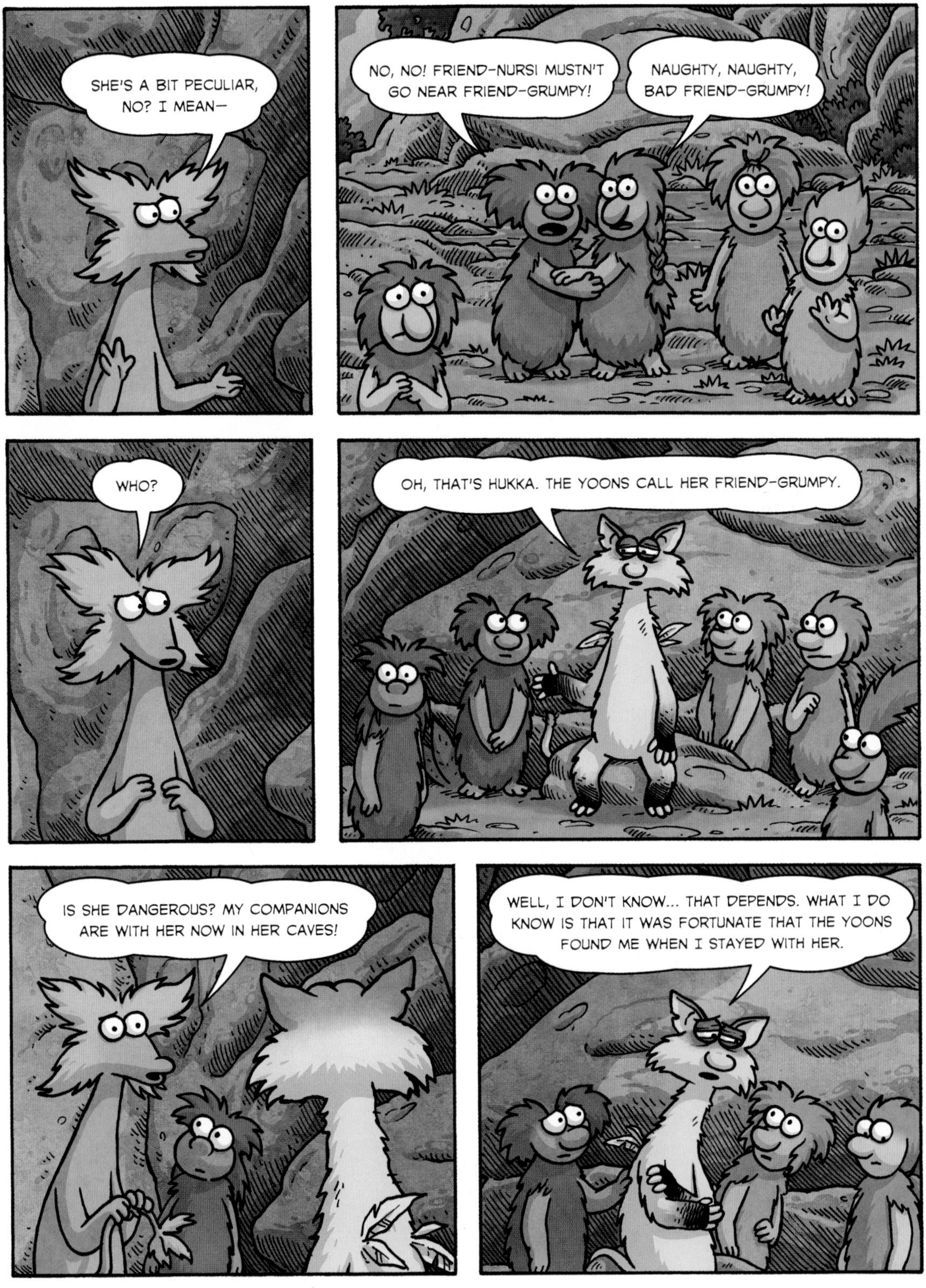
SHE'S A BIT PECULIAR, NO? I MEAN—
NO, NO! FRIEND-NURSI MUSTN'T GO NEAR FRIEND-GRUMPY!
NAUGHTY, NAUGHTY, BAD FRIEND-GRUMPY!
WHO?
OH, THAT'S HUKKA. THE YOONS CALL HER FRIEND-GRUMPY.
IS SHE DANGEROUS? MY COMPANIONS ARE WITH HER NOW IN HER CAVES!
WELL, I DON'T KNOW... THAT DEPENDS. WHAT I DO KNOW IS THAT IT WAS FORTUNATE THAT THE YOONS FOUND ME WHEN I STAYED WITH HER.

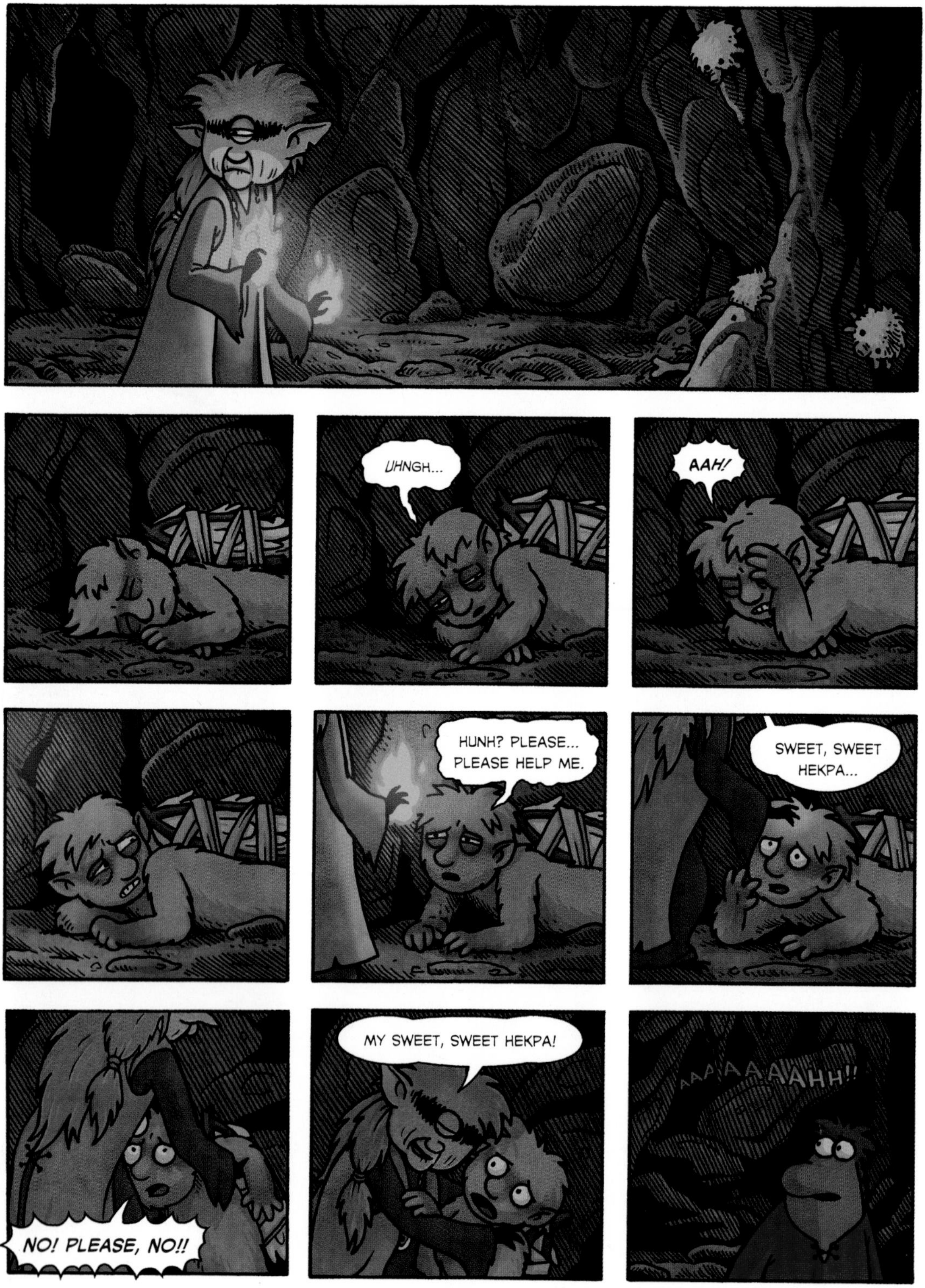
UHNGH...
AAH!
HUNH? PLEASE... PLEASE HELP ME.
SWEET, SWEET HEKPA...
NO! PLEASE, NO!!
MY SWEET, SWEET HEKPA!
AAAAAAAAHH!!

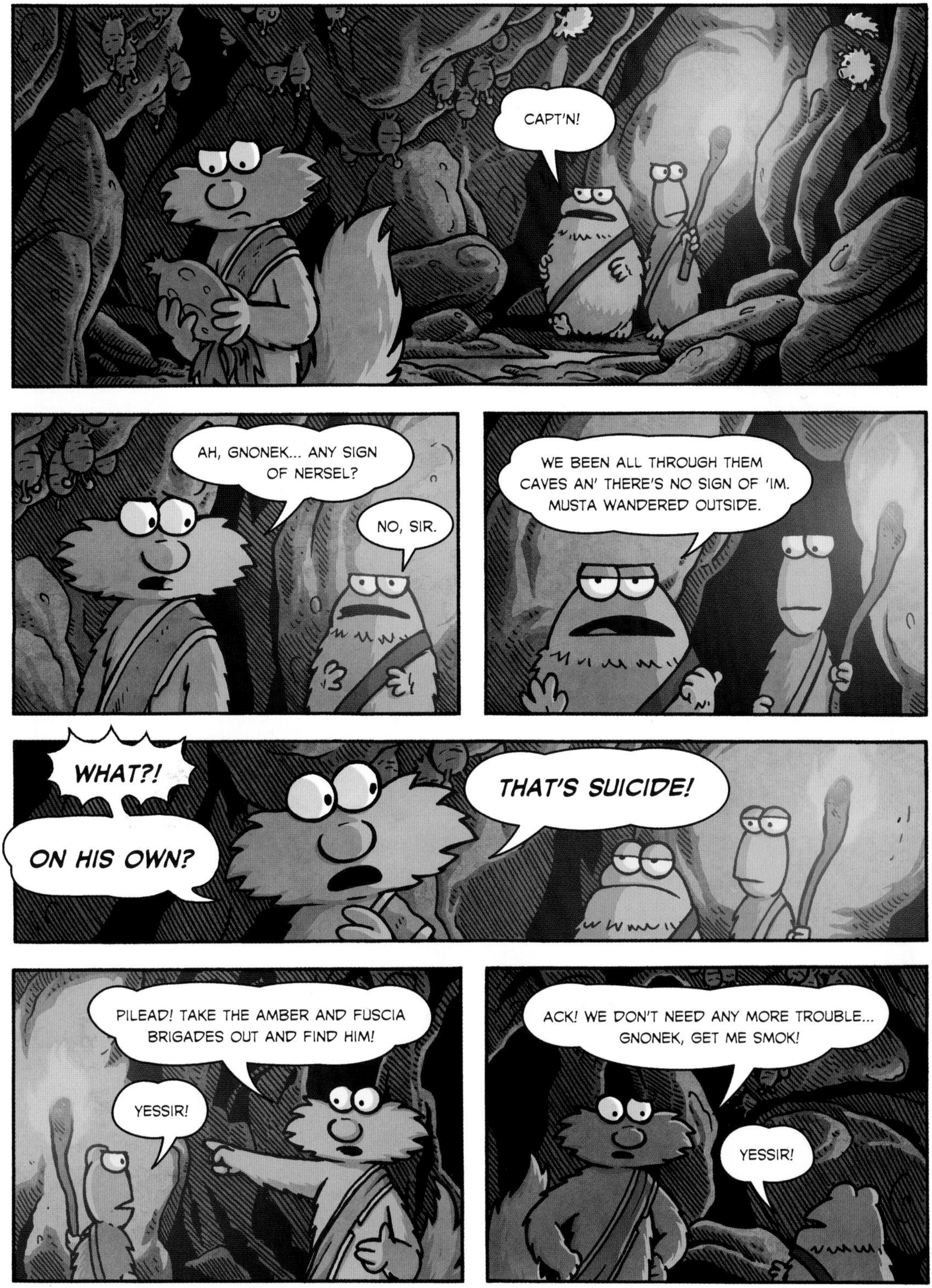
CAPT'N!
AH, GNONEK... ANY SIGN OF NERSEL?
NO, SIR.
WE BEEN ALL THROUGH THEM CAVES AN' THERE'S NO SIGN OF 'IM. MUSTA WANDERED OUTSIDE.
WHAT?!
ON HIS OWN?
THAT'S SUICIDE!
PILEAD! TAKE THE AMBER AND FUSCIA BRIGADES OUT AND FIND HIM!
YESSIR!
ACK! WE DON'T NEED ANY MORE TROUBLE... GNONEK, GET ME SMOK!
YESSIR!

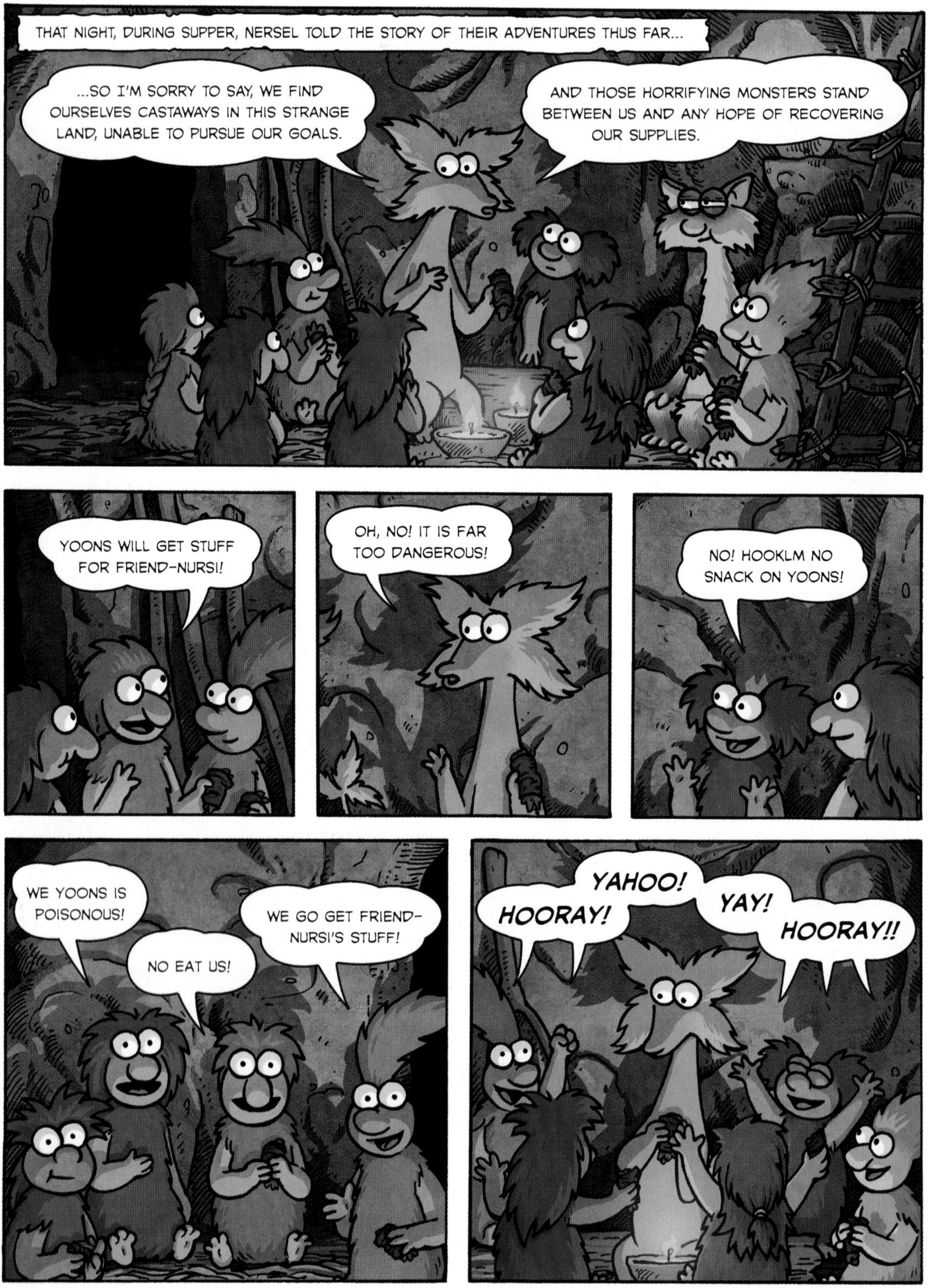
THAT NIGHT, DURING SUPPER, NERSEL TOLD THE STORY OF THEIR ADVENTURES THUS FAR...
...SO I'M SORRY TO SAY, WE FIND OURSELVES CASTAWAYS IN THIS STRANGE LAND, UNABLE TO PURSUE OUR GOALS.
AND THOSE HORRIFYING MONSTERS STAND BETWEEN US AND ANY HOPE OF RECOVERING OUR SUPPLIES.
YOONS WILL GET STUFF FOR FRIEND-NURSI!
OH, NO! IT IS FAR TOO DANGEROUS!
NO! HOOKLM NO SNACK ON YOONS!
WE YOONS IS POISONOUS!
NO EAT US!
WE GO GET FRIEND-NURSI'S STUFF!
HOORAY!
YAHOO!
YAY!
HOORAY!!

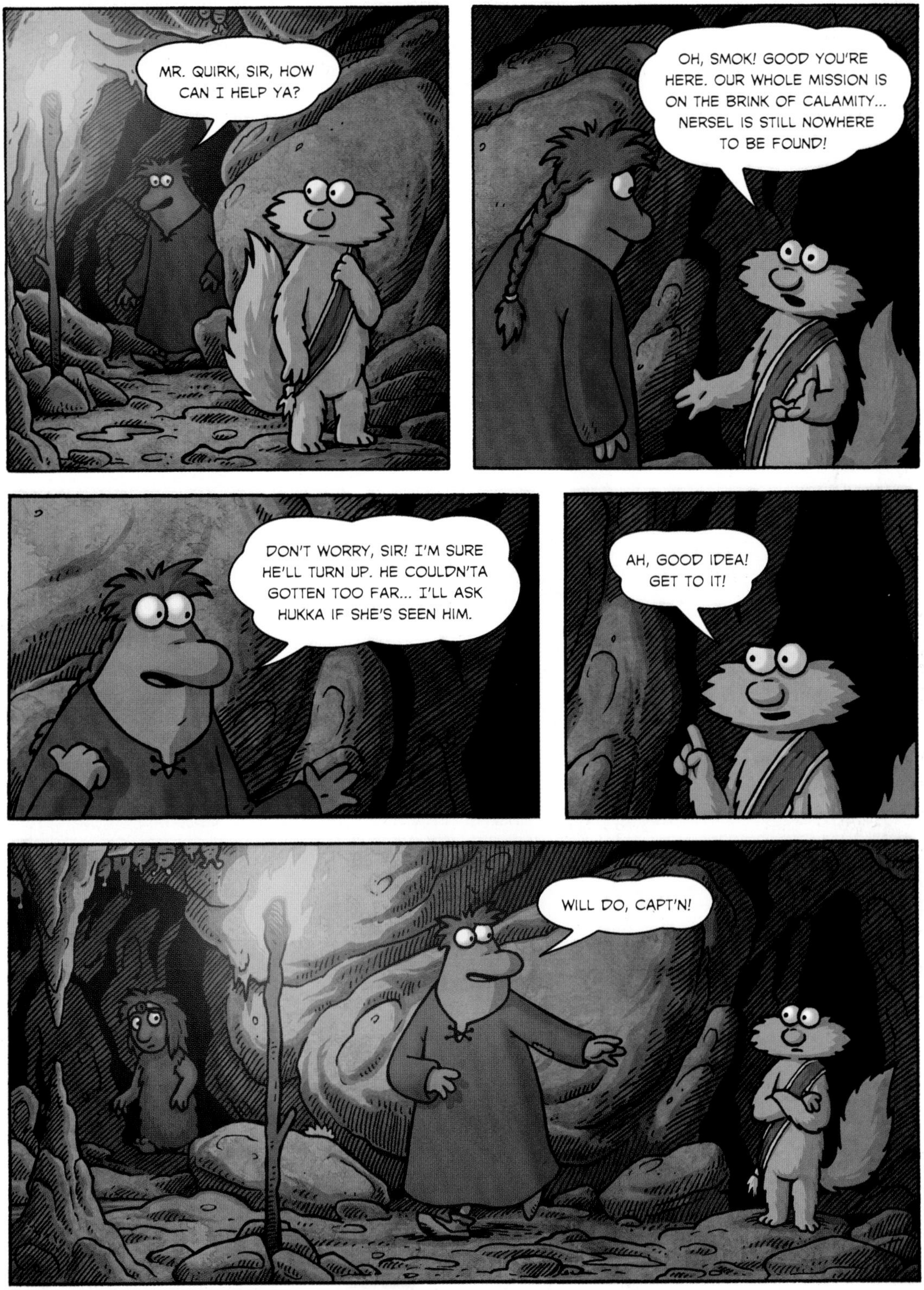
MR. QUIRK, SIR, HOW CAN I HELP YA?
OH, SMOK! GOOD YOU'RE HERE. OUR WHOLE MISSION IS ON THE BRINK OF CALAMITY... NERSEL IS STILL NOWHERE TO BE FOUND!
DON'T WORRY, SIR! I'M SURE HE'LL TURN UP. HE COULDN'TA GOTTEN TOO FAR... I'LL ASK HUKKA IF SHE'S SEEN HIM.
AH, GOOD IDEA! GET TO IT!
WILL DO, CAPT'N!

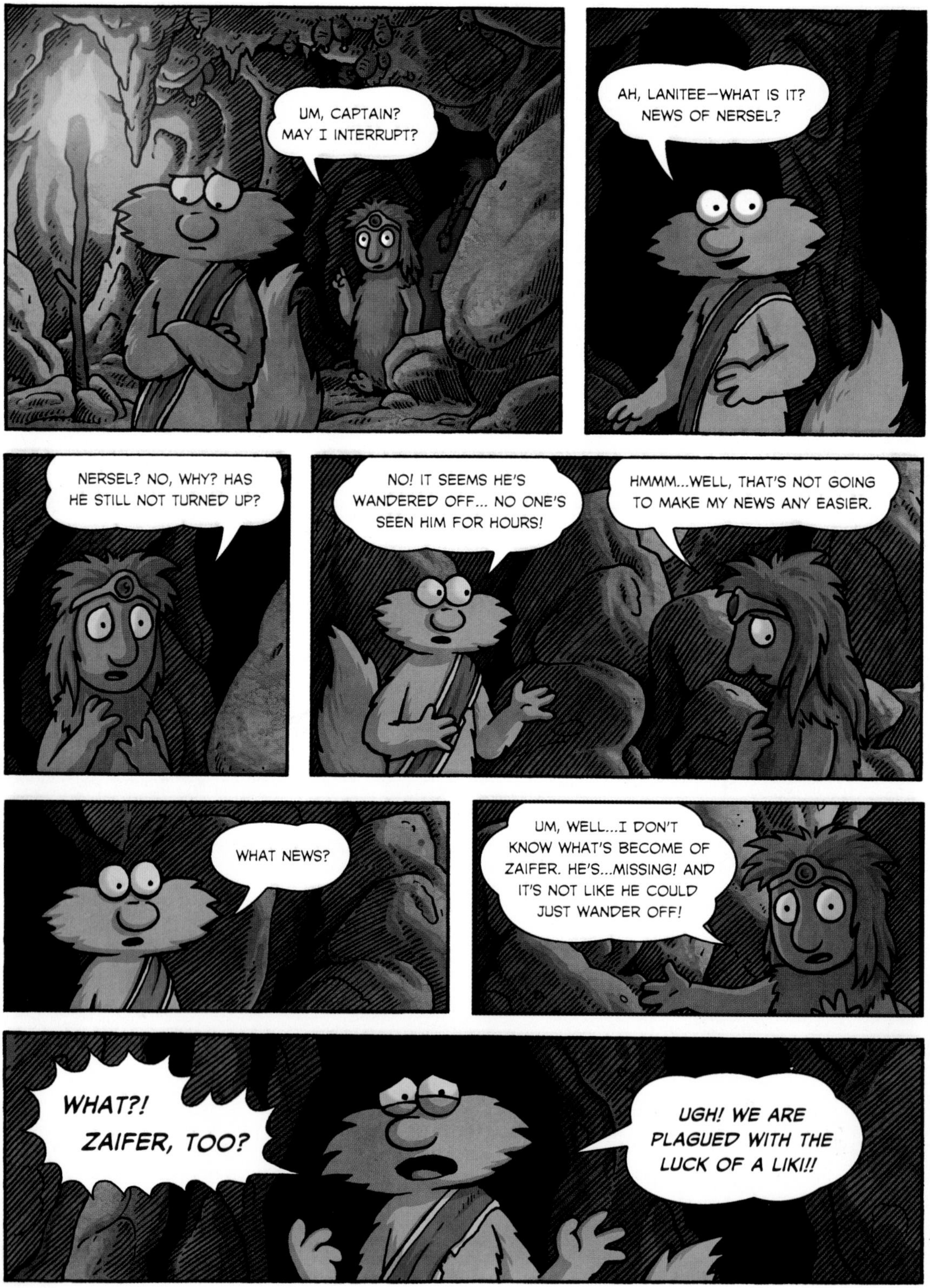
UM, CAPTAIN? MAY I INTERRUPT?
AH, LANITEE—WHAT IS IT? NEWS OF NERSEL?
NERSEL? NO, WHY? HAS HE STILL NOT TURNED UP?
NO! IT SEEMS HE'S WANDERED OFF... NO ONE'S SEEN HIM FOR HOURS!
HMMM...WELL, THAT'S NOT GOING TO MAKE MY NEWS ANY EASIER.
WHAT NEWS?
UM, WELL...I DON'T KNOW WHAT'S BECOME OF ZAIFER. HE'S...MISSING! AND IT'S NOT LIKE HE COULD JUST WANDER OFF!
WHAT?! ZAIFER, TOO?
UGH! WE ARE PLAGUED WITH THE LUCK OF A LIKI!!

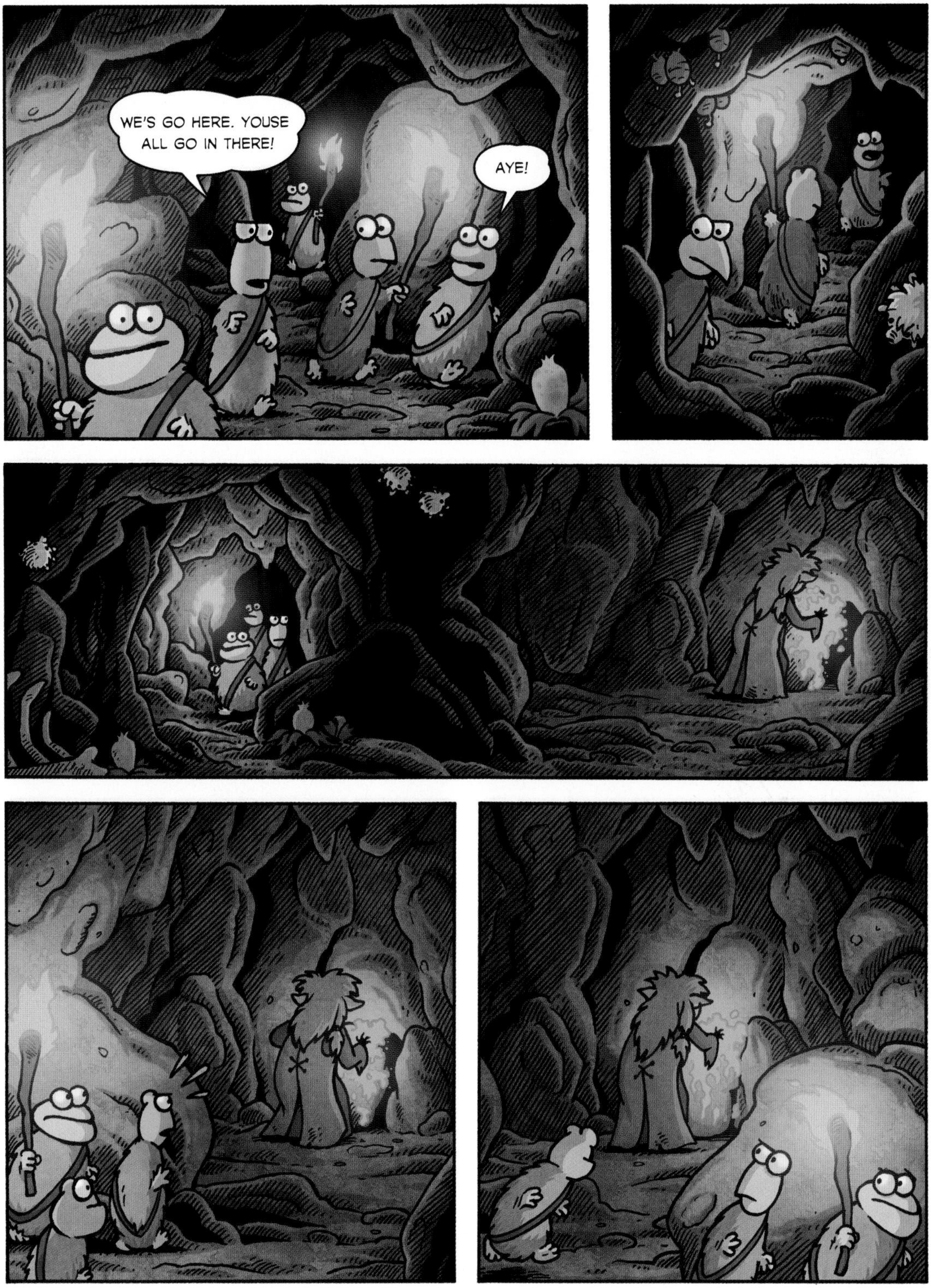
WE'S GO HERE. YOUSE ALL GO IN THERE!
AYE!

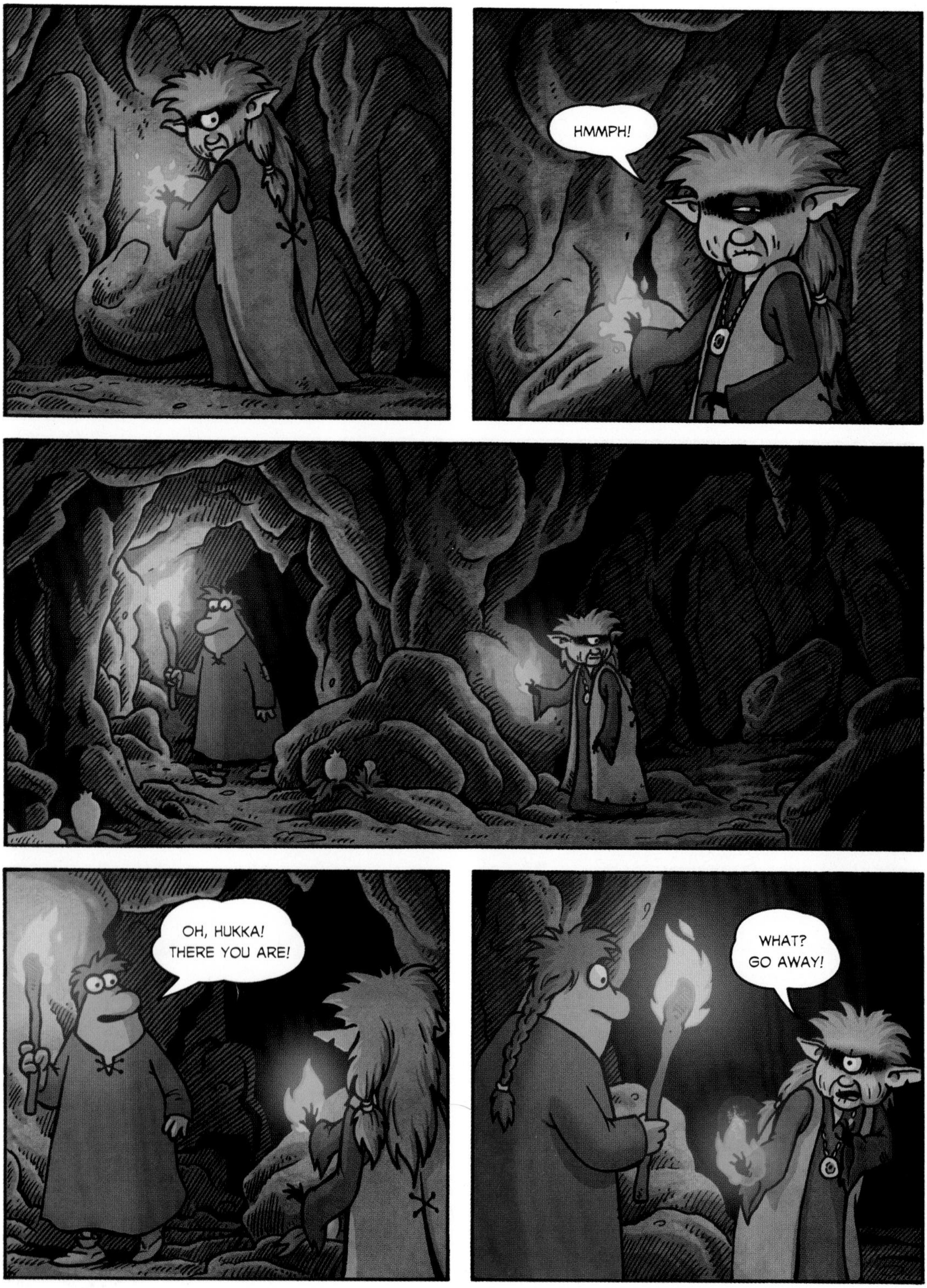
HMMPH!
OH, HUKKA! THERE YOU ARE!
WHAT? GO AWAY!

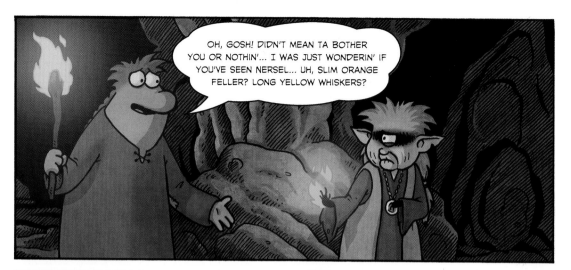

OH, GOSH! DIDN'T MEAN TA BOTHER YOU OR NOTHIN'... I WAS JUST WONDERIN' IF YOU'VE SEEN NERSEL... UH, SLIM ORANGE FELLER? LONG YELLOW WHISKERS?

NO! NO! THERE'S TOO MANY OF YOU! NO WONDER YOU LOST HIM!

MAYBE THE HOOKLM GOT HIM. IT'S NOT MY PROBLEM! *NOW LEAVE ME ALONE!!*

UH, ALL RIGHT...THANKS ANYWAY.

UNHHH...

63

EARLY THE NEXT MORNING, THE YOONS OF LUKKI'S GROTTO SET OFF TO RETRIEVE WHAT WAS LEFT OF THE H.M.S. GWANIIMANDER'S CARGO FROM THE HOOKLM...

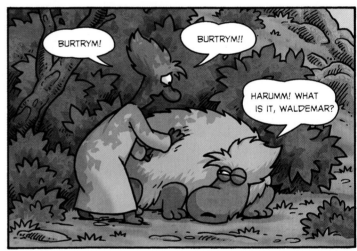

BURTRYM!

BURTRYM!!

HARUMM! WHAT IS IT, WALDEMAR?

THOSE...THOSE LITTLE CRITTERS ARE STEALING OUR STUFF!

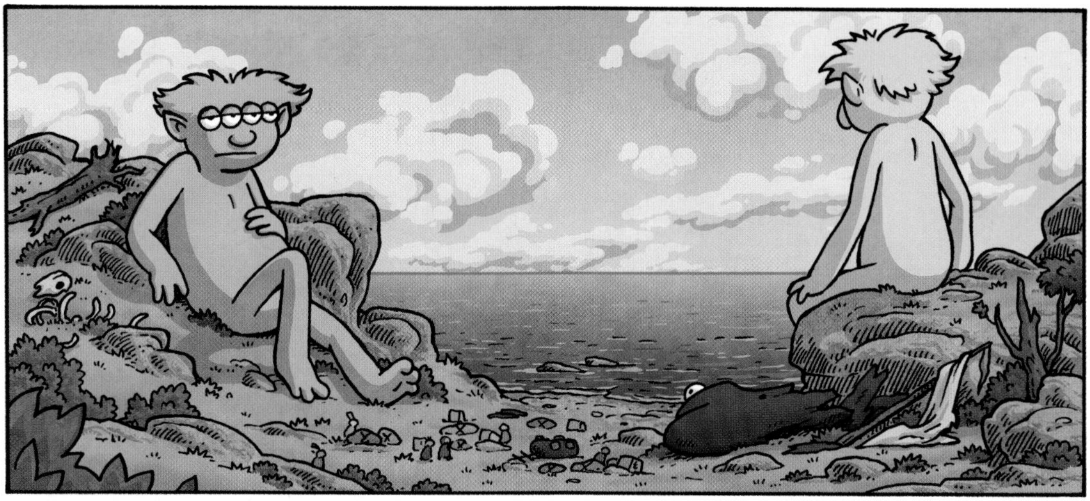

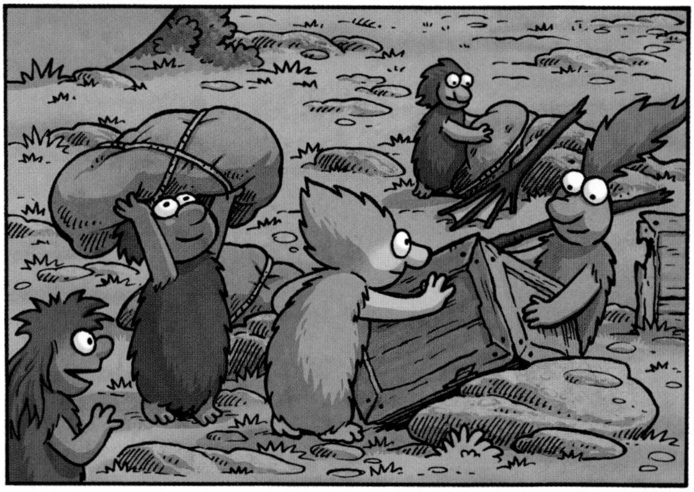

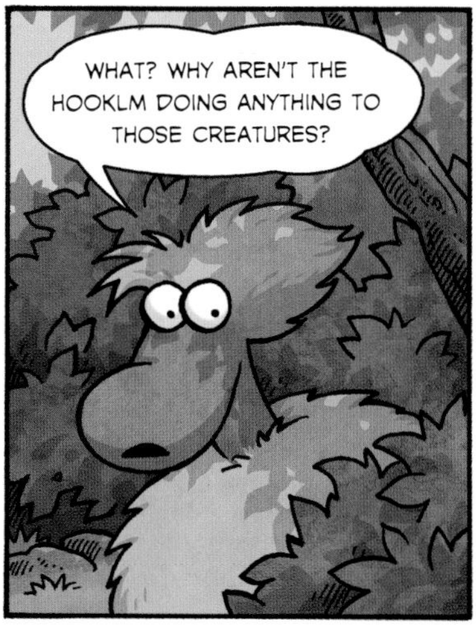
WHAT? WHY AREN'T THE HOOKLM DOING ANYTHING TO THOSE CREATURES?

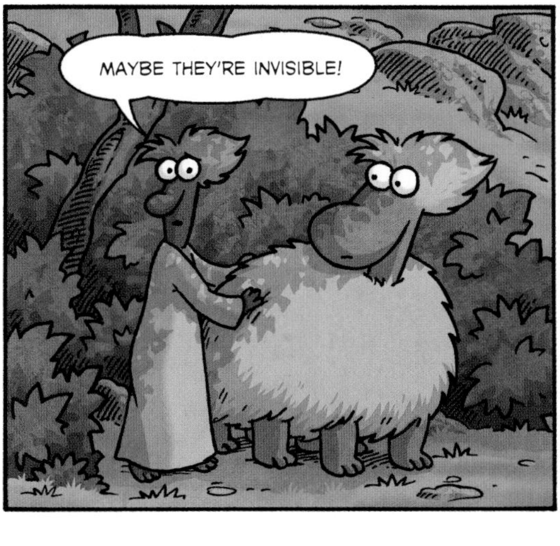
MAYBE THEY'RE INVISIBLE!

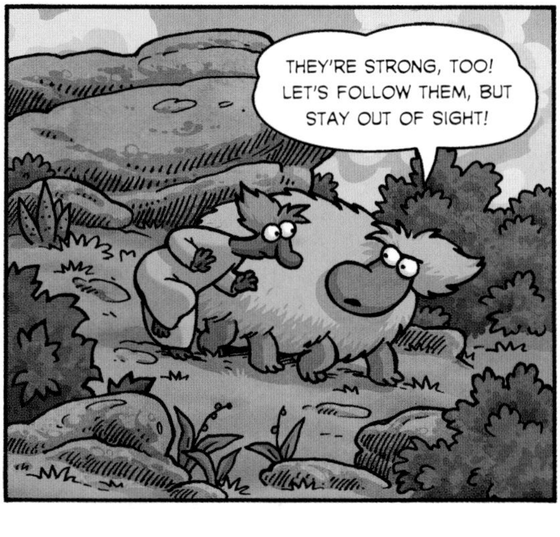
THEY'RE STRONG, TOO! LET'S FOLLOW THEM, BUT STAY OUT OF SIGHT!

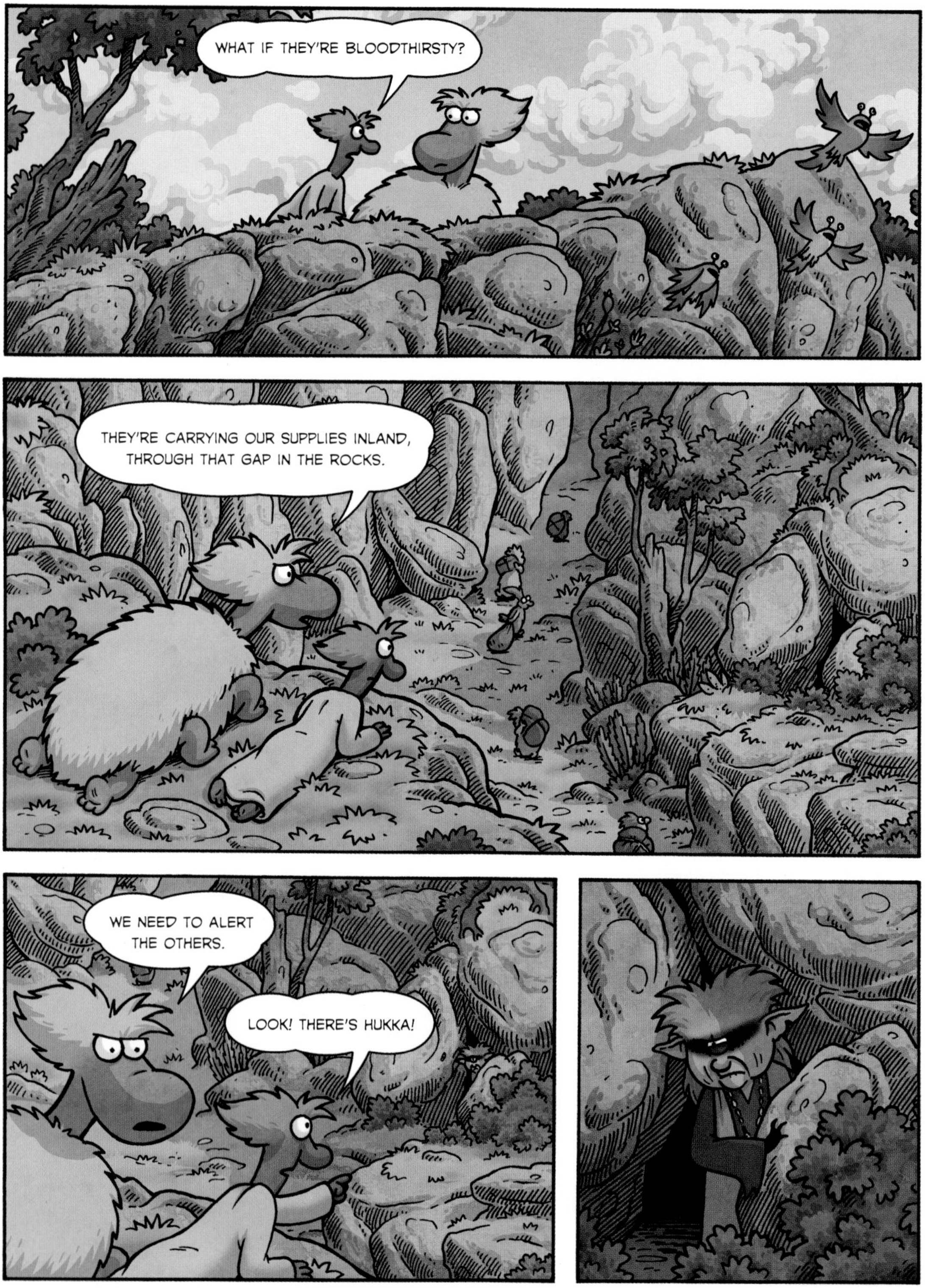
WHAT IF THEY'RE BLOODTHIRSTY?
THEY'RE CARRYING OUR SUPPLIES INLAND, THROUGH THAT GAP IN THE ROCKS.
WE NEED TO ALERT THE OTHERS.
LOOK! THERE'S HUKKA!

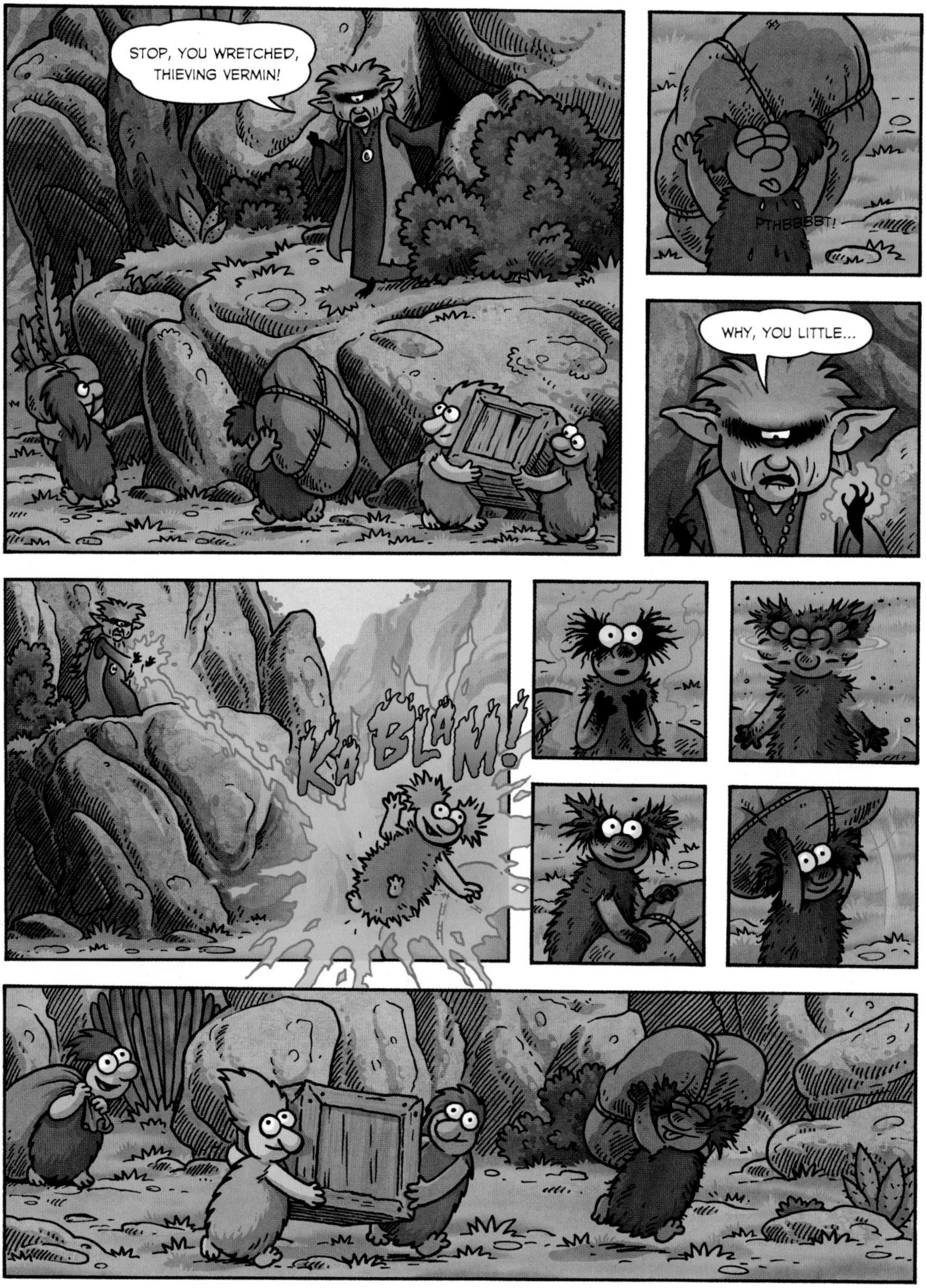
STOP, YOU WRETCHED, THIEVING VERMIN!
PTHBBBBT!
WHY, YOU LITTLE...
KA BLAM!

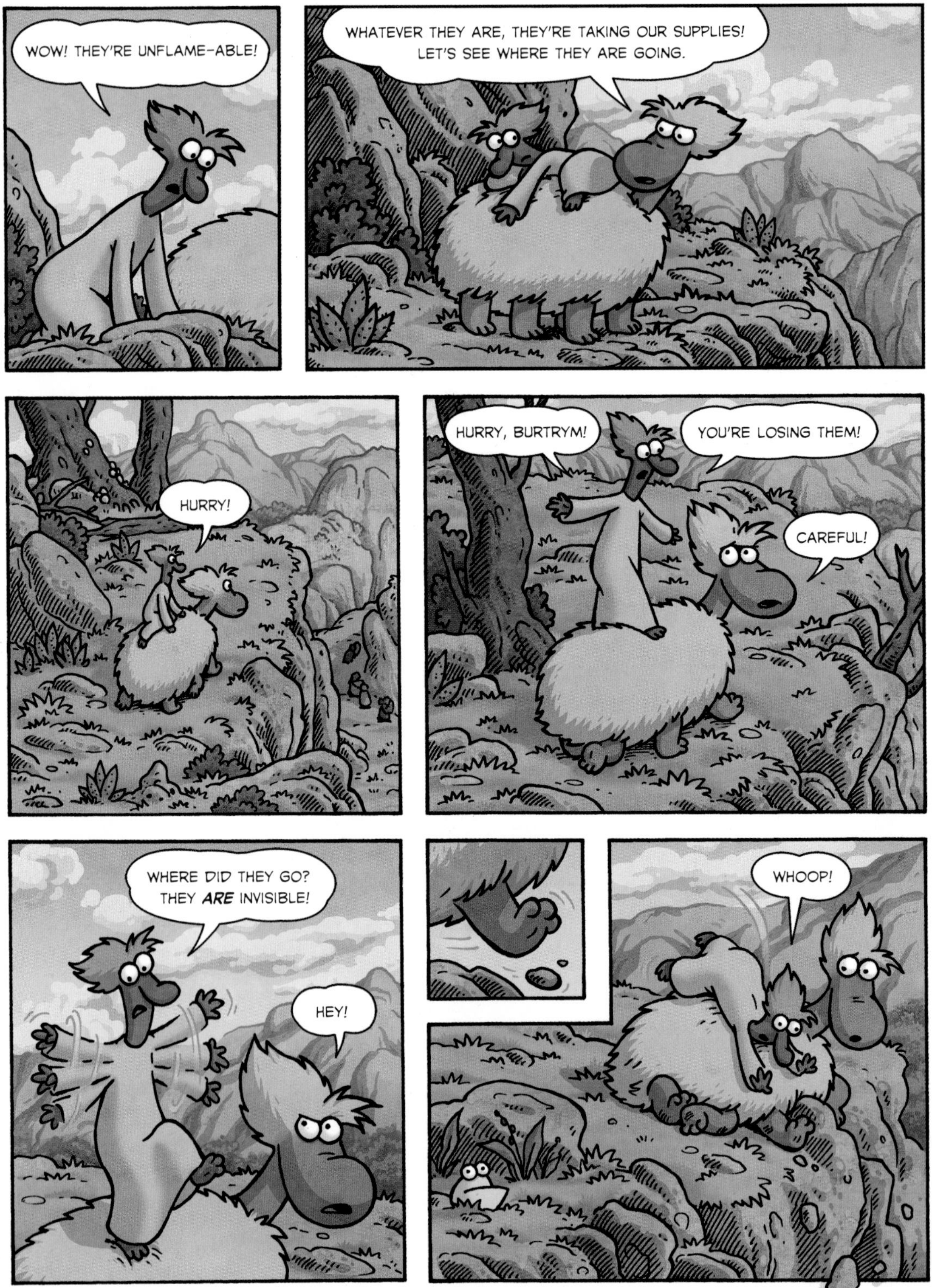
WOW! THEY'RE UNFLAME-ABLE!
WHATEVER THEY ARE, THEY'RE TAKING OUR SUPPLIES! LET'S SEE WHERE THEY ARE GOING.
HURRY!
HURRY, BURTRYM!
YOU'RE LOSING THEM!
CAREFUL!
WHERE DID THEY GO? THEY ***ARE*** INVISIBLE!
HEY!
WHOOP!

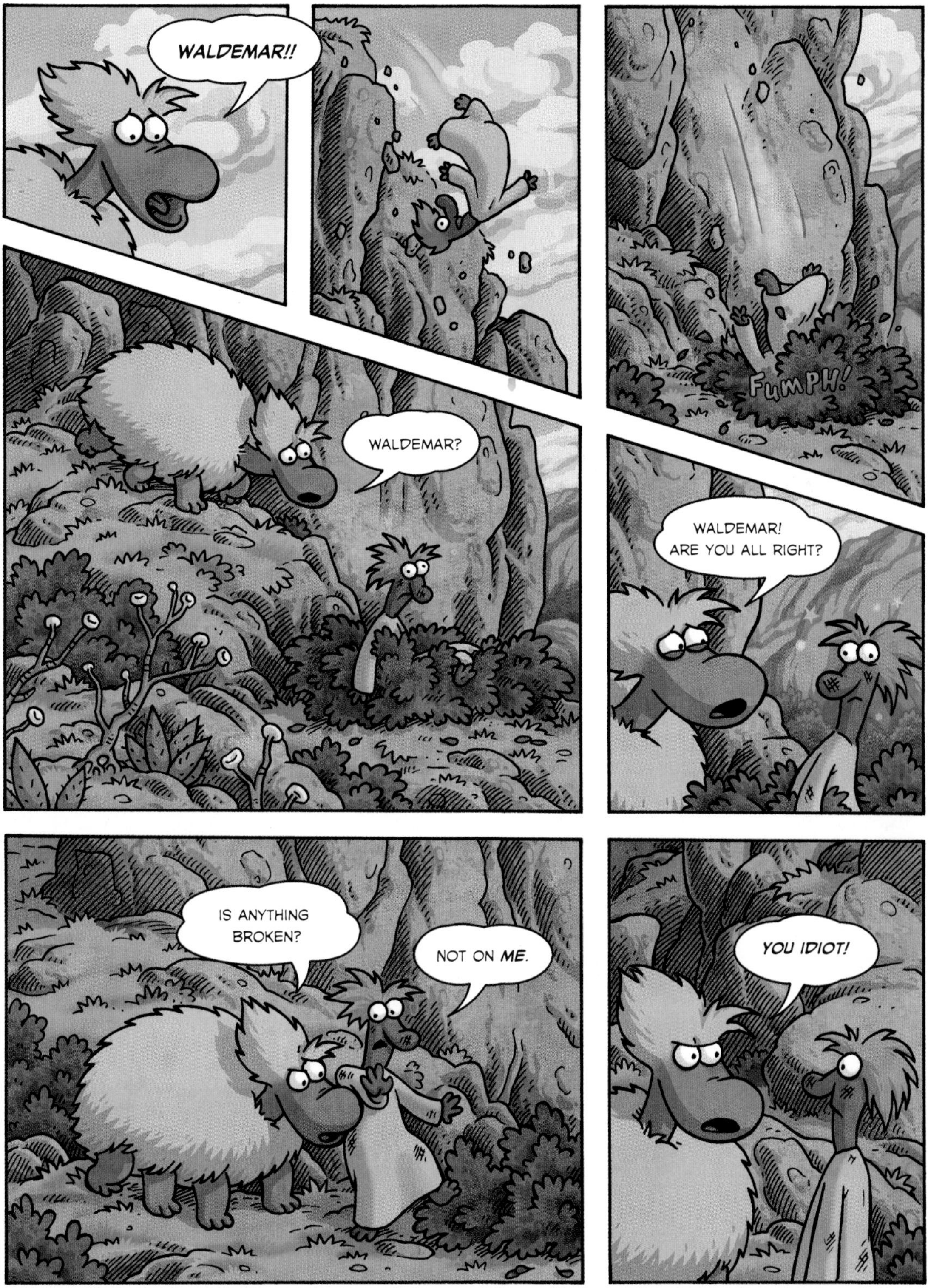
WALDEMAR!!
FUMPH!
WALDEMAR?
WALDEMAR!
ARE YOU ALL RIGHT?
IS ANYTHING BROKEN?
NOT ON ME.
YOU IDIOT!

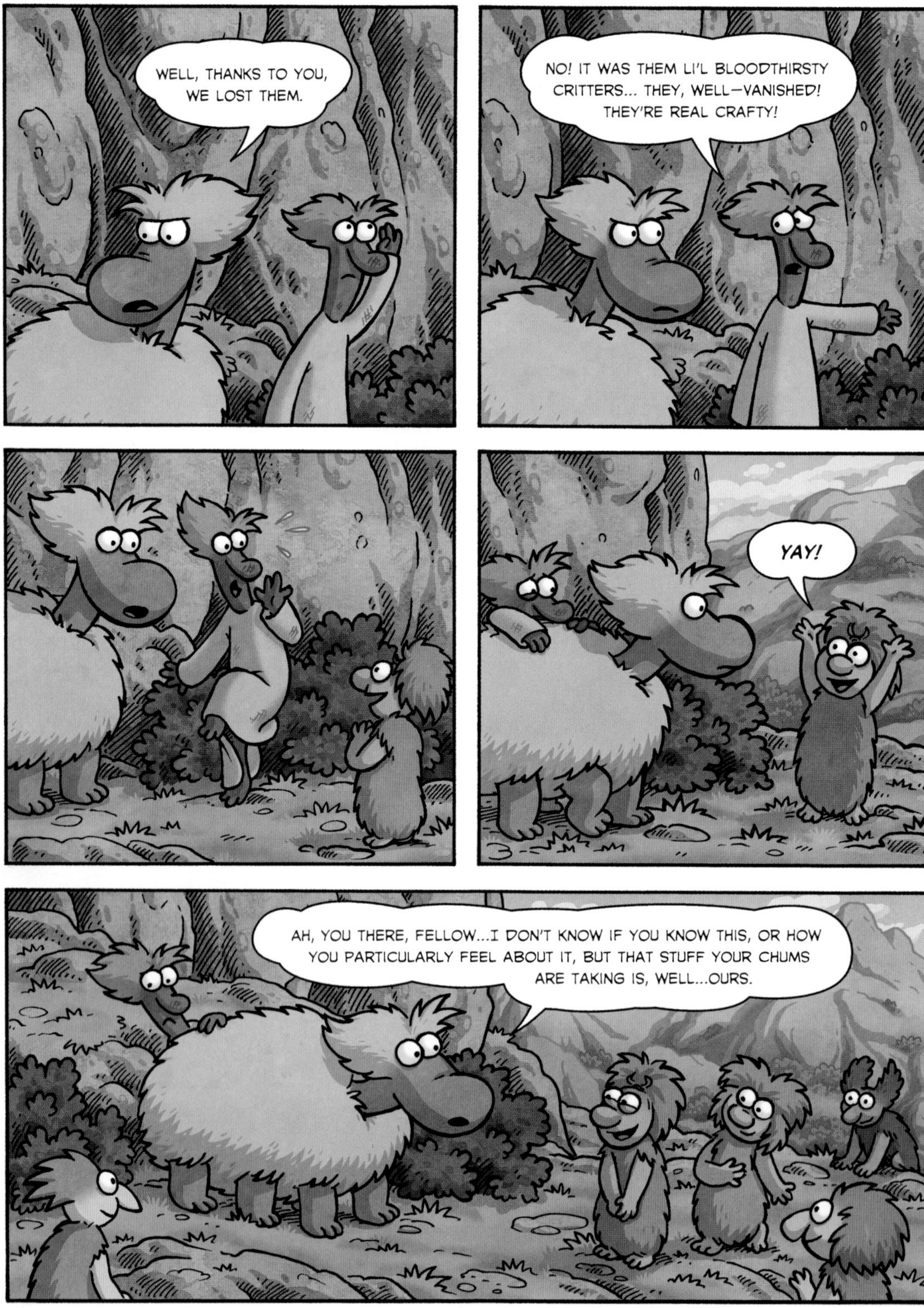

WELL, THANKS TO YOU, WE LOST THEM.
NO! IT WAS THEM LI'L BLOODTHIRSTY CRITTERS... THEY, WELL—VANISHED! THEY'RE REAL CRAFTY!
YAY!
AH, YOU THERE, FELLOW...I DON'T KNOW IF YOU KNOW THIS, OR HOW YOU PARTICULARLY FEEL ABOUT IT, BUT THAT STUFF YOUR CHUMS ARE TAKING IS, WELL...OURS.

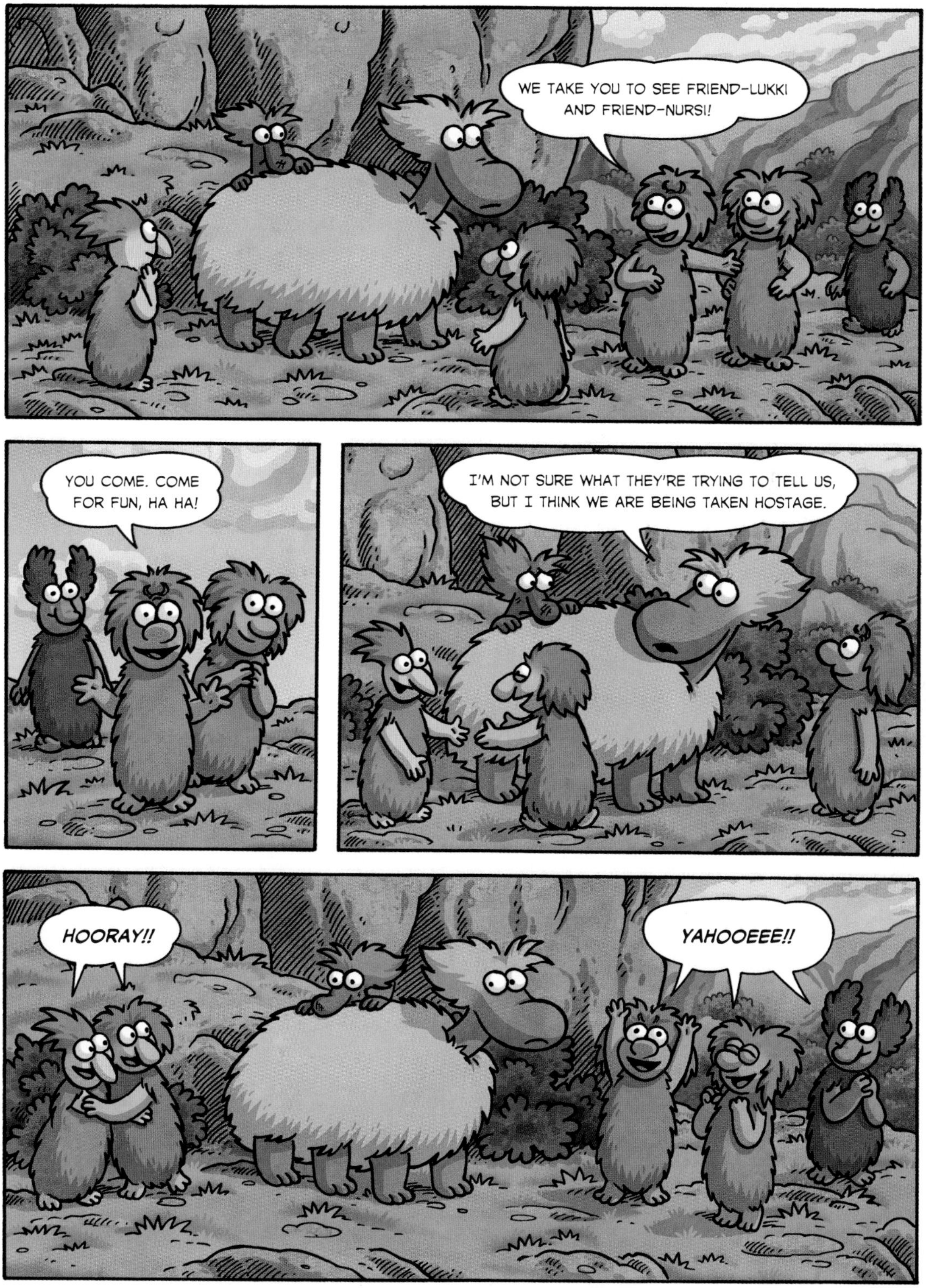
WE TAKE YOU TO SEE FRIEND-LUKKI AND FRIEND-NURSI!
YOU COME. COME FOR FUN, HA HA!
I'M NOT SURE WHAT THEY'RE TRYING TO TELL US, BUT I THINK WE ARE BEING TAKEN HOSTAGE.
HOORAY!!
YAHOOEEE!!

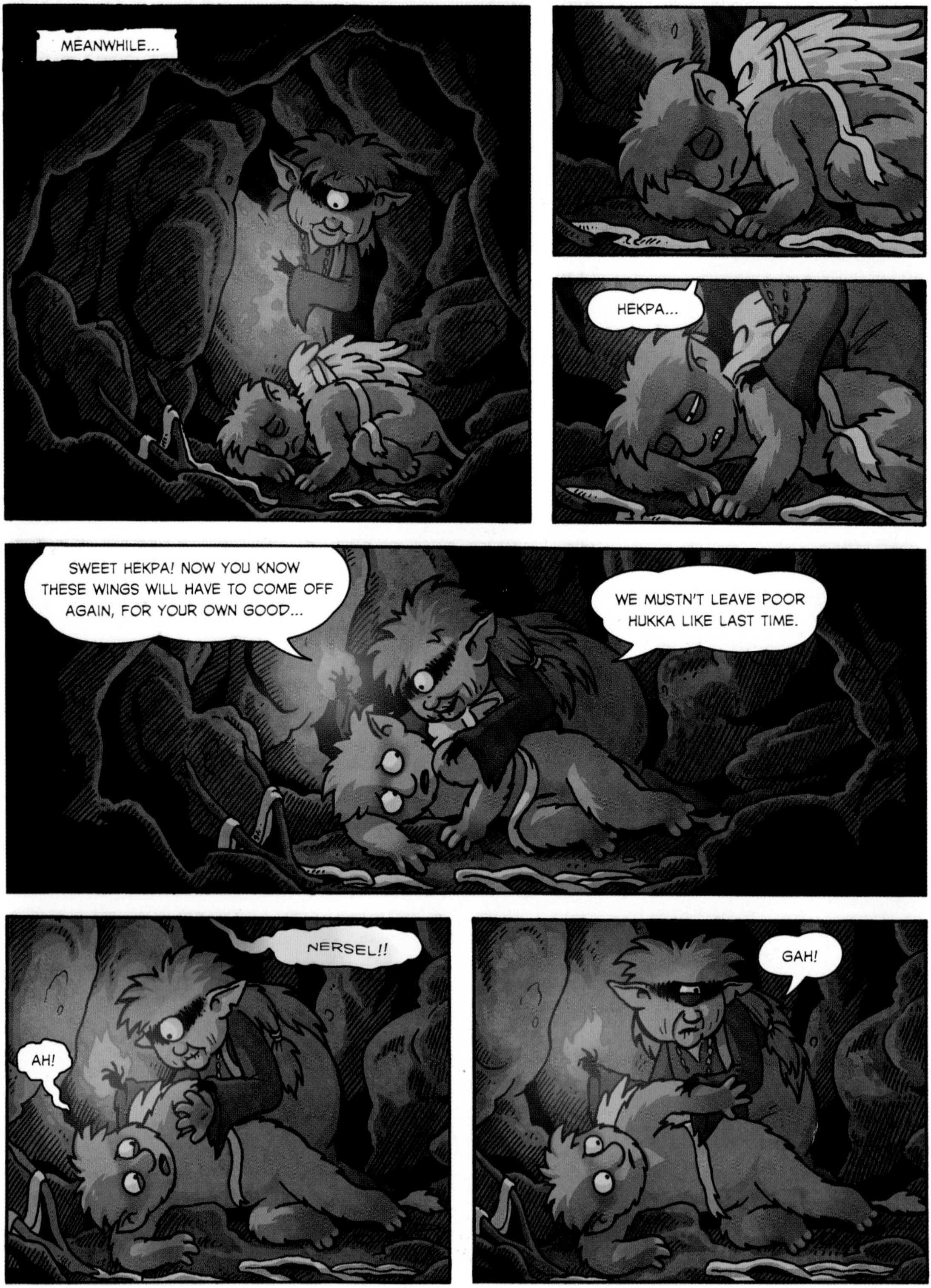
MEANWHILE...
HEKPA...
SWEET HEKPA! NOW YOU KNOW THESE WINGS WILL HAVE TO COME OFF AGAIN, FOR YOUR OWN GOOD...
WE MUSTN'T LEAVE POOR HUKKA LIKE LAST TIME.
AH!
NERSEL!!
GAH!

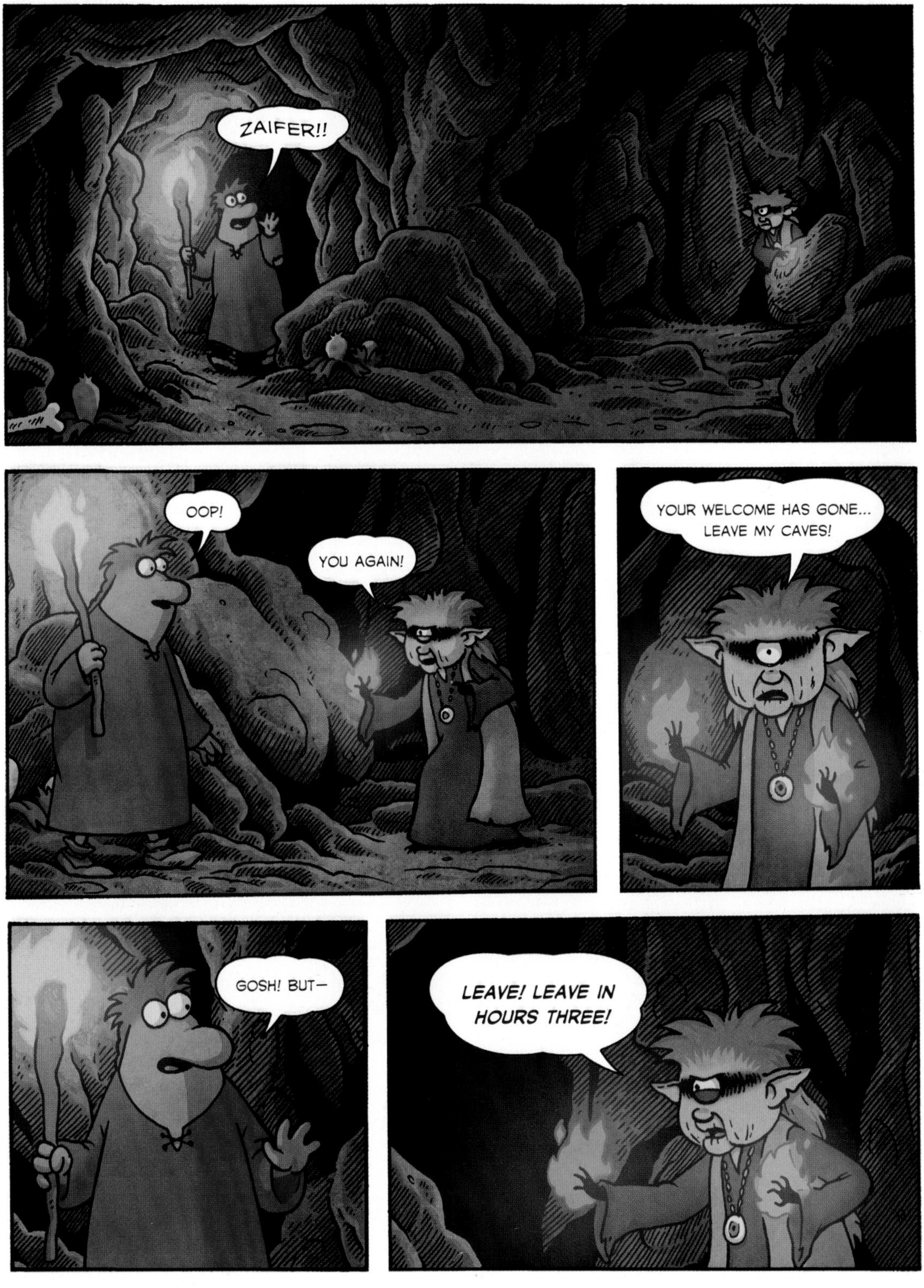
ZAIFER!!
OOP!
YOU AGAIN!
YOUR WELCOME HAS GONE... LEAVE MY CAVES!
GOSH! BUT—
LEAVE! LEAVE IN HOURS THREE!

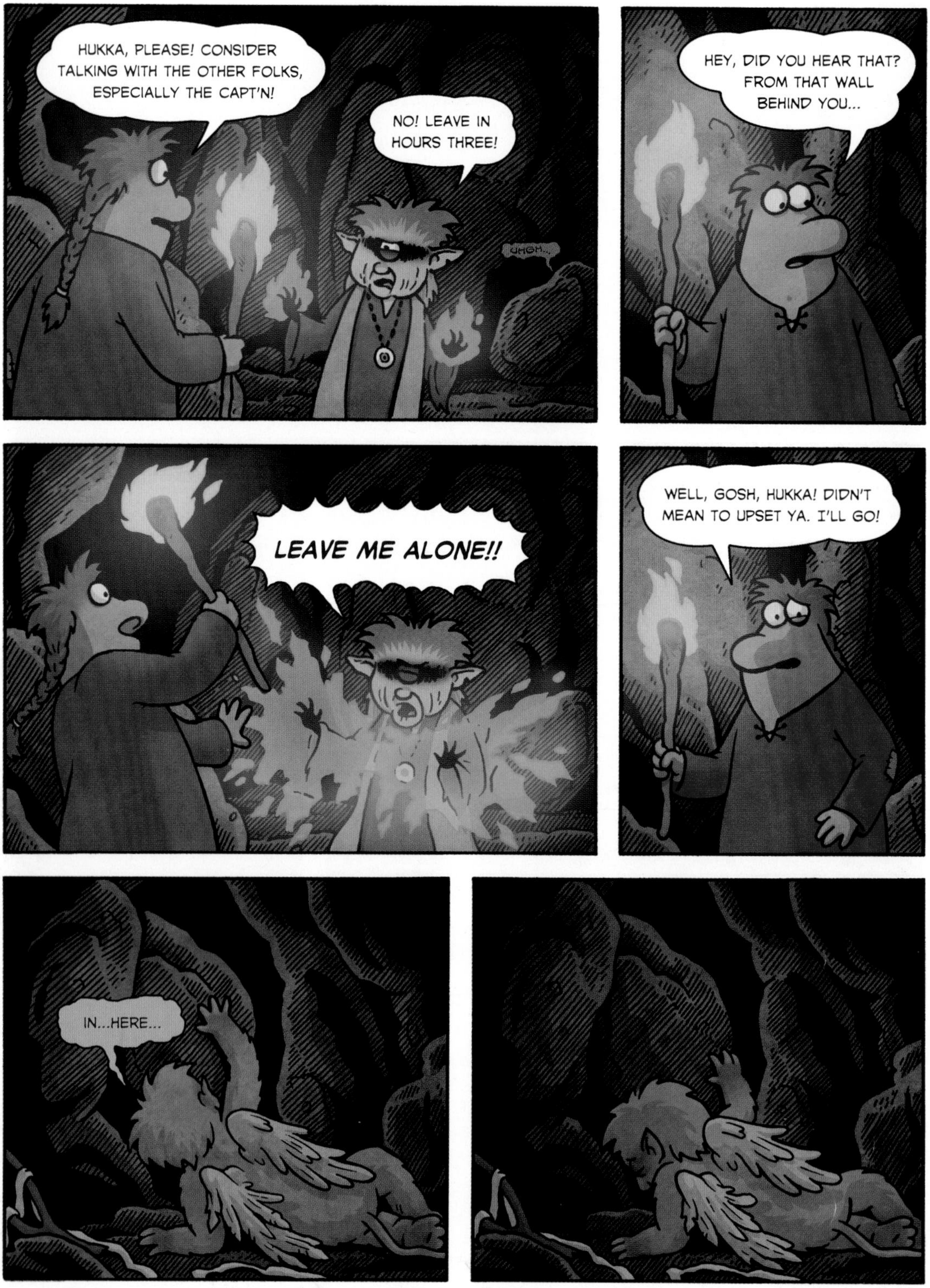
HUKKA, PLEASE! CONSIDER TALKING WITH THE OTHER FOLKS, ESPECIALLY THE CAPT'N!
NO! LEAVE IN HOURS THREE!
UHGH...
HEY, DID YOU HEAR THAT? FROM THAT WALL BEHIND YOU...
LEAVE ME ALONE!!
WELL, GOSH, HUKKA! DIDN'T MEAN TO UPSET YA. I'LL GO!
IN...HERE...

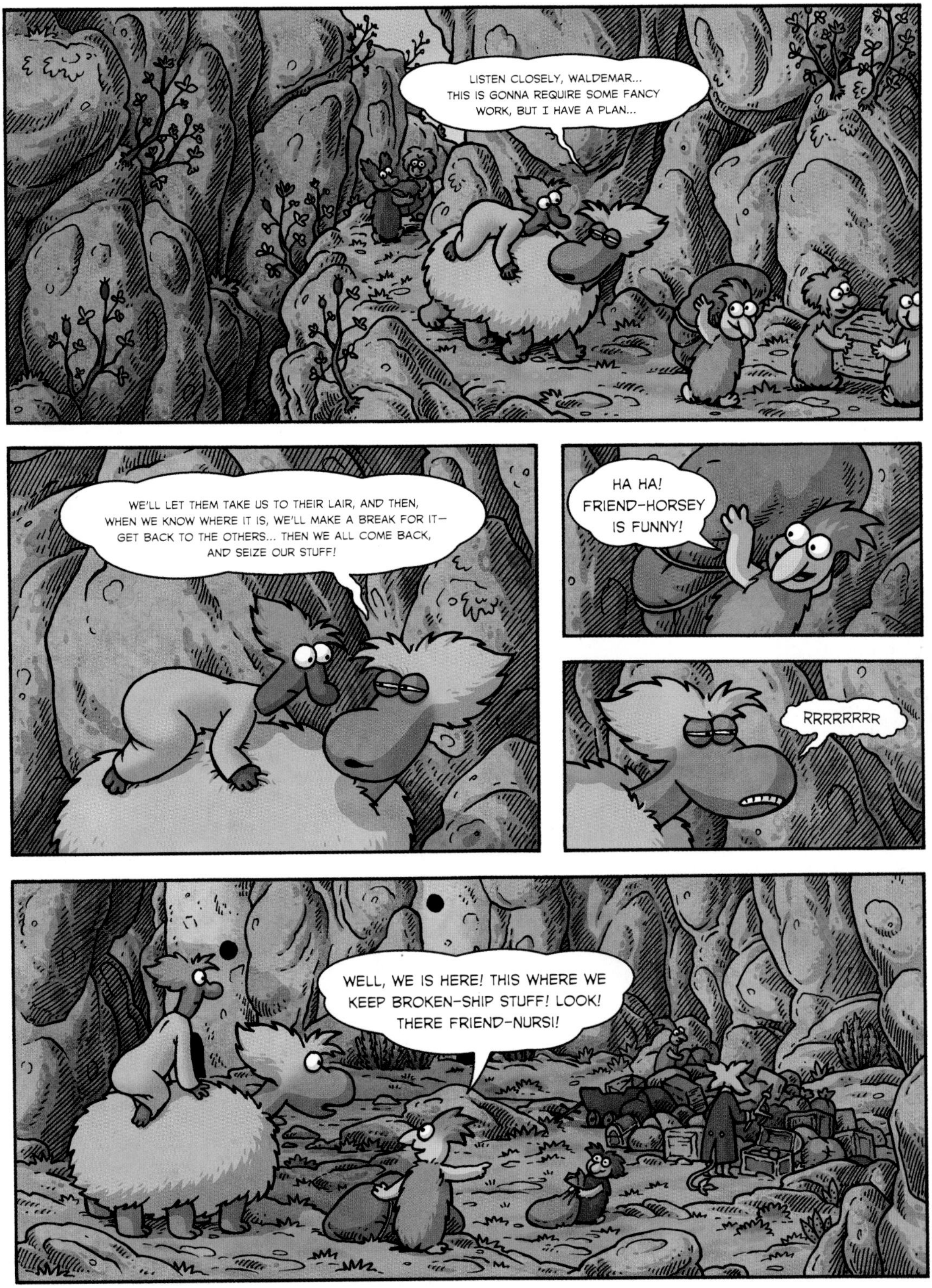
LISTEN CLOSELY, WALDEMAR... THIS IS GONNA REQUIRE SOME FANCY WORK, BUT I HAVE A PLAN...
WE'LL LET THEM TAKE US TO THEIR LAIR, AND THEN, WHEN WE KNOW WHERE IT IS, WE'LL MAKE A BREAK FOR IT— GET BACK TO THE OTHERS... THEN WE ALL COME BACK, AND SEIZE OUR STUFF!
HA HA! FRIEND-HORSEY IS FUNNY!
RRRRRRRR
WELL, WE IS HERE! THIS WHERE WE KEEP BROKEN-SHIP STUFF! LOOK! THERE FRIEND-NURSI!

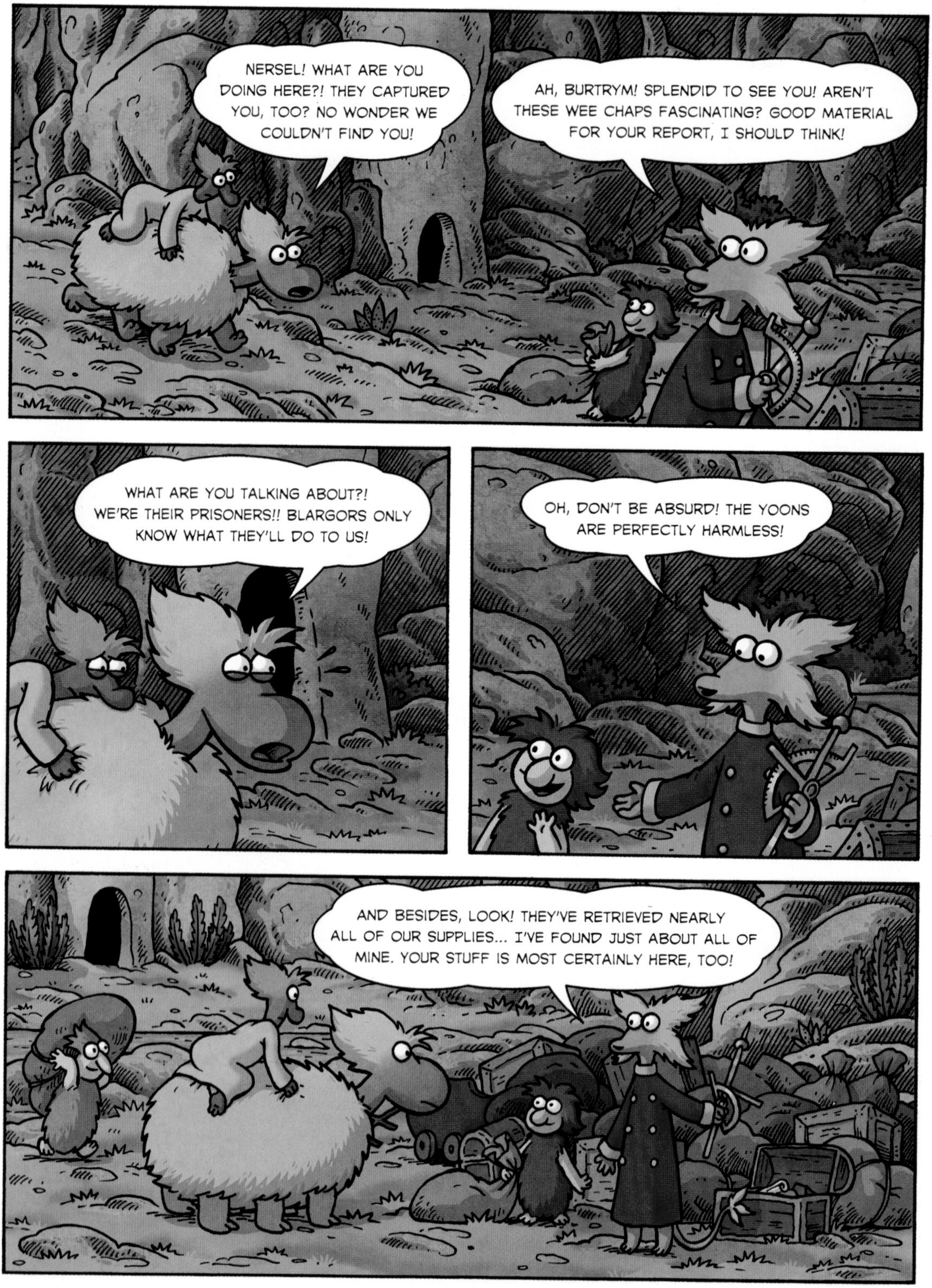
NERSEL! WHAT ARE YOU DOING HERE?! THEY CAPTURED YOU, TOO? NO WONDER WE COULDN'T FIND YOU!
AH, BURTRYM! SPLENDID TO SEE YOU! AREN'T THESE WEE CHAPS FASCINATING? GOOD MATERIAL FOR YOUR REPORT, I SHOULD THINK!
WHAT ARE YOU TALKING ABOUT?! WE'RE THEIR PRISONERS!! BLARGORS ONLY KNOW WHAT THEY'LL DO TO US!
OH, DON'T BE ABSURD! THE YOONS ARE PERFECTLY HARMLESS!
AND BESIDES, LOOK! THEY'VE RETRIEVED NEARLY ALL OF OUR SUPPLIES... I'VE FOUND JUST ABOUT ALL OF MINE. YOUR STUFF IS MOST CERTAINLY HERE, TOO!

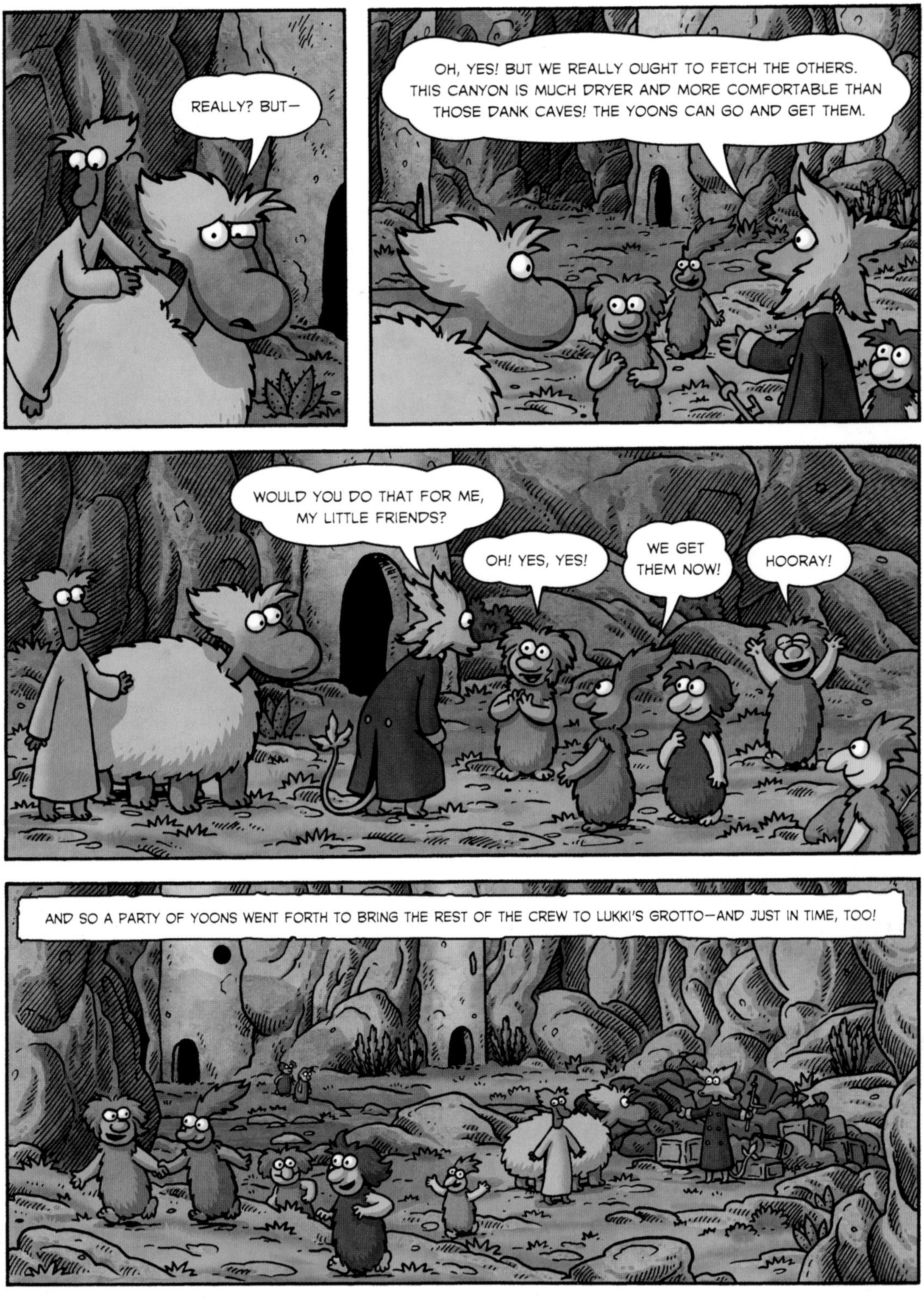
REALLY? BUT—
OH, YES! BUT WE REALLY OUGHT TO FETCH THE OTHERS. THIS CANYON IS MUCH DRYER AND MORE COMFORTABLE THAN THOSE DANK CAVES! THE YOONS CAN GO AND GET THEM.
WOULD YOU DO THAT FOR ME, MY LITTLE FRIENDS?
OH! YES, YES!
WE GET THEM NOW!
HOORAY!
AND SO A PARTY OF YOONS WENT FORTH TO BRING THE REST OF THE CREW TO LUKKI'S GROTTO—AND JUST IN TIME, TOO!

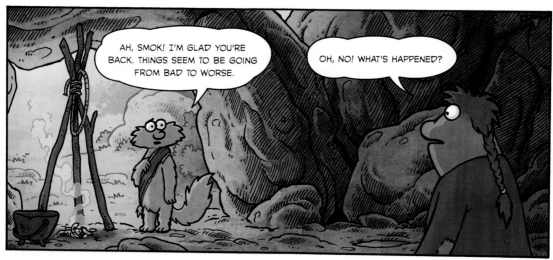

AH, SMOK! I'M GLAD YOU'RE BACK. THINGS SEEM TO BE GOING FROM BAD TO WORSE.

OH, NO! WHAT'S HAPPENED?

ON TOP OF OUR OTHER TROUBLES, NOW OUR SUPPLIES ARE BEING STOLEN! I'VE JUST BEEN BRIEFED BY GNONEK THAT SOME INDIGENOUS CREATURES ARE MAKING OFF WITH OUR CARGO.

THE AMBER BRIGADE HAS TRACKED THEM TO A CANYON NOT FAR OFF. I DON'T UNDERSTAND HOW THESE CREATURES GET PAST THE HOOKLM.

WHAT ABOUT YOU? DID YOU SPEAK TO HUKKA?

UM, UH...YES, SIR. I TRIED TO ASK HER, BUT SHE GOT ALL SURLY AND WOULDN'T LISTEN... IN FACT—

WHAT? WHAT HAPPENED?

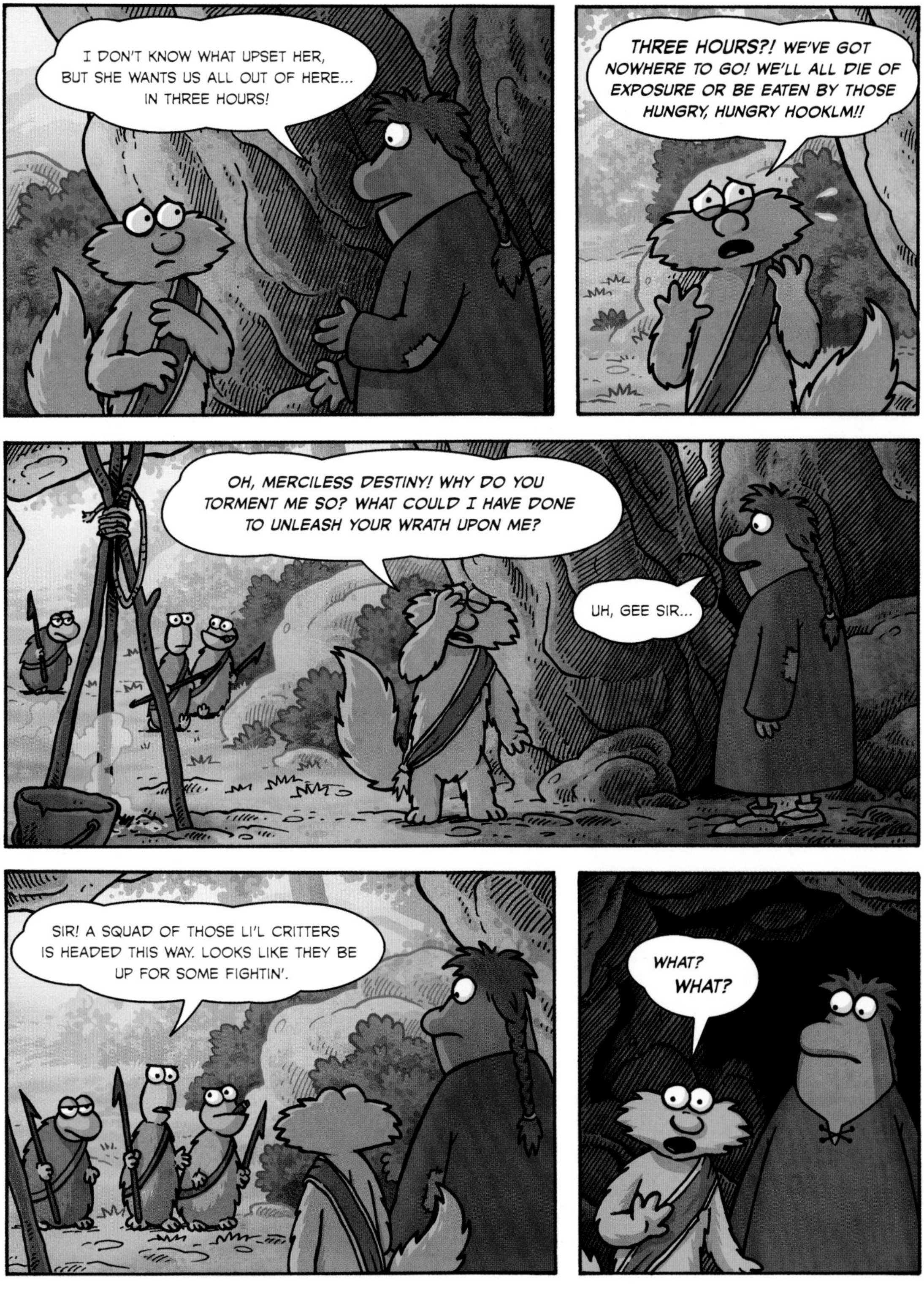
I DON'T KNOW WHAT UPSET HER, BUT SHE WANTS US ALL OUT OF HERE... IN THREE HOURS!
THREE HOURS?! WE'VE GOT NOWHERE TO GO! WE'LL ALL DIE OF EXPOSURE OR BE EATEN BY THOSE HUNGRY, HUNGRY HOOKLM!!
OH, MERCILESS DESTINY! WHY DO YOU TORMENT ME SO? WHAT COULD I HAVE DONE TO UNLEASH YOUR WRATH UPON ME?
UH, GEE SIR...
SIR! A SQUAD OF THOSE LI'L CRITTERS IS HEADED THIS WAY. LOOKS LIKE THEY BE UP FOR SOME FIGHTIN'.
WHAT?
WHAT?

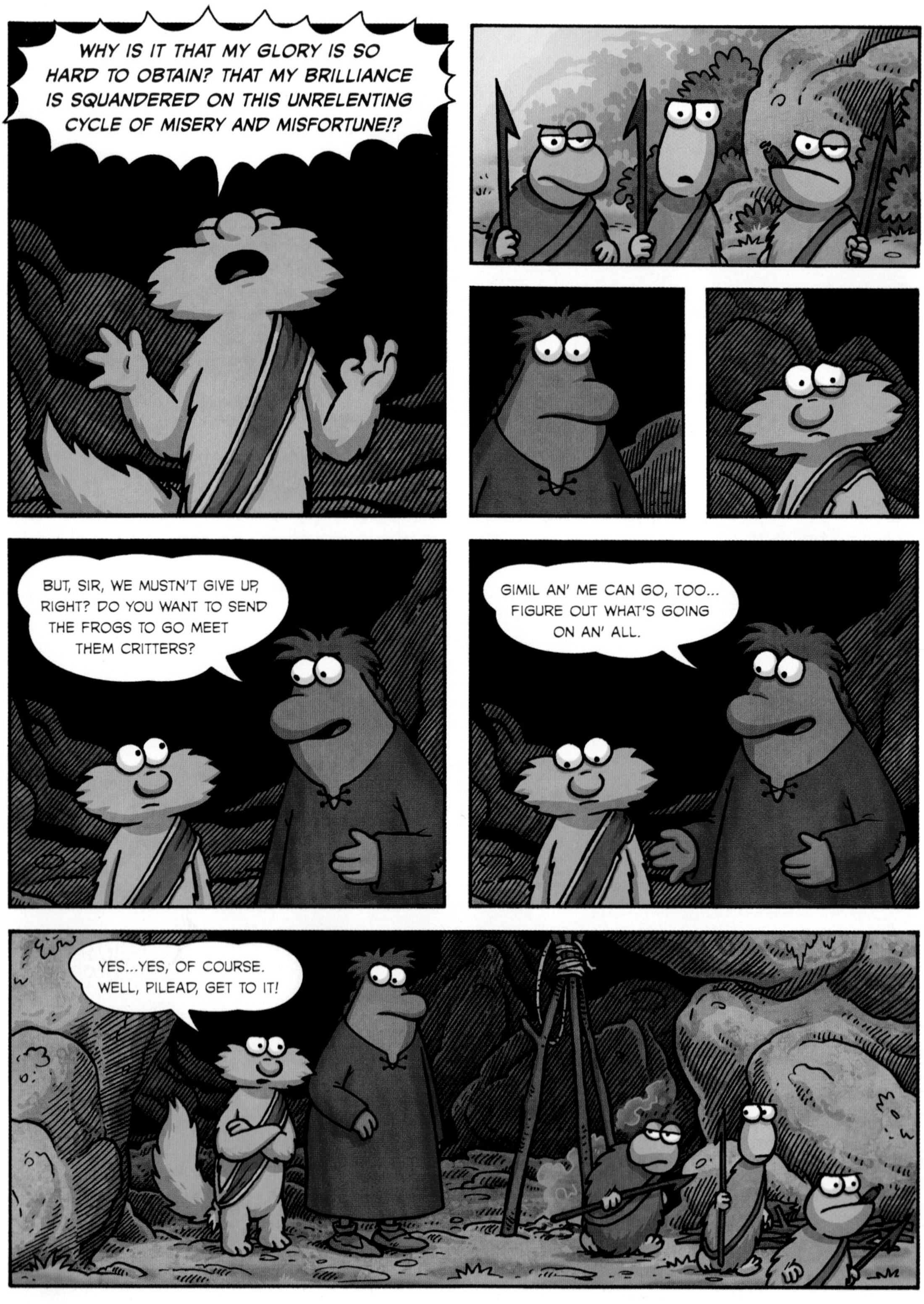
WHY IS IT THAT MY GLORY IS SO HARD TO OBTAIN? THAT MY BRILLIANCE IS SQUANDERED ON THIS UNRELENTING CYCLE OF MISERY AND MISFORTUNE!?
BUT, SIR, WE MUSTN'T GIVE UP, RIGHT? DO YOU WANT TO SEND THE FROGS TO GO MEET THEM CRITTERS?
GIMIL AN' ME CAN GO, TOO... FIGURE OUT WHAT'S GOING ON AN' ALL.
YES...YES, OF COURSE. WELL, PILEAD, GET TO IT!

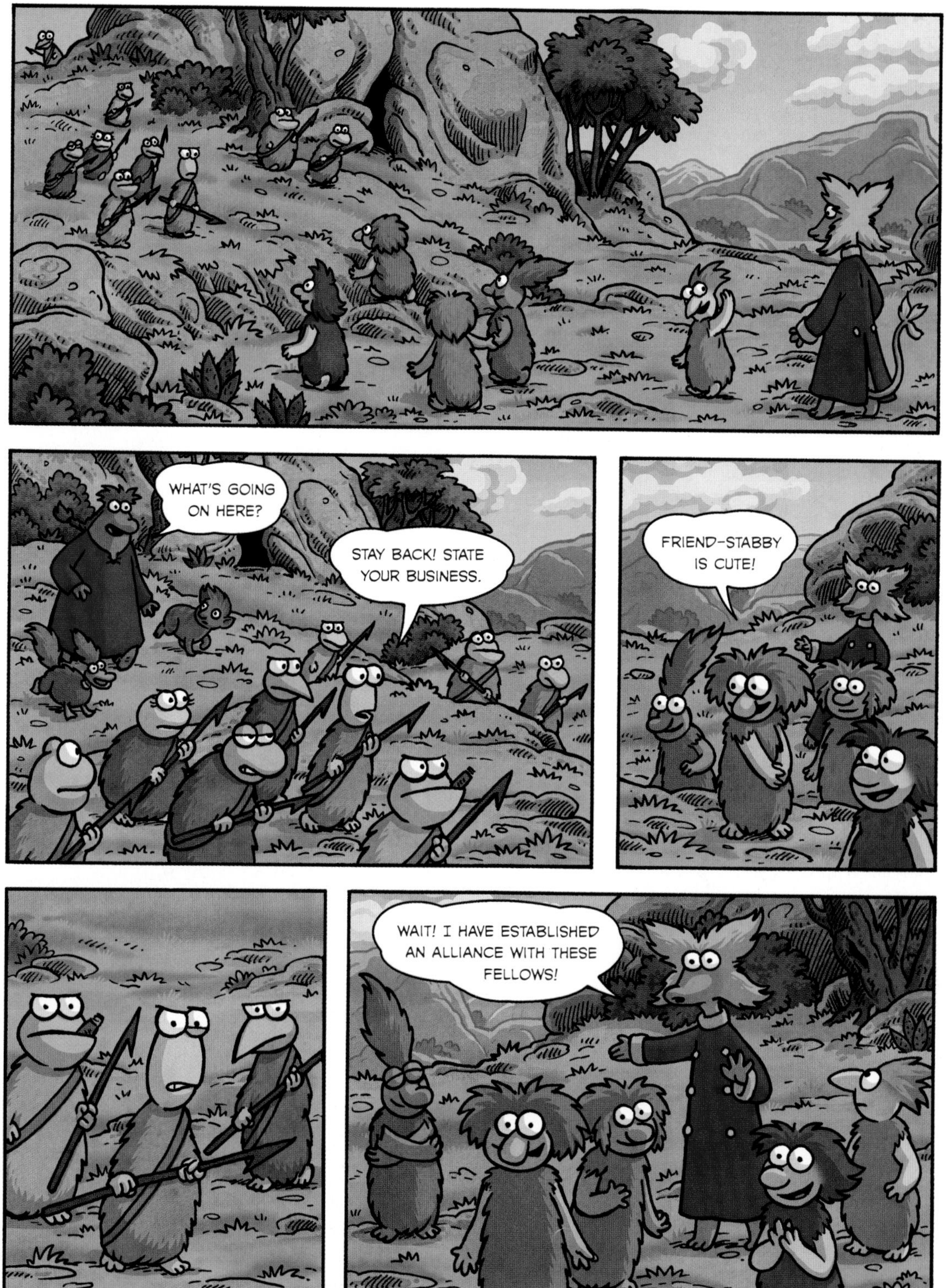
WHAT'S GOING ON HERE?
STAY BACK! STATE YOUR BUSINESS.
FRIEND-STABBY IS CUTE!
WAIT! I HAVE ESTABLISHED AN ALLIANCE WITH THESE FELLOWS!

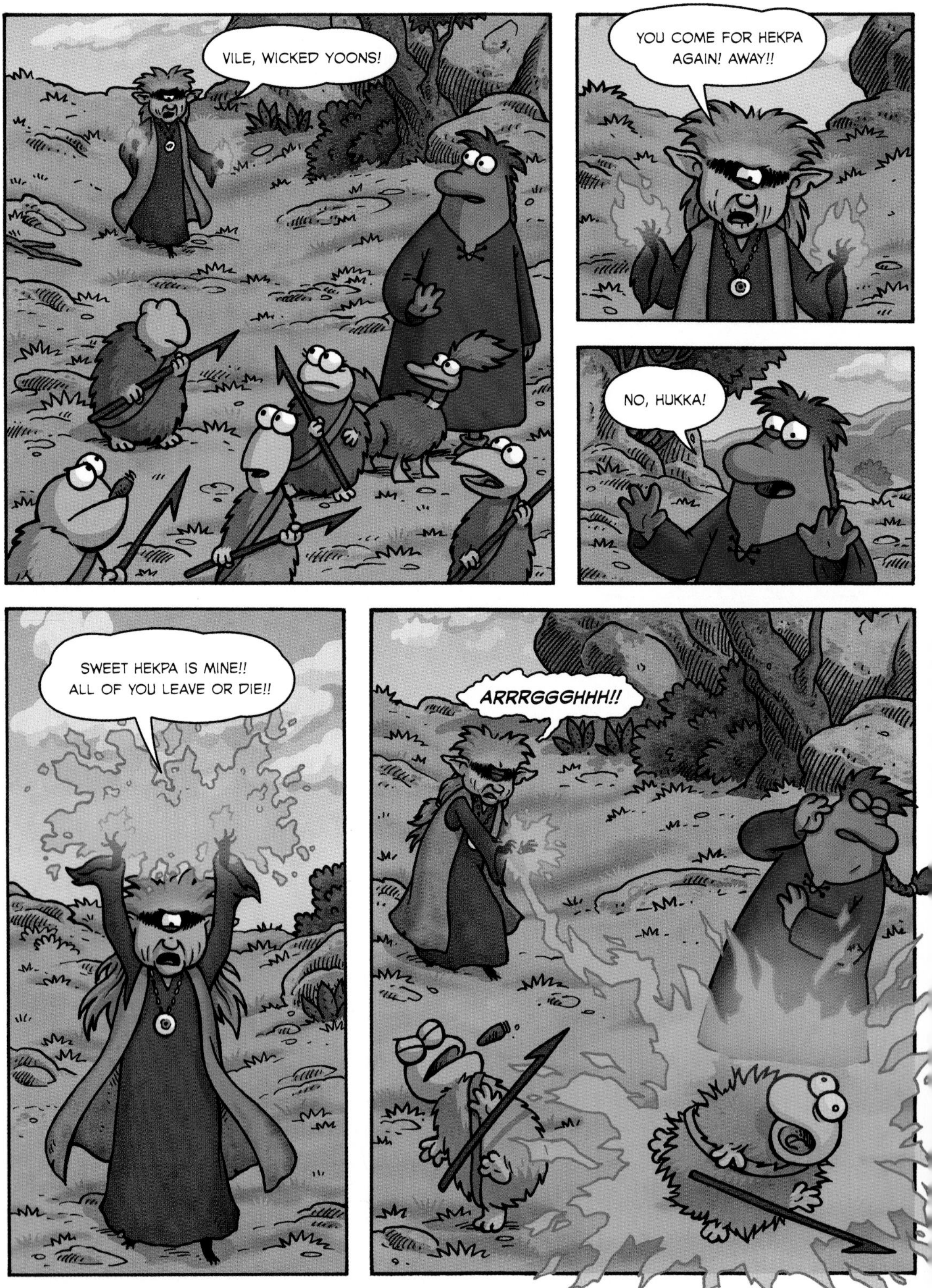
VILE, WICKED YOONS!
YOU COME FOR HEKPA AGAIN! AWAY!!
NO, HUKKA!
SWEET HEKPA IS MINE!! ALL OF YOU LEAVE OR DIE!!
ARRRGGGHHH!!

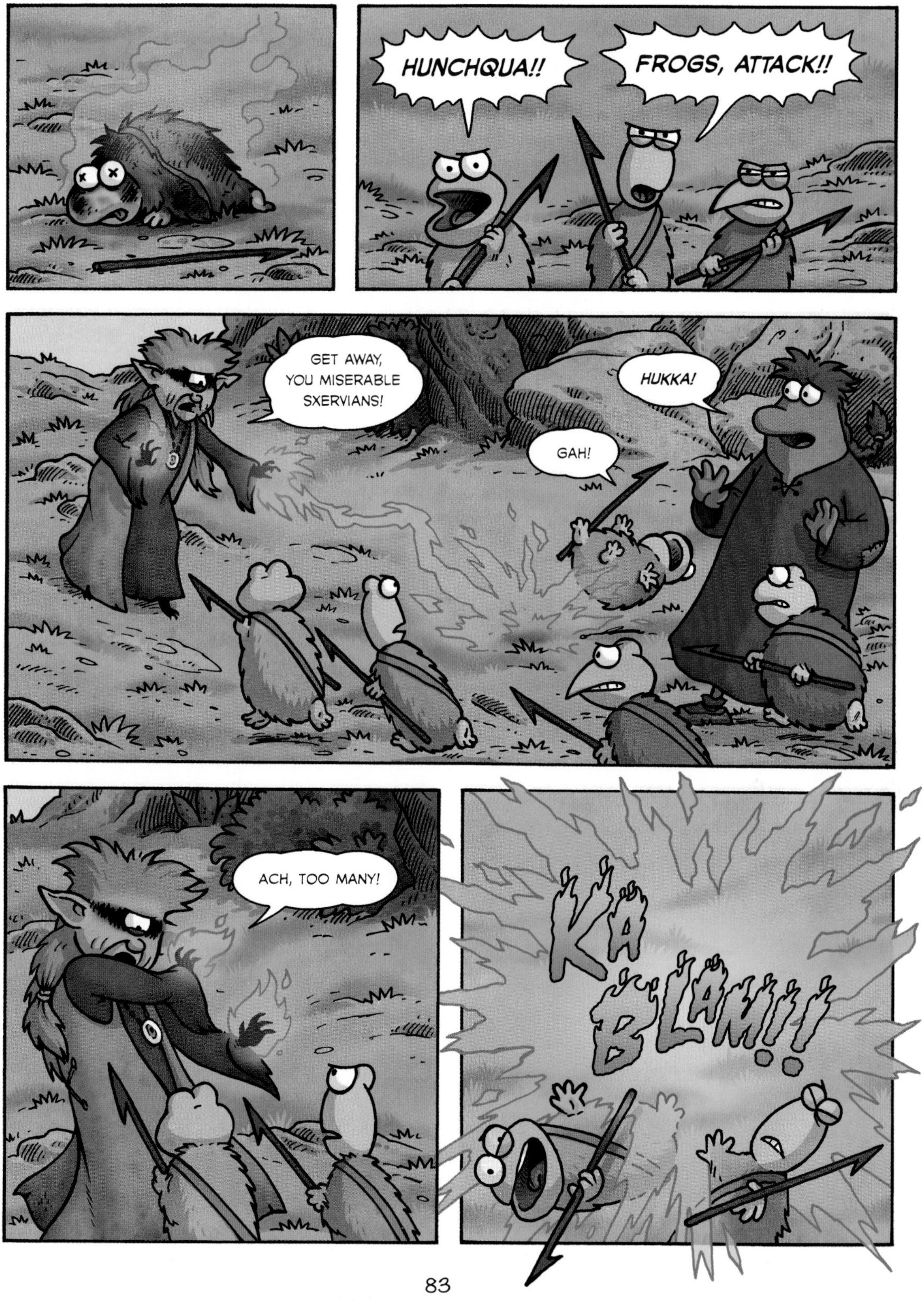
HUNCHQUA!!
FROGS, ATTACK!!
GET AWAY, YOU MISERABLE SXERVIANS!
HUKKA!
GAH!
ACH, TOO MANY!
KA BLAM!!

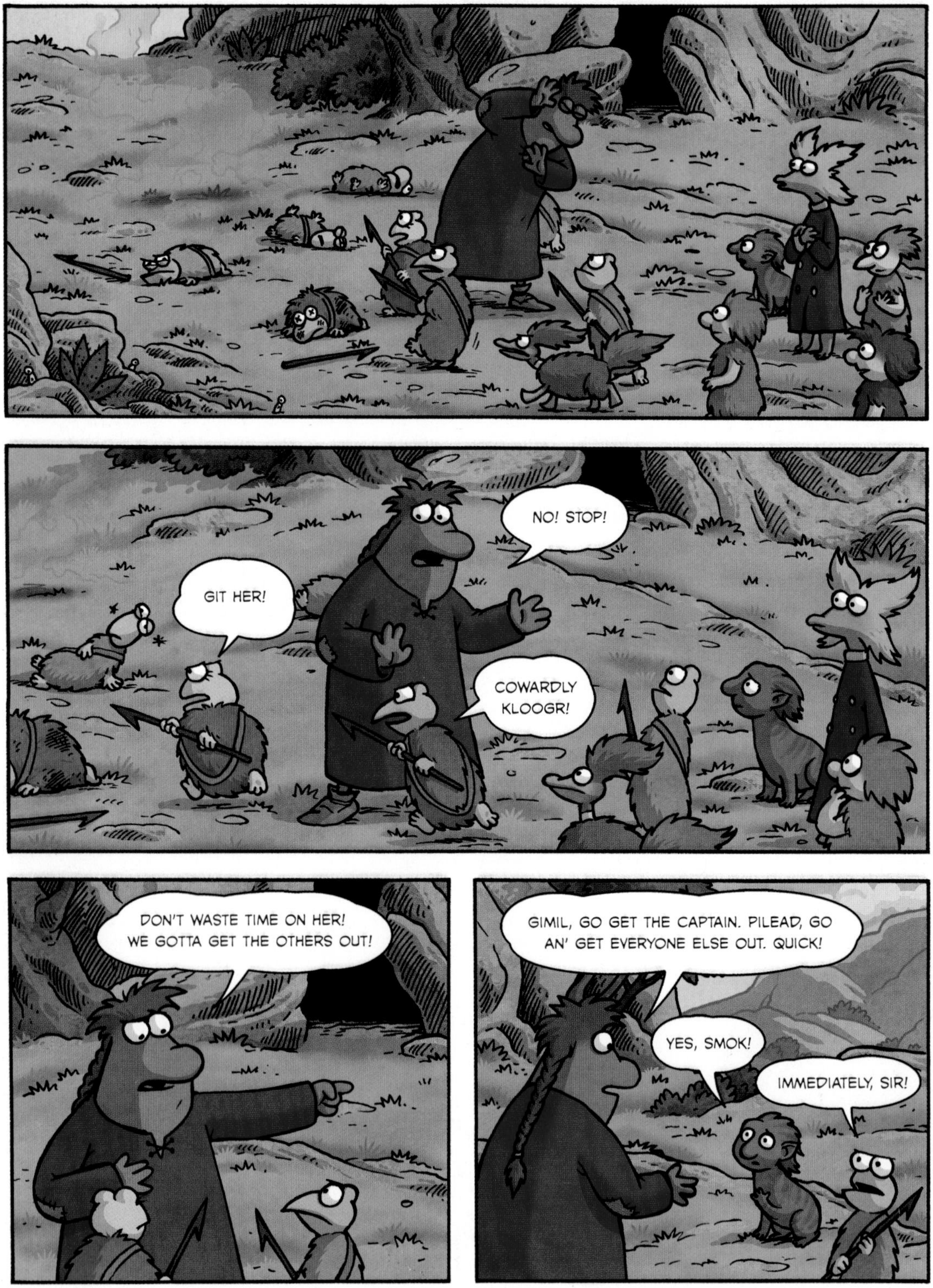
NO! STOP!
GIT HER!
COWARDLY KLOOGR!
DON'T WASTE TIME ON HER! WE GOTTA GET THE OTHERS OUT!
GIMIL, GO GET THE CAPTAIN. PILEAD, GO AN' GET EVERYONE ELSE OUT. QUICK!
YES, SMOK!
IMMEDIATELY, SIR!

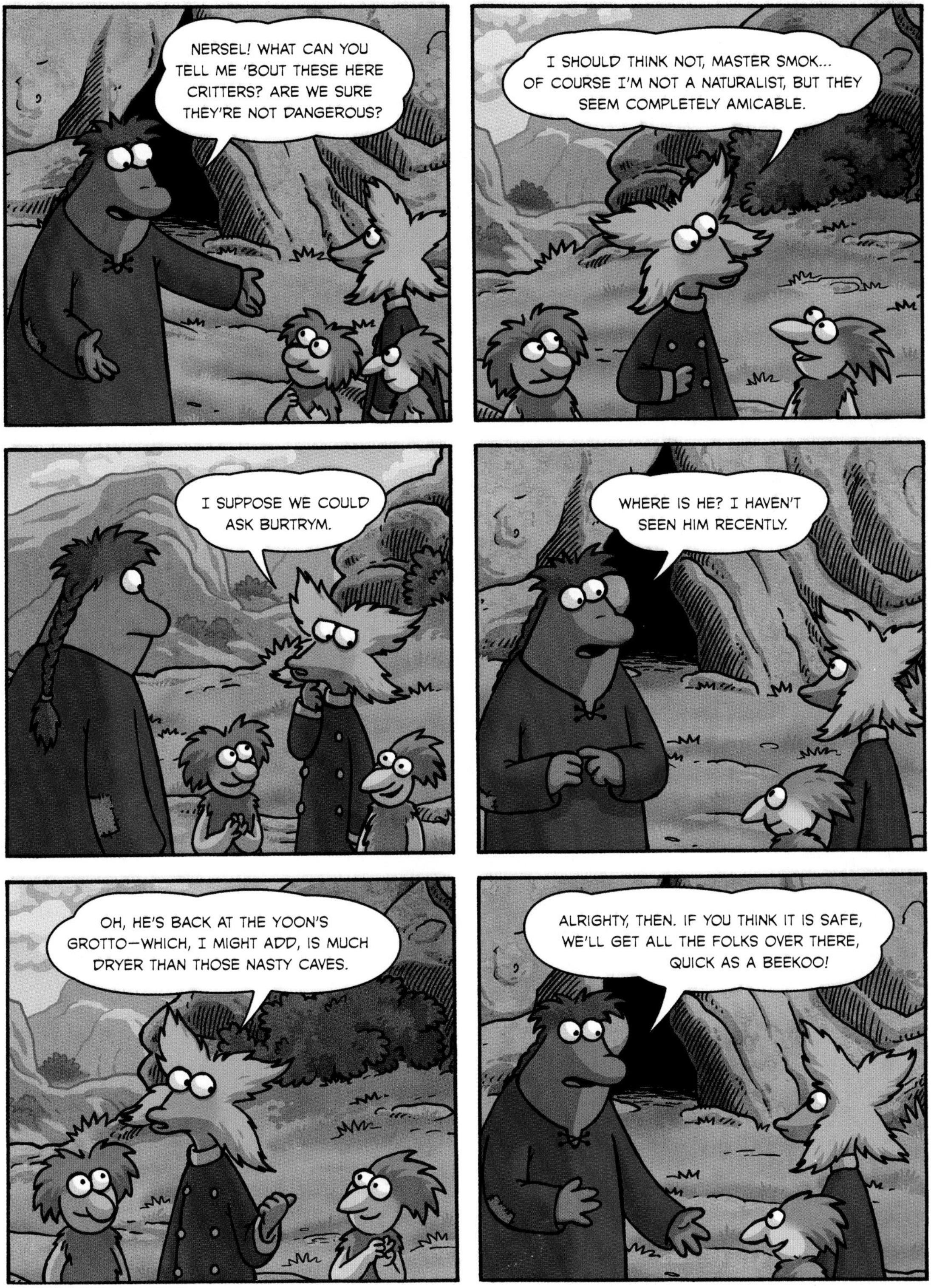
NERSEL! WHAT CAN YOU TELL ME 'BOUT THESE HERE CRITTERS? ARE WE SURE THEY'RE NOT DANGEROUS?
I SHOULD THINK NOT, MASTER SMOK... OF COURSE I'M NOT A NATURALIST, BUT THEY SEEM COMPLETELY AMICABLE.
I SUPPOSE WE COULD ASK BURTRYM.
WHERE IS HE? I HAVEN'T SEEN HIM RECENTLY.
OH, HE'S BACK AT THE YOON'S GROTTO—WHICH, I MIGHT ADD, IS MUCH DRYER THAN THOSE NASTY CAVES.
ALRIGHTY, THEN. IF YOU THINK IT IS SAFE, WE'LL GET ALL THE FOLKS OVER THERE, QUICK AS A BEEKOO!

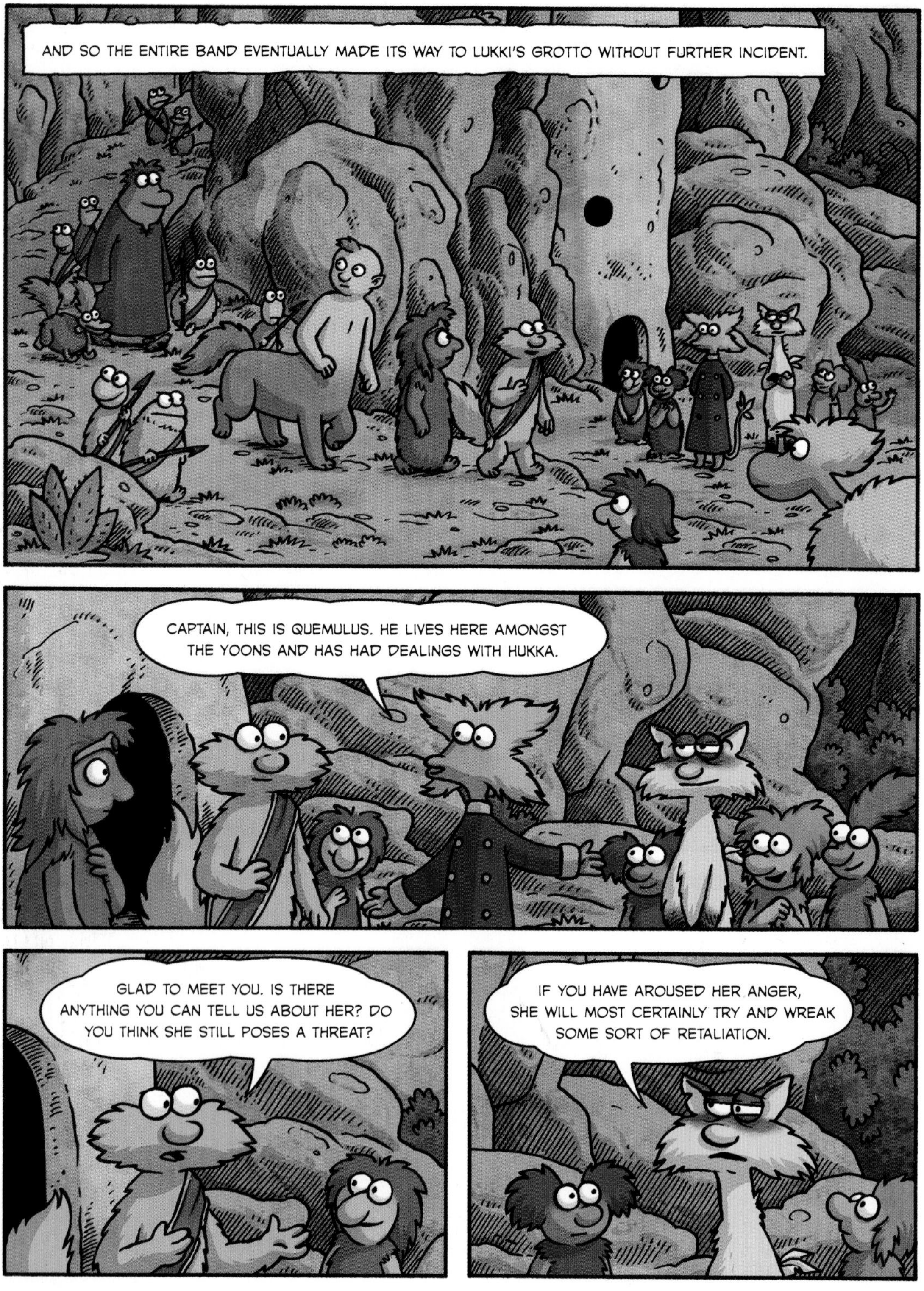
AND SO THE ENTIRE BAND EVENTUALLY MADE ITS WAY TO LUKKI'S GROTTO WITHOUT FURTHER INCIDENT.
CAPTAIN, THIS IS QUEMULUS. HE LIVES HERE AMONGST THE YOONS AND HAS HAD DEALINGS WITH HUKKA.
GLAD TO MEET YOU. IS THERE ANYTHING YOU CAN TELL US ABOUT HER? DO YOU THINK SHE STILL POSES A THREAT?
IF YOU HAVE AROUSED HER ANGER, SHE WILL MOST CERTAINLY TRY AND WREAK SOME SORT OF RETALIATION.

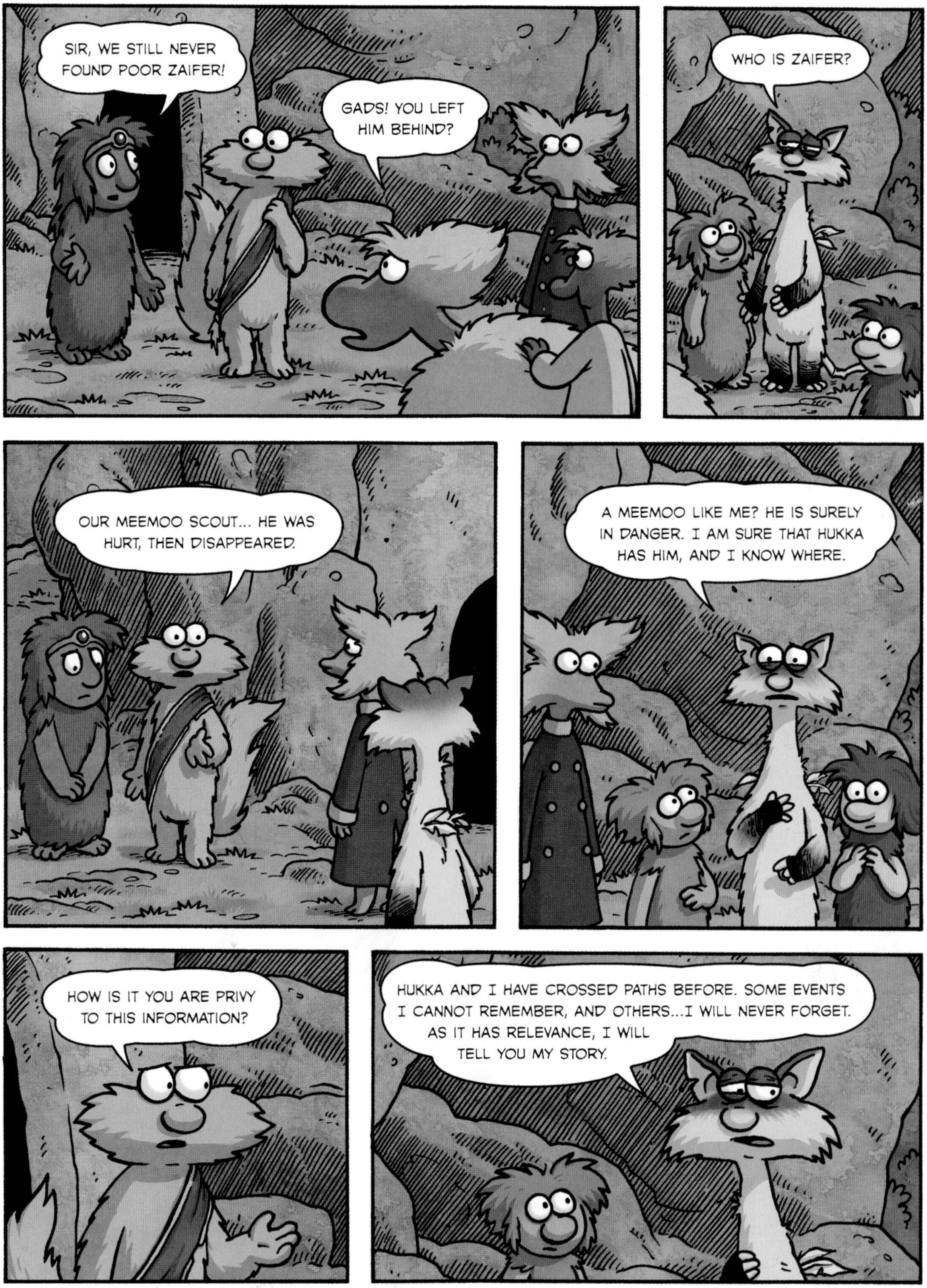
SIR, WE STILL NEVER FOUND POOR ZAIFER!
GADS! YOU LEFT HIM BEHIND?
WHO IS ZAIFER?
OUR MEEMOO SCOUT... HE WAS HURT, THEN DISAPPEARED.
A MEEMOO LIKE ME? HE IS SURELY IN DANGER. I AM SURE THAT HUKKA HAS HIM, AND I KNOW WHERE.
HOW IS IT YOU ARE PRIVY TO THIS INFORMATION?
HUKKA AND I HAVE CROSSED PATHS BEFORE. SOME EVENTS I CANNOT REMEMBER, AND OTHERS...I WILL NEVER FORGET. AS IT HAS RELEVANCE, I WILL TELL YOU MY STORY.

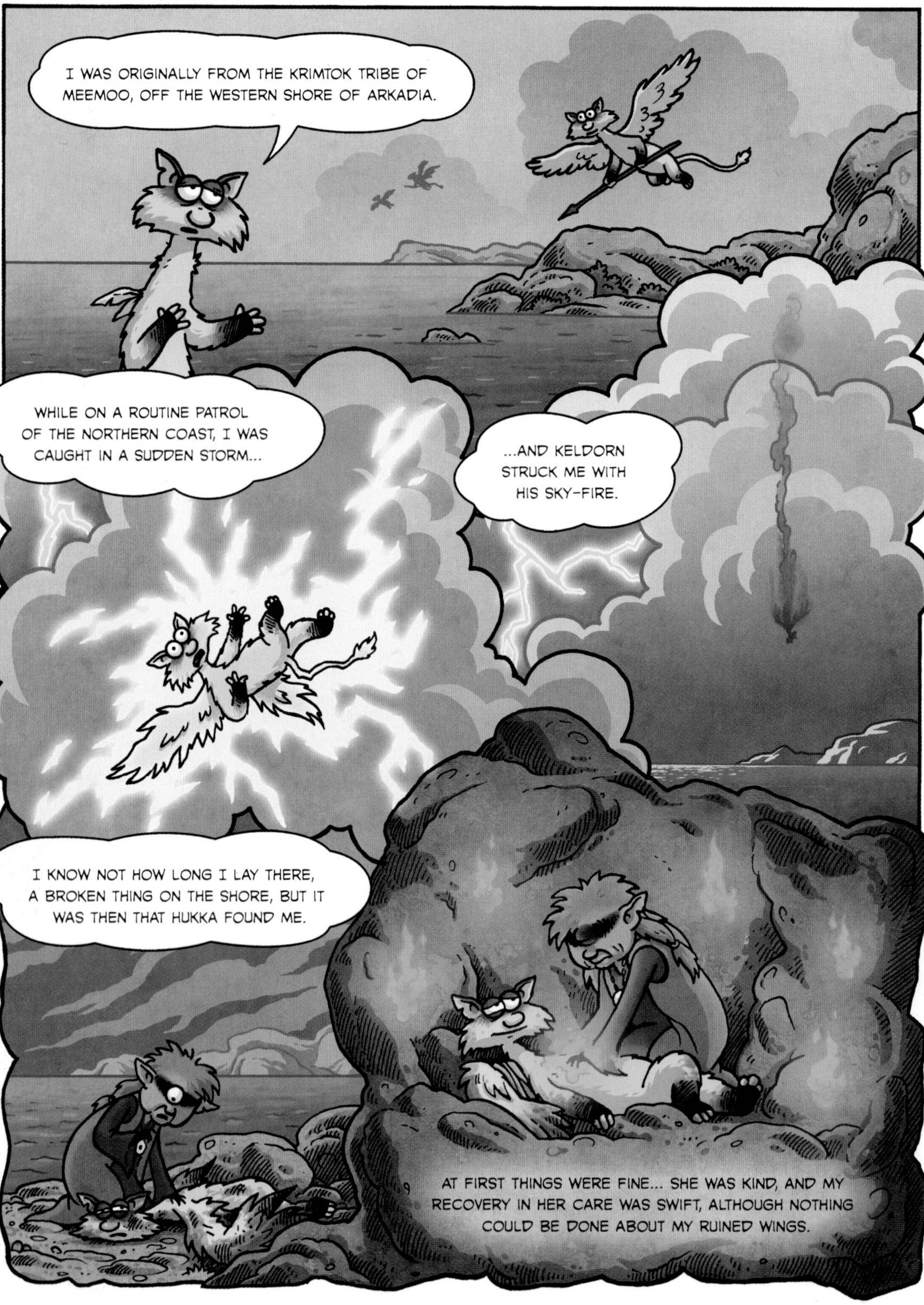
I WAS ORIGINALLY FROM THE KRIMTOK TRIBE OF MEEMOO, OFF THE WESTERN SHORE OF ARKADIA.
WHILE ON A ROUTINE PATROL OF THE NORTHERN COAST, I WAS CAUGHT IN A SUDDEN STORM...
...AND KELDORN STRUCK ME WITH HIS SKY-FIRE.
I KNOW NOT HOW LONG I LAY THERE, A BROKEN THING ON THE SHORE, BUT IT WAS THEN THAT HUKKA FOUND ME.
AT FIRST THINGS WERE FINE... SHE WAS KIND, AND MY RECOVERY IN HER CARE WAS SWIFT, ALTHOUGH NOTHING COULD BE DONE ABOUT MY RUINED WINGS.

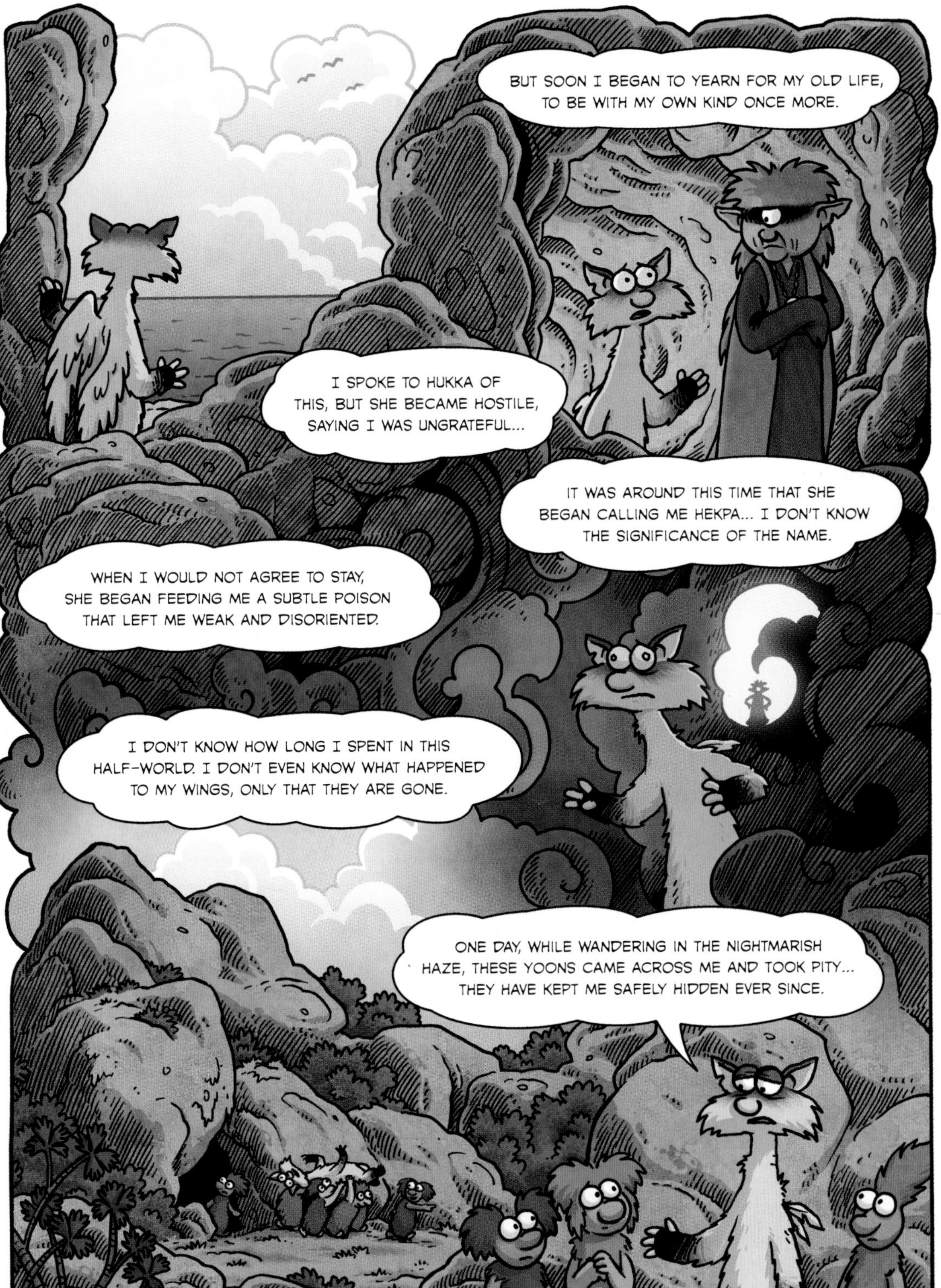
BUT SOON I BEGAN TO YEARN FOR MY OLD LIFE, TO BE WITH MY OWN KIND ONCE MORE.
I SPOKE TO HUKKA OF THIS, BUT SHE BECAME HOSTILE, SAYING I WAS UNGRATEFUL...
IT WAS AROUND THIS TIME THAT SHE BEGAN CALLING ME HEKPA... I DON'T KNOW THE SIGNIFICANCE OF THE NAME.
WHEN I WOULD NOT AGREE TO STAY, SHE BEGAN FEEDING ME A SUBTLE POISON THAT LEFT ME WEAK AND DISORIENTED.
I DON'T KNOW HOW LONG I SPENT IN THIS HALF-WORLD. I DON'T EVEN KNOW WHAT HAPPENED TO MY WINGS, ONLY THAT THEY ARE GONE.
ONE DAY, WHILE WANDERING IN THE NIGHTMARISH HAZE, THESE YOONS CAME ACROSS ME AND TOOK PITY... THEY HAVE KEPT ME SAFELY HIDDEN EVER SINCE.

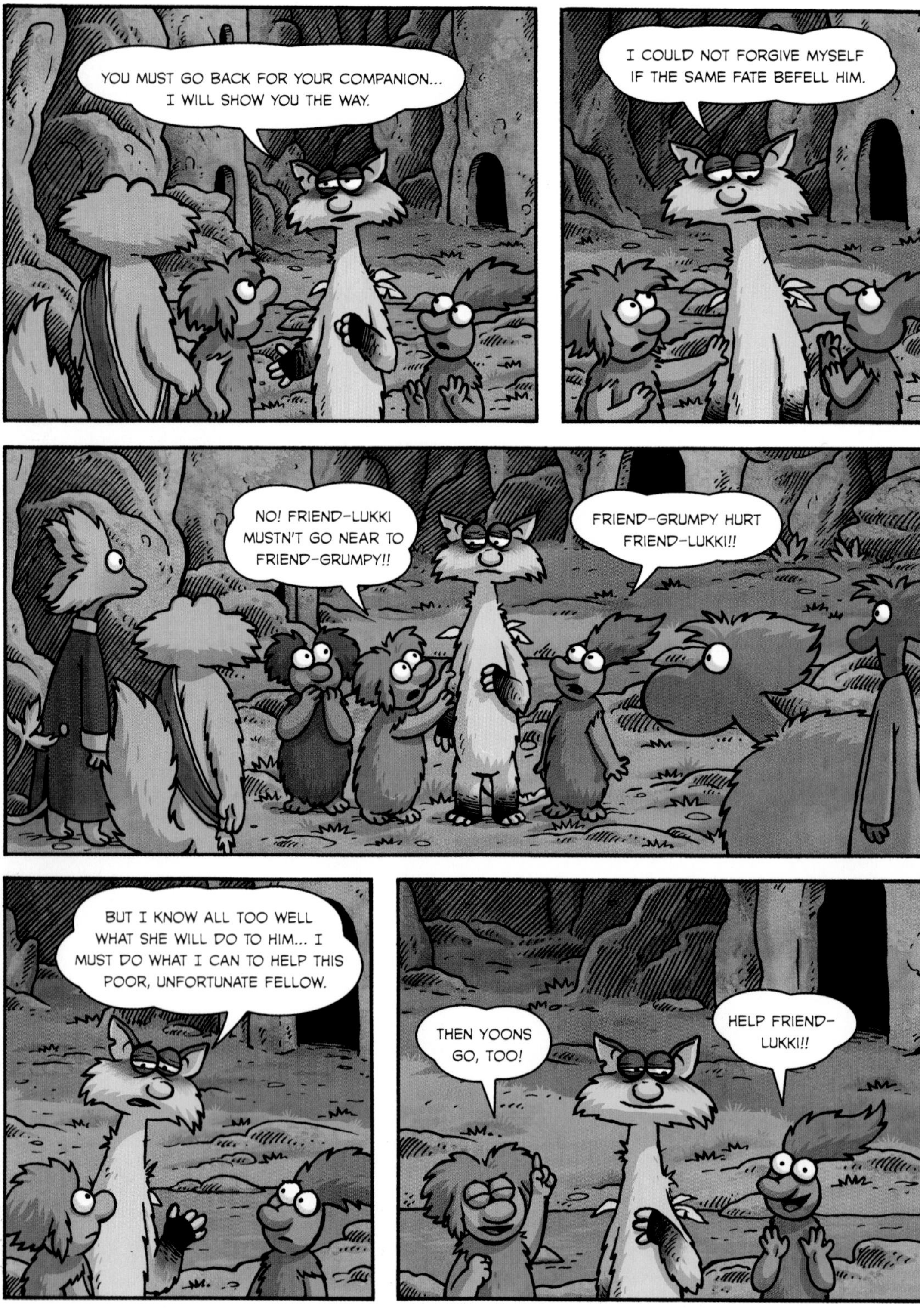
YOU MUST GO BACK FOR YOUR COMPANION... I WILL SHOW YOU THE WAY.
I COULD NOT FORGIVE MYSELF IF THE SAME FATE BEFELL HIM.
NO! FRIEND-LUKKI MUSTN'T GO NEAR TO FRIEND-GRUMPY!!
FRIEND-GRUMPY HURT FRIEND-LUKKI!!
BUT I KNOW ALL TOO WELL WHAT SHE WILL DO TO HIM... I MUST DO WHAT I CAN TO HELP THIS POOR, UNFORTUNATE FELLOW.
THEN YOONS GO, TOO!
HELP FRIEND-LUKKI!!

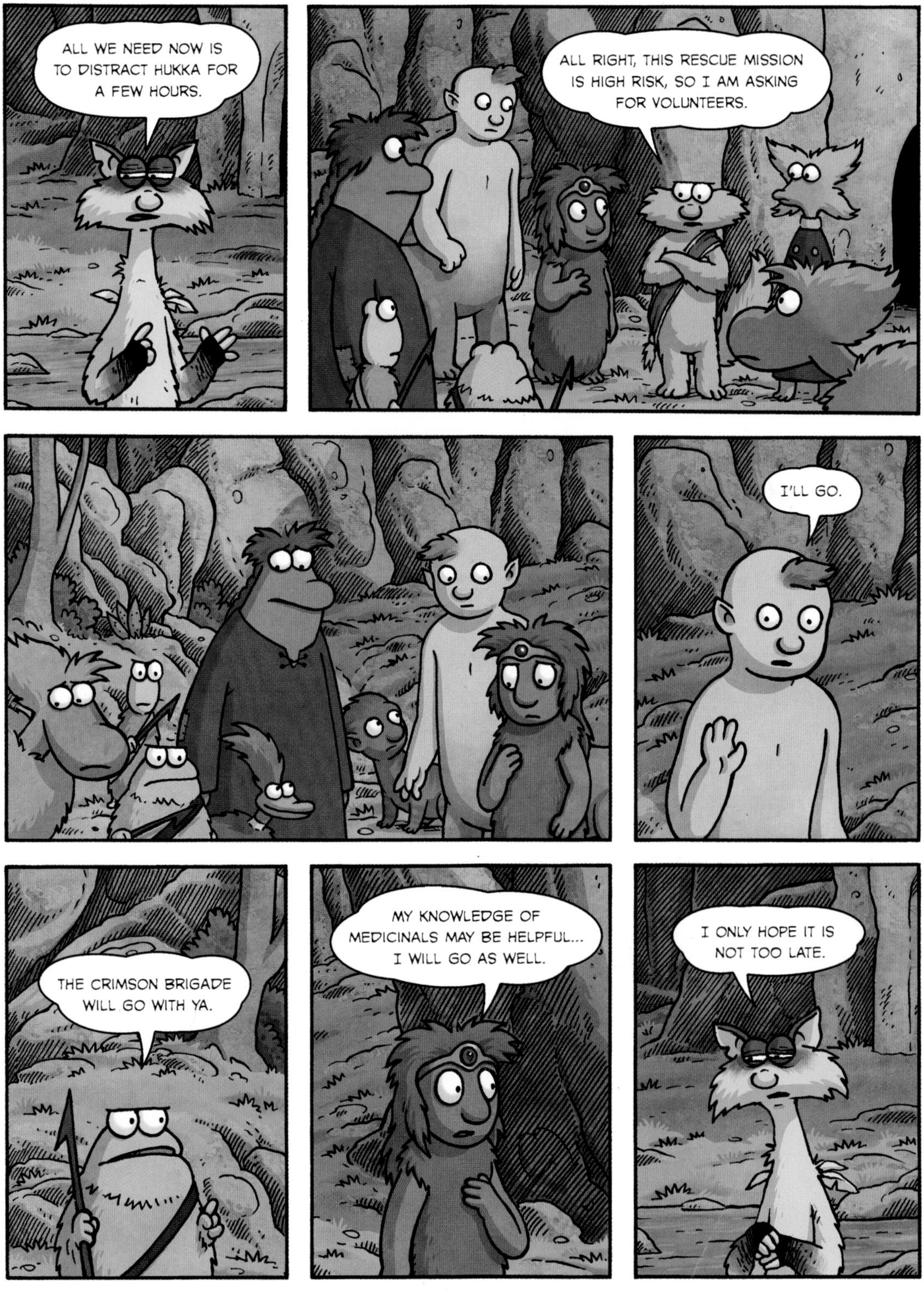
ALL WE NEED NOW IS TO DISTRACT HUKKA FOR A FEW HOURS.
ALL RIGHT, THIS RESCUE MISSION IS HIGH RISK, SO I AM ASKING FOR VOLUNTEERS.
I'LL GO.
THE CRIMSON BRIGADE WILL GO WITH YA.
MY KNOWLEDGE OF MEDICINALS MAY BE HELPFUL... I WILL GO AS WELL.
I ONLY HOPE IT IS NOT TOO LATE.

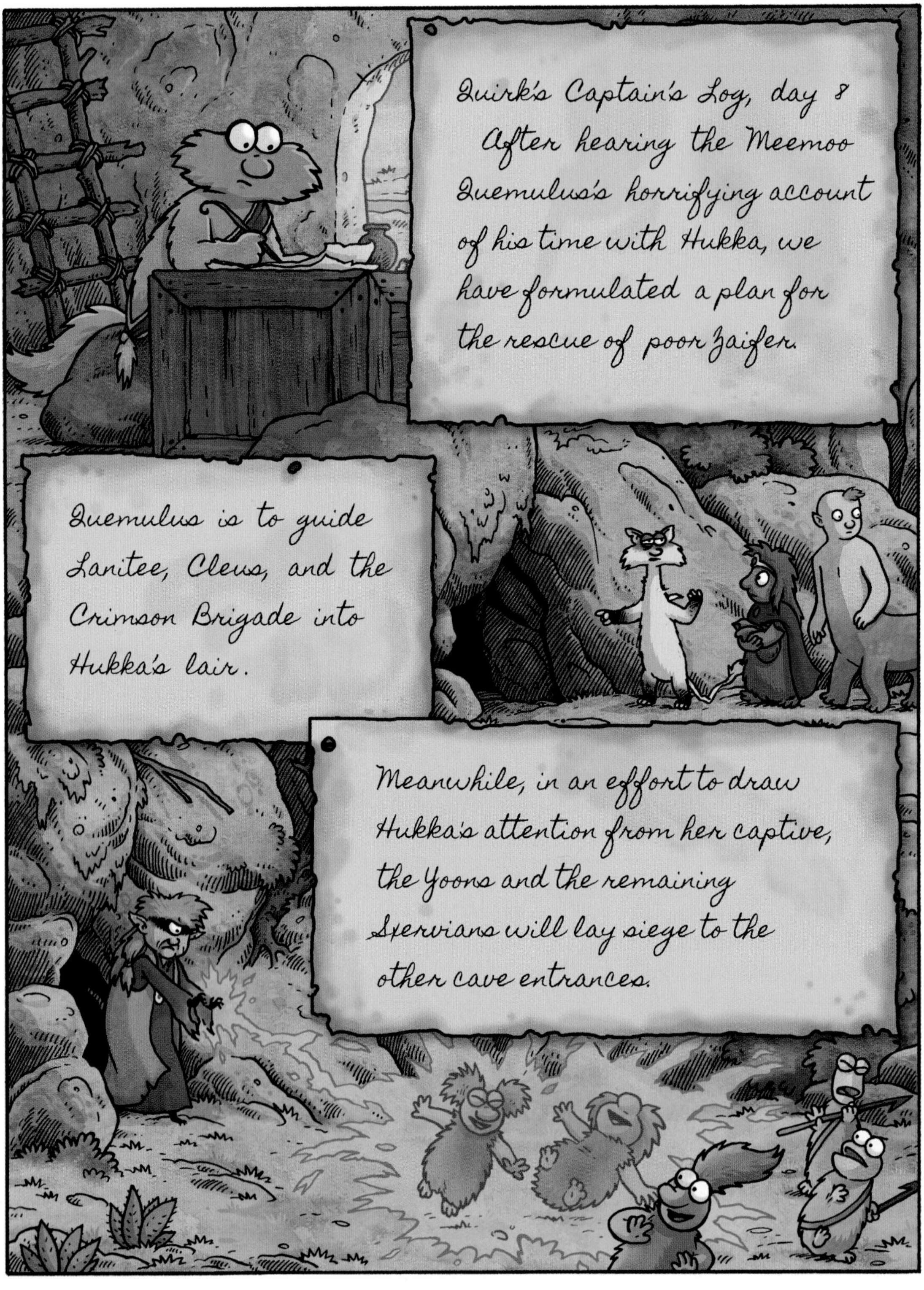
Quirk's Captain's Log, day 8
After hearing the Meemoo Quemulus's horrifying account of his time with Hukka, we have formulated a plan for the rescue of poor Zaifer.
Quemulus is to guide Lanitee, Cleus, and the Crimson Brigade into Hukka's lair.
Meanwhile, in an effort to draw Hukka's attention from her captive, the Yoons and the remaining Sxervians will lay siege to the other cave entrances.

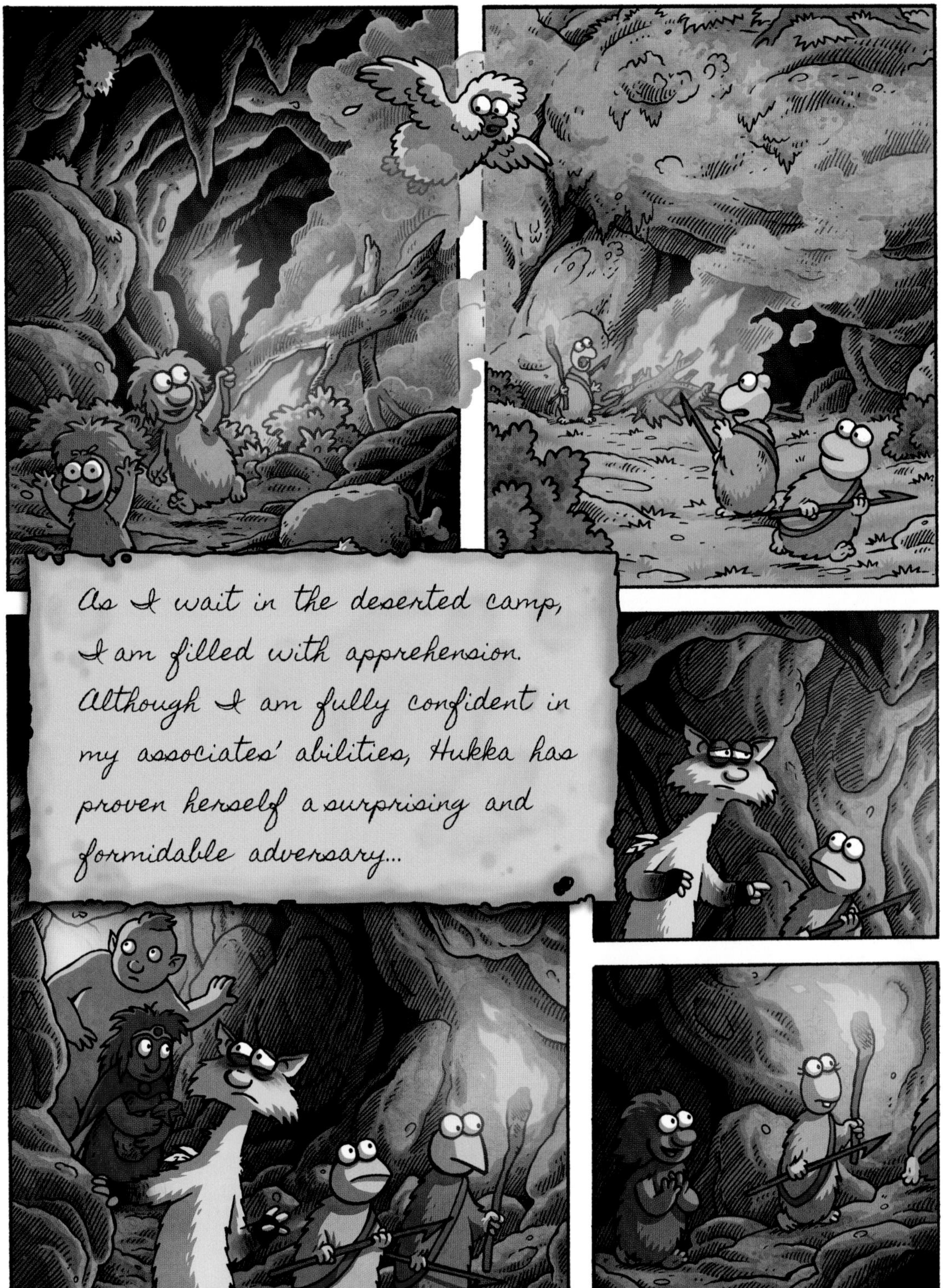
As I wait in the deserted camp, I am filled with apprehension. Although I am fully confident in my associates' abilities, Hukka has proven herself a surprising and formidable adversary...

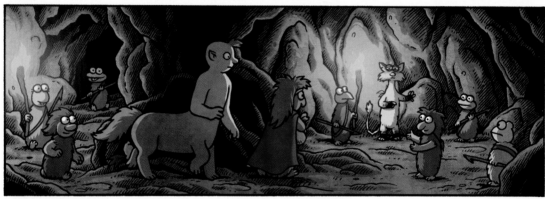

UNNGH! MMRF!

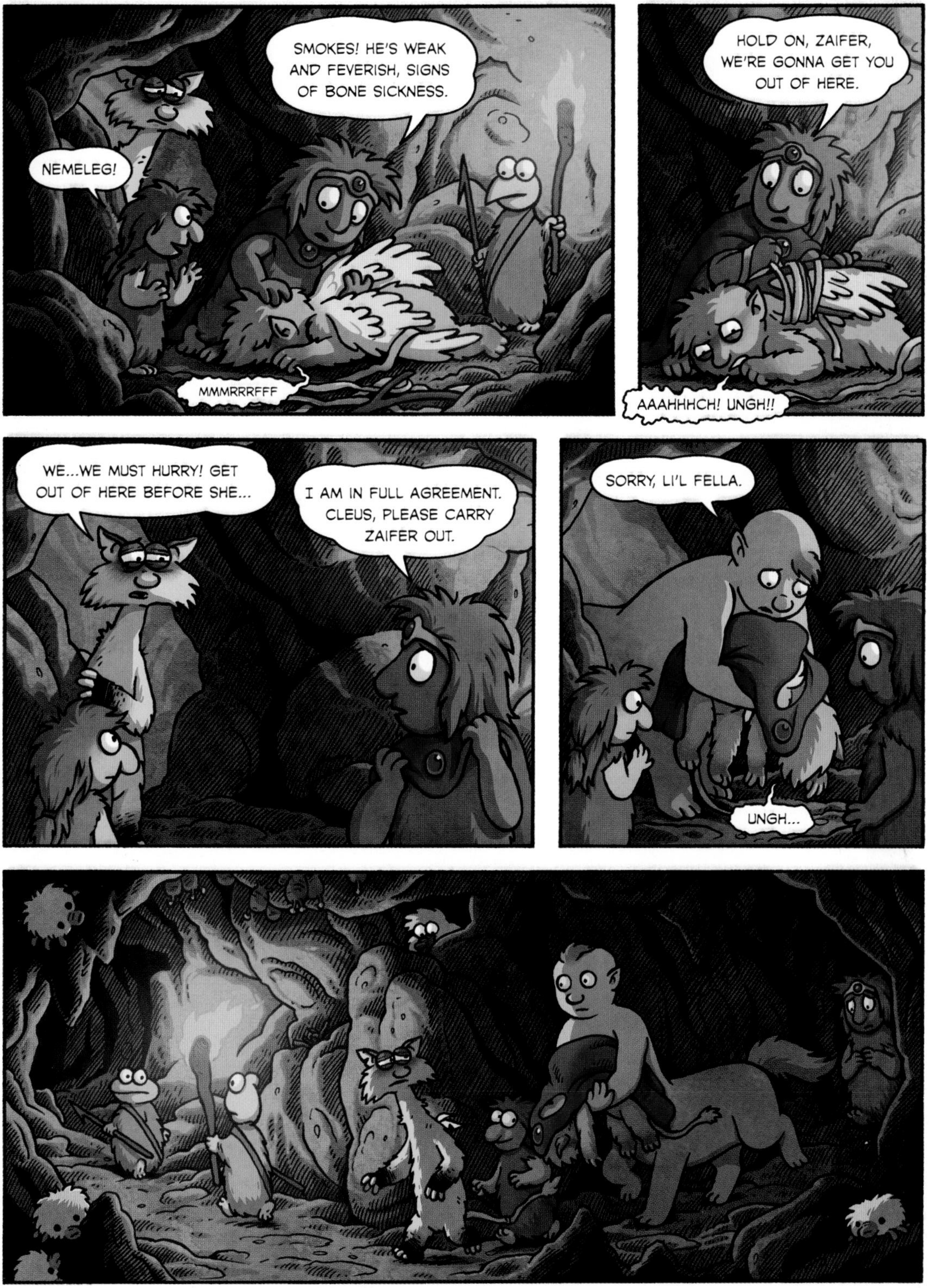
NEMELEG!
SMOKES! HE'S WEAK AND FEVERISH, SIGNS OF BONE SICKNESS.
MMMRRRFFF
HOLD ON, ZAIFER, WE'RE GONNA GET YOU OUT OF HERE.
AAAHHHCH! UNGH!!
WE...WE MUST HURRY! GET OUT OF HERE BEFORE SHE...
I AM IN FULL AGREEMENT. CLEUS, PLEASE CARRY ZAIFER OUT.
SORRY, LI'L FELLA.
UNGH...

BWWAAAAAAAAAAAAAAAHHH!!

HUH...HUKKA! SHE'S COMING!

I SUGGEST HASTE!

WHERE IS MY

HEKPA?!?

KABLAM!!

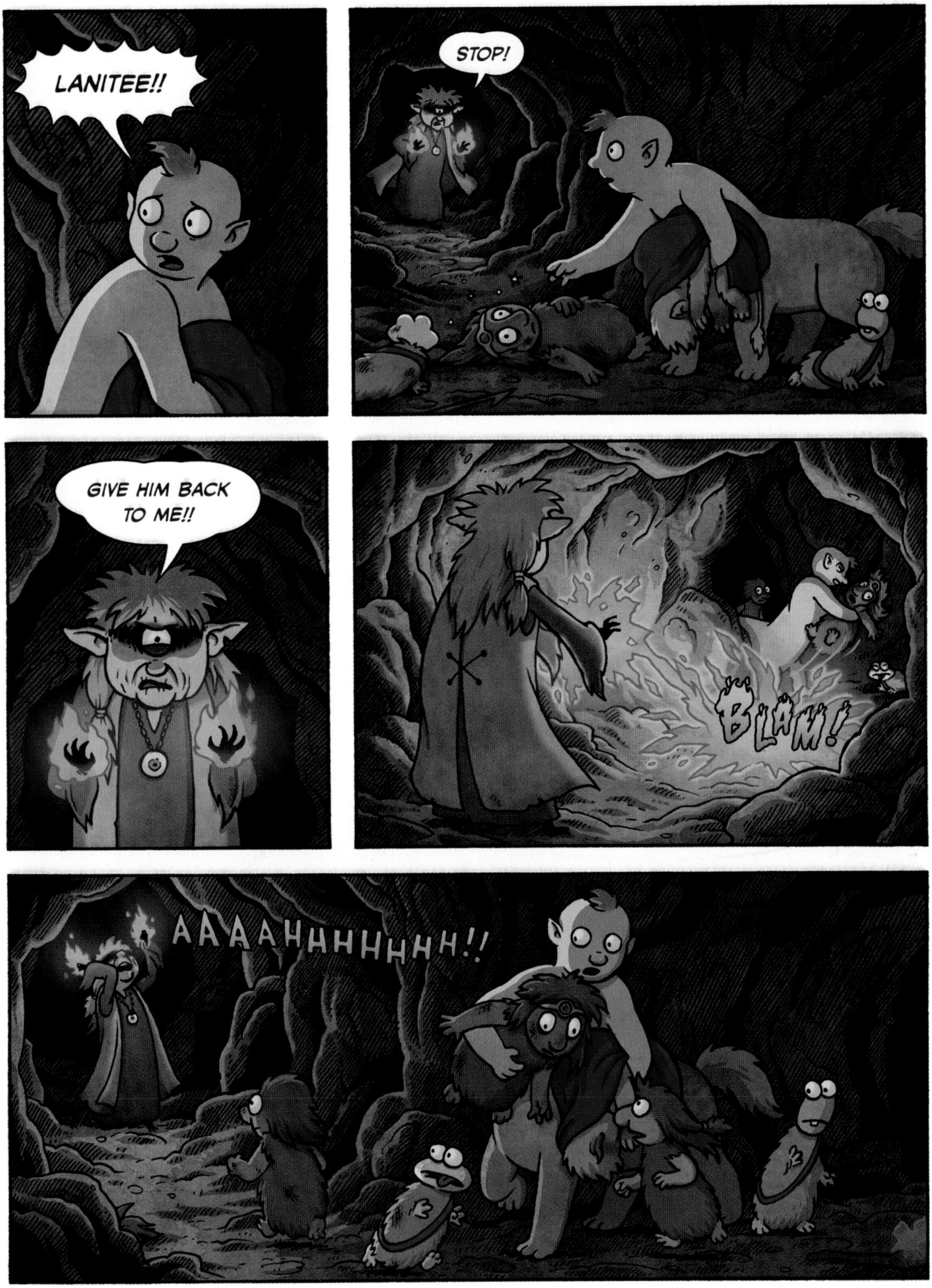
LANITEE!!
STOP!
GIVE HIM BACK TO ME!!
BLAM!
AAAAHHHHHHHH!!

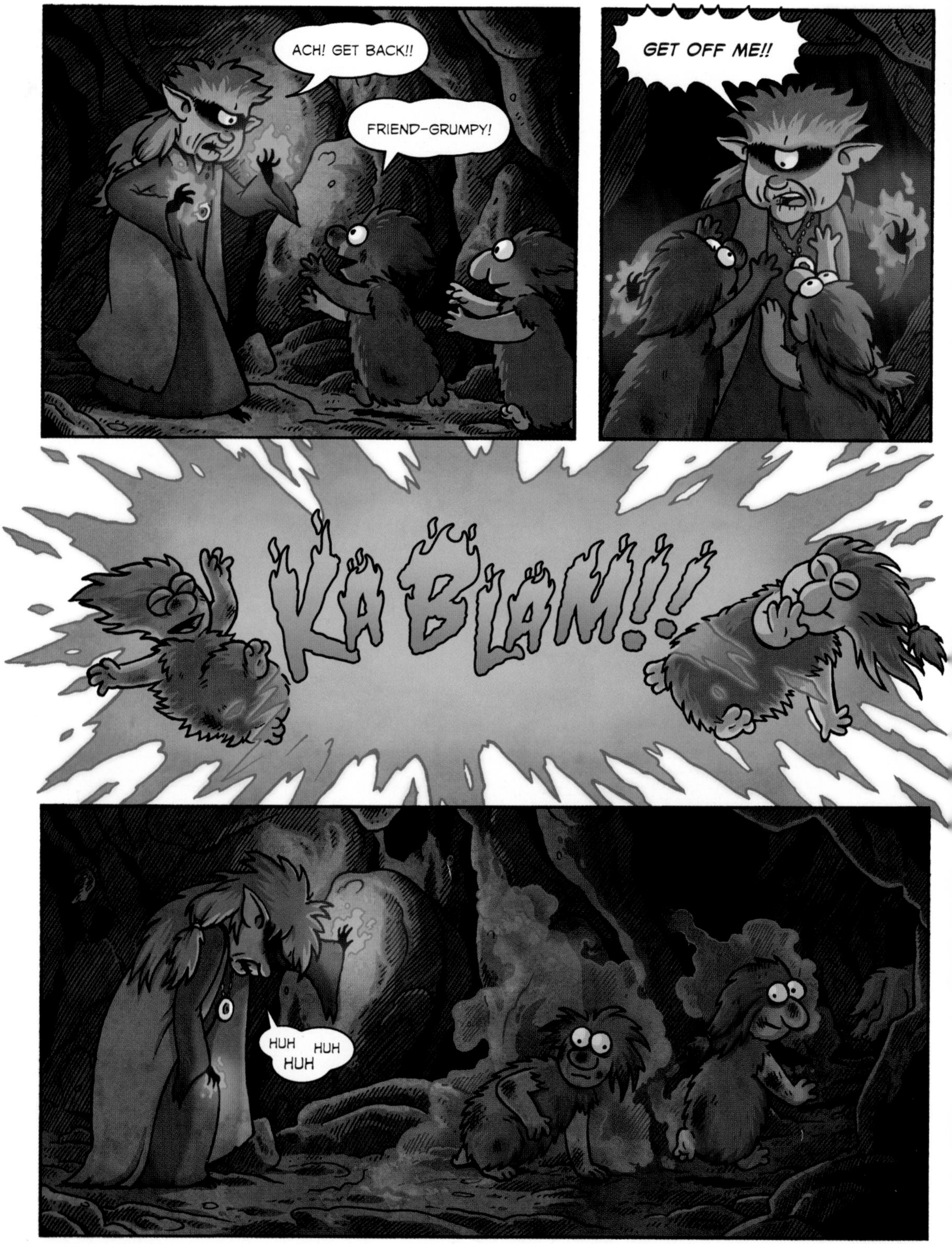
ACH! GET BACK!!
FRIEND-GRUMPY!
GET OFF ME!!
KA BLAM!!
HUH HUH HUH HUH

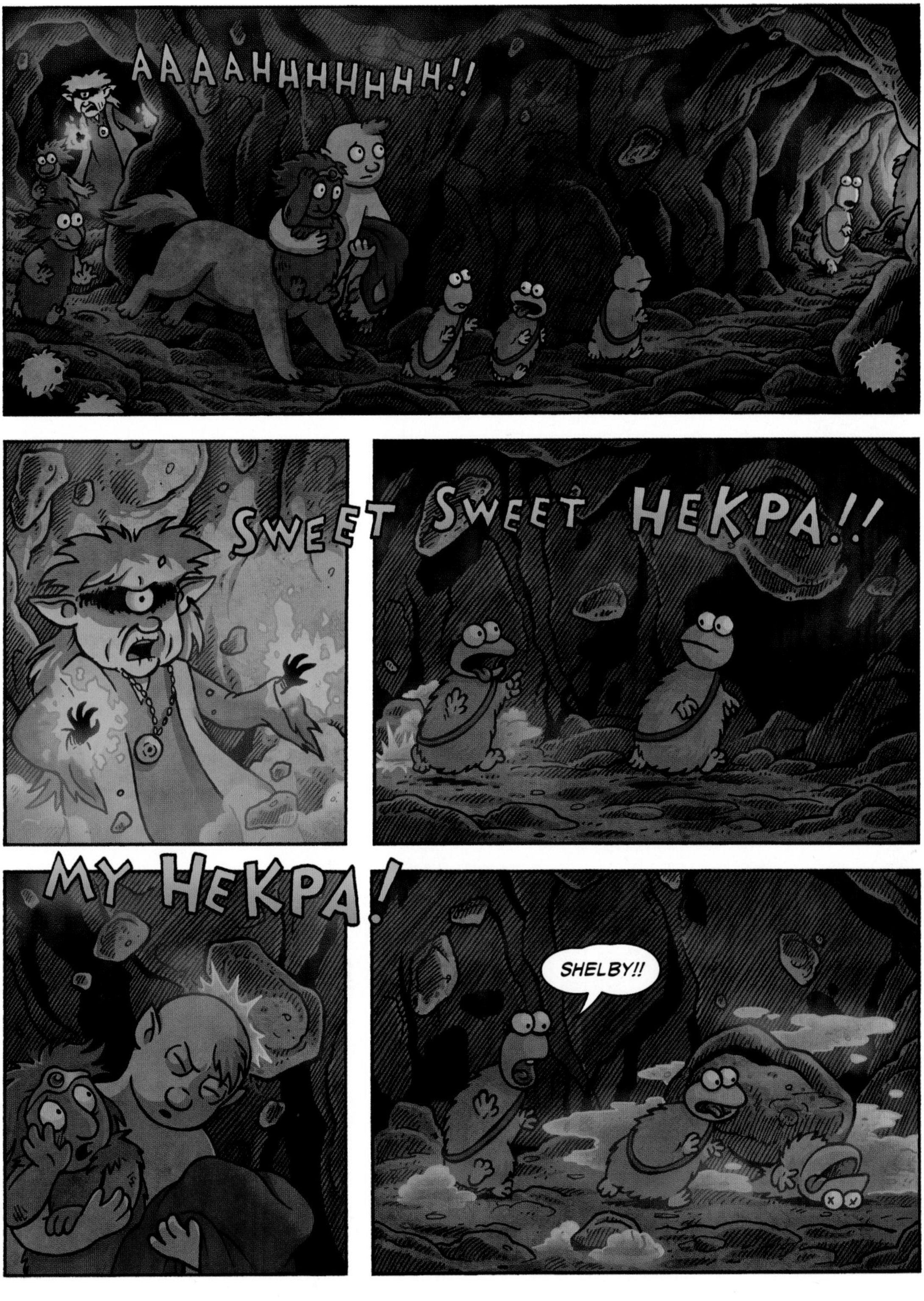
AAAAHHHHHHHH!!
SWEET SWEET HEKPA!!
MY HEKPA!
SHELBY!!

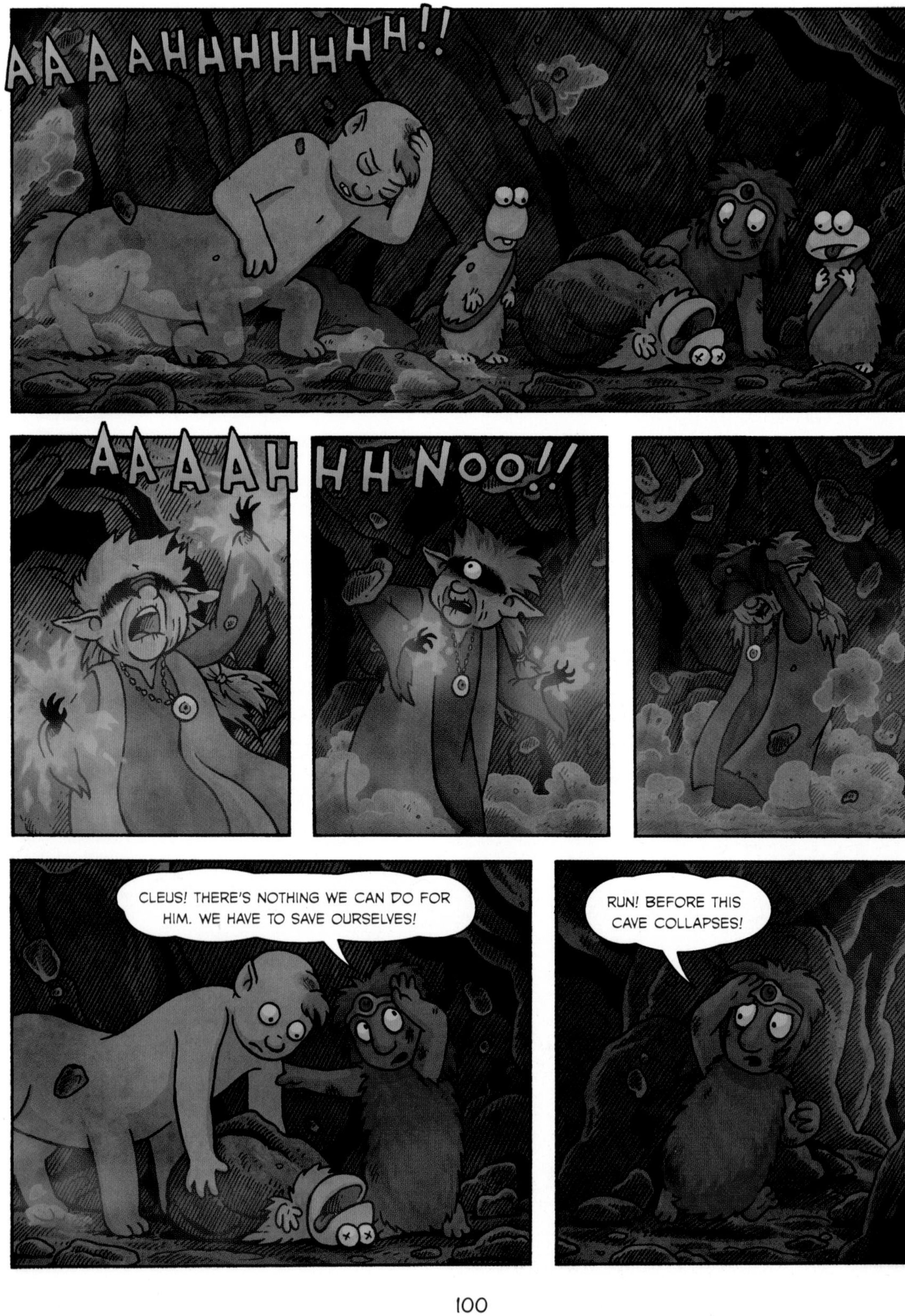
AAAAHHHHHHH!!
AAAAHHHNOO!!
CLEUS! THERE'S NOTHING WE CAN DO FOR HIM. WE HAVE TO SAVE OURSELVES!
RUN! BEFORE THIS CAVE COLLAPSES!

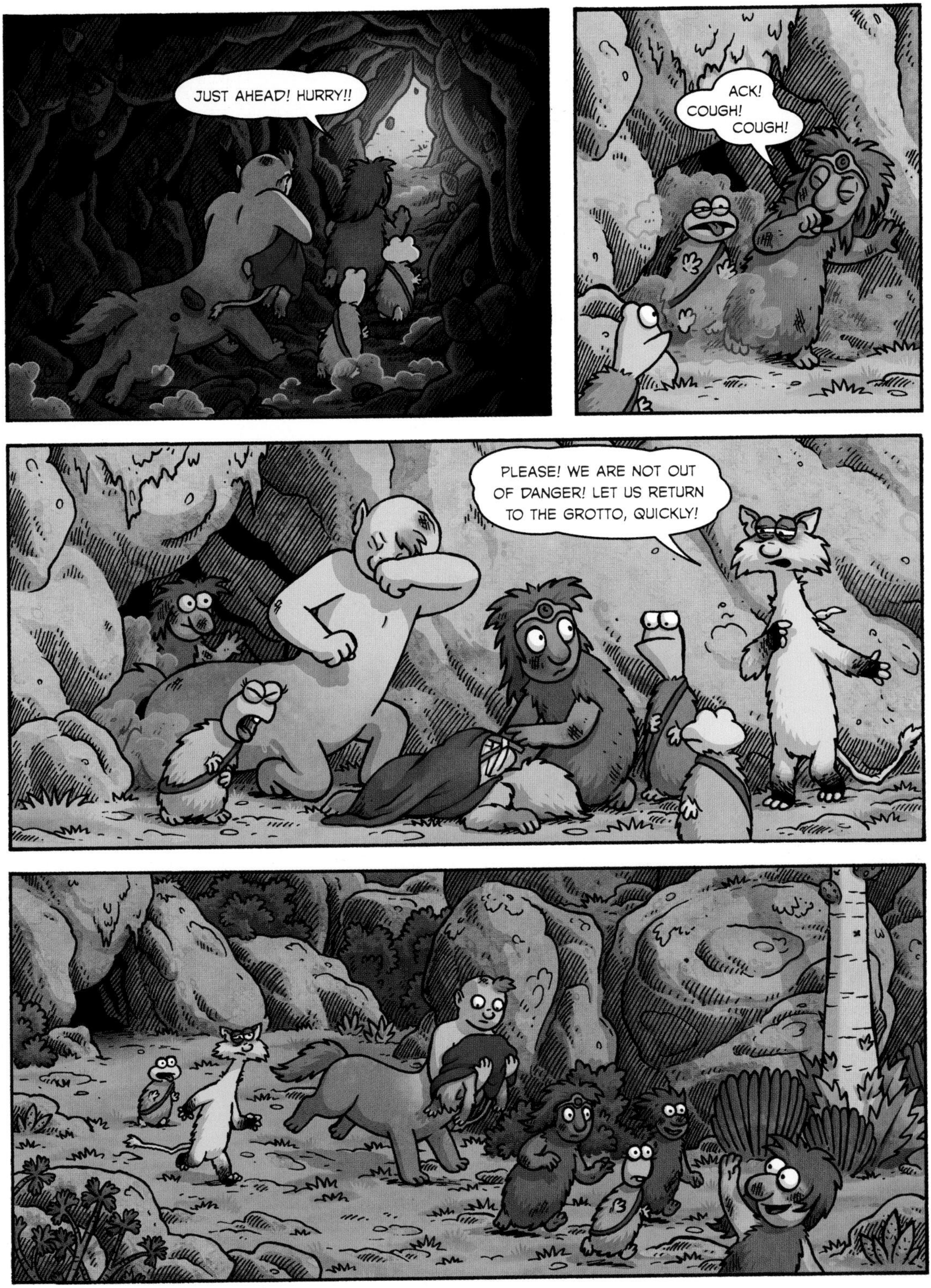
JUST AHEAD! HURRY!!
ACK! COUGH! COUGH!
PLEASE! WE ARE NOT OUT OF DANGER! LET US RETURN TO THE GROTTO, QUICKLY!

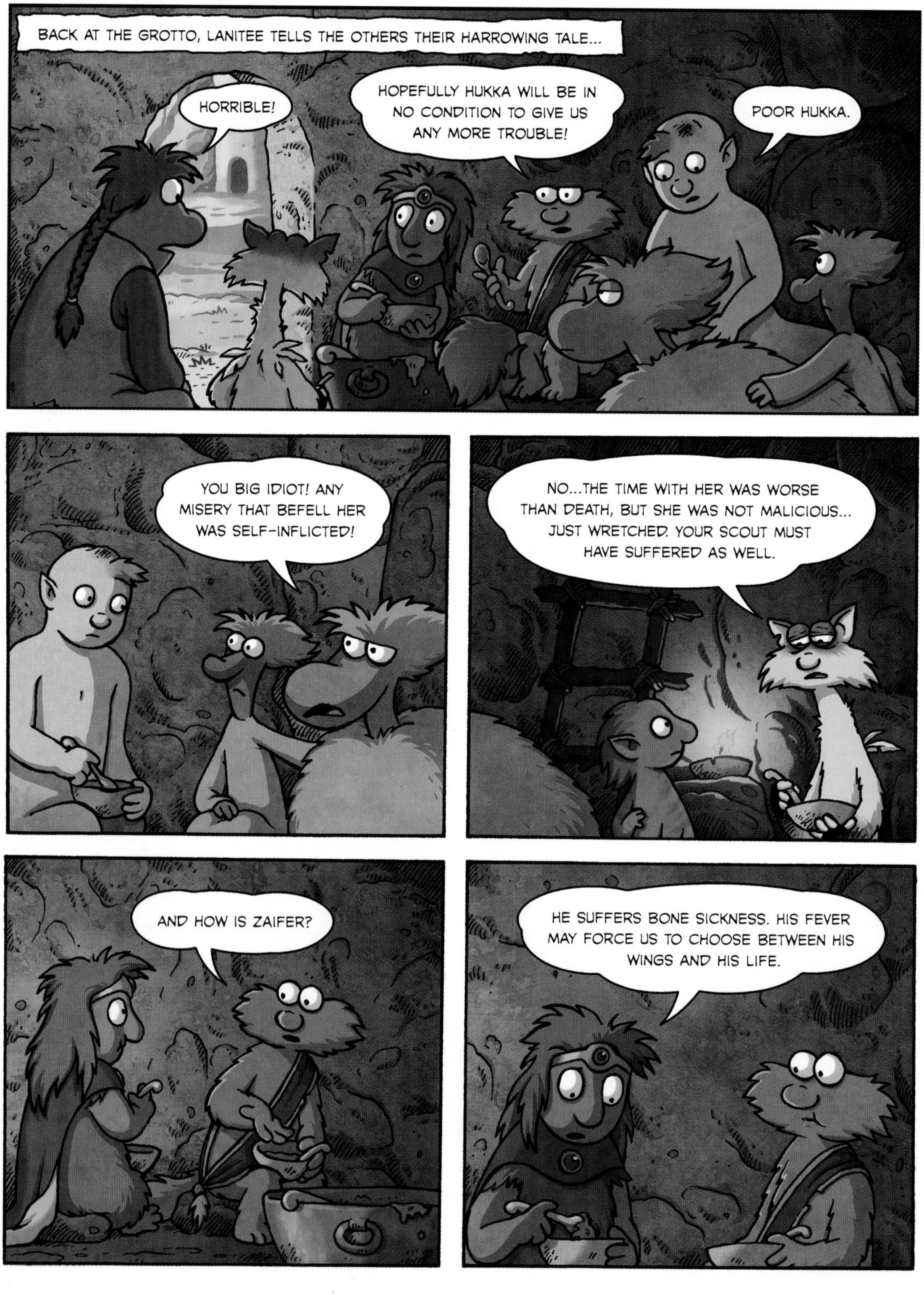

BACK AT THE GROTTO, LANITEE TELLS THE OTHERS THEIR HARROWING TALE...
HORRIBLE!
HOPEFULLY HUKKA WILL BE IN NO CONDITION TO GIVE US ANY MORE TROUBLE!
POOR HUKKA.
YOU BIG IDIOT! ANY MISERY THAT BEFELL HER WAS SELF-INFLICTED!
NO...THE TIME WITH HER WAS WORSE THAN DEATH, BUT SHE WAS NOT MALICIOUS... JUST WRETCHED. YOUR SCOUT MUST HAVE SUFFERED AS WELL.
AND HOW IS ZAIFER?
HE SUFFERS BONE SICKNESS. HIS FEVER MAY FORCE US TO CHOOSE BETWEEN HIS WINGS AND HIS LIFE.

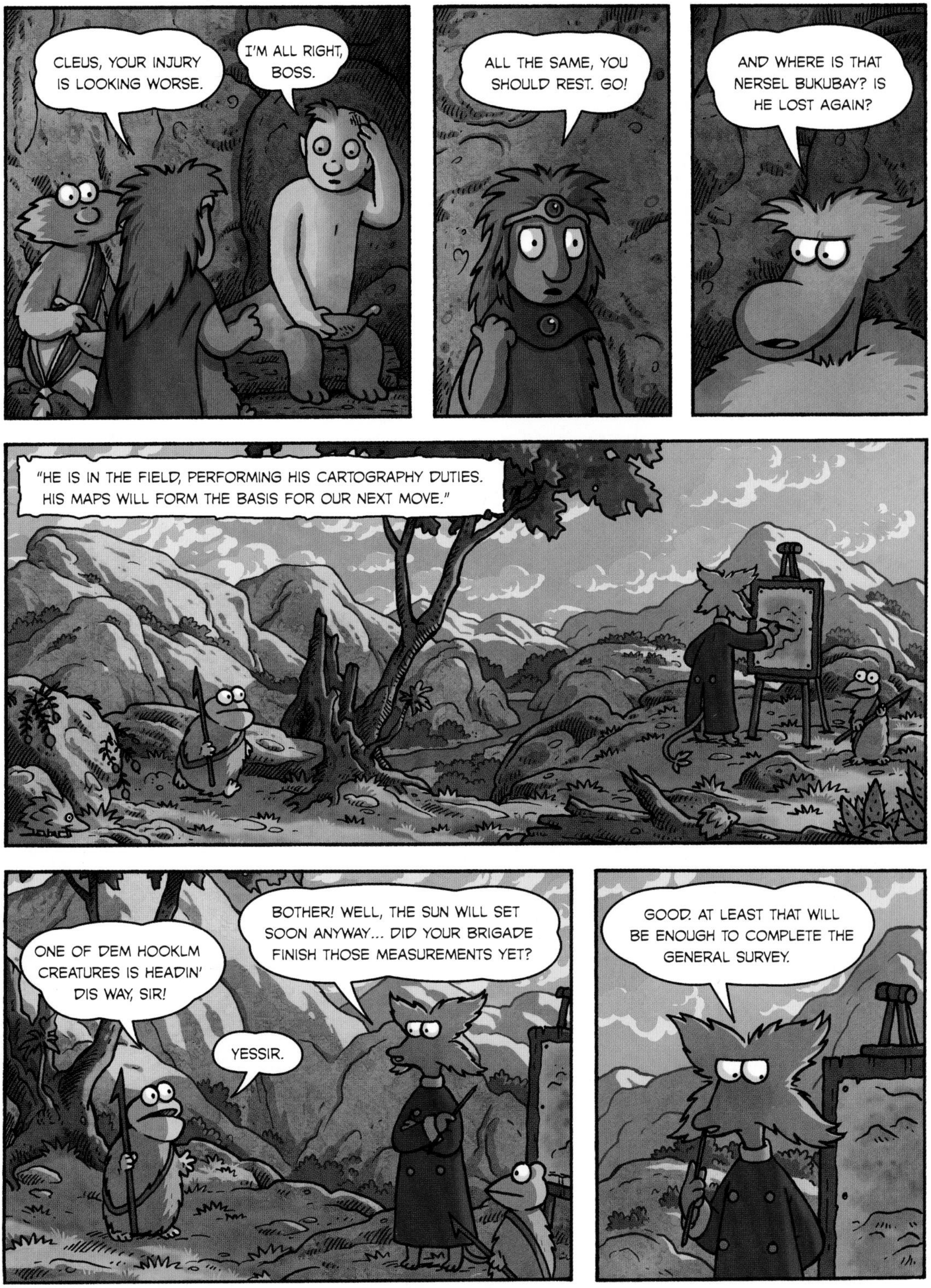
CLEUS, YOUR INJURY IS LOOKING WORSE.
I'M ALL RIGHT, BOSS.
ALL THE SAME, YOU SHOULD REST. GO!
AND WHERE IS THAT NERSEL BUKUBAY? IS HE LOST AGAIN?
"HE IS IN THE FIELD, PERFORMING HIS CARTOGRAPHY DUTIES. HIS MAPS WILL FORM THE BASIS FOR OUR NEXT MOVE."
ONE OF DEM HOOKLM CREATURES IS HEADIN' DIS WAY, SIR!
BOTHER! WELL, THE SUN WILL SET SOON ANYWAY... DID YOUR BRIGADE FINISH THOSE MEASUREMENTS YET?
YESSIR.
GOOD. AT LEAST THAT WILL BE ENOUGH TO COMPLETE THE GENERAL SURVEY.

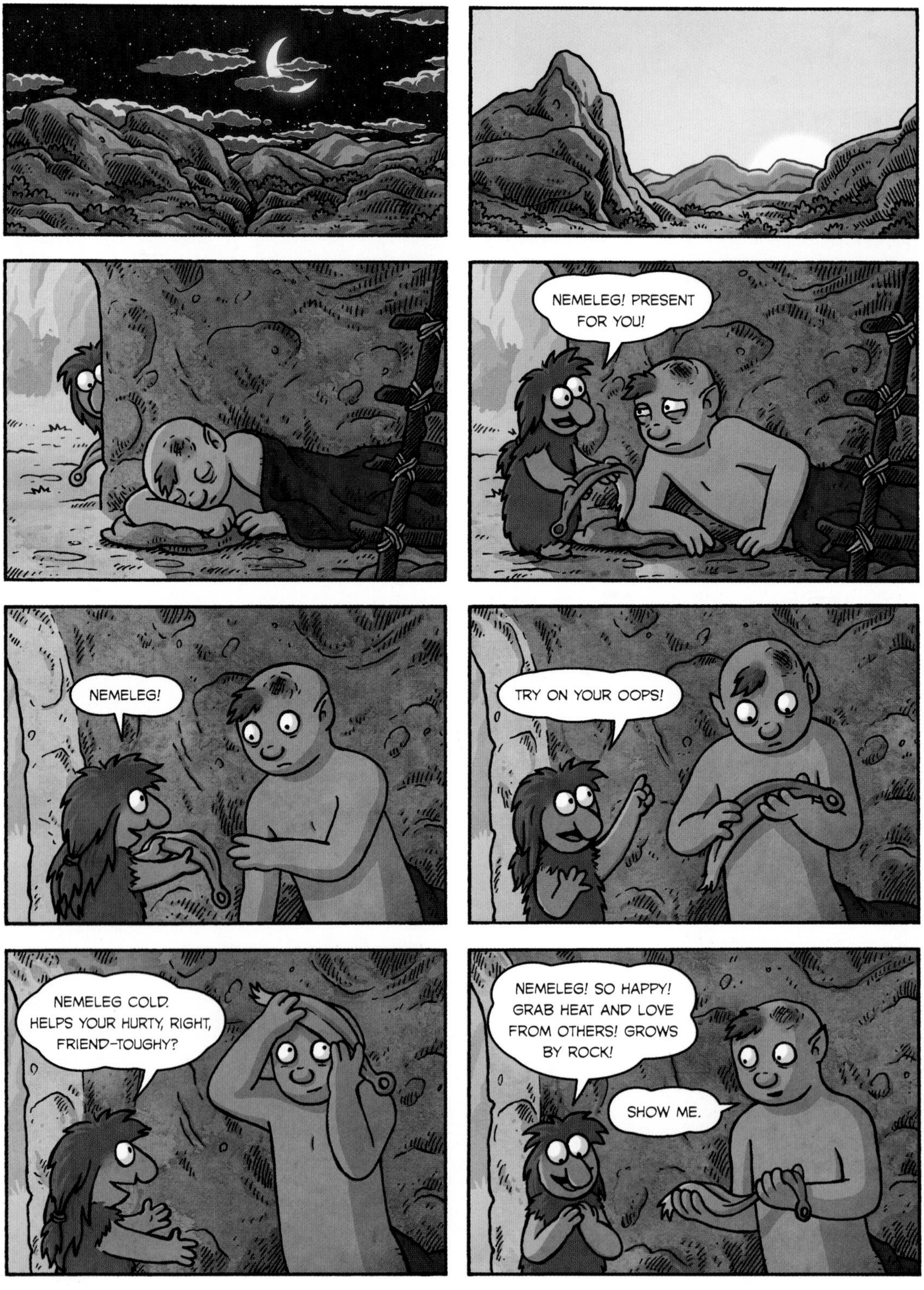
NEMELEG! PRESENT FOR YOU!
NEMELEG!
TRY ON YOUR OOPS!
NEMELEG COLD. HELPS YOUR HURTY, RIGHT, FRIEND-TOUGHY?
NEMELEG! SO HAPPY! GRAB HEAT AND LOVE FROM OTHERS! GROWS BY ROCK!
SHOW ME.

OTHERS SET TO WORK AS WELL...

HURRY UP, WALDEMAR...
FINISH UP THOSE SKETCHES.

HOORAY!

WHOOP!

YAHOOEE!!

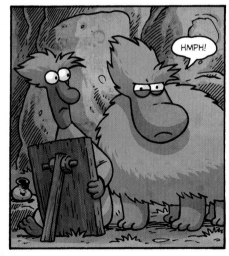

HMPH!

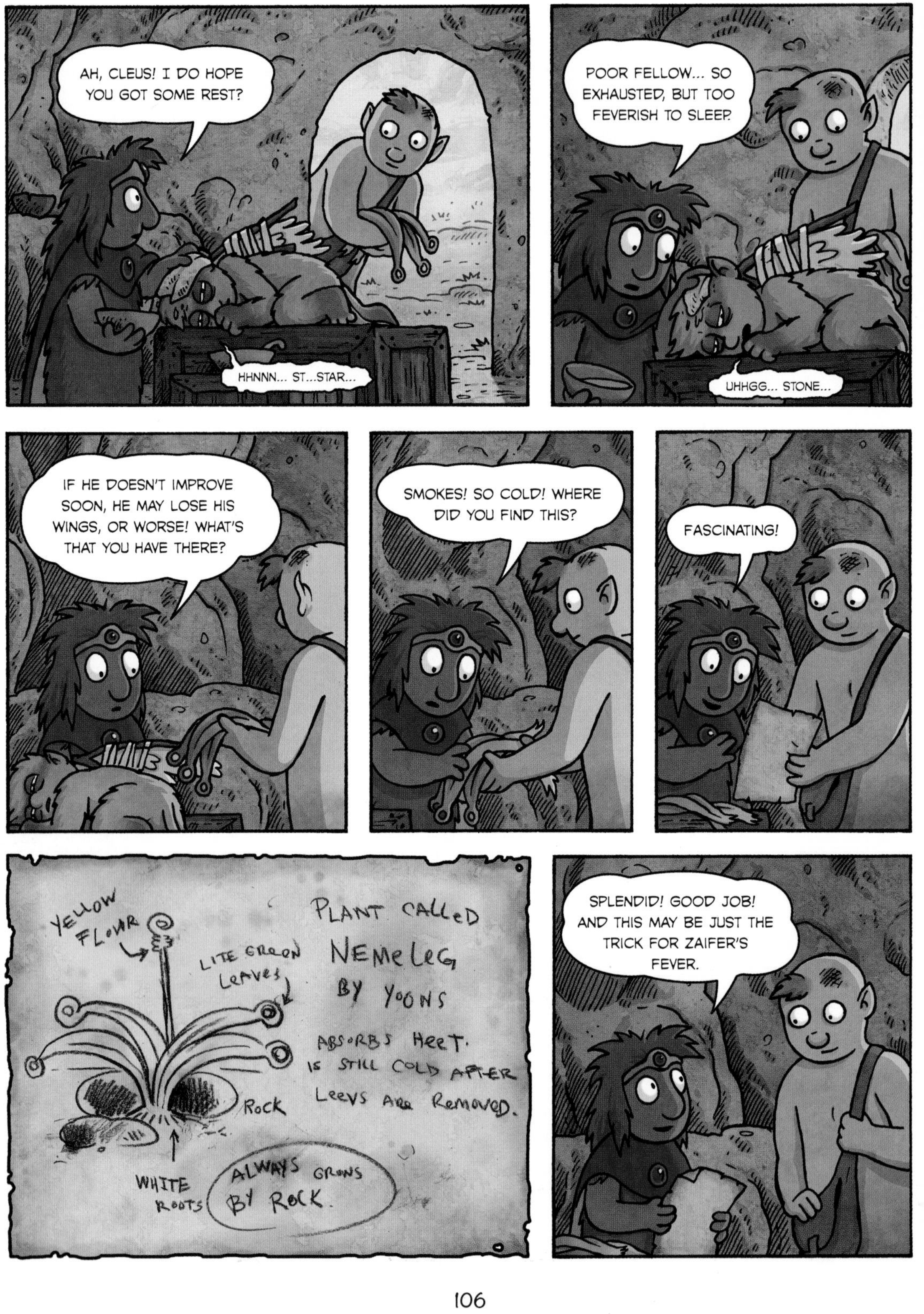
AH, CLEUS! I DO HOPE YOU GOT SOME REST?
HHNNN... ST...STAR...
POOR FELLOW... SO EXHAUSTED, BUT TOO FEVERISH TO SLEEP.
UHHGG... STONE...
IF HE DOESN'T IMPROVE SOON, HE MAY LOSE HIS WINGS, OR WORSE! WHAT'S THAT YOU HAVE THERE?
SMOKES! SO COLD! WHERE DID YOU FIND THIS?
FASCINATING!
YELLOW FLOWR
LITE GREEN LEAVES
PLANT CALLED NEMELEG BY YOONS
ABSORBS HEET. IS STILL COLD AFTER LEEVS ARE REMOVED.
ROCK
WHITE ROOTS
ALWAYS GROWS BY ROCK.
SPLENDID! GOOD JOB! AND THIS MAY BE JUST THE TRICK FOR ZAIFER'S FEVER.

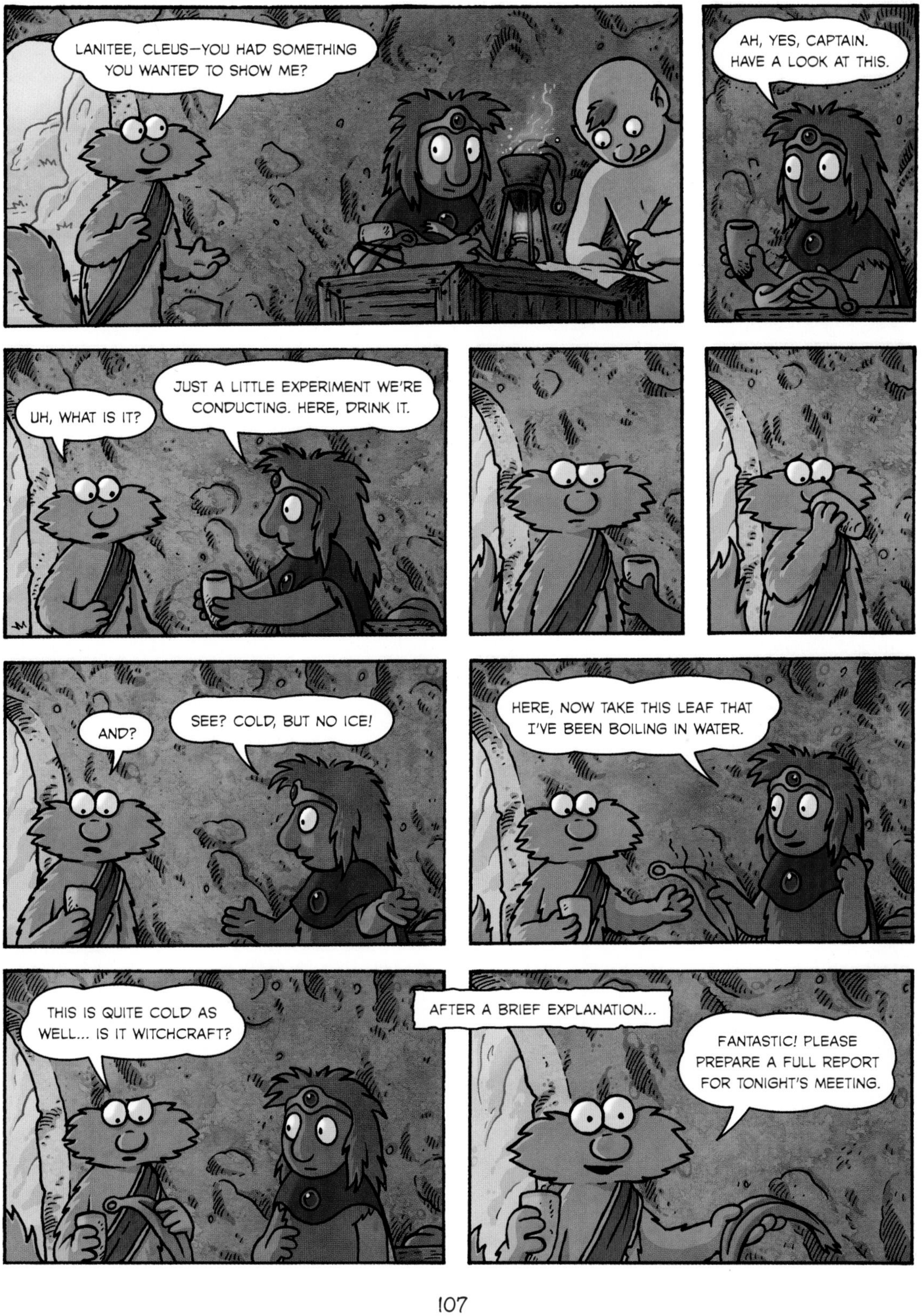
LANITEE, CLEUS—YOU HAD SOMETHING YOU WANTED TO SHOW ME?
AH, YES, CAPTAIN. HAVE A LOOK AT THIS.
UH, WHAT IS IT?
JUST A LITTLE EXPERIMENT WE'RE CONDUCTING. HERE, DRINK IT.
AND?
SEE? COLD, BUT NO ICE!
HERE, NOW TAKE THIS LEAF THAT I'VE BEEN BOILING IN WATER.
THIS IS QUITE COLD AS WELL... IS IT WITCHCRAFT?
AFTER A BRIEF EXPLANATION...
FANTASTIC! PLEASE PREPARE A FULL REPORT FOR TONIGHT'S MEETING.

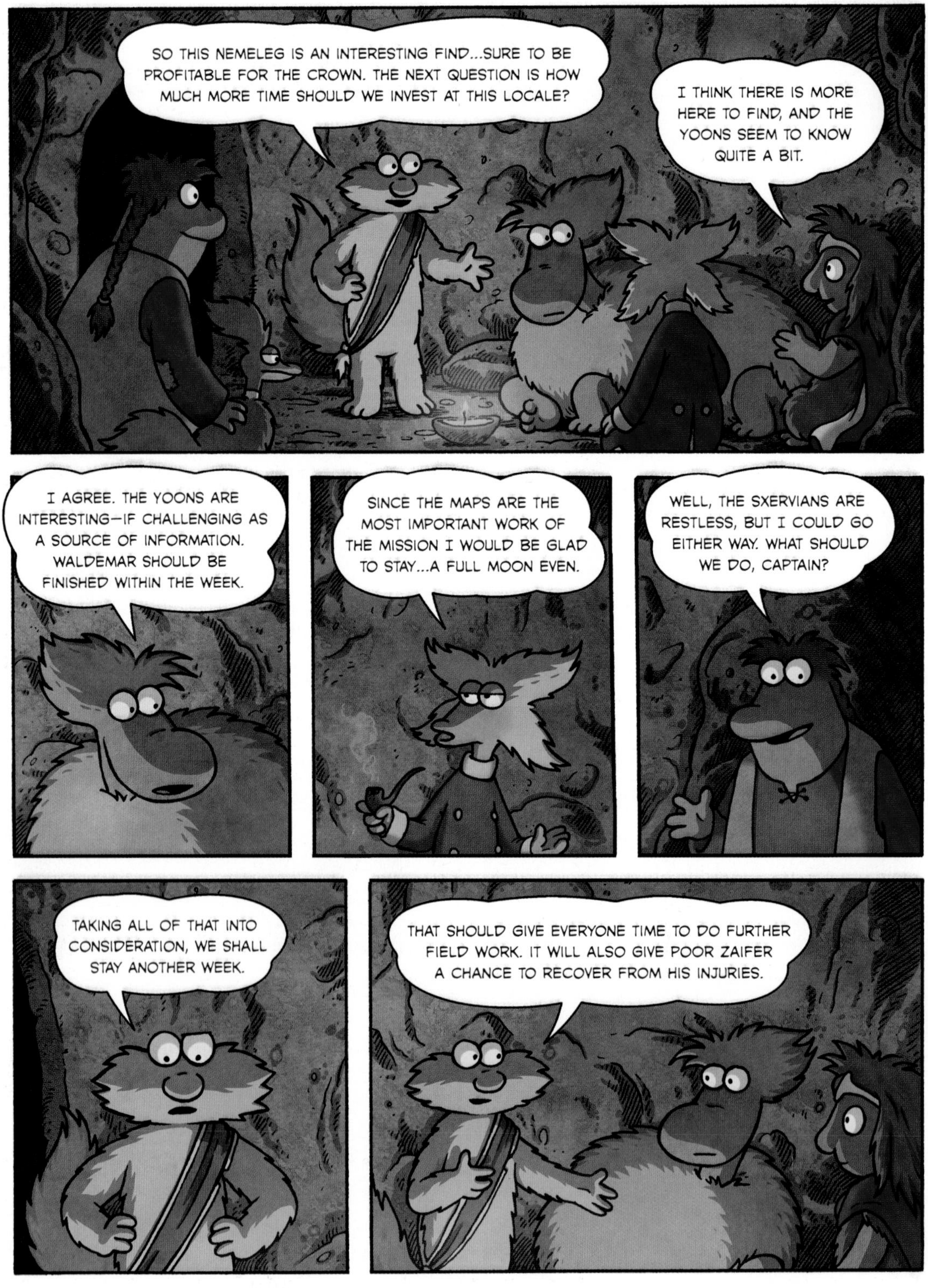
SO THIS NEMELEG IS AN INTERESTING FIND...SURE TO BE PROFITABLE FOR THE CROWN. THE NEXT QUESTION IS HOW MUCH MORE TIME SHOULD WE INVEST AT THIS LOCALE?
I THINK THERE IS MORE HERE TO FIND, AND THE YOONS SEEM TO KNOW QUITE A BIT.
I AGREE. THE YOONS ARE INTERESTING—IF CHALLENGING AS A SOURCE OF INFORMATION. WALDEMAR SHOULD BE FINISHED WITHIN THE WEEK.
SINCE THE MAPS ARE THE MOST IMPORTANT WORK OF THE MISSION I WOULD BE GLAD TO STAY...A FULL MOON EVEN.
WELL, THE SXERVIANS ARE RESTLESS, BUT I COULD GO EITHER WAY. WHAT SHOULD WE DO, CAPTAIN?
TAKING ALL OF THAT INTO CONSIDERATION, WE SHALL STAY ANOTHER WEEK.
THAT SHOULD GIVE EVERYONE TIME TO DO FURTHER FIELD WORK. IT WILL ALSO GIVE POOR ZAIFER A CHANCE TO RECOVER FROM HIS INJURIES.

SMOK, IF THE FROGS NEED SOMETHING TO DO, HAVE THEM WORK WITH GIMIL AND SCOUT OUR NEXT MOVE...FOCUSING SOUTH AND WESTWARD.

YES, SIR!

EXCELLENT! I DO BELIEVE OUR FORTUNE HAS FINALLY SHIFTED!

Quirk's Captain's Log, mission day 10

After the tumultuous events following our mishap, we have set up a base camp in the southern end of "Lukki's Grotto." The Yoons, while quite primitive by our standards, have an extensive and well established settlement here. In their own and sometimes simplistic way, they can tell us a great deal about this forbidding land. They keep Burtrym and Waldemar quite busy...

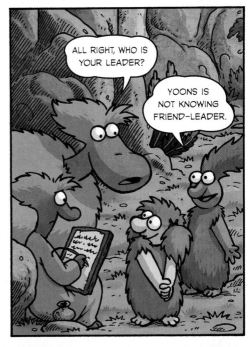

ALL RIGHT, WHO IS YOUR LEADER?

YOONS IS NOT KNOWING FRIEND-LEADER.

DON'T BE RIDICULOUS! SURELY YOU MUST HAVE A LEADER...A CHIEF, PERHAPS?

ME NOT KNOW FRIEND-CHIEF, TOO!

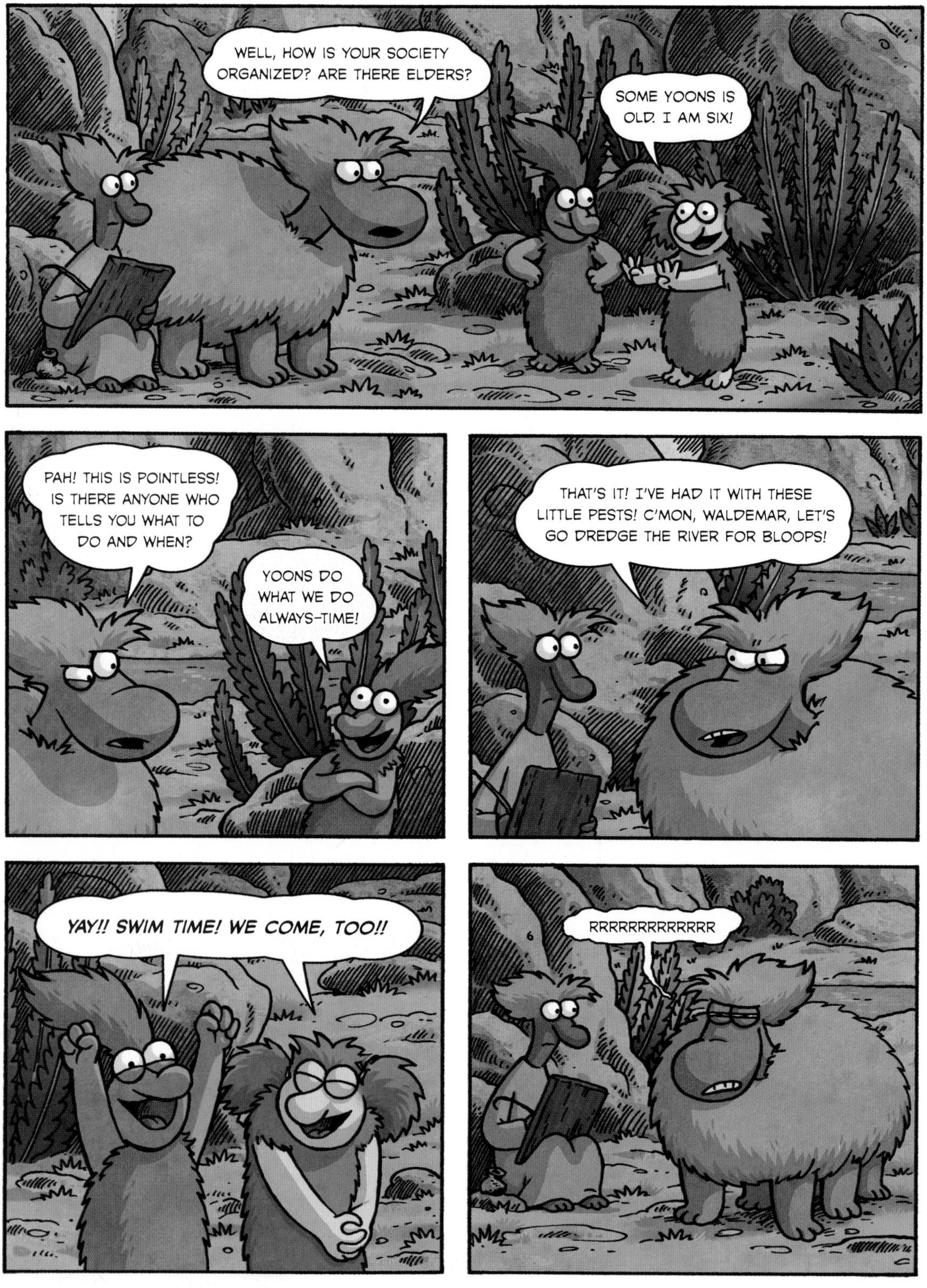
WELL, HOW IS YOUR SOCIETY ORGANIZED? ARE THERE ELDERS?
SOME YOONS IS OLD. I AM SIX!
PAH! THIS IS POINTLESS! IS THERE ANYONE WHO TELLS YOU WHAT TO DO AND WHEN?
YOONS DO WHAT WE DO ALWAYS-TIME!
THAT'S IT! I'VE HAD IT WITH THESE LITTLE PESTS! C'MON, WALDEMAR, LET'S GO DREDGE THE RIVER FOR BLOOPS!
YAY!! SWIM TIME! WE COME, TOO!!
RRRRRRRRRRRRR

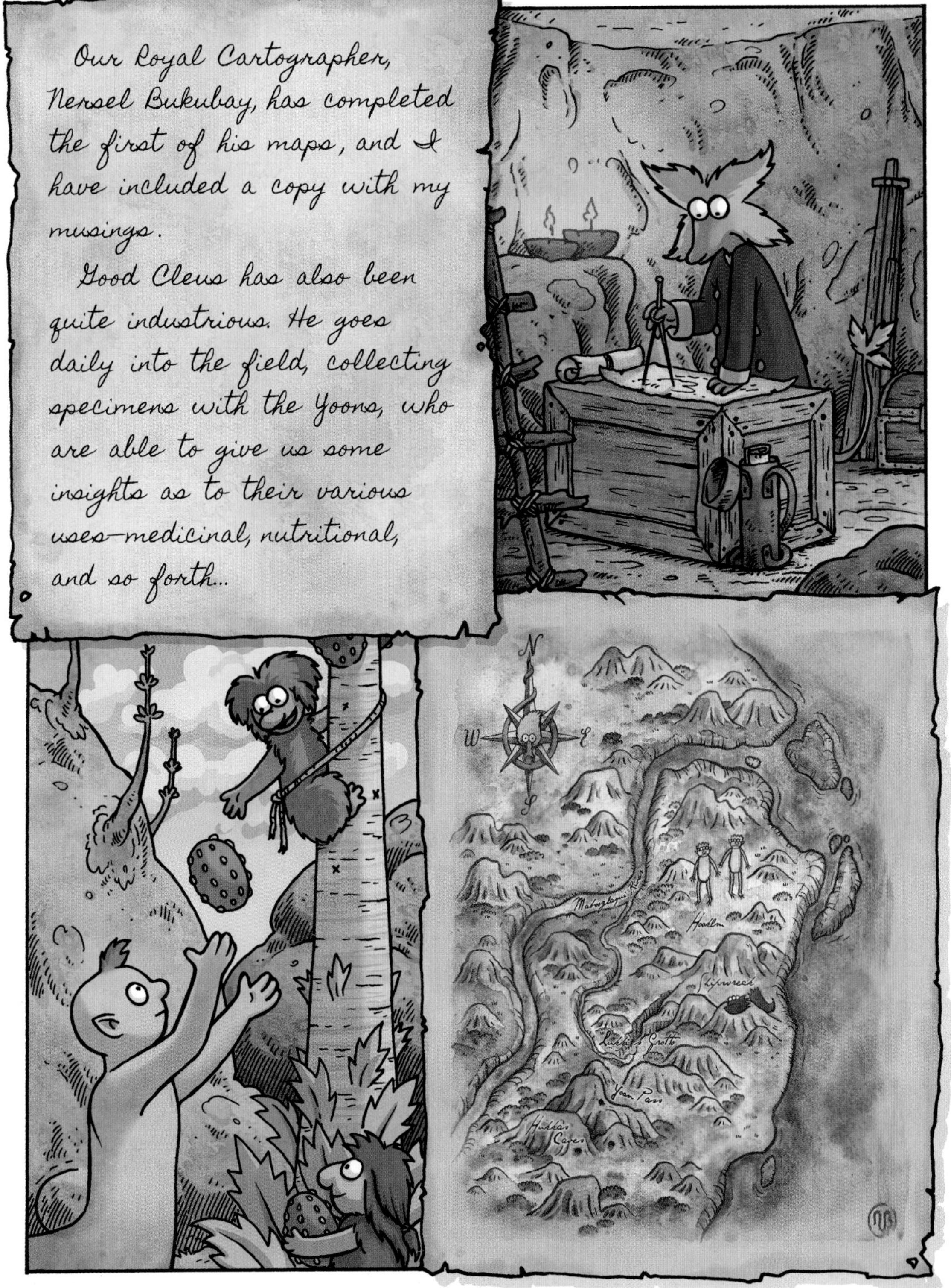
Our Royal Cartographer, Nersel Bukubay, has completed the first of his maps, and I have included a copy with my musings.
Good Cleus has also been quite industrious. He goes daily into the field, collecting specimens with the Yoons, who are able to give us some insights as to their various uses—medicinal, nutritional, and so forth...
N
W
E
S
Shipwreck
Yoon Pass
Hukka's Caves

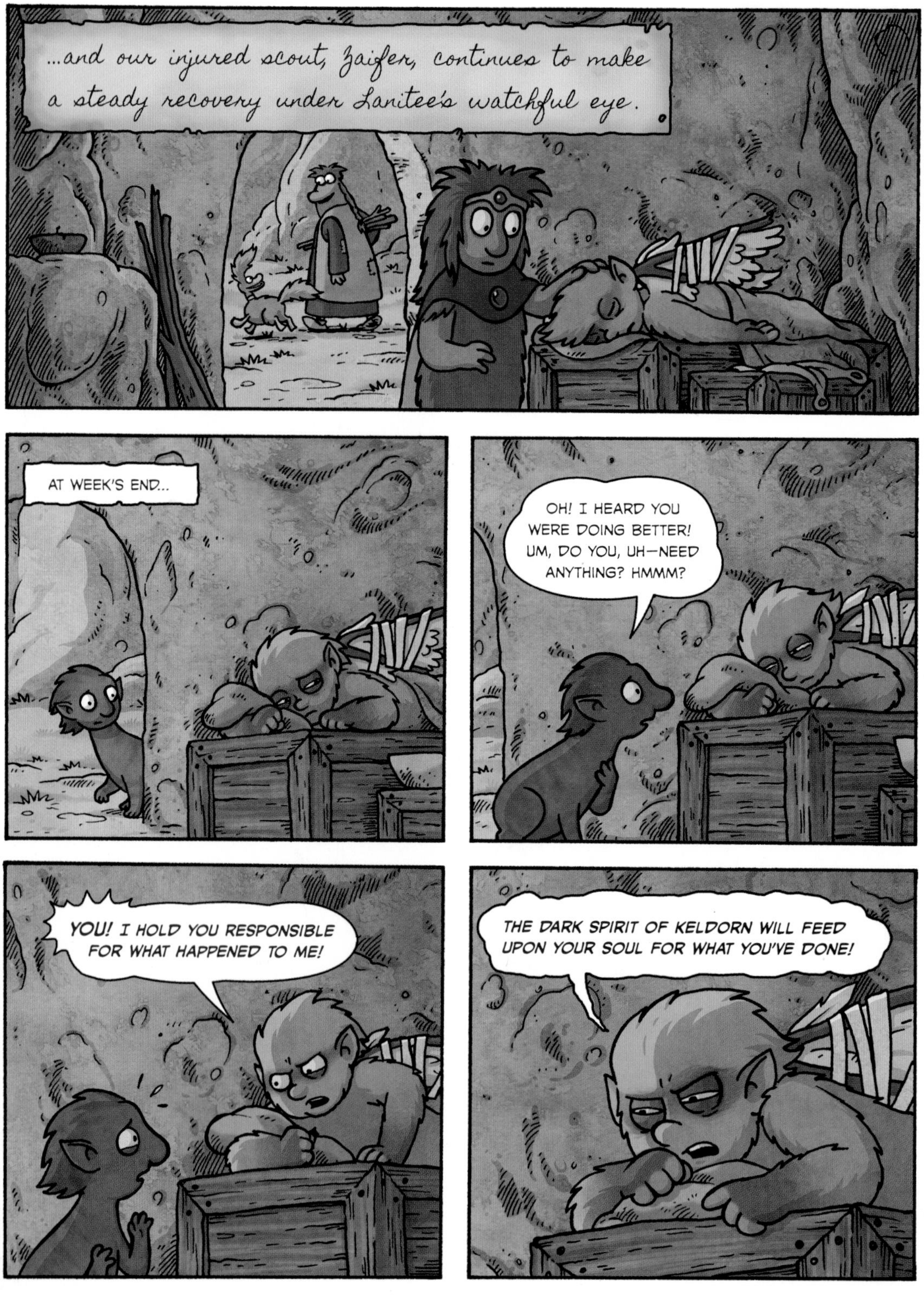
...and our injured scout, Zaifer, continues to make a steady recovery under Lanitee's watchful eye.
AT WEEK'S END...
OH! I HEARD YOU WERE DOING BETTER! UM, DO YOU, UH—NEED ANYTHING? HMMM?
YOU! I HOLD YOU RESPONSIBLE FOR WHAT HAPPENED TO ME!
THE DARK SPIRIT OF KELDORN WILL FEED UPON YOUR SOUL FOR WHAT YOU'VE DONE!

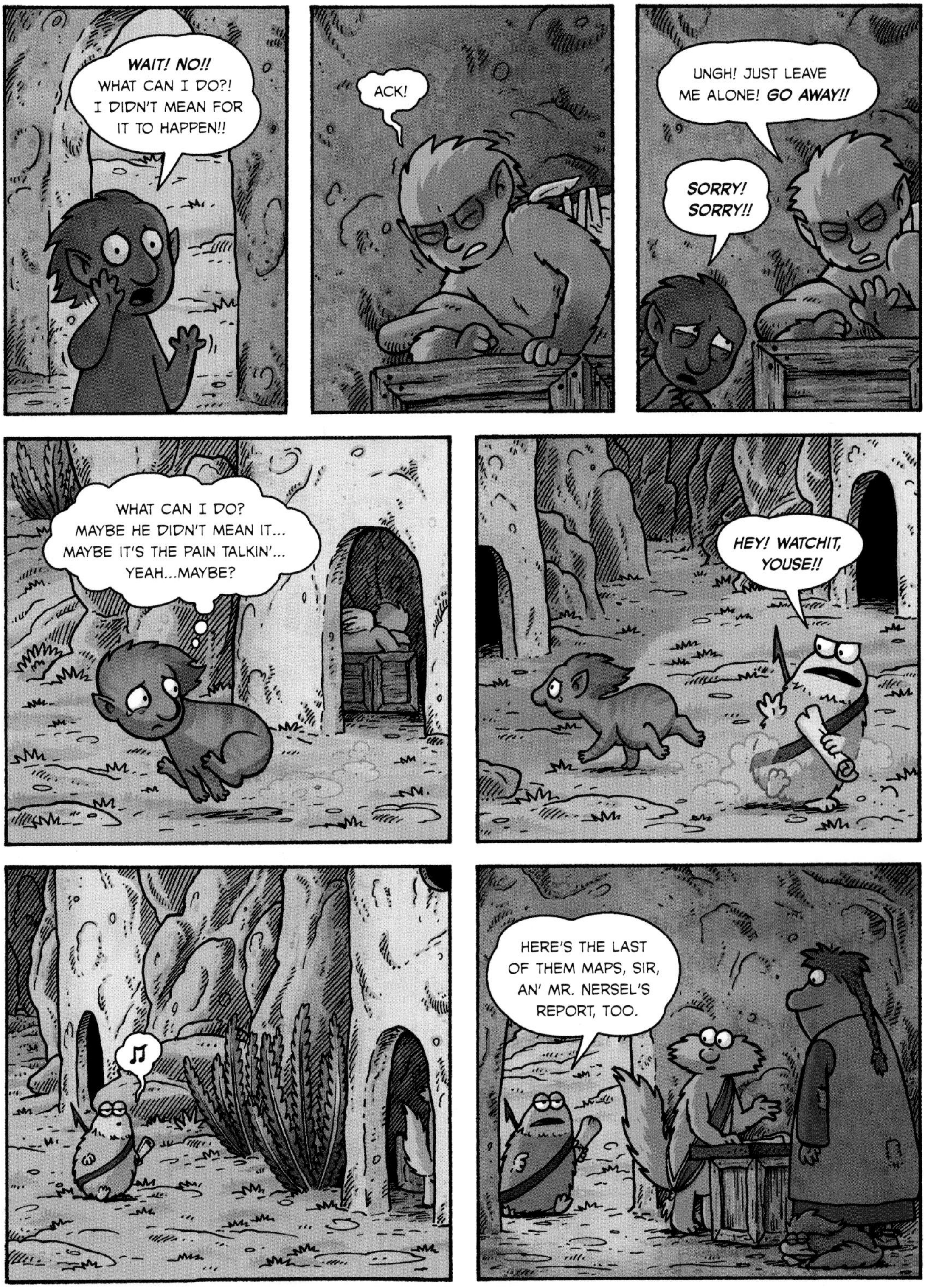
WAIT! NO!! WHAT CAN I DO?! I DIDN'T MEAN FOR IT TO HAPPEN!!
ACK!
UNGH! JUST LEAVE ME ALONE! GO AWAY!!
SORRY! SORRY!!
WHAT CAN I DO? MAYBE HE DIDN'T MEAN IT... MAYBE IT'S THE PAIN TALKIN'... YEAH...MAYBE?
HEY! WATCHIT, YOUSE!!
♫
HERE'S THE LAST OF THEM MAPS, SIR, AN' MR. NERSEL'S REPORT, TOO.

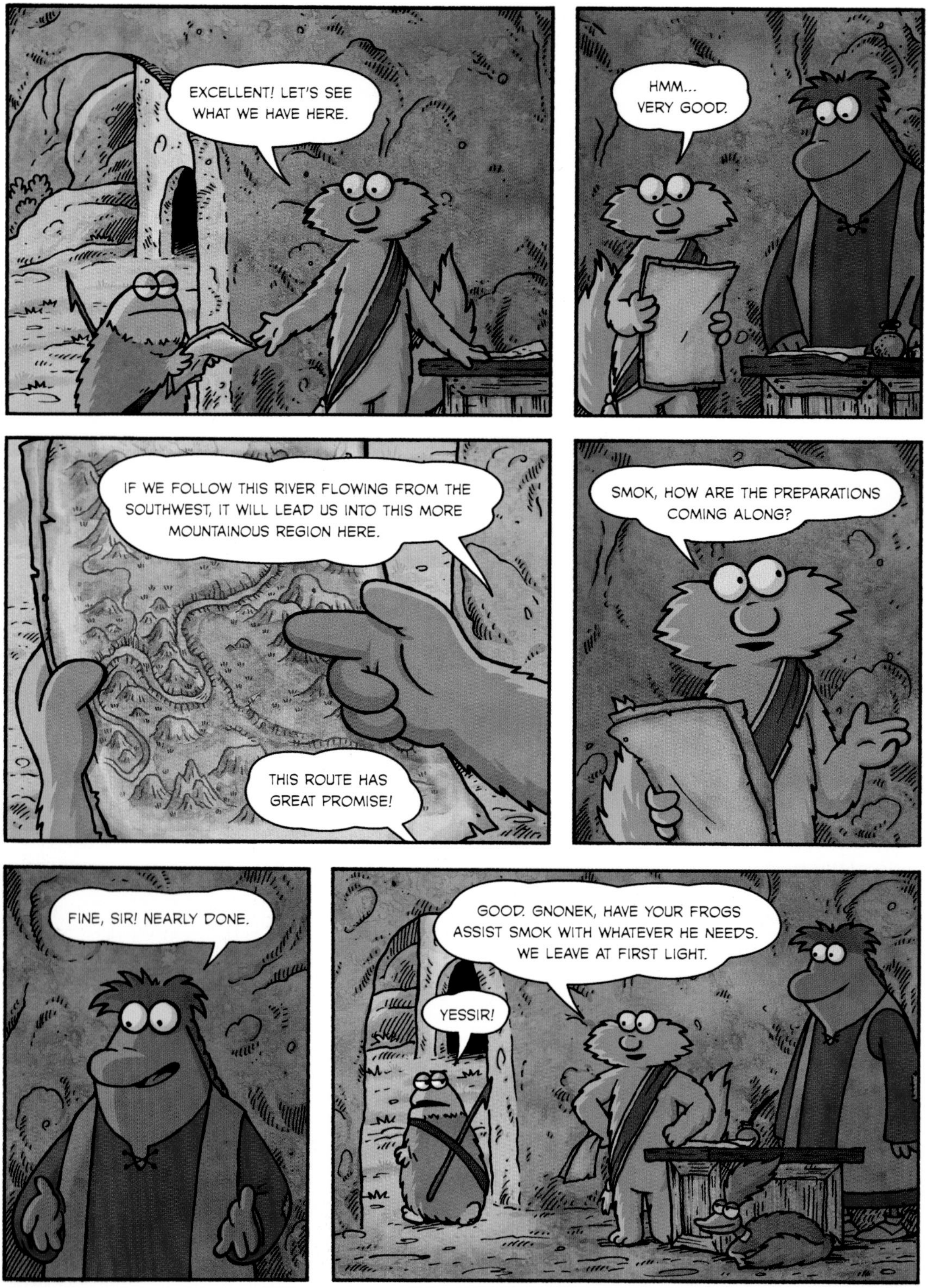
EXCELLENT! LET'S SEE WHAT WE HAVE HERE.
HMM... VERY GOOD.
IF WE FOLLOW THIS RIVER FLOWING FROM THE SOUTHWEST, IT WILL LEAD US INTO THIS MORE MOUNTAINOUS REGION HERE.
THIS ROUTE HAS GREAT PROMISE!
SMOK, HOW ARE THE PREPARATIONS COMING ALONG?
FINE, SIR! NEARLY DONE.
GOOD. GNONEK, HAVE YOUR FROGS ASSIST SMOK WITH WHATEVER HE NEEDS. WE LEAVE AT FIRST LIGHT.
YESSIR!

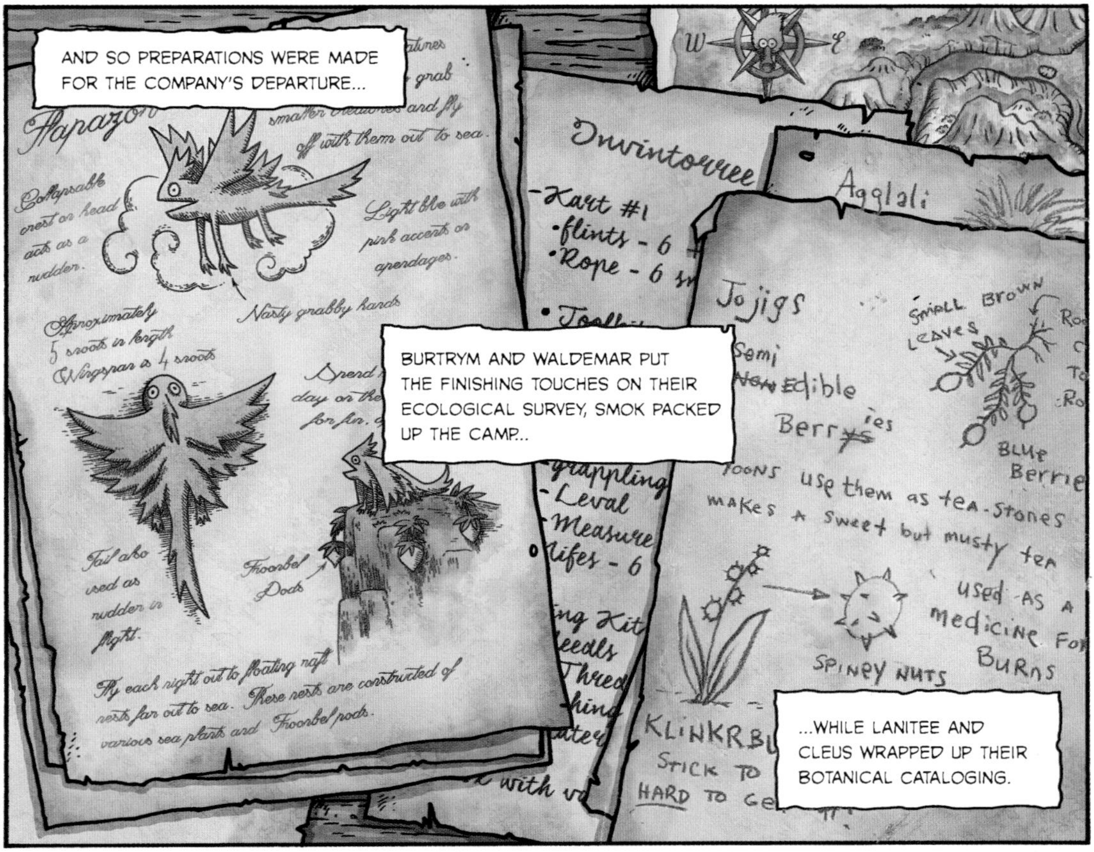
AND SO PREPARATIONS WERE MADE FOR THE COMPANY'S DEPARTURE...
Flapazon
smaller creatures and fly off with them out to sea.
Collapsable crest on head acts as a rudder.
Light blue with pink accents on apendages.
Nasty grabby hands
Aproximately 5 sroots in length
Wingspan is 4 sroots
Tail also used as rudder in flight.
Froorbel Pods
Fly each night out to floating raft nests far out to sea. These nests are constructed of various sea plants and Froorbel pods.
Invintorree
-Kart #1
·flints - 6
·Rope - 6
-grappling
-Leval
-Measure
Agglali
BURTRYM AND WALDEMAR PUT THE FINISHING TOUCHES ON THEIR ECOLOGICAL SURVEY, SMOK PACKED UP THE CAMP...
Jojigs
Semi Edible
Berries
SMALL BROWN LEAVES
BLUE Berries
YOONS USE THEM AS TEA-STONES
MAKES A SWEET BUT MUSTY TEA
USED AS A MEDICINE FOR BURNS
SPINEY NUTS
KLINKRB
STICK TO
HARD TO GE
...WHILE LANITEE AND CLEUS WRAPPED UP THEIR BOTANICAL CATALOGING.

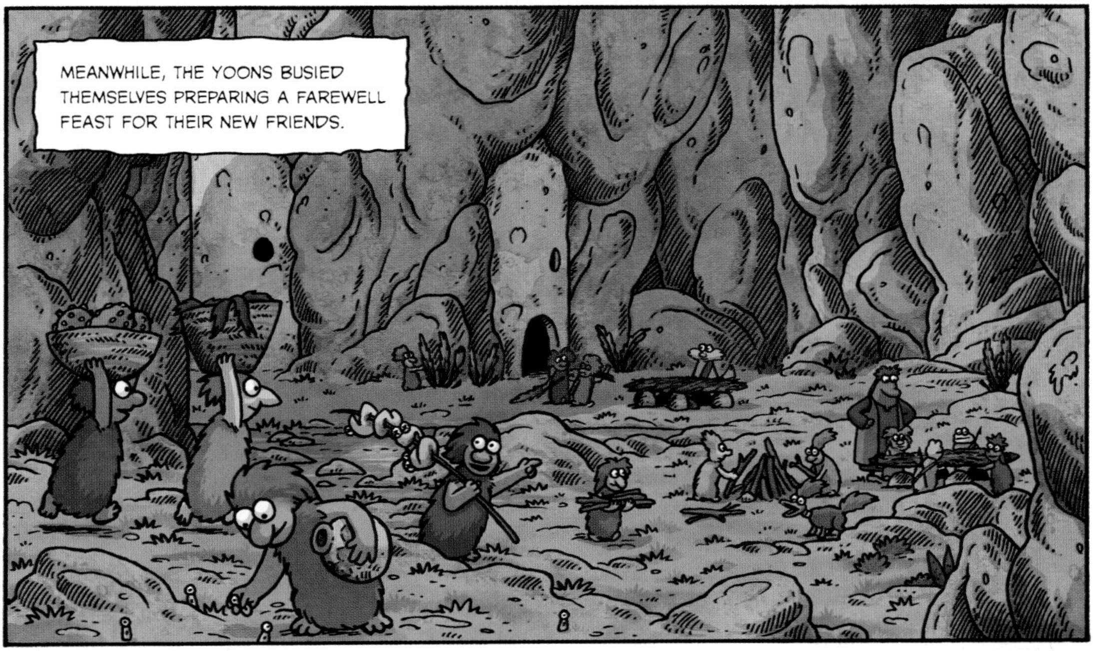
MEANWHILE, THE YOONS BUSIED THEMSELVES PREPARING A FAREWELL FEAST FOR THEIR NEW FRIENDS.

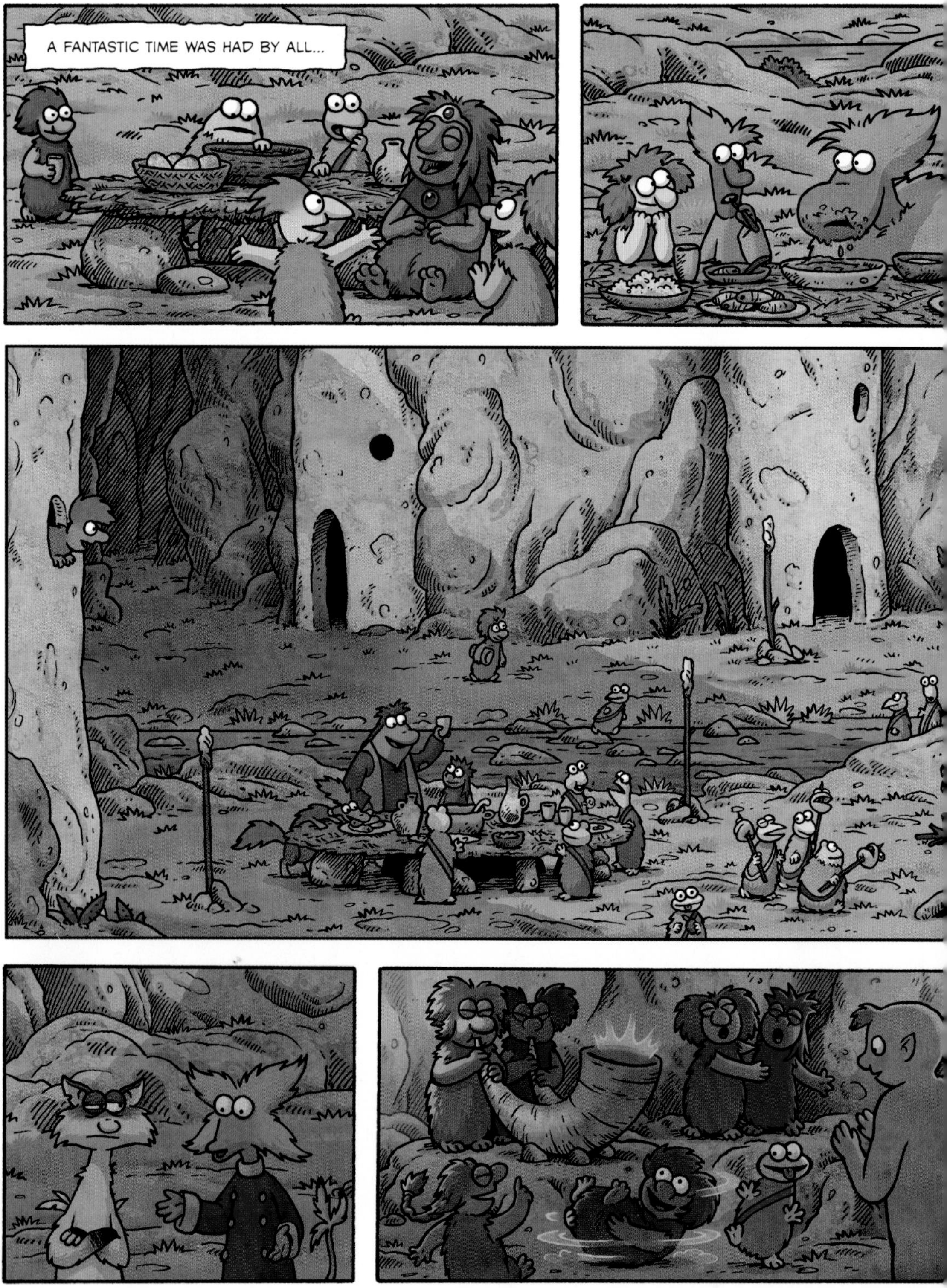
A FANTASTIC TIME WAS HAD BY ALL...

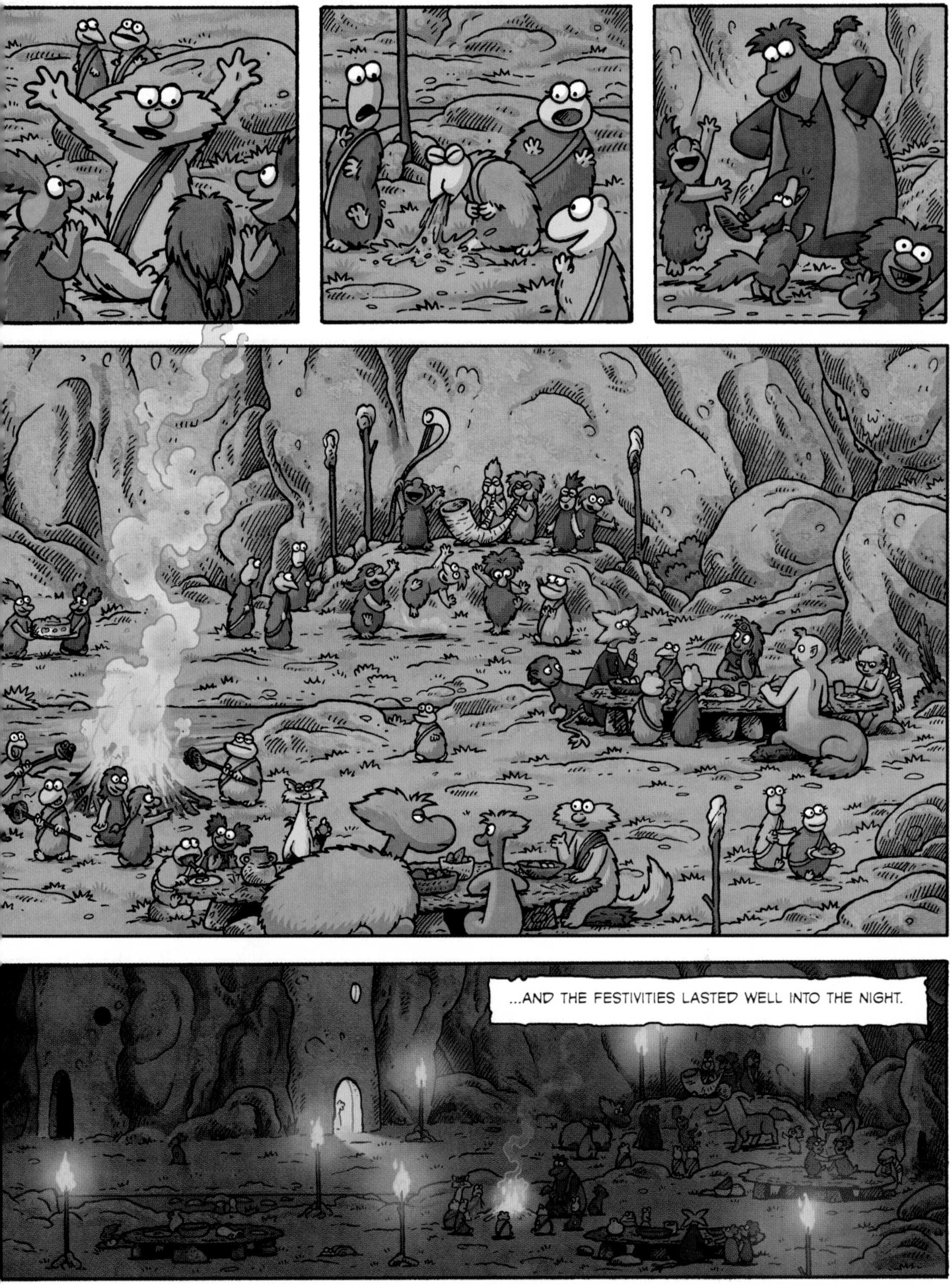
...AND THE FESTIVITIES LASTED WELL INTO THE NIGHT.

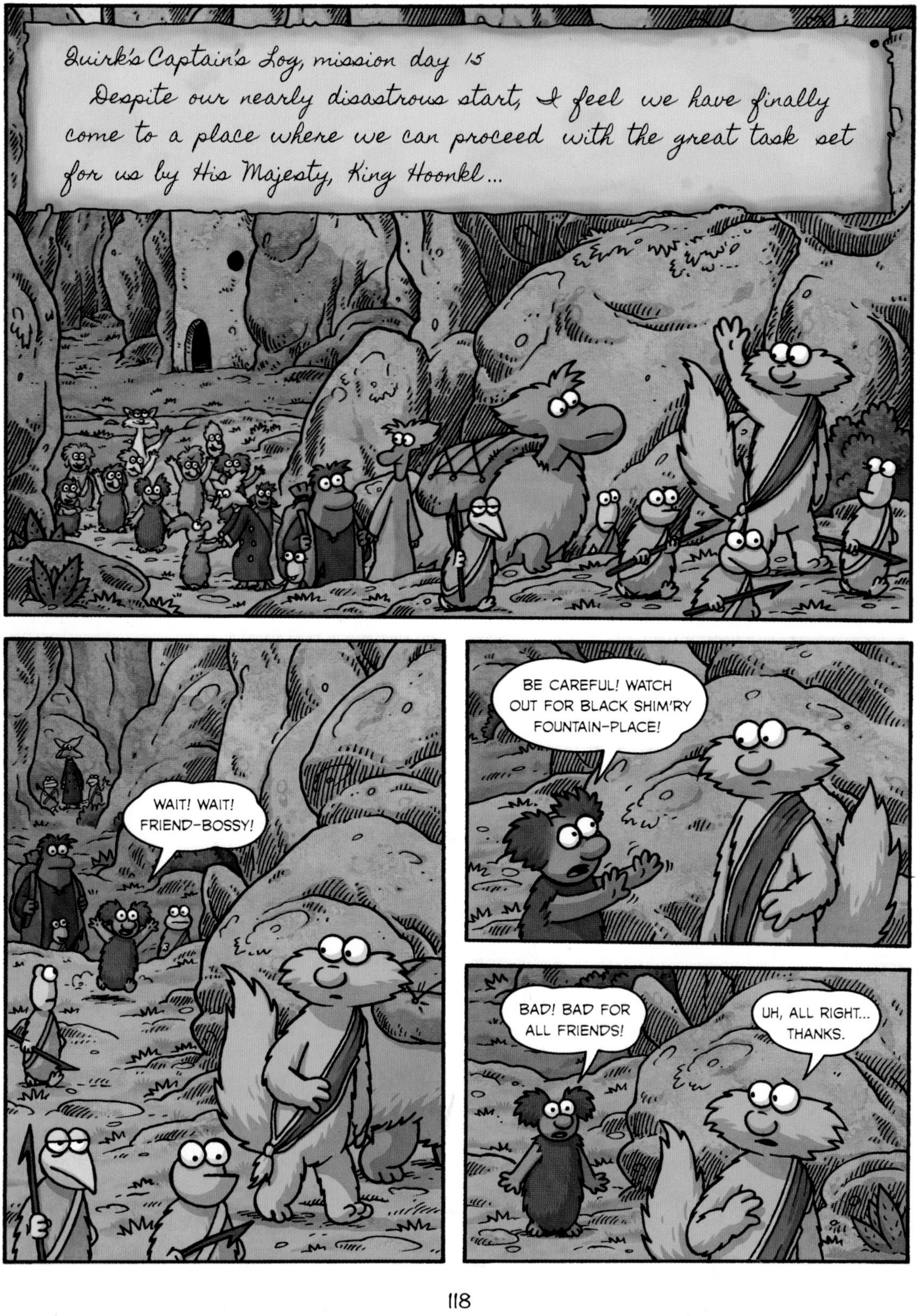
Quirk's Captain's Log, mission day 15
Despite our nearly disastrous start, I feel we have finally come to a place where we can proceed with the great task set for us by His Majesty, King Hoonkl...
WAIT! WAIT! FRIEND-BOSSY!
BE CAREFUL! WATCH OUT FOR BLACK SHIM'RY FOUNTAIN-PLACE!
BAD! BAD FOR ALL FRIENDS!
UH, ALL RIGHT... THANKS.

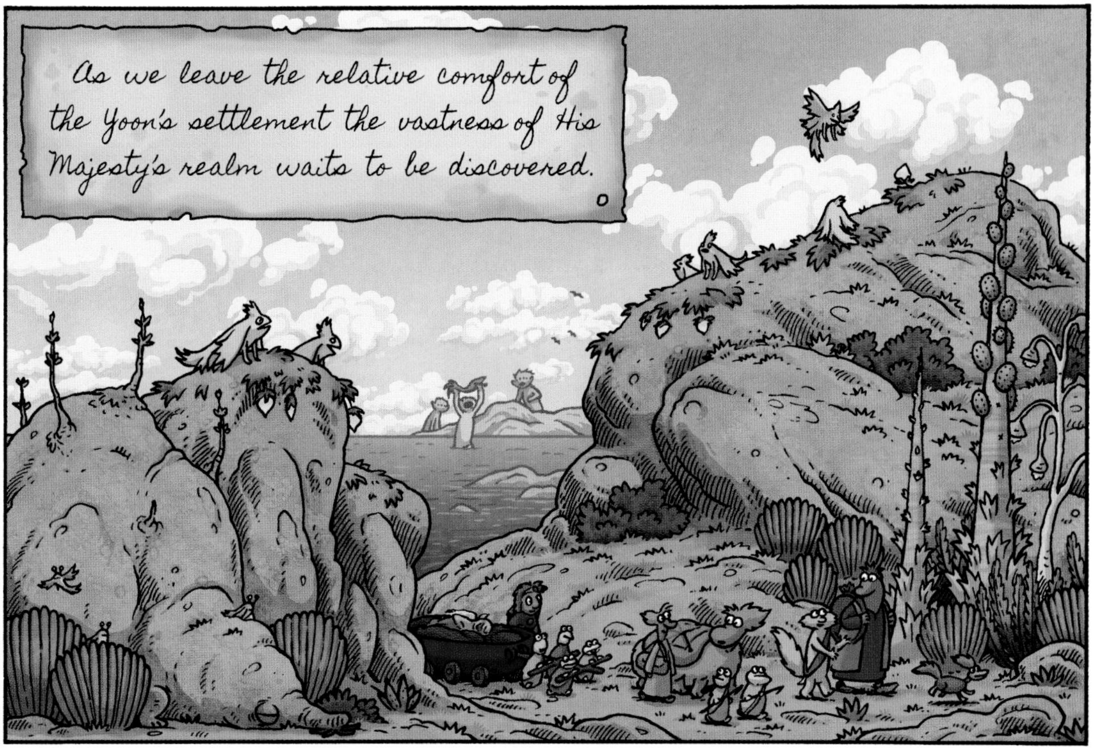
As we leave the relative comfort of the Yoon's settlement the vastness of His Majesty's realm waits to be discovered.

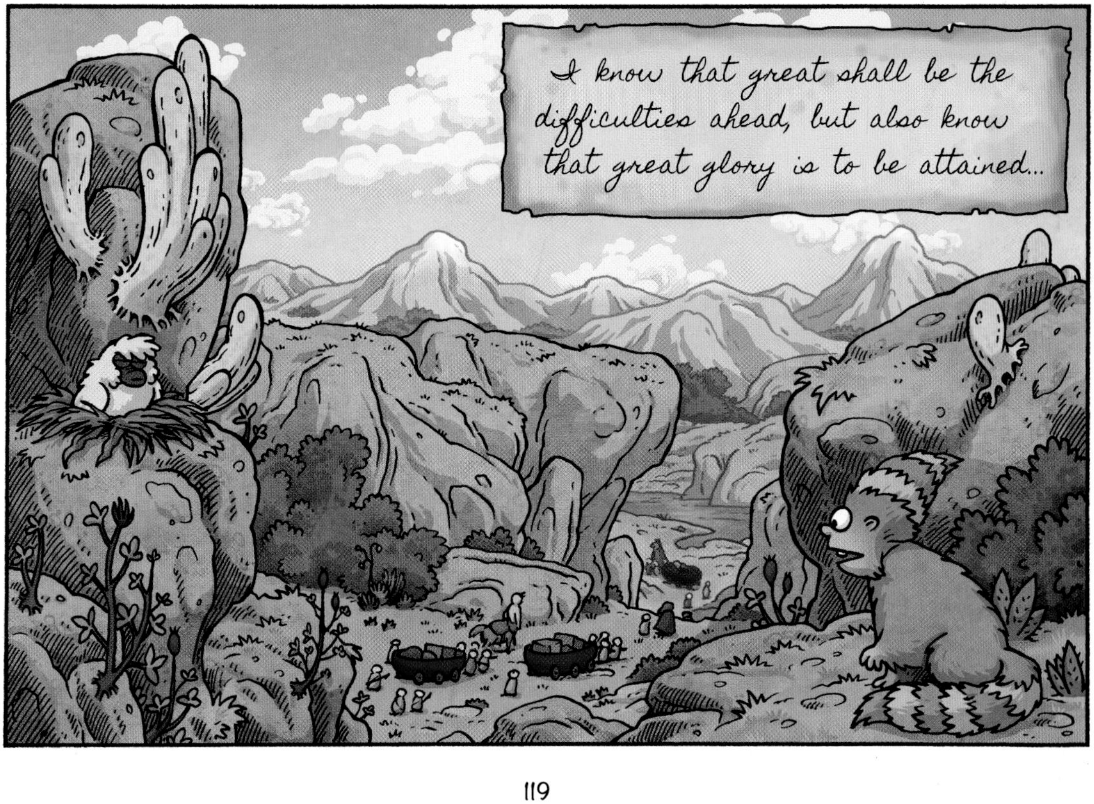
I know that great shall be the difficulties ahead, but also know that great glory is to be attained...

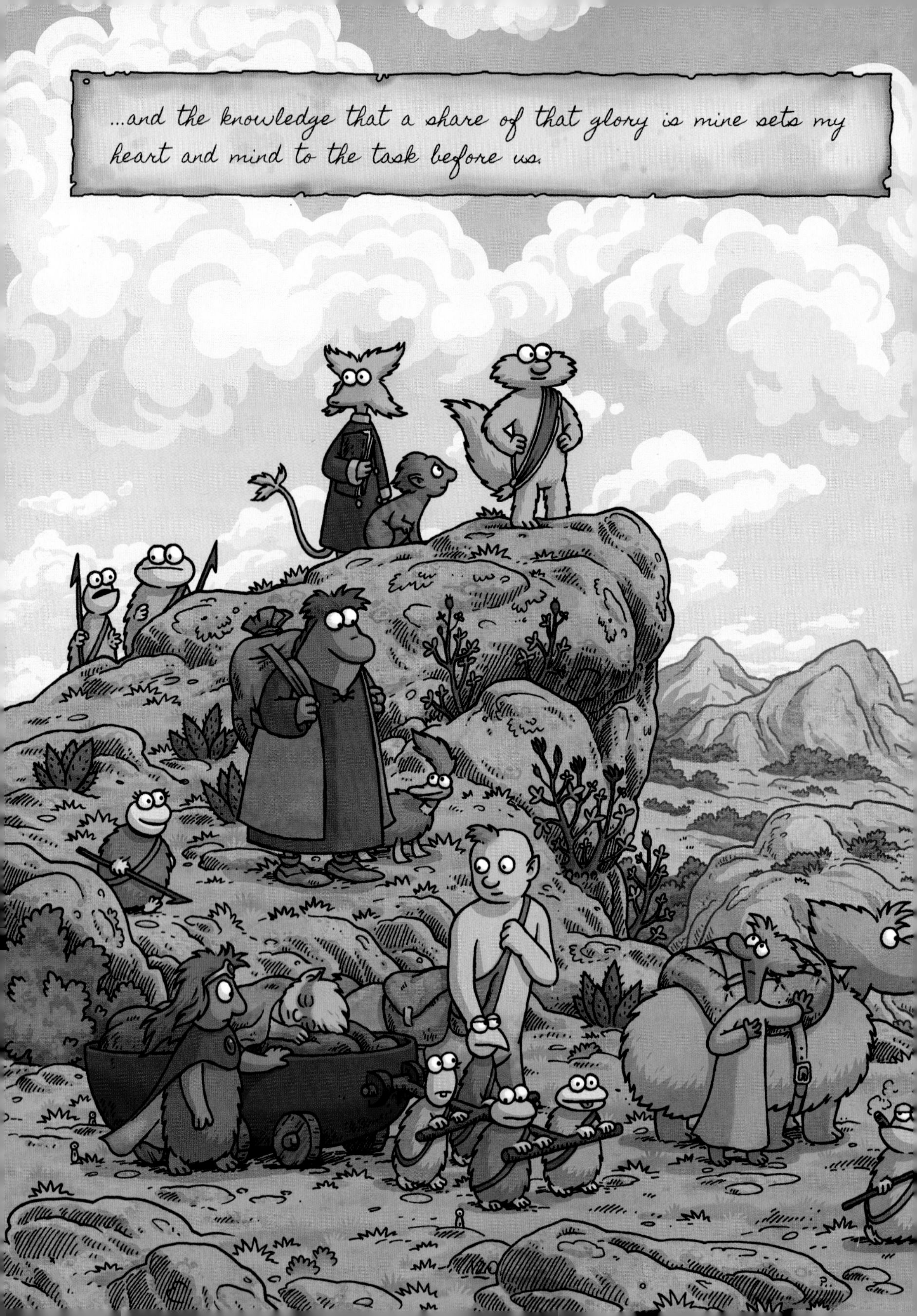
...and the knowledge that a share of that glory is mine sets my heart and mind to the task before us.

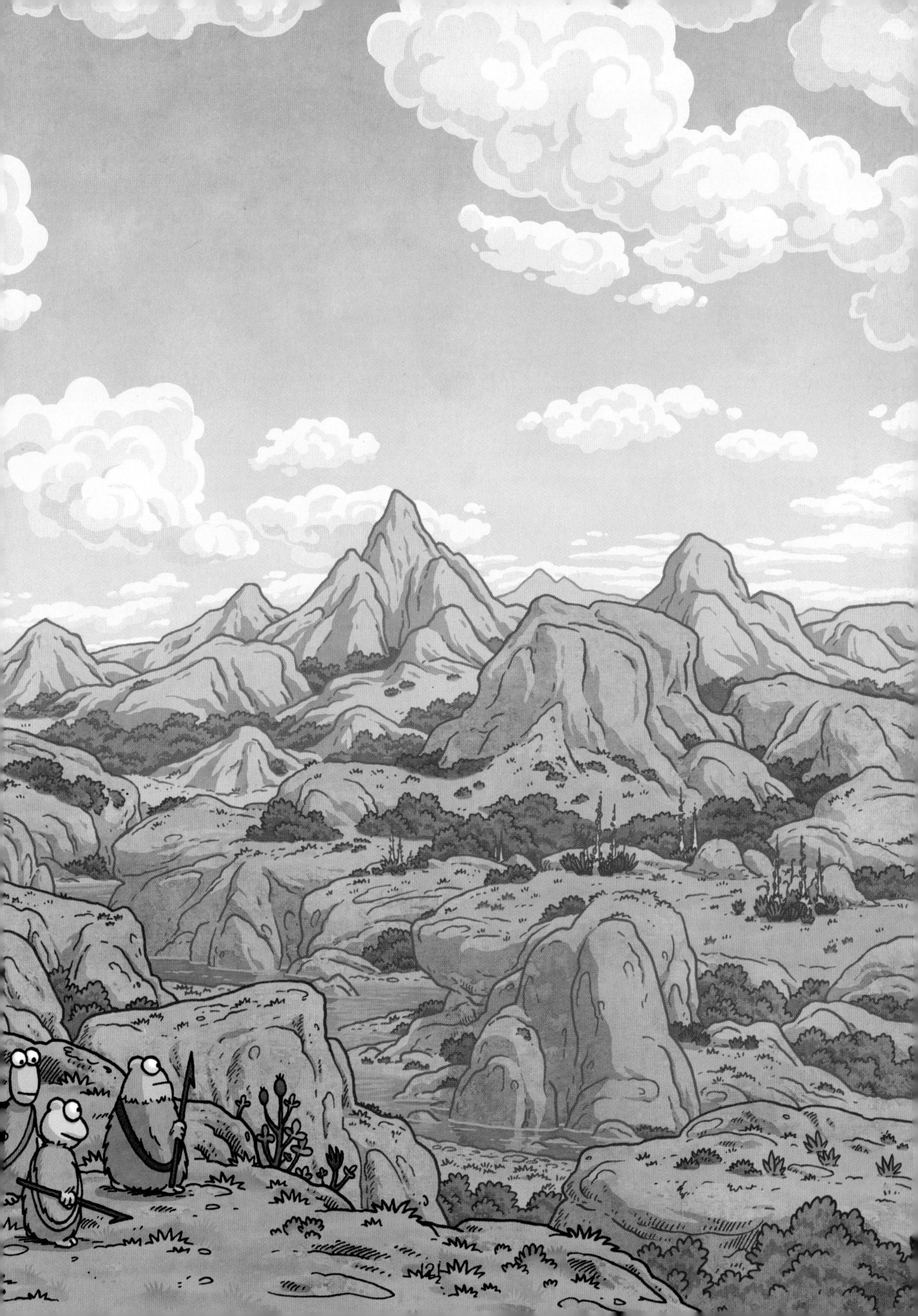

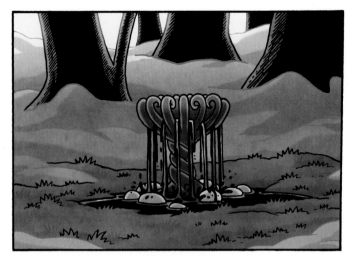

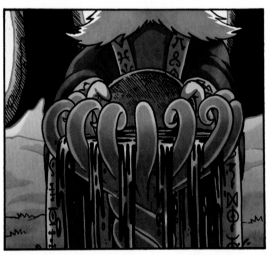

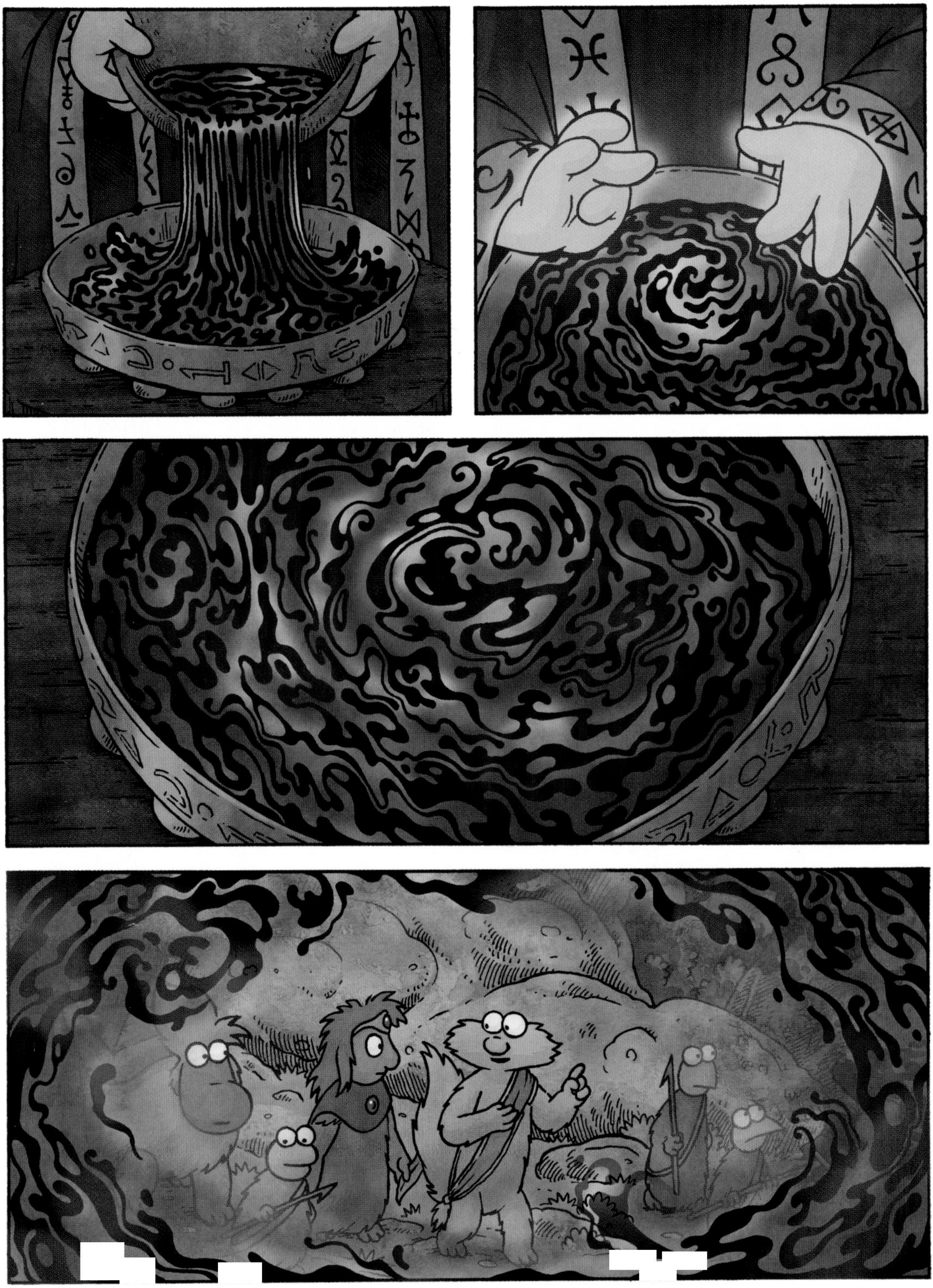

Characters of Note

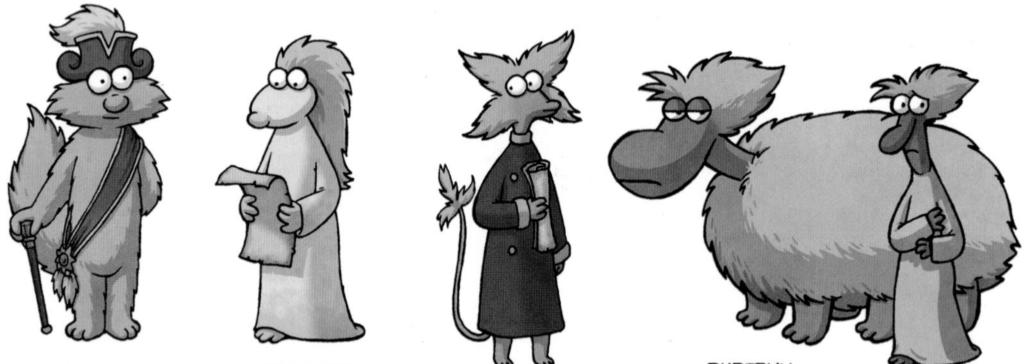

CAPTAIN QUENTERINDY QUIRK
CAPTAIN, MISSION LEADER

DELECHUS
CAPTAIN'S ASSISTANT

NERSEL BUKUBAY
CARTOGRAPHER ROYAL

BURTRYM
ECOLOGIST

WALDEMAR
ECOLOGIST

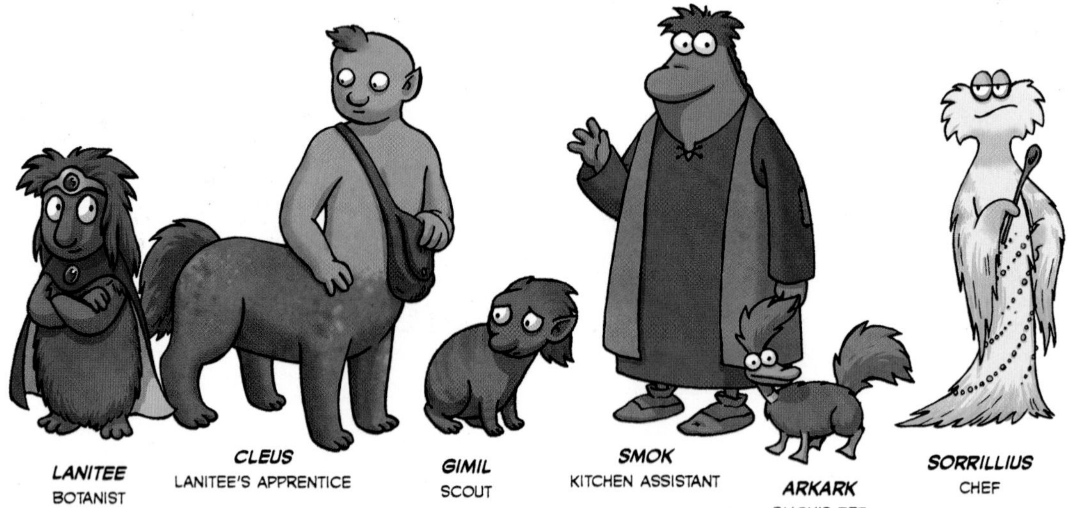

LANITEE
BOTANIST
(PRIESTESS/HEALER)

CLEUS
LANITEE'S APPRENTICE

GIMIL
SCOUT

SMOK
KITCHEN ASSISTANT

ARKARK
SMOK'S PET

SORRILLIUS
CHEF

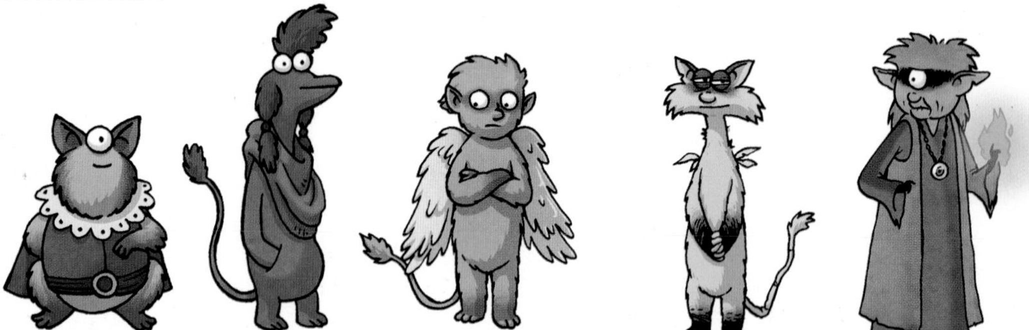

POMFRITZ
SURVIVAL EXPERT

INKTON TIKLOR
ARCHIVIST

ZAIFER
SCOUT

QUEMULUS

HUKKA
RECLUSE/SORCERESS

Sxervian Frog Brigades

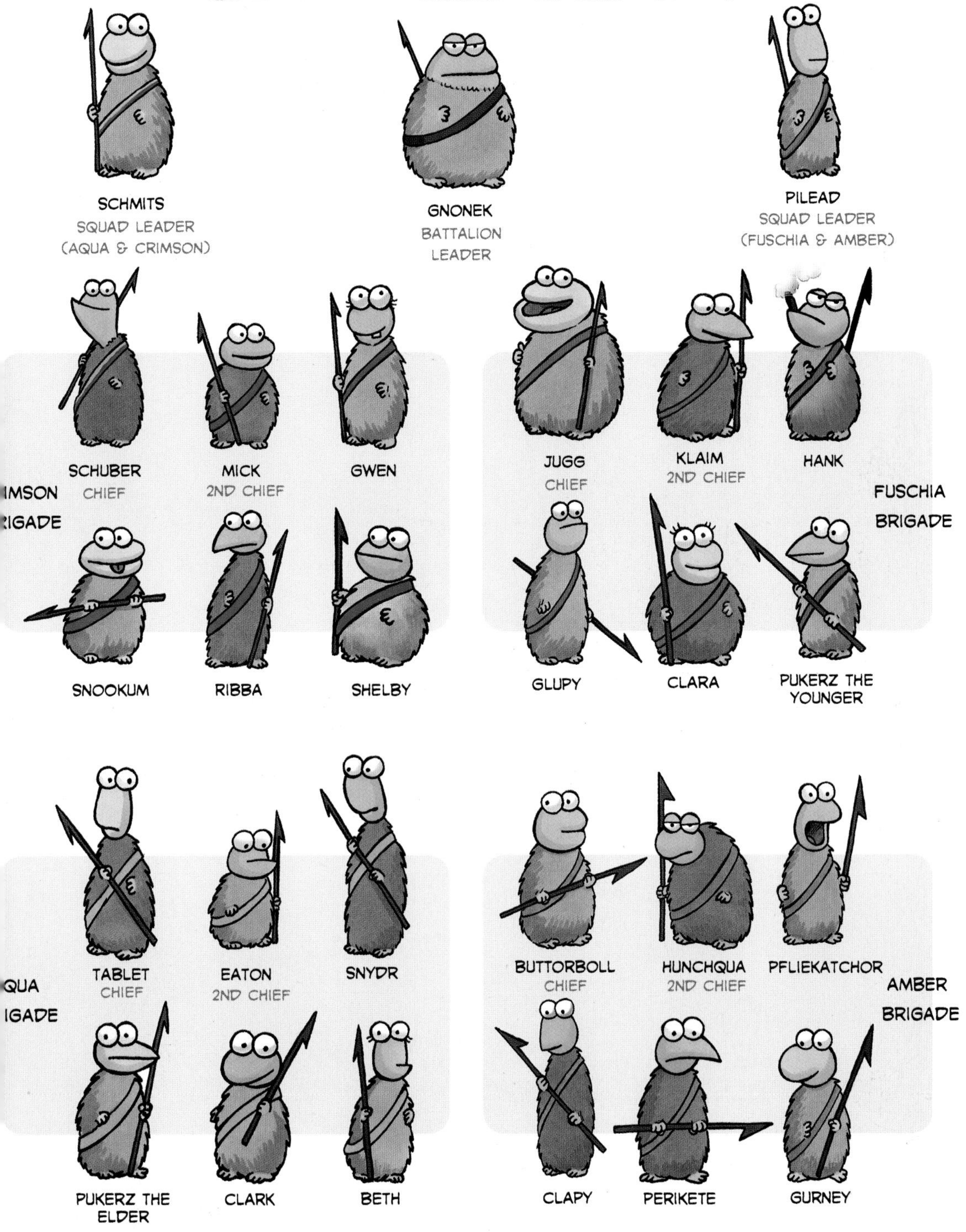

SCHMITS
SQUAD LEADER
(AQUA & CRIMSON)

GNONEK
BATTALION
LEADER

PILEAD
SQUAD LEADER
(FUSCHIA & AMBER)

CRIMSON
BRIGADE

SCHUBER
CHIEF

MICK
2ND CHIEF

GWEN

SNOOKUM

RIBBA

SHELBY

JUGG
CHIEF

KLAIM
2ND CHIEF

HANK

FUSCHIA
BRIGADE

GLUPY

CLARA

**PUKERZ THE
YOUNGER**

AQUA
BRIGADE

TABLET
CHIEF

EATON
2ND CHIEF

SNYDR

**PUKERZ THE
ELDER**

CLARK

BETH

BUTTORBOLL
CHIEF

HUNCHQUA
2ND CHIEF

PFLIEKATCHOR

AMBER
BRIGADE

CLAPY

PERIKETE

GURNEY

Map of the Landing Site
by Nersel Bukubay, Cartographer Royal

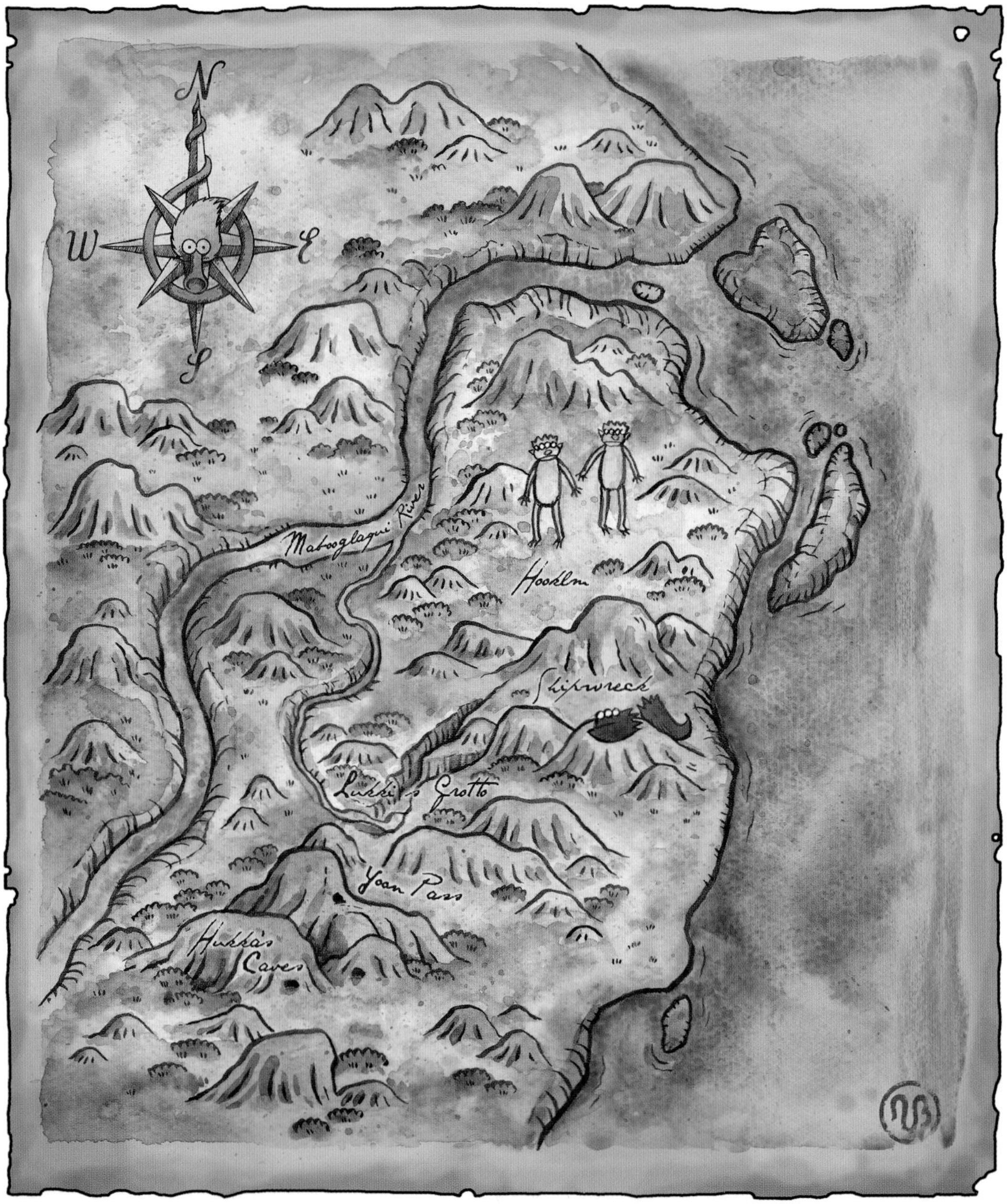

N
W
E
S
Mabooglaqui River
Hooklm
Shipwreck
Lukki's Grotto
Yoan Pass
Hukka's Caves

Growing up on Long Island, **Robert Christie** spent most of his waking hours obsessively drawing anything and everything, except cars. While taking cover from a lunchroom food fight, he met Deborah Lang, and shortly thereafter they conspired to create Crutonia. Ever since, they have been writing stories set in their quirky, made-up world. After earning his BFA in St. Louis, he moved to Jersey City, where he makes his living as an illustrator, painter, and prop maker for major motion pictures, Broadway, and fashion photo shoots. He has been writing and further developing Crutonia with Deborah for more than three decades, and *Into the Outlands* is their first published graphic novel.

Deborah Lang is a cartoonist, scientific illustrator, and molecular biologist. She was born in New York City, but eventually moved to Long Island purely to meet up with Rob Christie to create Crutonia. Her earliest published drawings include advertisements in *Pennysaver* and monthly comic strips in her college newspaper. She has published illustrations and papers in international science journals. Deborah spent many years in Philadelphia during college and grad school and presently lives in Chicago.

Acknowledgments

We thank the many people who have supported this work throughout the years. Firstly, the Andys: Andy Fair, Andy J. Fair, and Andrew McIlvaine. We thank Kim Fudge and Vincent McIlvaine for their support and patience. Thanks to Russell Lehrer and David Rosen for their support and hospitality. A big thank you to all the Crutonians, including founding CCLF members Jason Catanzariti and Kerrin Hutz, MaryAnn Taylor, and Nancy Cummings Ahola. Our gratitude to our families: parents, siblings, and the mini crew. We are grateful to our wonderful circle of friends (more than we can list). We greatly appreciate the mentorship of Matt Madden and Tom Hart, C.M. Butzer, and Bob Mecoy. Finally, we are very thankful to our First Second family, especially Mark Siegel for seeing the potential for our work and for giving us this great opportunity.

First Second
New York

Published by First Second
First Second is an imprint of Roaring Brook Press,
a division of Holtzbrinck Publishing Holdings Limited Partnership
175 Fifth Avenue, New York, New York 10010

Library of Congress Control Number: 2015951856

ISBN: 978-1-62672-233-0

Our books may be purchased in bulk for promotional, educational, or business use. Please contact your local bookseller or the Macmillan Corporate and Premium Sales Department at (800) 221-7945 ext. 5442 or by email at MacmillanSpecialMarkets@macmillan.com.

FIRST EDITION

First edition 2016

Book design by Rob Steen

Printed in China by Toppan Leefung Printing Ltd., Dongguan City, Guangdong Province

10 9 8 7 6 5 4 3 2 1

Drawn with 2H Sanford Turquoise pencils and inked with 03, 05, and 08 mm Micron pens on HP Premium Choice Laser Paper and Strathmore 400 Series Bristol Board. Colored digitally using Photoshop CC and a Wacom Intuos Pro tablet. Additional texture created with Dr. Ph. Martin's Synchromatic Transparent Watercolors on Strathmore 400 Series cold press watercolor paper. Nersel's maps hand-painted with FW acrylic ink and Windsor & Newton Artists' Watercolors using Princeton 0 and 2 watercolor brushes on Canson Montval cold press watercolor paper.

BY ART WE LIVE